the Professor

and Other Writings

Also by Terry Castle

The Apparitional Lesbian:
Female Homosexuality and Modern Culture

The Female Thermometer: Eighteenth-Century
Culture and the Invention of the Uncanny

Boss Ladies, Watch Out! Essays on Women and Sex

The Literature of Lesbianism: A Historical
Anthology from Ariosto to Stonewall

the Professor

and

Other Writings

TERRY CASTLE

HARPER

An Imprint of HarperCollins*Publishers*
www.harpercollins.com

THE PROFESSOR AND OTHER WRITINGS. Copyright © 2010 by Terry Castle.
All rights reserved. Printed in the United States of America. No part of this book
may be used or reproduced in any manner whatsoever without written permission
except in the case of brief quotations embodied in critical articles and reviews.
For information, address HarperCollins Publishers, 10 East 53rd Street,
New York, NY 10022.

HarperCollins books may be purchased for educational, business, or sales
promotional use. For information, please write: Special Markets Department,
HarperCollins Publishers, 10 East 53rd Street, New York, NY 10022.

FIRST EDITION

Designed by Eric Butler

Library of Congress Cataloging-in-Publication Data has been applied for.

ISBN 978-0-06-167090-9

10 11 12 13 14   OV/RRD   10 9 8 7 6 5 4 3 2 1

To Blakey

Author's Note

SEVERAL OF THE ESSAYS COLLECTED in this volume were produced for specific publications. I am deeply grateful to the sympathetic editors who commissioned and indeed helped me to polish them—notably Mary-Kay Wilmers at the *London Review of Books*, a spectacularly generous reader and critic of my work over the years, and the equally inspiring Benjamin Schwarz and Jon Zobenica at the *Atlantic*. I also wish very much to thank Rakesh Satyal and Tina Bennett, whose discerning comments and suggestions—on the long final piece especially—have been indispensable. Blakey Vermeule, Margo Leahy, and Beverley Talbott have likewise been of inestimable assistance. Needless to say, all errors, infelicities, and lapses in judgment are my own.

The essays appear in the order they were written. The earliest, "Courage, Mon Amie," is from 2002; the latest, "The Professor," was written just last year. All have autobiographical elements. Having labored in the dusty groves of academe for over twenty years, I felt—as a new millennium unfolded—a desire to write more directly and personally than had previously been the case.

It should also be noted that in several essays, notably the title-piece, "The Professor," I have changed names, places, and other details to protect the privacy of various individuals involved.

Contents

the Professor

and Other Writings

Courage, Mon Amie

Lewis Newton Braddock

A YEAR AGO THIS PAST autumn—a year before the old life so shockingly blew away—I made a long-contemplated trip to France and Belgium to see the cemeteries of the First World War. My quest, though transatlantic, was a modest, conventional, and somewhat geeky one: I hoped to locate the grave of my great-uncle, Rifleman Lewis Newton Braddock, 1st/17th (County of London) Battalion (Poplar and Stepney Rifles), the London Regiment, who had died in the war and was buried near Amiens. Facts about him are scarce. My grandmother, whose only brother he was, has been dead now for twenty years. No one else who knew him is still alive. By stringing together odd comments from family members, I've learned that he worked as a greengrocer's boy in Derby before joining up in 1915;

that he served first in the Sherwood Foresters; that he managed to survive three years before getting killed during the final German retreat in June 1918. My mother, born eight years after his death, claims to have heard as a child that he was shot accidentally, "by his own guns." But my uncle Neil, her only brother, can't believe "they would have told the family that." Newton was said to be artistic: two dusty little green-gray daubs, both of them Derbyshire landscapes, are among his surviving effects. There are two photographs of him in uniform, one from the beginning of the war, the other from the end. In the first he looks pale, spindly, and rather stupid: a poorly-fed late-Victorian adolescent overfond of self-abuse. In the second, the one with the mustache, he is stouter, tougher, dreamier, and looks distressingly like both my mother and my cousin Toby. My companion Blakey says he looks like me. I don't see it. I've been fascinated by him—and the Great War—since I first heard of him, at the age of six or so. I'm now forty-eight.

Somebody should write about women obsessed with the First World War. Everybody knows Pat Barker, of course, but there's also Lyn Macdonald, a former BBC producer whose dense, addictive, exhaustively researched oral histories of the war (*1914: The Days of Hope, 1915: The Death of Innocence, Somme, They Called It Passchendaele, The Roses of No Man's Land, To the Last Man: Spring 1918*) are a fairly devastating moral education for the reader. And once you begin to delve, as I have done, into the netherworld of popular military history—battlefield guides, memorial volumes, regimental histories, military-souvenir Web sites—it is peculiar how many lady-archivists you encounter. Some of these, it's true, are part of husband and wife teams: the prolific Valmai Holt, for example, author with her husband of *My Boy Jack? The Search for Kipling's Only Son* (1998). (John Kipling died in his first half-hour in action—at the age of eighteen—at Loos in 1915. Though his stricken father carried on a twenty-year search for his grave, his remains were not found until

1992.) When not writing, the Holts run a sprightly operation known as Major & Mrs. Holt's Battlefield Tour Company. "Their Battlefield Guide to the Somme and Battlefield Guide to Ypres," reads one cheery promotional blurb, "have brought these areas to life for tens of thousands of people."

Other female obsessives work in austere isolation. The late Rose E. B. Coombs, MBE, former special collections officer at the Imperial War Museum, is the author of *Before Endeavours Fade: A Guide to the Battlefields of the First World War* (1976 and 1994). Miss Coombs's bleak volume, illustrated with her own amateur snaps, is a necrophile's delight: photograph after photograph in tiny, eye-straining black and white of crosses, graves, plaques, inscriptions, bombed-out blockhouses converted into monuments, decaying trench relics, dank rows of cypresses, grassed-over mine and shell craters, obscene-looking barrows, and yet more crosses and graves. Some of the photos show boxy 1970s cars parked in the background—a peculiarly depressing sight—and anonymous male tourists with period comb-overs and long sideburns. I bought my secondhand copy through the mail from a military book dealer in Dorset and its once-glossy pages reek of must and damp.

My own war fixation is equally grim and spinsterish; its roots primal and puzzling. My first awareness of the Great War came, quite literally, with the crackup of my parents' marriage. They had emigrated from England to California in the early 1950s and divorced ten years later, in 1961. (I was born in San Diego in 1953.) It was a bit of a mess, my mother had been having an affair with a lieutenant in the Navy, and in the convoluted aftermath my irascible grandfather, a former buyer for the co-op in St. Albans, prevailed on her, the Extremely Guilty Party, to come back to England and rehabilitate herself in some respectable, out-of-the-way spot. My baby sister and I were bundled onto a plane at 4:00 a.m., me sobbing dolefully at the breakup of my little world. Gone into transatlantic blackness—forever, it seemed—my cowboy hat and Mickey Mouse books, the pixie-cutted members of my Brownie troop, our blue and white Rambler, and the sunny back patio where my father had, in happier days, filmed me in vivid Kodachrome disporting in a blow-up plastic pool.

Our first few months in England were spent in my grandparents' little brick bungalow at the foot of Caesar's Camp, near Folkestone. (Their house and lane have since disappeared, razed to make way for the stark, moonscaped run-up to the Channel Tunnel.) It was in those lonely, quiet days—the clock ticking on the mantelpiece, the adults discoursing in another room—that I first examined my great-uncle's bronze memorial disk, which stood on a bookshelf next to my grandmother's Crown Derby. It was six inches across, heavy-ish, and the same greeny-gold color as a three-penny bit, a piece of coinage with which I had recently become acquainted. I was imme-diately charmed by its glint, its inscriptions, its palpable seriousness. It seemed to have survived, like a dense, tooth-breaking wafer, from some unknown time and place. I asked my mother, only slightly babyishly, to ask my grandmother if I could have it for my new col-lection of oddments, begun when our plane had stopped in Iceland for refueling and my mother bought me a ceramic puffin from the tiny airport gift shop. This request, received with embarrassed laughter, was not granted.

The following three years in England, a stagnant time character-ized mainly by my mother's depression and sexual loneliness, deepened my war curiosity without clarifying it. We moved to our own little bungalow in nearby Sandgate, at the top of a rise just below the Shorn-cliffe Army Camp. There were several new things here. I saw my first person without a leg, an old man with a horrible stump in Sandgate High Street, and though I never mentioned him to anyone, I was terri-fied for months we would run into him again. The village had its own little grime-blackened war memorial (standard vintage and style) and an air of lugubrious decay unlike anything I had encountered before. The gray waves of the Channel flopped endlessly and drearily on the shingle beach that ran alongside the High Street. This blighted strand, impossible to walk on in bare feet, bore no resemblance to the palm-studded sands of infancy and toddlerhood. I fixated on orange-flavored Aero chocolate bars as a means of survival.

My primary school, Sir John Moore's, was part of the Shorncliffe Camp. I have no recollection of the sun shining during my sojourn there. Each day I walked to school and back past deserted, dusky parade grounds, the occasional ghostly soldier in puttees looming up out of the mist. Except for a few barracks and the red brick officer quarters, all dating from Napoleonic days, the place seemed largely uninhabited. Once in a while an army truck lumbered up Artillery Road. My first suicidal fantasy had to do with flinging myself under one in the presence of my horrified parents, now strangely reunited, as if by magic carpet, to witness the act. This, I know, makes it all sound bad, but Sir John Moore's wasn't really so awful—our teacher once took us out to make bark rubbings—and I soon developed a powerful aesthetic attraction to the various uniforms I saw, the officers' peaked caps and regimental insignia especially.

But when I dream of the place—and sometimes I still do—my brain usually fixes on the baleful rituals of Armistice Day. Nothing was explained. Who, or what, was an *armastiss*? It was never made very clear. Nonetheless, schoolmates and I were duly instructed to bring cut flowers from home, the bottoms of the stems to be moistened with a wrapper of wet tissues in aluminum foil. My mother obliged—I'm not sure how, given that nothing very posy-like grew in the leftover building rubble around our house. And intriguing, too, the break in school-day routine. At half-past ten we mustered in the playground by the toilets—no talking, straight lines, wipe your noses, please—then set off through the camp. We passed by Sir John Moore's poky little museum, the Folkestone bus stop, and the abandoned cinema.

We trundled across playing fields, skirted stinging nettles, rounded unknown corners, then ascended a rolling procession of new-old Kentish hills, hills that must have been close by, but, uncannily, never seemed to exist except on that particular day. At the top of these, the sky suddenly lifting, an astonishing vista broke out before us: greensward and chalk and Lear-like white cliffs, the cold massy sea and lofting gulls, the distant line of France, and everywhere, like some vibrant, disturbing retinal trick, hundreds of identical graves, sweeping down in rows to the cliff's edge, as far as the eye could see.

We stayed near the top, of course, our teacher deploying us in little ranks till each of us ended up with our own white marker to stand in front of. The grave at one's feet at once prompted animistic dread. Were you supposed to stand right on the spot under which the dead person lay? Could he feel your presence through the grass? If so, it was creepy, possibly even foolhardy, to be there. Might he not, late at night, get up from his grave, glide down Artillery Road, and seek you out? Southern California, a place entirely lacking in cemeteries, offered no precedents. The scariest thing back there had been a Time-Life book of my father's with a picture of a grim, tiny-eyed shark, jaws open wide in prehistoric eagerness. This was far worse: a ghastly corpse-face at the bedroom window! The tattered rendition of the Last Post, by a pair of insect-buglers on the hill opposite didn't help. A prayer was said; the bouquets deposited; the tremors persisted. I had yet to see any *Night of the Living Dead* movies at this point; but when I did, back in San Diego a few years later, alone in the cheerless TV den of the house my father now shared with his new wife and stepdaughters (the same place I was sitting when I saw Oswald get shot), I realized I already knew all about them.

All very sad and picturesque (poor little female-Terence!); but enough to explain a forty-year Craving for More? For just such a craving—acquisitive, pedantic, and obscurely guilt inducing—is what I ended up with. Not all at once, of course; like most obsessions, this one took a while to get going. In my twenties, as a literature student, I read and acquired the obvious classics: Graves, Owen, Sassoon, Remarque, Barbusse, Brittain, Fussell. But I had lots of other fads and hobbies going, too: opera, Baroque painting, Kurosawa films, the Titanic, the Romanovs, trashy lesbian novels. Sometimes my preoccupations overlapped. I became fascinated, for example, with the long World War I sequence in Radclyffe Hall's *The Well of Loneliness*. I read up on butch lady–ambulance drivers at the Western Front. But the world had not yet retracted to a gray, dugout-sized, lobe-gripping monomania.

Then, starting in my thirties, things seemed to intensify. I was in England teaching in my university's overseas program in 1989, as it happened, on the seventy-fifth anniversary of the start of the war. An item on the news one evening, showing tottery, beribboned veterans saluting at the Menin Gate, reduced me to sudden tears. I began absorbing ever more specialized fare: Macdonald's books, Taylor and Tuchman on the political background, battle histories of Gallipoli, Verdun, and Passchendaele, books about Haig and Kitchener, VAD nurses, brave dead subalterns, and monocled mutineers. I read Michael Hurd's desolating biography, *The Ordeal of Ivor Gurney*, on the train to Edinburgh, the city where the nerve-wracked composer, on his way to insanity and death, was hospitalized after being gassed in 1917. I stared at the few surviving pictures of him: the one in a private's tunic (2nd/5th Gloucesters); the one where he's standing, in ill-fitting civvies, alone and blank and looking down at the grass, in the grounds of his asylum in 1922.

And more and more I began investigating the filthy minutiae of 1914–18 trench warfare. John Keegan, the *Face of Battle* man, was my trench guru. I read all his books. I became an armchair expert on Lewis guns and enfilade fire, shrapnel and mortars, wiring parties, trench raids and listening posts, the tricky timing of the creeping barrage. I pondered the layout of dugouts and communication trenches, the proper distance between parapet and parados, the placement of machine gun nests. (They're always called "nests.") It seemed at the time, I realized, an odd obsession for a girl. But it seemed to go along with various other un-girlish things about me: my vast bebop collection and dislike of skirts, my aversion (polite) to sleeping with men.

I remember a conversation with a famous feminist poet in the late 1980s in which I grandly pronounced it a "disgrace" that so few women knew anything about military history. In an apotheosis of pomposity (and also to see if it would get her goat) I boasted about my great-uncle and proudly asserted that I could never have been a pacifist in August 1914.

Over the past ten years the *folie* has only become more involved. A couple of years ago I started collecting first editions of World War I books (latest Internet bandersnatch: a battered copy of Reginald Berkeley's *Dawn*, a patriotic tear-jerker, complete with garish pictorial dust jacket, about the martyrdom of Nurse Cavell).

I've got several faded trench maps and a tiny, pocket-sized "Active Service Issue" book of psalms and proverbs, issued by the Scripture Gift Mission and Naval and Military Bible Society in 1918. Every year, when I go to London, I load up on greasy wartime postcards in one of the memorabilia shops in Cecil Court ("Helping an Ambulance through the Mud," *"Armée Anglaise en Observation,"* "The Destruction at Louvain, Belgium," "Tommy at Home in German Dugouts!"). I've got a whole shelf on war artists: C.R.W. Nevinson, Paul Nash, William Roberts, Wyndham Lewis, and the skullishly named Muirhead Bone. I've got books about Fabian Ware and the founding of the Commonwealth War Graves Commission. I've a 1920 *Blue Guide to Belgium and the Western Front* and a Michelin Somme guide from 1922, both published for the so-called pilgrims— the aged, widowed, and dead-brothered—who flooded France and Flanders after the war seeking the graves of the lost. I have scratchy recordings of "Pack up Your Troubles" and "The Roses of Picardy";

a tape of a (supposed) German bombardment; and yet another of a Cockney BEF veteran describing, rather self-consciously, the retreat from Mons. I have videos and documentaries: Renoir's *Grande Illusion*, Wellman's *Wings*, Bertrand Tavernier's *Life and Nothing But*, and a haunting excerpt from Abel Gance's famous antiwar film *J'Accuse*. And then, too, there are all my mood-setting "highbrow" CDs: the songs of Gerald Finzi, Vaughan Williams, George Butterworth, Gurney, Ernest Farrar. (The baritone Stephen Varcoe is unsurpassed in this repertoire.) I have but to hear the dark opening bars of Finzi's "Only a Man Harrowing Clods" to dissolve in sticky war nostalgia and an engorged, unseemly longing for things unseen.

Yet something about my fixation has always bewildered me, as it indubitably has those friends and bedmates forced to enthuse over grimy mementos and the latest facts. (Thanks to a trawl around at www.fallenheroes.co.uk I recently discovered, for example, that Shorncliffe Camp was a major Great War jumping-off point, notably for the Canadian units who went on to fight, with appalling losses, at Vimy Ridge in 1917. The soldiers in the cemetery were mostly men who had died of wounds or sickness in nearby military hospitals after returning from the front. But a few graves hold other kinds of casualties: a small group of Belgian refugees, a single Portuguese soldier, several members of the Chinese Labor Corps, some civilian victims of a daylight air raid on Folkestone on May 25, 1917, in which ninety-five people were killed and 195 injured.*) I guess an obsession

---

* John Keegan on the unhappy exploits of the Portuguese army in World War I: "Portugal, historically Britain's oldest ally, declared war on Germany and Austria in March 1916. It eventually sent two divisions to the Western Front, armed and equipped by the British. Put into the line at Neuve-Chapelle, in the British sector south of Ypres, they were attacked during the second great German offensive of 9 April 1918, broke and ran. Large numbers of prisoners were taken. The Portuguese, an unsophisticated and rural people, were unsuited to the strains of industrial warfare and it was unwise of the Portuguese Government to have taken sides. It would have been better advised to imitate Spain in standing apart." *An Illustrated History of the First World War* (2001).

is defined, crudely enough, by the fact that one doesn't understand it. Even as it besets, its determinants remain opaque. (The word "obsession," interestingly, is originally a military term: in Latin it signified a siege action, the tactical forerunner of trench warfare.) The obsessions of others embarrass and repel because they seem to dehumanize, to make the obsessed one robotic and alien and unavailable. It's like watching an autistic child humming or scratching or banging on a plate for hours on end.

I suppose it was some desire to get free of a certain robot feeling in myself that prompted my trip to France and Belgium. Not that I was planning on renouncing my books or my collections. (Nor have I.) It was more a matter of, Okay, you've been talking about it forever; go find him. Blakey was teaching and couldn't go, but Bridget could, and wanted to, even though she is not from the Braddock side of the family. She turned out to be the ideal companion. She's my first cousin, a South Londoner by way of Ipswich. Our estranged fathers are brothers. We knew each other as children—for a brief time, before my mother took us back to San Diego—but then I didn't see her for two decades until I looked her up one day in the London telephone book. (After my parents' divorce I'd let all the Castle relatives go to hell.) Bridget, it turned out, had been in the Army for eleven years, in Germany and Belfast, and was now running the transport department for a London borough. She is slangy and brusque and ultracompetent—knows all about plumbing and engines and dogs—and regards me, the Prodigal Bluestocking, as a bit feckless. A couple of years ago we went down to Dungeness to see Derek Jarman's garden and ran into a man with his wife and mother-in-law whose car had got stuck in the wet gravel. Bridget had it hitched up in a trice and dragged it free, while the man stood by looking utterly flummoxed and outdone. ("Ex-military," she said, by way of explanation.) Anyway, Bridget set it all up: our Chunnel car-ticket, the package-deal hotel in Ghent, our route map. Needless to say, she drove all the way from Herne Hill to the outskirts of Ypres, with me a slightly cranked-up presence in the passenger seat.

I'd been hoping, obviously, that the trip might bring some new understanding, might clarify both my relationship with my dead great-uncle and my war fixation. But no such *éclaircissement* took place, at least not immediately. On the contrary. Though a "success" from a practical standpoint—we found Newton's neat little grave and red geraniums on the second day—the journey seemed only to provoke more disorientation. As Bridget gamely motored us from one memorial to the next, the freezing rain walloping down on the windscreen ("Hooge Crater is just up here"), I found myself less and less able to grasp what I was doing there. I felt misty, numb, a bit ghoulish. I was the Big Girl-Expert: an Unusual and Fascinating Person Now at Last Visiting the Western Front. (She's slept with more women than her father has!) But I felt increasingly disgusted with myself. I started thinking that probably a lot of people I knew didn't really like me, were only pretending to.

The nadir came on the second day. We'd spent the first day in and around Ypres, visiting Tyne Cot and neighboring cemeteries, moping around the In Flanders Fields museum. Ypres itself is a huge bummer, fake and nasty and foul, with machine-cut cobblestones and dead-eyed people everywhere. Numerous renovations were going on, presumably to make the spot more of a "target" destination for European Community tourists (though it's already been flattened and rebuilt more times than anyone can count). We found a Great War souvenir shop, run by a surly Falklands War vet, but I couldn't bring myself to buy anything, not even one of the dull gold cap badges or orphaned tunic buttons. That night we retreated in a downpour to our Ibis in Ghent Zentrum, the only good news being the charred steak and frites we gobbled down in a place near the cathedral. The hotel was filled with paunchy Benelux businessmen who took one look and didn't bother giving us the eye; the bedroom was cramped and small, with two narrow beds about a foot apart. I got horribly self-conscious at having to undress in front of Bridget, and started blushing. The Incest Taboo, in one of its weirder manifestations, seemed to descend thickly, like a cloud of odorless gas.

The next day we zipped south on a motorway, Moby on the CD player, huge container trucks from Holland and Germany careening by in the rain. Coffee in Albert, a quick gander in the drizzle at the French war memorial in the town square, then on to the giant Lutyens monument to the Missing of the Somme at Thiepval. It was midmorning, and we were the only people there apart from a sullen group of French lycée students playing around on the steps of the thing. (They all had the same annoyed-teenager look: *We're too old to be standing around here!*) The memorial itself is a massively ugly parody-arch in the middle of nowhere. You see it coming up on the horizon from miles away. ("The majestic Memorial to the Missing," says Miss Coombs, "stands amid fields still scarred with the trench lines of the Leipzig Redoubt.") Blakey would call it fugly. Loads of Castles among the 73,000 or so incised names, though nobody known to us. One of them had been in the Bicycle Corps, which made us laugh because it was all so Edwardian and English and pathetic. "He died heroically, his bicycle shot out from under him." Housman could have written a poem about it.

Uncle Newton, it turned out, was not far off, halfway between Amiens and Albert, in a pretty little walled "extension" cemetery at Franvillers filled mainly with Australians. The cemetery was on a small rise, presumably close to the place where he had died, and impeccably maintained. It had three or four farmhouses around it, probably built in the 1960s. I figured I was the fifth person to visit him in the eighty years since his death, the other four being my grandmother, her sister Dolly, her sister's daughter Sue, and my uncle Neil (on his way back from the Italian Front in 1945). As Bridget and I unlatched the gate and went in, the sun came out, just like in a Jane Austen novel when the heroine is about to get proposed to. We walked around; we scrutinized the inscription on the Blomfield Cross of Sacrifice. We read the homely greeting-card messages in the memorial book. ("Sleep well, lads!" "We'll never forget you!" "Thinking of you always with love and gratitude." "Always with us.") Bridget took a photograph of me by the grave—glum and fat and respectful—and that was that.

But even as we began winding back north towards Calais and home in the late afternoon, I suppose we were getting close to having had enough. I started to feel broody and compulsive and "Urne Buriall"-ish; the sky got dark and pent again. I asked Bridget, as we drove, if she thought soldiers buried in tidy little battlefield cemeteries like my great-uncle's occupied separate plots. True, they had their individual headstones; but might they not, in the hurry and chaos of war, have simply been piled willy-nilly into a single burial pit somewhere in the vicinity of the present markers? A mass grave, if you like. Bridget said, "Yes, I'm afraid so," and kept her handsome gray-blue eyes on the road. We both hunkered down. Then back toward Ypres we decided on one last stop: a little old-fashioned war museum that, according to the guidebook, incorporated some vestiges of front-line trench—something, for all of our perambulations, we hadn't yet seen. We followed an ancient Roman track a mile or two across sodden beet fields; made several bumpy turns up a hill and into a copse; then rolled up, even as the rain started again, in the little dirt parking lot.

Dank thoughts in a dank shade. In the front of the "museum"—a little cluster of dilapidated houses and sheds—was a café, deserted inside except for a couple of bloated Flemish men with wet black mustaches. Empty beer glasses. The drill here was: buy your ticket in the café; walk through the two side rooms where the "exhibits" were; then out into the back garden where the bit of old trench was; then back again. The bleary-eyed proprietor, likewise with mustache, looked like that Belgian serial killer who got caught by Interpol a while ago. He contemplated us briefly with deep alcoholic hatred. *How yoo ʒhay in Inghlissh? Who arrhh ʒeeeʒ two fhucking dykes?* The place was damp and cold and dirty—old spiked Uhlan helmets and things lined up on a shelf behind him—and smelled like hell.

The place, I learned afterward, is famously horrible. Stephen O'Shea, the wonderful Canadian writer, has a stark riff on it in *Back to the Front*, his extraordinary 1996 account of hitchhiking the entire length of the Western Front. (O'Shea is another catastrophe junkie: one of his later books is on the Cathars.) But Bridget and I needed no guidebook to alert us to the vibe. Down one side of the display room we proceeded, dutifully examining the fly-blown war photos on the wall. They got worse as you went along. Battlefield shots first—mudslides, craters, collapsing limbers and dead horses—then a switch to British and German wounded laid out in hospital beds. The photographer, "Ferdinand of Ypres," had signed each picture in a flowery chemical script. (An early example of diversification no doubt: the Ypres *carte de visite* business must have fallen off dramatically when the place got pulverized in November 1914.) The last two were clearly Ferdinand's masterpieces: tight, nauseating close-ups of men with ghastly facial injuries, jaws and mouths gone, rubbery slots for noses, an eye or an ear the only human thing left. The one other person in the room with us was a pale young man in a windbreaker, one of the Four Horsemen on his day off. He was busy taking photos of the photos and smiling delightedly.

We passed next through a kind of garage with rusty stuff piled all around: shell casings, barbed wire, rotting Sam Browne belts, a pair of ludicrous French shop dummies gaily attired in mismatched officers' uniforms. Then on out to the display trenches, snaking off into the woods behind the building. These had a neat, generic, recently packed-down aspect, the corrugated iron supports looking as if they'd just come from the Lille DIY store. Not much to see really, once you'd peered down into them or clambered in—as Bridget briefly did—so we went back in the house and down the other side of the exhibit room. Here was further war debris: ammunition boxes, ancient bully-beef tins and, jarringly, some bits of Nazi regalia and Hitler junk (a blotted letter to him at the front from his grandmother). I knew Hitler had fought—valiantly—in a Bavarian infantry regiment near the Messines Ridge, but this part of the show seemed nonetheless a mite too enthusiastic. A big dusty swastika banner, sorely in need of dry-cleaning, was draped in a corner, like a prop from the Hall of the Grail scene in Syberberg's postmodern *Parsifal*.

But they saved the best till last. *Zhose ughly girls get snooquered Beeg Time!* Along the far wall by the exit was a long wooden work desk with five or six seats attached, rather like a junior high school science class setup. Mounted at each seat was a beautiful old-fashioned viewing machine—a kind of antique stereopticon—made of brass and polished wood, with a double eyepiece and hand crank. It was all too exquisite and Proustian to resist. Like silent film cameramen, Bridget and I took our seats and eagerly began to crank.

Yet hellish indeed what assailed us. Trench-pix again, in lots of twenty, but now eternally fixed in a lurid, refulgent, Miltonic 3-D. Sickening and brain-twisting. A clicking, clacking kaleidoscope of atrocities. Don't forget the vertigo. Even as I sat and stared I felt myself lurching forward, into the bright intolerable sunshine of some ruinous as usual summer day in 1917. The light itself was a somatic wedge tilting one into the past. The cerebellum went walkabout.

Granted, the light preserved in old photographs can be unnerving at the best of times. I have a picture in one of my books of Mahler and Richard Strauss stepping out into bright sunlight after a matinee of *Salomé* in Graz in 1906. The Old World sun glinting off the side of Mahler's polished shoe, the sharp edge of Strauss's boater, the geometric shadows thrown onto the wall behind them: these teleport one instantly into the scene. You start remembering what the day was like. But here the illusion of reality was fearsomely, even fiendishly intensified. The febrile glare, conjoined with the stereoscopic depth of field, equaled My God They're Right There. A corpse with flies. A headless body upside down in the sand. Two skulls on a battlefield midden. An obscure something or other in *feldgrau*. I got up in disgust after seeing yet another moribund horse, its intestines spilled out and glistening.

In the weeks and months that followed, nothing made very much sense. (After a surreal shopping spree at the vast Eurostar mall outside Calais, Bridget and I got back to Herne Hill without incident.) I confess I was moody. I was on sabbatical; I should have been happy. But I maundered and malingered. On the flight home to San Francisco I stopped for the weekend in Chicago to see Blakey. She politely admired the absurd keychain I'd brought her from Flanders: a laminated reproduction of a 1914 recruiting poster. A cadre of shrewish females exhorting their unfortunate men, "Women of Britain Say—Go!" (I myself had a plastic, finger-pointing Kitchener, the brave homo-warlord bristling like a 1980s Castro Street clone.) We took my photos of Tyne Cot and Franvillers to be developed at the Walgreens on Michigan Avenue. But then we had a big blow-up fight that evening and she rushed out of her apartment building in a rage. I had to ask the Polish doorman which way she'd gone and ran after her, gesticulating like a Keystone Cop, up Lake Shore Drive.

When I got back to California, friends asked about the trip. I gave brief, potted, cousin-rich recountings; sometimes I even described the stereopticon. But I felt like a bit of a sociopath, especially when one of my colleagues looked at me with revulsion as I related the itinerary. At the same time I became irrationally indignant when listeners seemed insufficiently captivated by my odyssey of death. In March I gave a lecture at an esteemed university where I hoped to get a job. (The people there knew that Blakey and I wanted to be together; I had been asked to apply.) The talk had to do with the war and writers of the 1920s: Wyndham Lewis, Woolf, the Sitwells. I showed slides of Claud Lovat Fraser's sad little trench drawings and expressed, all too dotingly, my love for them. I even mentioned (obliquely) Uncle Newton. It was not a success. The department Medusa—a steely Queer Theorist in bovver boots—decided I was "wedded to the aesthetic" and needed "nuking" at once. And so I was. Hopes dashed, I fell into a pompous, protracted, maudlin depression, like Mr. Toad when he finds the stoats and ferrets have taken over Toad Hall. Friends kept saying "But they are the ones who look bad!" But I couldn't get over the ghastly cruelty of it all. I felt like a bullet-ridden blob. The cemetery trip had done something to me—induced a kind of temporary insanity?—but I couldn't get a grip on how or why. I was cabin'd, cribb'd, confin'd, and bound in to saucy doubts and fears.

My resolution's plac'd, and I have nothing
Of woman in me; now from head to foot
I am marble-constant, now the fleeting moon
No planet is of mine.
  —*ANTONY AND CLEOPATRA*, V.II. 237–40

A clue to the nature of my feelings came only this past autumn, haltingly, in the wake of the attacks on the East Coast. Even in balmy California there was no escaping what had happened. Televisions—especially the silly little army of them suspended above the treadmills at the gym I belong to—became existential torture devices. No more *Frasier* reruns or baseball; just Peter Jennings and dirty bombs.

The boys with tattoos flexed nervously. Even the female-to-male transsexuals looked shaken. (It's a gay gym.) I went through my own quiet days feeling gusty, shocked, and forlorn. Blakey was still in Chicago. One evening I broke down and called my father for the first time in months. He was surprised to hear from me. I mumbled that

I was "calling to see how he was," that I was upset by the attacks. Long, baffled pause. He allowed that he was fine. Silence, followed by clotted *hmmms.* He seemed to apprehend that I wanted something. I started raging inwardly. After a long silence, as if goaded by tiny jumper cables, he morosely acknowledged that when he and his brother were evacuated to the North of England in 1940, he thought it was "the end of the world." Two weeks later, though, he was feeling "somewhat better." Glum Larkinesque half-chuckle. Now, this was all unprecedented self-revelation, but didn't help much. I asked after his wife and the trombone-playing nephew. He sank back into his customary Arctic mode. I hung up, swearing as always never to call again.

I'd got off the World War I thing after the job fiasco—couldn't bear to look at my lecture notes, had tried to put everything out of my mind. But now it came inching back. I was desperate for something to read in those disordered weeks, something to match up with the lost way I was feeling. I galloped through Ann Wroe's book on Pontius Pilate, but it was too weird and dissociated. I ordered Kenneth Tynan's diaries from Amazon but found I was in no mood for high camp and dominatrixes. I wanted something stolid and sad. With a sense of oh-what-the-hell, I finally picked up a book I'd bought on the trench trip and then instantly lost interest in: a new paperback edition of Vera Brittain's Great War diary, the very diary she later transmuted into her celebrated 1933 war memoir, *Testament of Youth.*[*]

Brittain was hardly an unknown quantity. I'd read *Testament of Youth* in my twenties and had never forgotten the intensity with which she related the primal bereavements of her early years. (I had once observed my grandmother surreptitiously dabbing at her eyes while reading it in the 1970s; her own Great War losses—of fiancé

---

* *Chronicle of Youth: Great War Diary 1913–17*, edited by Alan Bishop (Phoenix, 2000).

and only brother—duplicated Brittain's exactly.) Yet I couldn't say I had ever exactly warmed to Brittain, as either author or woman. For all the pain and horror she had suffered—and for all the integrity of her subsequent personal and political commitments—she struck me as abrasive and conceited. I tended to agree with Woolf, who, after devouring *Testament of Youth*, applied the usual backhanded praise in a comical diary entry from the 1930s:

> *I am reading with extreme greed a book by Vera Brittain. Not that I much like her. A stringy metallic mind, with I suppose, the sort of taste I should dislike in real life. But her story, told in detail, without reserve, of the war, and how she lost lover and brother, and dabbled her hands in entrails, and was forever seeing the dead, and eating scraps, and sitting five on one WC, runs rapidly, vividly across my eyes.*

And as I started in, it all began coming back to me: the Head Girl self-righteousness; the smug rivalry with other women; the grue-some fascination with period bores like Mrs. Humphry Ward and Olive Schreiner. (In her wartime letters to the doomed Roland Leigh-ton, her nineteen-year-old fiancé, Brittain is forever comparing their poetical puppy love to that of the unfortunately named "Lyndall and Waldo" in *Story of an African Farm*.) Nor did I find much at first to obviate my ill humor. I've got big irritable underlinings, I see, at just that point early in 1915 when Brittain, still at Somerville, contem-plates enlisting as a VAD nurse:

> *Janet Adie came to tea to help me learn to typewrite. She is feel-ing very busy because she now has the secretaryship of one of those soup-kitchen affairs on her shoulders. It does not sound very strenu-ous an occupation; these people who never had anything to do before don't know the meaning of work . . . I was told I ought to join this &*

that & the other. Everyone seems to be so keen for me to give up one kind of work for another, & that less useful, but more understandable by them. The general idea seems to be that college is a kind of pleasant occupation which leads to nothing—least of all anything that might be useful when the results of war will cause even graver economic problems than the war itself. If only I can get some work at the Hospital in the summer. I wonder what they will say when they see me doing the nursing which seems to exhaust them all so utterly, & my college work as well! I always come out top in the end, & I always shall.

Yet as I continued to read, something else began coming through too—something less rebarbative. I started noticing, amid all the boasts and bitchiness and careening *ressentiment*, a more vulnerable side to Brittain's personality. I hadn't remembered—at all—what a phobic and self-critical woman she was, or indeed how deeply she had had to struggle, throughout the First World War, with what she felt to be her own pusillanimity. Now among the myriad painful feelings the attacks of September 11 had evoked in me—grief, despair, outrage—perhaps the most shame-making had been a penetrating awareness of my own cowardice. I worried incessantly about crashes, bombs, sarin gas, throat slitting, eye gouging, burning, jumping, falling. I brooded over horrific illnesses—anthrax, smallpox, radiation sickness, plague—and imagined my own blood, teeming with bacteria, oozing thickly from my pores. I became afraid of bridges and tall buildings and the incendiary, blue-gold beauty of the city in which I lived. My childhood fear of flying revivified, I shed tears of self-disgust when I saw the pregnant Mrs. Beamer, whose husband had died on United Flight 93, take the same flight a few weeks later to show her resilience in the face of disaster. While straining to appear normal, I felt a vertiginous dread—of life itself—soar and frolic within me, like an evil biplane on the loose. I was not brave, it seemed, as men were, or even semi-stoical. I struggled with hysterical girlishness. It was an archaic and humiliating problem. I was female—and a wretched poltroon.

Yet signs of similar struggle—against girl-frights of such magnitude that she "ached," she said, "for a cold heart & a passionless indifference"—were everywhere in Vera Brittain's journals. And perhaps because I was already alert to the theme, I found myself peculiarly affected by her testimony. I rapidly consumed the remaining diaries; reread *Testament of Youth* in a single great dollop; then turned to Paul Berry and Mark Bostridge's excellent Brittain biography of 1995. Before I knew it, I was up to my ears again in Great War matériel, but this time with a difference. I was getting a weensy bit more honest. To confess in public that you are afraid of death—and violent death especially—is to break a powerful taboo. Simple people will pity you and say nothing; the sophisticated will accuse you of being insufferably bourgeois. ("Spirited men and women"—or so maintains the title character in Bellow's *Ravelstein*—"were devoted to the pursuit of love. By contrast the bourgeois was dominated by fears of violent death.") Yet precisely in Brittain's unsentimental revelation of her fear and candid hankering after the kind of physical bravery she saw in the men she knew at the front, I found not only a partial clue to the meaning of my war obsession, but a necessary insight into my own less admissible hopes and fears.

Brittain's own anxieties, to be sure, were to some degree part of a difficult family inheritance. As Berry and Bostridge point out, she was a delicate woman: small and gamine in appearance, even in her starched VAD uniform. (Her brother Edward, who won a Military Cross on the first day of the Somme and died in June 1918, a few days after my Uncle Newton, towers over her by at least a foot in family photographs.) And in many ways she was delicate in spirit, too. Insanity ran in the family—she worried greatly as an adult about a "bad, bad nervous inheritance" in the Brittain line—and she was prone all her life to irrational frights and fancies. In an unfinished autobiographical novel from the 1920s she recalls the panic produced in her as a child by the sight of a "leering" full moon:

> *The little girl in the big armchair had gazed at it, tense with fear, till at last it grew into a face with two wicked eyes & an evilly grinning mouth. Unable to bear it any longer, she hid her face in the cushions, but only for a few moments; the moon had a dreadful fascination which impelled her, quite against her will, to look up at it again. This time the grin was wider than ever & one great eye, leering obscenely at her, suddenly closed in a tremendous & unmistakable wink. Four-year-old Virginia was not at any time remarkable in her courage . . . Flinging herself back into the chair, she burst into prolonged & piercing screams.*

Similar hallucinations plagued her later in life. In one of the stranger asides in *Testament of Youth*, she describes a "horrible delusion" she suffered after being demobilized in 1918. Returning to her studies at Somerville, traumatized and embittered by her war losses, she seemed to perceive, each time she looked at herself in the mirror, a "dark shadow" on her face, suggestive of a beard. For eighteen months she was tormented by this "sinister fungus" and feared she was becoming a witch. In the memoir she attributes the fantasy to the strain she was under and passes over it relatively quickly. ("I have since been told that hallucinations and dreams and insomnia are normal symptoms of over-fatigue and excessive strain, and that, had I consulted an intelligent doctor immediately after the war, I might have been spared the exhausting battle against nervous breakdown which I waged for 18 months.") Yet one has a sense, here and elsewhere, of a woman painfully susceptible to mental distress. Despite her subsequent achievements as journalist, public speaker, and political activist—or so say Berry and Bostridge—Brittain had always "to fight hard for what little confidence she achieved, and even in old age the predominant impression she created among those meeting her for the first time was of a woman who seemed to be in a state of almost perpetual worry."

But cowardice, as Brittain herself knew well, was also something more or less imprinted on women. By coddling and patronizing its female members, society enforced in them a kind of physical timidity; then, with infuriating circularity, defined such timidity as effeminate and despicable. Both practically and philosophically, Brittain rebelled against the linkage. In *Testament of Youth* she recalls, broodingly enough, the violent "inferiority complex" she felt in the early days of the war with regard to her lover Roland. He had enlisted in the Norfolks and would soon have his courage "tested" in the most literal way possible. Yet while fearing for his safety, Brittain envied him the trial. When he admitted in a letter how proud he was to be going to the front—it relieved him of the appearance of a "cowardly shirking of my obvious duty"—she declared, with palpable chagrin, that "women get all the dreariness of war, and none of its exhilaration." By "exhilaration" she meant, among other things, a certain exemption from self-contempt. Women got to hand out white feathers—notoriously—but the gesture took on its odium precisely because women themselves epitomized "cowardly shirking" so perfectly. They were the skulkers and moochers and tremulous babies of modern life, emasculated beings in need of protection, forbearance, and forgiveness.

Everyone knows what Brittain did: made herself as manly as possible by becoming a nurse on the Western Front. (Her subsequent beard-in-the-mirror fantasy suggests the psychic intensity of her rejection of conventional femininity.) It was as if by getting as close to the fighting as she could—within striking distance of long-range German artillery—she sought to subject herself to the same practical test of bravery imposed on Roland and her brother Edward. Her war diaries make unabashedly clear the impinging wish: to act as a man would and be emboldened thereby. "I had no idea she would get so thrilled as she seemed about the nursing," she writes in 1915 after telling her classics tutor at Somerville that she is signing up for war service; "she seemed to put it quite on the level of a man's deed by agreeing with me that I ought not to put the speedy starting of my career forward as an excuse, any more than a man should against enlisting." Joining up was doing something "on a level" with a man—facing up to fear like a soldier—and "all part of the hard path I have assigned myself to tread."

Which is not to say that Brittain entirely mastered her fearfulness. During her two years of nursing she was often afraid, and sometimes abjectly so. On her way by ship to Malta, her first foreign posting, she dreaded being blown up by enemy mines. During an air raid on Etaples during the final German advance in 1918, her teeth "chattered with sheer terror." But always there to sustain her was the faith that one might be inspirited—as if by magic—simply by mimicking, as far as possible, the stoic attitudes of men. Men had a certain *mana*, it seemed, a native supply of aplomb and insouciance that a courage-hungry woman might draw on. Blood transfusion technology, sadly, had yet to be perfected at the time of the First World War; thousands of soldiers who died from blood loss at casualty clearing stations might easily have been saved in later wars. Yet if hemoglobin could not be transfused, valor might be. By placing herself in harm's way, or as near to it as she could get, Brittain seems to have hoped to absorb, as if by osmosis, the palpable gallantry of the men she loved and admired.

After Roland's death in 1915 by sniper bullet near Louvencourt, Brittain immediately elevated him, talismanically, to the role of chief exemplar and courage infuser. Since his death was less than glorious (he seems merely to have lifted his head up inopportunely while slithering on his stomach through No Man's Land on a routine nighttime patrol), Brittain's posthumous exaltation of him depended on some ambitious mental maneuvers. In the weeks after his death, she repeatedly sought to assure herself that despite the humiliating manner of his demise he was as brave an English warrior as any Arthurian knight. "I had another letter tonight from Roland's servant," she writes in February 1916,

> *giving a few more illuminating details of His death. It proves Him conclusively not to have thrown His life away recklessly or needlessly. He was hit because he was the last man to leave the dangerous area for the comparative safety of the trench, and so was at the post where the Roland we worship would always have wished to be when he met Death face to face.*

"Worship" is the operative word. In *Testament of Youth*, Brittain presents herself as godless and disillusioned, but it is clear from the ardent tributes to Roland in the diaries that she viewed him, for a time at least, as a sort of new Jesus Christ, whose martial self-sacrifice had made possible the "salvation" of others—including her own. Almost as soon as Roland was killed, she began referring to him with a God-like "He": "Whether it was absolutely necessary for Him to go [on the fatal patrol] is questionable, but He would not have been He if He had not, for not only did He like to do everything Himself to make sure it was done thoroughly, but He would never allow anyone, especially an inferior, to take a risk he would not take Himself." She herself became "His" principal devotee and disciple, the mystic practitioner of a new sort of *imitatio Christi*, as her entries from 1916 make clear:

SUNDAY, 2 JANUARY.

> *We had more details today—fuller, more personal, more interesting, & so much sadder . . . Two sentences—one in the Colonel's letter & one in the Chaplain's hurt me more than anything. The*

*Colonel says, "The Boy was wonderfully brave," and the Chaplain,
"He died at 11 p.m. after a very gallant fight." Yes, he would have
been wonderfully brave; he would have made a gallant fight, even
though unconsciously, with that marvelous vitality of his. None ever
had more to live for; none could ever have wanted to live more . . . I
can wish to do nothing better than to act as He has acted, right up
to the end.*

MONDAY, 31 JANUARY.

*There was very much of a Zeppelin scare tonight. The Hospital
was in utter darkness, passages black, lamps out, blinds down.
I stood at the window of my ward, feeling strangely indifferent to
anything that might happen. Since He had given up all safety, I was
glad to be in London, which is not safe.*

SUNDAY, 22 OCTOBER.

*We had a simple sermon comparing harvest with the Resurrec-
tion of the Dead, & sang the hymn "On the Resurrection Morning"
to end with. I don't believe half the theology implied in these things,
of course, & yet it is all a reminder. "I could not if I would forget"—
Roland. But I never would, since in all this hard life He is my great
& sole inspiration, & if it were not for Him I should not be here.*

In 1917, when Roland's old school friend Victor, blinded by a
bullet at Arras, lies dying in a London hospital, she admits that one
reason she can't bear to lose him is because in his "accurate, clear
& reverent memory of Him, Roland seems to live still." "All that I
ask," she concludes, "is that I may fulfill my own small weary part
in this War in such a way as to be worthy of Them, who die & suffer
pain."

In the nervy state that gripped me after September 11, such re-
flections struck me with new and incriminating force. Had I resisted

Brittain for so long—cast her off as an important Not-Me—precisely because, deep down, I felt so much like her? I found out now, with a sudden embarrassed poignancy, precisely how much I sympathized, both with her anxiety and with the florid hope that the men she knew might infect her, so to speak, with physical courage. Not very butch of me, I know. Not very feminist. But I had to confess it: I admired and coveted—quite desperately at times—the insane, uncomplaining, relentless bravery of men.

I hear the shrieks. I write this knowing full well that some readers will find such veneration wholly charmless, part of an objectionable idealization of war or some absurd reversion to worn-out sex roles. So let me try to be a bit more precise. It seems to have something to do, first of all, with walking. Walking, paradoxically, is one of the great leitmotifs of the First World War. (I say "paradoxically" because we are so used to imagining the nightmarish stasis of the trench world—a stasis more notional, perhaps, than actual. Even in times of relative quiet the typical front-line trench was an ant heap of comings and goings.) Under normal conditions British soldiers traveled to the battle sector by troop train; contemporary accounts of "going up the line" are full of descriptions of men crammed into creaking boxcars, and the slow, juddering rides towards Abbeville or Béthune. (How often the physical imagery of the First War anticipates, diabolically, that of the Second.) But on disembarking, soldiers usually had to march—sometimes for ten or twenty miles—toward billets, reserve trenches, and other staging-areas behind the lines. "This in fact," Malcolm Brown writes in *Tommy Goes to War*, "was the classic progress 'up the line': train to the railhead, after which the Tommy had to fall back on the standard means of troop-transportation in the First World War—his own feet." All the famous soldier songs of the time—"Here We Are," "Tipperary," "Mademoiselle from Armentières"—were first and foremost marching songs.

The route was long, exhausting, and often indelibly frightening, especially for the tyro soldier seeing warfare up close for the first time. "Yesterday as we were jingling over the cobbles past the danger zone," one subaltern quoted by Brown wrote,

> sure enough, away to the right came Ponk! Ze-e-e-e-e-e-ee-E-Bang! right over our heads. Again: Ponk: Ze-e-e-e-ee-E-Bang! A little nearer. The road just there is bare of cover, but a little way along on the right was a large barn, shell-holed. I would have given quids and quids just to run to that barn: but I am in front of my column, so I merely glance up in a casual way (what an effort) as if I'd been reared on shrapnel, whereas it's my baptism!

Another described his company being scattered by a German shell on their first march up the line near Bailleul: "My back and pack were struck by a shower of debris and flying dirt while quite a number of men fell and bled for their country. Jack Duncan was in front of me and he received a severe wound from this, our first shell. He was carried onto the pavement and left for the attention of the doctor."

Getting into the front-line trench itself meant further dreadful walking: a crabbed, head-down slog along battered communication trenches or over rotting duckboards, sometimes under heavy shelling or machine-gun fire. The journey to the front lines around Ypres—invariably made at night, through pools of mud and the reamy stench of dead animals and men—was notoriously ghastly. "The boards," Leon Wolff writes in *In Flanders Fields*,

> were covered with slime, or submerged, or shattered every few yards. The heavy laden troopers (60 lb of clothing, equipment and weapons were carried per man) kept slipping and colliding. Many toppled into shell-craters and had to be hauled out by comrades extending rifle-butts. And falling into even a shallow hole was often revolting, for the water was foul with decaying equipment, excrement, and per-

*haps something dead; or its surface might be covered with old, sour
mustard gas. It was not uncommon for a man to vomit when being
extricated from something like this.*

And many fell, never to be dragged out. At Passchendaele, in the
satanic months of October and November 1917, soldiers going up the
line would often see the heads or hands of hapless predecessors pro-
truding from the muck.

Animals, it seems, knew better—that such walking was intolerable. "In one official history," Wolff notes, "there is a picture . . . cap-
tioned 'Bogged,' of a mule in a shell-hole. His hindquarters are deep
in the mud; only his head and shoulders protrude. In utter despair his
head rests in the mud, eyes half-closed. Many mules had panicked,
had fought merely to stand on visible portions of the planking, and
could be made to move only with much coaxing and punishment."
The collapsing pack mule is a vignette out of Sterne's *A Sentimental
Journey*—but here gone awry and nightmarish.

The most celebrated walking of all was that of soldiers going "over
the top." In order to stay in sync with the barrage and each other, attacking troops were strictly enjoined not to run. Once up over the
parapet and into No Man's Land, they were required to proceed in
a stylized, almost courtly fashion—one man every two yards, rifles
at the port, bayonets fixed, everyone moving forward in slow and
regular waves. And thus unfurled what one writer calls "the classic
drama of the Western Front," the solemn, pavane-like motion of men
towards machine-gun fire and death:

*In the flame and clamour and greasy smoke the British slogged for-
ward deliberately, almost unhurriedly. They moved from crater to
crater, but even in the craters they were not safe, for the German
gunners streamed bullets against the edges of the holes and wounded
many men lying near the rims. As the British walked, some seemed*

to pause and bow their heads; they sank carefully to their knees; they rolled over without haste and then lay quietly in the soft, almost caressing mud.

There is something beyond uncanny in such scenes. On the first day of the Somme, defending German gunners watched in amazement as row upon row of British soldiers plodded calmly towards them, only to be cut down in swathes. For the oncoming troops, it took every ounce of courage not to break formation—even as hellfire raged, crumps exploded, and ground churned up around them. For the few who survived, the dream-like walk towards enemy trenches remained ever after, in the words of one historian, "an intensely personal journey etched in [the] memory like the Stations of the Cross."

As Paul Fussell long ago pointed out, the passage over No Man's Land was indeed a Christ-like transit, a hideous stroll into the Valley of Death. Like the assault on the Somme, the Passion begins— kinesthetically and archetypally—in heroic pedestrianism: the tedious trudge "up the line" to the boneyard known as Golgotha. Jesus is the first man in history to walk unwaveringly towards his own death. And ultimate masculine fortitude—at least in the modern West— has never lost its association with this Christ-like, goal-oriented walking. It is striking how many accounts of the destruction of the World Trade Center obsessively replay the image of doomed firemen and police walking into the towers and up the fatal stairwells— with exactly the same steady, flowing motion of attacking soldiers in the Great War. In a 2001 *Newsweek* report on the last minutes of Bill Feehan, a deputy commissioner of the New York City Fire Department killed in the collapse of the North Tower, he is seen exhorting his subordinates to walk just so:

Feehan's men—Guidetti, Goldbach and two other deputy commissioners, Tom McDonald and Tom Fitzpatrick—began rushing

to the elevator. "Now, hold it, guys," said Feehan, wearing a wry
smile, holding his arms to the side and waving his palms down, like
a teacher calming rambunctious schoolchildren. "Do we really want
to run to this? Or should we walk to it?" Feehan was following an
old dictum: "Firemen should never run." It was important to stay
calm, to size up the job before rushing in.

Panic-stricken civilians making their way down were staggered—
or so one reads again and again—by the sight of "firefighters loaded
with gear, trudging their way up the stairs. Everyone stepped aside to
let them pass, watching them in awe." Onward, Christian soldiers.

Cynics will no doubt want to debunk the heroic image of World
War I walking: they will call attention to the fact that men who
balked at the whistle—the signal for the start of the assault—faced
being shot on the spot by their commanding officers. True enough.
It's also true that other frightened soldiers simply faded from the
scene, only to be caught and punished later. (The Ypres museum has
a sad little pamphlet for sale commemorating the 306 British troops
officially tried and "shot at dawn" for cowardice or desertion.) Kipling—Kipling!—has the following wrenching couplet in his *Epi-
taphs* (1919):

I could not look on Death, which being known,
Men led me to him, blindfold and alone.
("The Coward")

Yet, relatively speaking, very few men seem to have failed thus in
their duty. Those who did so were usually blatantly shell-shocked or
otherwise unfit. However amazing in retrospect, the vast majority
of ordinary soldiers accepted the martial tasks assigned them, even
when such tasks were plainly suicidal. The most moving British novel
to come out of the war, Frederic Manning's *Her Privates We* (1930),

may be taken as a fitful, yet forceful, demonstration of this fact. The hero, a laconic private soldier named Bourne, commits himself to a nighttime trench raid, though he knows it is doomed to fail. When asked by his foolish commanding officer if he has any objection to going, Bourne feels "something in him dilate enormously, and then contract to nothing again," but says only that he is "quite ready" to go. He goes; he dies; and the book ends.

If you're a woman—and a woman haunted by feelings of cowardice—it's hard to know where to stand with all of this. You regret the appalling, absurd waste of life. You excoriate the madness of the system. You rail against war. You see the savage toll the cult of heroism takes—has always taken—on men and boys. But painful, too—at times exorbitantly so, once you become sensitized to it—the near-total exclusion of your own sex from such primal dramas of unflinching physical courage. You feel at a moral deficit. You wonder, perhaps dubiously, if you would be capable of such nobility under the circumstances: of moving forward calmly. You fear the worst. For Brittain was right: women have seldom been asked to exert their valor in this direct, theatrical, entirely wasteful, and (yet) sublime fashion. Certainly I never have.

From early childhood I have searched with little success for a woman who might show me, in some comparable and quite literal way, how to walk towards death. Few have offered themselves as models. A psychoanalyst I know says this is because women are preeminently concerned with "life." Children and the raising of children. They have no interest in walking towards death. Given half a chance, they walk away from death. It's "pure and simple biology," the shrink says. But whence my own odd questing? Some retardation of normal development? Some sad hormonal jousting with the male of the species? Some dissatisfaction with simply staying put and waiting for things to happen? Last week I went to see the film version of *Lord of the Rings*—not having thought much about Tolkien since I was twelve. The trilogy's a death-trip of course—a long weary trudge through mud, mines, ravaged woods, and orc-infested caves. As I pondered the dire, cacophonous, corpse-laden wastelands through which Frodo and his friends are forced to travel—now digitalized and Dolby-ized and fiercely estranging (like video games and cyberterrorism)—I found myself wondering whether Tolkien had been a soldier on the Western Front. Couldn't remember. Got home and looked him up: he fought on the Somme with the Lancashire Fusiliers.

True, a woman on her way to public execution in some degree resembles a soldier going over the top. As a child, I uncovered a few such women, and studied them as best I could. But a certain intimacy, kinship—even friendliness—was almost always lacking. They never felt like comrades. There was Joan of Arc, but I found her celebrated visions freakish and her personality aloof. I was not raised a Catholic, so stories of female saints and martyrs made little or no impression. I was too young for the terrible dramas of the Holocaust and Resistance. There was the aforementioned Edith Cavell—her fate, I find, is luridly described in a children's *Pageant of History* book I still have on my shelves—but it would take a while before I understood her actions in context. (Calling me, not long ago, from the grotty pay phone near the latter's memorial at the foot of Charing Cross Road, Blakey had to endure me squeaking away, at eight thousand miles' distance, *But of course she was a spy! The Germans had every right to shoot her! She knew it!* etc.) Only now do I begin to find the high starched collar, iron-gray hair, and sweeping black cape oddly alluring. No, sir, I do not require a blindfold.

The French Revolution, to be sure, offers instances of almost picturesque feminine gallantry—though it's hardly fashionable to say so. Madame Roland was famously poised on the scaffold: she let Lamarche, a feeble old man being executed with her, go first so he would not have the sight of her own headless corpse before him as he approached the guillotine. Marie Antoinette, former *cocotte*, was even more so. Hounded, half-starved, white-haired, and decrepit at the age of thirty-four (from chronic menstrual flux and the gross abuse of her jailers), the no-good *Autrichienne* became quite staggeringly noble in her final moments. David's harrowing sketch of her, set down from life as she rolled by in the death cart on her way to execution, is the unexpected emblem of a stupendous and electrifying heroism.

The French Revolution is also the setting for the only major work of art—the only one that I can think of at least—devoted profoundly and entirely to the topic of feminine courage: Francis Poulenc's 1957 opera *Dialogues of the Carmelites*. Based on a play by Bernanos and a novel by Gertrud von Le Fort, *Die letzte am Schafott* ("The Last to the Scaffold"), the opera turns on the struggle of Sister Blanche de l'Agonie du Christ, a novice in the Carmelite order at Compiègne, to master the dread that assails her when the sisters of the convent are arrested during the Terror. The plot has its origin in fact: Marie de l'Incarnation, a Carmelite nun who survived the Revolution, tells a similar story in her memoirs. (And how odd, the WWI freak notes, that it should all have taken place at Compiègne: British GHQ during the retreat from Mons and site of the signing of the Armistice in 1918.)* When the other sisters take a vow of martyrdom, Blanche runs away and hides for several weeks at her father's house. Mortified by her own cowardice, however, she secretly follows her fellow nuns when they are taken to Paris for execution. In the opera's final moments, as the condemned women march to the guillotine singing the Salve Regina—a voice falling out with each ferocious slice on the

---

* Like Sarajevo, Belfast, and Dallas, Compiègne would seem to be one of the strangely doom-laden minor cities in history. My 1920 *Guide to Belgium and the Western Front* notes that Joan of Arc was captured and turned over to the English there in 1430; Marie Antoinette, aged fifteen, met her future husband the Dauphin there in 1770; and Tsar Nicholas and the Tsarina were received by President Loubet at the famous nearby château in 1901.

cymbals—Blanche suddenly materializes from the crowd and joins in the procession. Hers is the only voice left, soaring up in triumph, when the last blade stroke comes down and the curtain drops.

But Blanche is a bit of a pill, too—a sexless high soprano and one of those blonde, seraphic goody-goodies one could never stand at school. Charlotte Brontë would have loathed her. And for every Blanche, it seems, there are always women like the unhappy Lange Vaubernier, better known as Madame du Barry, the one-time mistress of Louis XV. On her way to execution, according to Lamartine's *Histoire des Girondins* (1847), the aging harlot flung back her veil "in order that her countenance might move the people" and "did not cease to invoke pity, in the most humiliating terms." The poet, spokesman of the People, is extravagantly contemptuous:

> *Tears flowed incessantly from her eyes upon her bosom. Her piercing cries prevailed over the noise of the wheels and the clamor of the multitude. It seemed as if the knife struck this woman beforehand, and deprived her a thousand times of life.*
>
> *"Life! Life!" she cried; "life for my repentance!—life for all my devotion to the Republic!—life for all my riches to the nation!"*
>
> *The people laughed and shrugged their shoulders. They showed her, by signs, the pillow of the guillotine, upon which her charming head was about to sleep. The passage of the courtesan to the scaffold was but one lamentation. Under the knife she still wept. The Court had enervated her soul. She alone, among all the women executed, died a coward, because she died neither for opinion, for virtue, nor for love, but for vice. She dishonored the scaffold as she had dishonored the throne.*

Poor old Lange. *See yah. Wouldn't wanna be yah.*

At a certain point one just gives up and decides to go with the men. They're so much closer to home, after all. Unless one is insane or a sex fanatic, it's impossible to identify much with Joan of Arc or Marie Antoinette; whereas one's estimable Uncle Newton, soft mustache and all, seems just a few decades and a Chunnel trip away. I sometimes feel I could call him up on the phone. He lives in the same world as I do, the familiar vale of sorrows, fuck-ups, and relentless, chain-reaction human disasters. (How acutely one feels the 9/11 violence to be, like so much else in our time, simply one of the hundreds of geopolitical aftershocks of the First World War. Palestine, after all, began its long, sad modern history in 1917, when Allenby's Army drove off the Turks at Gaza and occupied Jerusalem.)* And compelling indeed is the knowledge that I myself can now walk exactly where he walked. The worst signs of battle have long disappeared from the Western Front but the war tourism industry battens still on the morbid hankering of visitors to stroll freely about those very places (Loos, Menin, Hooge, Stuff Trench, Polygon Wood, Vimy, Festubert, Beaumont Hamel, Gheluvelt, Neuve-Chapelle) where walking (of any sort) was once so foul and frightening. One can now wander unimpeded over spots formerly blasted by gun and shell fire; where lifting one's head above the parapet, even by an inch, meant getting it blown off. One feels floaty and tall and invulnerable, like a ghost. You imagine getting hit all over—positively laced with bullets—but it doesn't hurt at all.

And then, too, there's the *mana* effect: the hope that by treading just so, on the very spot, some ancient family backbone will be magically imparted. (After I came back from my trip, I found it oddly difficult to brush the Somme mud off my hiking shoes.) Traveling through Picardy and Flanders, it's hard to forget that the soil itself is full of once-sentient matter, now dissolved but still in situ. We are

---

* Siegfried Sassoon, in *Memoirs of an Infantry Officer* (1930): "Markington had gloomily informed me that our [War] Aims were essentially acquisitive, what we were fighting for was the Mesopotamian Oil Wells. A jolly fine swindle it would have been for me, if I'd been killed in April for an Oil Well!"

inclined to make fun of Rupert Brooke–style animism these days, perhaps because his creepy brand of dirt-magic is still so weirdly potent:

> *There shall be*
> *In that rich earth a richer dust concealed;*
> *A dust whom England bore, shaped, made aware,*
> *Gave, once, her flowers to love, her ways to roam,*
> *A body of England's, breathing English air,*
> *Washed by the rivers, blest by suns of home.*

Yet it's only a short step from Brooke's patriotic composting to
fantasies of an even more atavistic sort. Almost as soon as the first
Great War cemeteries were opened to the public, sentimental grave
visitors sought to absorb the magical rigor of the dead. In *The Un-
ending Vigil* (1967), his history of the Commonwealth War Graves
Commission, Philip Longworth relates a saccharine tale of a French
child at Versailles—a "heroic little thing . . . doomed by a disease of
the spine"—who insisted on tending the graves of her *"chers soldats
anglais"* until her sickness defeated her. The punning import of the
story is so obvious as to be risible: how else to ward off "spineless-
ness" in the face of mortality? I've got her number, and she, undoubtedly, has mine.

So I want my great-uncle to make me brave; is that what it boils
down to? To place his hand in the small of my back and give me that
first shove up onto the fire-step? To start me off on my wind-up-
toy-like way into No Man's Land? That's an answer for the moment,
I suppose, but no more than that. It would be nice to be sturdier and
less addled, not such a twit on wheels. It would be gratifying to impress everyone with my handsome, jut-jawed selflessness. ("I now
perceive one immense omission in my Psychology," William James
once wrote; "the deepest principle of Human Nature is the craving
to be appreciated.") Somewhere, it seems, there must be a lost baby

picture of me—at my father's perhaps?—in which I look just like Mel Gibson in *Gallipoli. Huɀɀah, matey!*

At the same time, I see how kooky and notional it all is. How can I be sure, for example, that my great-uncle even died bravely? His service record seems to have disappeared; according to the Public Record Office Web site, it looks to have been one of the hundreds of thousands of such records destroyed during the Blitz. Perhaps he was a puny little time-serving fellow who just happened to be in the wrong place at the wrong time. My mother's vague recollection of him being shot by "his own guns" is worrying: perhaps he was sitting in a dugout drinking a cup of tea, or nibbling on a piece of chocolate (the family vice), and simply got blown up by accident. Perhaps he was picked off by an errant bullet while using the company latrine. Perhaps he started jabbering in terror one day and his sergeant-major just had to brain him in homicidal exasperation. Such things were all part of the "normal wastage" of the war. I have a great deal invested, I realize, in the image of him not being wasted. I prefer to view him stalking forward coolly, his fellow Poplar and Stepney Rifles at his side, across the muddy, blood-drenched plains of the Ancre.

But even if my fantasy about him is accurate, do I really need him to show me the way? I've gotten this far, after all, on my own two feet. Might it not be the case, terrors notwithstanding, that most people end up "walking towards death" in a fairly resolute fashion whether they plan to or not? One of the few times, paradoxically, I've found myself in apparent physical danger, when a bomb warning sounded deep in one of the Tube tunnels at Charing Cross and everyone had to evacuate in a hurry, I not only remained calm but felt peculiarly philosophical. The long-legged platform guard skedaddled at once—I can still see him bounding up the escalator steps two or three at a time—leaving a little group of tourists and children and old-age pensioners to scramble along after him. I ran about a third of the way up the escalator, panting horribly—it was one of those extra long ones and for some reason wasn't moving—then thought: *oh fuck this, I'm too tired to run anymore! I don't care if I get blown up!* It was like the old French and Saunders skit: my leg bones have gone away. So I walked the rest of the way, more or less sedately, ultimately surfacing in Trafalgar Square. The crowds and the pigeons were bustling about as usual. No bomb went off, that week or later.

Silliest of all perhaps: whom do I hope to impress with my virile equipoise? My mother? My father? Siegfried Sassoon? Vera Brittain? Miss Coombs? None, I confess, has ever asked for such a proof of character. Blakey couldn't care less. She's staying with me till next September, working away in the downstairs room, where she's just figured out a way to type on a laptop while lying down. The dog loves it because he gets to spend the whole day snoozing on the bed with her while she muses. She's stuck with me all this dreary past year, though I'm not sure what she really thinks, either about my war obsession or the "walking towards death" stuff. She is interested in evolutionary psychology and selfish genes. Given such an intellectual framework, the First World War, like all genocidal conflicts, poses certain conceptual difficulties. How could it have been possible for millions of men to squander their DNA in such a reckless fashion? It's a stumper, I agree.

The other day we looked at an old photo in one of my books of a parade of volunteers, still dressed in their civilian clothes, marching down a London street in August 1914. War has just been declared. The men look tough and expectant; a military band is playing and women gaze down from balconies and windows. I had just realized to my great excitement that the narrow roadway in the picture (at first generic-looking Edwardian) was actually Villiers Street, the busy pedestrian thoroughfare that runs down from the Strand to Embankment. There on one side of the picture, clearly visible once you get your bearings, is the dark, somewhat dusty façade of Gordon's Wine Bar. It looks almost exactly as it does now.

I went there the first time, I recall, with Bridget, one late autumn night in 1987, during the honeymoon phase of our cousinhood. (It was the same night, we discovered later, as the terrible fire at King's Cross.) Down steep wooden steps into a smoky medieval crypt where they served up our burgundy and plonk. Strange, as always, the curving back of time. One of the worst things about the First World War, from the vantage point of 2002, is that you think you've got to the end of thinking about it, then something makes you start all over again. This picture, for instance. I would prefer to move on and out—from gloomy 1918 especially—but I keep getting sent back to the beginning, as if stuck in some kind of Möbius loop. It's totally unlikely, as I said to Blakey, that my great-uncle could be one of the men in the parade, coming from the Midlands as he did. (The new Sherwood Forester battalions of 1914 and '15 formed up in Derby and Newark.) But that didn't keep me, as soon as Blakey went back to work, from screwing in my monocle and inspecting the men like a staff general. It was a tough job: I had first to remove all the cloth caps and boaters, add rifles and packs and khaki, then connect the fatal dots. And even then, all I could really see—staring crazily upward, as if already dazed by the fumes from the dugout brazier—was my own once-boyish face.

My Heroin Christmas

Living without love is like not living at all.
—ART PEPPER, 1958

Art Pepper, 1960

WRITING THIS IN SAN FRANCISCO, having just come back from San Diego and a heroin Christmas at my mother's. Not that I used any—there was definitely *not* any blowing, horning, tasting, fixing, goofing, getting loaded, or laying out. I've always been afraid of serious drugs, knowing my grip on "things being okay" was pretty tenuous already. Back in high school in the early seventies when everyone else was dropping acid, I refrained, mainly out of fear that I would be the inevitable freak-with-no-friends who would end up curled up for life in a psychotic ball, or else spattered in ribbony pieces, having flung myself through a plate-glass window. I also wanted to get perfect grades. No: the major dissipations this holiday were candy and coffee and buying things online with just one click. Before I left, Blakey had given me some chocolate cigarettes, and at night, lying on my back under the covers with the laptop on my stomach—my mother had put me in the little upstairs room that used to be Jeff's—I would reach over and unroll one in a smarmy, bourgeois, sugar-dazed languor.

It was a heroin Christmas because I was reading the greatest book I've ever read: the jazz musician Art Pepper's 1979 autobiography *Straight Life: The Story of Art Pepper*. It knocked my former top pick, *Clarissa*, right out of first place. As Art himself might say, *my joint is getting big just thinking about it*. I realize there may be a few lost souls who've never heard of him. Forget the overrated (and vapid-looking) Chet Baker. Art Pepper (1925–1982) was an authentic American genius. One of the supreme alto saxophone players of all time, Charlie Parker included. A deliriously handsome lover boy in the glory days of his youth. A lifelong dope addict of truly Satanic fuck-it-all grandeur. A natural writer of brazen, comic, commanding virtuosity. A proud long-term denizen of the California prison system. And now, no doubt, a tranquil if desiccated corpse. As his third and last wife, Laurie, notes in the epilogue to *Straight Life*, "Art . . . was afraid to be buried in the ground; he was afraid of the worms. But he was terrified of fire. So I had him interred in a crypt at the Hollywood Cemetery, like Rudolph Valentino. He would have enjoyed the location, the company, and that creepy word, crypt." If my mother—now seventy-seven, curious, and freakishly adept at Internet navigation—ever looks me up on Google and sees what I'm writing now, I doubt if she'll be pleased.

Some of my liking, I confess, arises from sheer Southern California white-trash fellow feeling. Pepper was born near Los Angeles and spent most of his rackety life (as I have) on the West Coast. His father was a shipyard worker and nasty alcoholic. His mother, a dim-witted teenage bride, didn't want him and late in her pregnancy tried to abort him by leaping off a table. For what it's worth, my cross-eyed stepsister Lee did something similar when *she* got pregnant at sixteen in San Diego in 1967: made my younger stepsister Linda (around ten at the time) jump off a sofa onto her stomach to make it "pop." As with Mrs. Pepper's desperate *jeté*, the gambit failed to produce the desired effect. Lee had to have the baby in a Catholic place for unwed mothers and left it with an adoption agency. She later married Greg, a telephone installer from San Bernardino with a mammoth Nietzsche-style mustache, and became a compulsive gambler and grocery coupon–clipper before dying of drink at forty-six in 1996.

Unlike Art, however, I never mastered a musical instrument. (Plinking guitar accompaniments to "Love Is Blue" and "If I Had a Hammer"—grimly laid down as puberty loomed—don't count.) Pepper was a child prodigy. Though forgotten and unloved (his parents split up and basically dumped him), he got hold of a clarinet and taught himself to play. By the age of fourteen he was sitting in on clarinet and sax in jazz clubs all around L.A. After a short stint in the army— Pepper was stationed in London after the D-Day invasion—he joined the Stan Kenton Orchestra and traveled around the country as Kenton's lead alto. You can hear one of his very first recorded solos—brief, free, characteristically ductile—three breaks in after the famous scat-singing vocal by June Christy on Kenton's thunderous account of "How High the Moon" on the recent Proper Box compilation, *Bebop Spoken Here*.

After his first small-group recordings in the early fifties, discerning jazz fans recognized Pepper as a post-bop player of unusual beauty, subtlety, and warmth. The fact that he was white, like many other major West Coast jazz musicians, was not generally held against him. Astonishing to discover, especially given how few people outside music know much about him now, that he came in second after Charlie Parker in a 1951 *DownBeat* readers' poll for Best Alto Sax Player Ever. Even the most partisan Bird fanciers acknowledged that Pepper's tone was the most ravishing ever heard before on alto. Parker received 957 votes and Art almost tagged up with 945.

But things got wrenching soon enough. Having begun as an alcoholic and pothead in his teens, Pepper got hooked on heroin while on the road with Kenton's orchestra in 1950. He had found—as he relates in his memoir—that junk was precious indeed, the only thing that made him feel "at peace" with his frightening talent and the unstable world around him.

> *I felt this peace like a kind of warmth. I could feel it start in my stomach. From the whole inside of my body I felt the tranquility. It was so relaxing. It was so gorgeous. Sheila said, "Look at yourself in the mirror! Look in the mirror!" And that's what I'd always done: I'd stood and looked at myself in the mirror and I'd talk to myself and say how rotten I was—"Why do people hate you? Why are you alone? Why are you so miserable?" I thought, "Oh, no! I don't want to do that! I don't want to spoil this feeling that's coming up in me!" I was afraid that if I looked in the mirror I would see it, my whole past life, and this wonderful feeling would end, but she kept saying "Look at yourself! Look how beautiful you are! Look at your eyes! Look at your pupils!" I looked in the mirror and I looked like an angel. I looked at my pupils and they were pinpoints; they were tiny, little dots. It was like looking into a whole universe of joy and happiness and contentment.*

In the mid-fifties Pepper was arrested numerous times on possession charges and spent over a year in various jails and rehabilitation centers. (He inevitably used his devious charm to hoodwink his dopey docs into thinking he had cleaned up, even though he never did; in jail he shot up all the time.) Out on parole and divorced from his first wife—she'd dumped him over drugs—he took up with a clingy, bouffant-haired Filipina cocktail waitress named Diane, whom he married in 1957. (He wasn't in love with her, he confesses; she was dumb and slovenly: "Diane—the Great Zeeeero." "I just wanted to have chicks I could ball when I wanted to ball.") She too soon had a huge habit. (She became suicidal and died a few years later.) For a while Pepper still got paying gigs, and some of his best recordings—*Art Pepper Plus Eleven*, *Modern Art*, *The Return of Art Pepper*, and the sublime *Art Pepper Meets the Rhythm Section* (with Miles Davis's nonpareil late-fifties rhythm section)—were made while he was high. But after he and poor Diane began nodding out for days at a time, blissfully insensible to the strangulated yips of their miniature French poodle, Bijou, no one would hire him. He started doing solo hold-ups and boosts to keep them supplied, cruising past East L.A. construction sites and making off with unguarded power tools. He got caught with a condom full of dope after one of these farcical heists and when he refused to rat on his dealer, was sent to San Quentin, where he spent five brutalizing years.

Pepper was released in 1968—middle-aged, chapfallen, penniless, and still addicted, his numerous scars and track marks supplemented with a conglomeration of scary and absurd prison tattoos. He describes these droll insignias in a typically deadpan passage in his autobiography:

> One guy did one of Pan. Pan played his little horn and all the women followed him. He'd take them into a cave and ball them, and then the women would disappear. They'd never find them again. I had Pan put on my left forearm, and then—I've always like Peanuts—a guy put Snoopy and Linus inside my left forearm. I got the smiling and the sad masks on my right forearm. On my right bicep I got a Chinese skull, with a long mustache and a Van Dyke beard, smoking an opium pipe. Above my left breast I got a naked lady, a rear view of her squatting, but that one faded. And then on my back I got a chick doing the limbo, going under the bar, with little black panties on. That one came out nice. Just before I got released, I was going to get a vampire. A guy had done a drawing of Dracula, and it was going to

be on my right arm over my vein. The mouth would be open over the vein, and then when I fixed I could say, "Hey, wait a minute! I gotta feed mah man! He's hungry, jack!" You know. "Come on, baby, I gotta go first. Mah man's hungry. He needs some blood!'

You can see some of the tattoos in the supergrotty ex-felon pic of him—a cadaverous Nan Goldin–style mug shot—on the cover of *Art Pepper: Living Legend* (1975). The LP should perhaps have been called *Semi-Living Legend*.

But the story has the teensiest little glimmer of a happy ending. After hitting the skids yet again, rupturing his spleen on stage (he'd started playing intermittently with the Buddy Rich band) and nearly dying, Pepper managed to get himself into Synanon, the celebrated Santa Monica drug-rehabilitation center and *Atlas Shrugged*–style beach commune. He lived there for several years in the early seventies and met Laurie, the young woman who became his third wife. He gradually cleaned up, at least partially, and began a heroic if truncated musical comeback. He made some new records, started touring again, and as quasi-rehabilitated *éminence grise,* gave jazz workshops at colleges and universities (even in his worst dope fiend days he had enjoyed tutoring young saxophonists). He played in Japan in the late seventies and developed there a new and enraptured cadre of fans. "My reception," he notes in a revealing aside at the end of his memoir, "was overwhelming and frightening. I feel a strong obligation to return to Japan again and again and to justify, in my playing and recording, the devotion of the Japanese fans." Accepting the love of others was always painful for him, but toward the end of his life he managed to open up a little bit.

He also began dictating *Straight Life* to Laurie, a kind and meticulous young woman who, along with being a fellow Synanon resident, had fortuitously trained as an anthropologist. (The title *Straight Life*—addict argot for living without heroin—is the name of one of Pepper's musical compositions from the 1950s.) Once he'd laid out the basic narrative for her, a strange uncensored flow of childhood reminiscence, jazz and junk lore, obscene sexual anecdotes, and fearless, often japing self-revelation, Laurie, with Pepper's permission, asked some of his old bandmates, producers, drug dealers, prison cronies, and girlfriends to add their own insightful (and often unflattering) comments into the mix. The resulting feuilleton came out in 1979. It was hailed at once as a poetic masterpiece: a kind of riffing, scabrous, West Coast *Season in Hell*. As Whitney Balliett, doyen of American jazz critics, wrote at the time in *The New Yorker*, Pepper had "the ear and memory and interpretive lyricism of a first-rate novelist." Balliett was right. But unfortunately the literary glory was short-lived. Though mostly off junk, Pepper continued to consume pills in great quantities and shot up, quite brazenly, with coke and methadone to the last day of his life. He died in Panorama, California, of an exploding brain in June 1982 at the age of fifty-six.

Which isn't to say I meant to get hooked on Art this holiday; I had tons of other things to do. I was worrying about shoulder-fired missiles and water supplies. I was trying, despite the exigencies of the season, to pay down my astronomical credit card debt. I was brooding over various intellectual and personal failings. I was also supposed to be writing a *London Review of Books* essay about Madame de Pompadour. The big exhibit of Pompadour pictures at the National Gallery was almost over and I was embarrassingly late with my piece. I'd invited my ex, Bev, to go with me to San Diego— Blakey was flying off to visit her dad—and so we ended up taking Bev's cushy, landau-like Ford Taurus, the tiny trunk of my two-seater being comically insufficient for everything that needed transporting: a Santa Claus–sized sackful of presents for my mother and the cats; numerous bottles of boutique olive oil for Tracy and Gilbert; the melancholy Charlie, small yet dignified in his plastic pet carrier; piled-up copies of the *TLS* and the *New Yorker*; the computer and its many accoutrements; a space cult's worth of junk food (it's a ten-hour drive); the Goncourt brothers. I was hoping that Edmond and Jules would help me get somewhere with the Pompadour and all those ghastly Bouchers.

I also threw in an unopened copy of *Art Pepper Meets the Rhythm Section*, picked up on a whim a few evenings earlier at the Stanford Shopping Center. (I once spotted Condoleezza Rice there, smoothly circumnavigating the potted ferns and plashing fountains, a well-dressed zombie on a mission.) I'd found it—somewhat surprisingly, along with the paperback of *Straight Life*—in one of those depressing HEAR CD stores, so evocative of the late nineties U.S. economic boom, where you put on headphones and sample various glossily repackaged "classics" while sipping on your Starbucks. Some poor drone in the stock department must have let these hipster items in by mistake. I'd been on a private little jazz kick for a while, and had in fact just finished Ashley Kahn's absorbing history-of-a-date, *A Love Supreme: The Making of John Coltrane's Signature Album*. Trane was a nice sheets-of-sound antidote to the ormolu, love nests, and scheming courtiers of the ancien régime. Yet despite having a workable assortment of Mulligans and Bakers and Konitzes, I was also feeling vaguely dissatisfied with the West Coast "cool" side of my collection. Wasn't it a bit thin and dilettantish? And wasn't the whole school, pre- and post-Getz, in need of (my) reconsideration? I had known about Art Pepper vaguely; but as I riffled through the pages of his autobiography and saw he was writing about Oceanside and Norwalk and Huntington Beach—all those exit signs just up the freeway from my birthplace—I suddenly decided, with a certain prim sententiousness, that *I'd have to explore his work*.

There was also, I admit, the lesbian factor: I found him madly attractive. I'd never seen a picture of Art before, and here he was, on both CD cover and book, in the sort of dapper outfit that must have driven dykey lady–jazz lovers of the fifties insane with covetousness. He stood outdoors, leaning up against a eucalyptus tree, in a crisp open-necked pinky-white Coronet-style shirt (windowpane check) and a gorgeous pale tweed sports jacket dotted with tiny delicate flecks of brown and black. He held his alto gently in the crook of one arm. He smiled faintly at me—a low-rent Lucifer—and was humming quietly. *You'd be so-o-o-o—nice—to come home to!* He reminded me at once of those hunky young hard-drinking sailors, packed into fresh clean whites and reeking of Old Spice, whom my mother somewhat recklessly dated before she finally got together with Turk in 1967. When I wasn't riding my skateboard in front of our apartment, I was always jumping all over them in a passion.

In *Straight Life* Pepper is frank—and hilarious—on the subject of his looks. Detailing his stay in an expensive detox sanatorium in Los Angeles in the mid-fifties, he recalls prinking about in the nude after getting some huge shots of morphine to mitigate the symptoms of heroin withdrawal:

> *Here I was in this gorgeous room, comparable to any hotel I'd ever stayed in; I had my own private patio with flowers and lawn and birds chirping; and every four hours this pretty nurse would come in and give me an enormous shot of morphine. And I was just blind: I tripped out and sang to myself and made funny noises and looked at myself in the mirror. I stood in the bathroom for hours looking at myself and giggling, saying, "Boy, what a handsome devil you are!" I had a beautiful body. I'd get in the shower and bathe and get out and take a hand mirror and put it on the floor and look at my body from the floor. I'd look at my rear end and the bottom of my balls and the bottom of my joint, and I would play with myself until I got a hard-on and then gaze into this mirror and say, "What a gorgeous thing you are!"*

It's a fact: as soon as female-to-male transsexuals get their stubby new little tubercles, they instantly want to become gay men.

The problem with Bev's Taurus is no CD player (*author's note, 2010:* the iPod had yet to be invented), so I had unplugged my office boom box, crammed it with six giant new batteries and brought it along, too. In addition to all the jazz stuff—Bird, Dexter, Dizzy, Sonny, Miles, Ornette, Dolphy, the delectable Jimmy Giuffre—I'd filled several shopping bags with a small sampling of the *rest* of my CD collection, designed to satisfy whatever kind of recondite musical fix I might need on the road. Thus, all stacked up and ready to go were Conlon Nancarrow, Fatboy Slim, DJ Cheb I Sabbah, Ludwig Spohr, Amalia Rodriguez, Johnny Cash, Dame Myra Hess, Sigur Rós, *Verklärte Nacht*, Brenda Lee, Nusrat Fateh Ali Khan, *Gus Viseur à Bruxelles 1949*, the Pogues, some early Leontyne Price (yum), White Stripes, Charpentier, Delalande, *Coney Island Baby*, *Historic Flamenco*, *Rusalka*, the Bad Plus, Harry Smith's *Anthology of American Folk Music*, Son House, Reynaldo Hahn (the real guy, quavering away at the piano!), Busoni's Bach arrangements, Ginette Neveu, the Stanley Brothers, Tessie O'Shea, Milton Babbitt, *The Rough Guide to Rai*, Gladys Knight and the Pips, Charles Trenet, *Ska Almighty*, John Dowland, the organ music of Johann Fux (heh heh), Ian Bostridge, the Ramones, Astor Piazzola, *Ethel Merman's Disco Album*, Magnetic Fields, Flagstad and Svanholm in *Die Walkurie*, Lord Kitchener and the Calypso All-Stars, Sonic Youth, Youssou N'Dour, tons of the Arditti Quartet, Kurt Cobain, Suzy Solidor, John McCormack, Greek *rembetiko* music, Jan and Dean, *Los Pinguinos del Norte*, Shostakovich film scores, *Some Girls*, Wunderlich doing *Butterfly* (in luscious, spittle-ridden German), Cuban contredances, *Planet Squeezebox*, some croaky old Carter Family, Morton Feldman, Beatrice Lilly (and fairies at the bottom of the garden), Elmore James, *Giulio Cesare*, Miss Kitty Wells, *Vespro della Beata Vergine*, *South Pacific*, *Pet Sounds*, *Les Negresses Vertes*, *Dusty in Memphis*, Ferrier's *Kindertötenlieder*, Toots and the Maytals, *Têtes Raides*, Lulu, *Lulu*—even Gurdjieff's potty piano ramblings. He always makes me think of Katherine Mansfield.

But things went AWOL from the start. Stopping for gas at Casa de Frutta, between Highways 101 and 5, I found the batteries in the boom box weren't working. I'd held off on playing anything up to that point because it was too early in the morning for serious listening— we'd left at dawn—but now, after coffee, I was craving something. Imprecations, followed by ferocious jerking out of batteries in the Chevron parking lot. Fumbling attempts at reinstallation, in every possible permutation of plus and minus—even, despairingly, plus to plus. Bev, watching patiently, said, well, we can listen to my tapes. *Tapes!* I glared at her and peered into the shoebox of dusty old cassettes in the trunk. Could I survive for ten hours solely on Sylvester, the soundtrack from *The Crying Game*, and *The Greatest Hits of Etta James?* Now, "Down in the Basement" is a major song and Etta one of the supreme live performers. Once, at a surreal outdoor concert at the Paul Masson Winery, marooned among pre-tech-stock-crash Silicon Valley yuppies dutifully sipping chardonnay, I watched her do the plumpest, most lascivious cakewalk imaginable. But I could hardly live on her for the rest of the day. I started squawking like an infuriated baby vulture.

Back in the Taurus it went from bad to worse: the dashboard tape deck wasn't working, either. Perhaps there had been a nuclear explosion somewhere—that, I knew, immediately shut down car electrical systems. We'd all have to swallow some potassium iodide. I resigned myself, imperfectly, to a day of protracted misery. Miles and miles of interstate wilderness (complete with a nasty tire blowout): wintry fields and irrigation ditches along 5, grayed-out almond orchards, the California state prison at Avenal. Then the three-hour eight-lane chaos of L.A.: Burbank, Glendale, Pasadena, Anaheim, Irvine, Long Beach, Oceanside, and Camp Pendleton. All along the southern coast the Marines were doing sea-to-land exercises. Bev, at the wheel and the long-suffering target of my ire, turned on the radio in self-defense at one point and began flipping from station to station with the seek button—derangingly—every two or three seconds. Burbly soft rock, stale oldies, Dean Martin singing Christmas carols, Mexican polka music, endless mirthless ads for Petco and Wal-Mart: the full auditory wasteland of American popular culture assailed us. Shades of when we used to be girlfriends. We bickered most of the rest of the way. By the time we rolled up, exhausted, in my mother's driveway, trundled in with the packages and admired the Christmas tree, so loaded with decorations and synthetic flocking you could hardly see the branches, my assaulted ears needed a thorough cleaning out with a washrag.

Yuletide in San Diego was the usual: sunny and soporific, the suburban ennui immediate, dazing, and total. The cats, senile and comatose, took up most of the available seating. (They had long ago given up trying to pull low-hanging ornaments off the tree.) Charlie moped in the yard under the orange tree; Bev read old copies of the *National Enquirer* and crunched on See's California Brittle. I found myself perusing *Via*, the official newsletter of the American Automobile Association, in a state of morose torpor. Every now and then an F-18 from Miramar Naval Air Station, just a couple of miles to the north, would scream over the house on one of its morning practice flights, rending the sky with a colossal sonic boom.*

My mother, oblivious to the booms, prattled away happily and brought up her favorite Web sites for us to look at on the television screen. Since Turk's death six years ago and the invention of Prozac, she's morphed into the Merry Widow. In 2001 she started subscribing to Web TV and now sits, portable keyboard perched on lap, two

---

* Morbid authorial note from 2010: in December 2008 one of these banshee F-18s crashed on my mother's street less than a block from her house. While the pilot ejected safely, four people were killed on the ground and four houses destroyed.

feet in front of her giant set, avidly surfing the Internet for seven or eight hours a day. She's got her "Brit Group" to talk to, a gang of elderly UK ex-pats who maintain a busy online chat room about the doings of the royal family and how to find Marmite in Kansas, as well as a small legion of Martha Stewart–ish arts and crafts sites that need checking out daily. My mother's heavily into polymer clay jewelry making and rubber stamp art. The day before Christmas, as a way of filling the time, she and I went to a craft supply shop in Old Town in search of fimo dough for the somewhat Neolithic-looking bead necklaces she'd begun making. (She cuts the strange stuff into slices using a pasta maker; makes little slugs out of the pieces; then slings them all into a toaster-oven.) I found some austere-looking rubber stamps with Vitruvian capitals on them, and bought several, along with some jet black ink. Robespierre would have approved. I figured I could decorate the page-proofs of my still yet-to-be written Pompadour essay with them. Or even make facetious greeting cards celebrating Thermidor and Fructidor.

At a certain point I realized that the Pompadour essay wasn't going to happen. The books I had been reading about her were perfectly fine but I was losing interest in the lady herself. She had become pink and odious. I started wondering if she had ever really existed. She *could* be a totally made-up person: some elaborate hoax, in effect. I got ratty and rough and churlish—so much so that one evening, after I blew my stack in the car on the way to the Indian restaurant, my mother was forced, like a weary civilian reaffixing a gas mask, to assume her classic Deeply-Wounded-by-Unpleasant-Daughter-but-Carrying-On-Bravely look. She said I needed anger management therapy. ("It's not just for men now—women get it, too.") I knew I wasn't being very festive. But the Goncourts weren't helping much either. Apart from reprising Diderot's great line on the Boucher portraits—"they have everything, Monsieur, but the truth"—the brothers seemed strangely dull, more feeble and syphilitic than I remembered.

Perhaps it was true: I was tiring of the eighteenth century. For twenty years it had been my academic meal ticket. But I seemed to be twisting, torquing away from it. Starting to like it only when it got marred and eccentric, a kind of broken, perverse, junk rococo. *Singerie*. Pockmarks. Freemasonry. Chess-playing automatons. Ultracreepy things like Marat's skin diseases. (He spent all his time in that hip bath on account of a maddening case of dermatitis.) Maybe because my psoriasis has flared up so badly this past winter—every morning when I woke up in San Diego I discovered a drift of huge white flakes on the pillowcase—I had developed an unwholesome interest in the epidermal problems of historical figures. My mother said my skin ailments were identical to hers. Naturally! Had Jack the Ripper preferred dandruff to intestines, she—and I—would have been the perfect victims.

But the jazz thing was also getting obsessive. My reveries were becoming increasingly boppish and monomaniacal. In one of the Pompadour books I'd been reading, the author had explained the fey jargon affected by Louis XV and his courtiers at Versailles: "Court language and pronunciation were quite different from that of Paris; courtiers said '*roue*' for '*roi*,' '*chev soi*' for '*chez soi*'; certain words and phrases were never used, '*cadeau*' should be '*présent*,' '*louis d'or*' should be '*louis en or*,' and so on." Lots of room here, obviously, for some *LRB*-ish, off-with-their-heads moralizing: *how we loathe the upper classes!* But what I found myself thinking of instead was the sad and dreamy little language invented by Lester Young—Absolute Monarch of the Swing Tenor—after his disastrous nervous breakdown in the U.S. Army in the 1940s:

> *Many claims, some of them vague and inflated, have been made about the linguistic originality of black American English, but in the case of Lester Young's language, such claims seem to have some substance. Buck Clayton believed Lester coined the usage of the word*

*"bread" to mean money, when he asked of a job, "How does the
bread smell?" To express his own hurt feelings he would say he had
been "bruised"—a frequently heard word in the Young vocabulary.
Another favorite expression was "Ivey Divey" which signaled a rather
bleak, stoic acceptance of some misfortune. Lester also used the title
"Lady," which he had bestowed on Billie Holiday, as a rather unnerving handle to the names of male friends and colleagues. It was
a habit which along with his rather languid, camp manner, gave the
wholly inaccurate impression that he was homosexual.**

Especially when my mother's jabs began hitting the mark, I found
myself moodily adapting some of Lester's plaints. "The other ladies
make all the bread." "I ain't groovy like the other ladies." "Those
LRB cats goin' to give all their reviewing gigs to the other ladies." It
was a struggle to be even halfway ivey-divey.

Art, it turned out, was my salvation—though not in the way
I expected. There's no CD player at my mother's: she's still got—
believe it or not—the same wacky fake-wood-grained cabinet-style
phonograph we had in the Buena Vista apartments in the 1960s. It has
spindly metal legs and space-age styling and looks like something the
Eameses might have designed on a not-so-good day. Granted, I can
get all weepy and nostalgic just looking at the thing. Back in the eighth
grade, I was so addicted to surreptitious music listening, I would get
up at 6:00 a.m. and in the hour or so before I had to go to school glut
myself (ever so quietly) on cherished selections from my small and
eccentric LP collection. (I had to keep the volume absurdly low so
not to wake up my mother or Tracy.) Prized possessions back then
were a budget Everest recording of Beethoven's Seventh, the complete works of Herb Alpert and the Tijuana Brass, some huge, breakers-
rolling-in-to-shore Rachmaninoff, and my favorite: *Elizabethan Lute*

_____

* David Perry, *Jazz Greats* (London: Phaidon, 1996), p. 139.

Songs. (My mother noticed the record jacket of the last-mentioned one day and opined, with a strange stare, that Julian Bream and Peter Pears were "pansies.") In my current technological fix, however, it was obvious that the ancient family sound machine wasn't up to much. The boom box was still non compos mentis. Forced to adopt emergency measures—under normal circumstances I loathe listening on headphones—I ended up buying an ugly red Walkman at the Rite-Aid on the morning of Christmas Eve.

I won't say too much about *Art Pepper Meets the Rhythm Section*: even the most garrulous bride needs to keep a few things about her wedding night a secret. Suffice it to note that as soon as I pressed the Walkman "play" button in bed that night I started having the Parsifal Reaction: the overpowering sense that I knew the music already, that it had been laid down in my heart in advance of my ever coming into consciousness, that I was somehow—uncannily—bringing it all into being as I listened. (Hearing the Wagner for the first time at a 1982 screening of Syberberg's adaptation, I became lost, in private druggy transport, for five straight hours.) I also knew that Art's moves were too beautiful and prodigious to absorb all in one go; I was going to have to ration him carefully in order to make him last a lifetime. Even the slightest, most gestural songs were like being delicately rocked in a cradle. *Life was warm and good!* I had to call Blakey to tell her. I quit listening on the fourth cut, "Waltz Me Blues," quite overmastered by the handsome jailbird's groove.

I began devouring *Straight Life* the same night and by the time I fell asleep had read a good 200 pages. Like his music, Pepper's verbal style was thrilling: licentious, colloquial, and so painfully human I could hardly bear it. Christmas turned into a get-through-it blur of leftover turkey and wrapping paper: for the next forty-eight hours, till Bev and I loaded up the car again for San Francisco on the twenty-sixth, I was mainlining Art nightly without shame. True, he was Orphic and amoral and narcissistic, prone to a kind of pervasive, mad, jazzy self-servicing. (In his introduction to the 1994 paperback reissue of *Straight Life*, the jazz critic Gary Giddins warns the reader that it is often hard to admire Pepper: "he whines, justifies, patronizes, and vilifies" and goes "overboard . . . with intimate revelations.") But along with the spleen and pussy lore, Pepper offered himself up with such astonishing vulnerability I found my eyes welling up repeatedly. I read away at a frenetic bebop pace—uptempo all the way—but also felt curiously mangled by the experience: inwardly appalled to realize just how contemptuous I could be, I'm afraid, toward people less fortunate or comfortable than myself. Yes, I had survived—*almost fifty and not dead yet!*—but at what cost? In my professional life I was becoming a mini bigwig. (Or perhaps a biggish mini wig.) So why in middle age was I still so frightened and so cruel? The usual cozy, bespectacled, reading-in-bed smirk kept getting wiped off my face.

Some of it was just the chastening rush of the style: so plain, blatant, and free. Startlingly, the epigraph to *Straight Life* was from Pound. "What is the use of talking and there is no end of talking. There is no end of things in the heart." But Pepper (or his amanuensis, Laurie) might easily have chosen something from Defoe or Swift, so blunt and Anglo-Saxon, pitiless and fine, his narrative of life's enormities. From the first pages on, a short dispassionate sketch of the shipwreck of his childhood, Pepper goes straight indeed to the heart of things that have no end:

During this period we lived in Watts, and my father continued going to sea. He hated my mother for what she had tried to do [abort her baby]. She was going out with this Betty; I don't know what they did. They'd drink. I'd be left alone. The only time I was shown any affection was when my mother was just sloppy drunk, and I could smell her breath. She would slobber all over me.

One time when my father had been at sea for quite a while he came home and found the house locked and me sitting on the front porch, freezing cold and hungry. She was out somewhere. She didn't know he was coming. He was drunk. He broke the door down and took me inside and cooked me some food. She finally came home, drunk, and he cussed her out. We went to bed. I had a little crib in the corner, and my dad wanted to get in bed with me. He didn't want to sleep with her. She kept pulling on him, but he pushed her away and called her names. He started beating her up. He broke her nose. He broke a couple of ribs. Blood poured all over the floor. I remember the next day I was scrubbing up blood, trying to get the blood up for ages.

After his parents split up, he relates, he was shunted off to his grandmother's, to the tiny redneck town where she lived with an aged swain:

Nuevo was a country hamlet. Children should enjoy places like that, but I was so preoccupied with the city and with people, with wanting to be loved and trying to find out why other people were loved and I wasn't, that I couldn't stand the country because there was nothing to see. I couldn't find out anything there. Still, to this day, when I'm in the country I feel this loneliness. You come face to face with a reality that's so terrible. This was a little farm out in the wilderness. There was this old guy, her second husband, I think. I don't even remember him he was so inconsequential. And there was the wind blowing.

(Not so far off again: I remember a hot dusty day in the mid-sixties when my mother drove us out to Poway see a friend of hers, a young woman named Donna, our former downstairs neighbor, who'd moved out of the apartments with her newborn baby when her husband Mike had shipped out to Vietnam. She'd found a kind of shack on a brush-covered slope where the rent was only fifty dollars a month, cheaper even than the apartments. Poway is a strip-mall suburb now, looped around with freeway sound walls and indistinguishable from the rest of the eastern San Diego County sprawl, but in 1966 the feeling of rural desolation was just as Pepper describes. I spent the afternoon reading *The Hobbit* and scratching in the dirt with a stick.)

Pepper's account of his early jazz and dope life, complete with stark portraits of some of the greatest talents of the era getting high and getting off (and often not getting back), was shocking in its matter-of-factness:

I was hanging around with Dexter Gordon. We smoked pot and took Dexedrine tablets, and they had inhalers in those days that had little yellow strips of paper in them that said "poison," so we'd put these strips in our mouths, behind our teeth. They really got you roaring as an upper: your scalp would tingle, and you'd get chills all over, and then it would center in your head and start ringing around. You'd feel as if your whole head was lifting off. I was getting pretty crazy, and right about that time, I think, Dexter started using smack, heroin.

And he was upfront—sometimes brutally—about yearning to imitate the flip, dandyish, hipster style that Gordon and other black postwar players cultivated so effortlessly:

Dexter Gordon was an idol around Central Avenue. He was tall. He wore a wide-brimmed hat that made him seem like he was about seven feet tall. He had a stoop to his walk and wore long zoot suits, and he carried his tenor in a sack under his arm. He had these heavy-lidded eyes; he always looked loaded, he always had a little half smile on his face. And everybody loved him. All the black cats and chicks would say, "Heeeeey, Dex!" you know, and pat him on the back, and bullshit with him. I used to stand around and marvel

*at the way they talked. Having really nothing to say, they were able
to play these little verbal games back and forth. I envied it, but I
was too self-conscious to do it. What I wouldn't give to just jump in
and say those things. I could when I was joking to myself, raving to
myself, in front of the mirror at home, but when it came time to do it
with people I couldn't.*

Here, with a jolt, I saw him pin it down: the mortifying craving
I (still) had for a certain uncensored verbal fluency. Nothing worse
than the puerile, inhibited, what-an-idiot-I-am sensation you get
when the words don't come out in time and the world, blast it to hell,
has moved on. And yet here he was acknowledging the failure, and in
the process somehow exorcizing it. It struck me that one wish impel-
ling autobiography since Rousseau must in fact be just this: the hope
of pulling out—however unexpectedly—some last-minute psychic
victory over *l'esprit de l'escalier.*

This said, I have to admit that what enthralled me most about
Straight Life were the sex parts. From the beginning Art could be
counted on to go way, *way* too far:

*I had my first sexual experience I can remember when I was four
or five. I was still living with my parents in Watts. They had some
friends who lived nearby, Mary and Mike, who had a daughter,
Francie, about four years older than me. Francie was slender, she
had black hair, she had little bangs cut across and a pretty face,
and she had a look about her of real precociousness. She had a devilish look about her, and she was very warm. Hot. She had nice
lips, her teeth were real white, a pink tongue, and her cunt was pink
and clean. A lot of little girls smell acid or stale, but . . . I remember sometimes we'd be playing together on the front lawn—there
would be other kids around—and she would sit on my face in her
little bloomers; nobody acted like they noticed anything. She's sit-*

ting there, and I'm sniffing her ass and her cunt and her bloomers,
and it always smelled real nice and sweet.

"Years and years later, when I was divorced from my first wife,"
he remarks, "I ran into Francie, and I wanted to ball her, but she was
in love and she wouldn't do it."

As an adult, Pepper screwed compulsively: waitresses and cocktail hostesses, women he met in all-night theaters, errant members of
his teenage fan club, a female prison clerk at San Quentin, druggie
chicks. He even went through a period as a Peeping Tom. (Once, he
says, he espied a woman masturbating in her bathroom and watched
her intently till he came in a burst, "all over my shorts and the top of
my pants." When she suddenly turned toward him—he was peeking
in through a high window—he jumped down in a hurry and hied off
down the street.) "Sex was in my thoughts all the time," he admits,
"and because of my upbringing I felt it was evil. That made it even
more attractive to me, and the alcohol and the pills I took made my
sex drive even stronger. I was obsessed."

An especially filthy yarn he recounts—about seducing a hotel
maid when he was on the road with Stan Kenton—reminded me of
the time when I came home from junior high and found Hopper, one
of the pre-Turk boyfriends, asleep and nude and snuffling in the little
single bedroom that my mother and sister and I then shared. (This
must have been on Waco Street.) It was only three in the afternoon
but Hopper obviously had had a lot to drink and was sleeping it off.
Maybe he was afraid that if he went back to the Navy base he'd get
busted back down to Seaman Third Class. (As a twelve-year-old,
I was obsessed with such details of service life. The whole setup
sounded marvelous to me.) In Art's story, the maid, a pretty young
Latina woman, arrives one morning to clean the room when he is
sitting in his bathrobe, hung over and bleary after a hard night of
bingeing and blowing:

She had green eyes. I'll never forget that, black hair and green eyes. I sat in a chair opposite the bathroom door. The door had a full-length mirror on it, and it was opened in such a way that I could see her in the mirror, but I was half in a daze. I really wasn't paying much attention because I had a heavy hangover. When I woke up I always had a hangover, and if I could get to a bar, I'd have a Bloody Mary. If not, I'd have a few shots in my room. So I was having a drink when I looked up and looked into this mirror, and I couldn't believe my eyes. She was cleaning the toilet bowl. She was standing, bent over but with her knees straight, which caused her dress to come up almost over her rear end, and she had black lace panties on, and I could see the beginning of this little mound and some wispy black hairs sticking out the sides of these little panties. She had gorgeous legs. It was a beautiful sight, and I thought, "This is too good to be true!" When she came in, she'd closed the door behind her. Some of them leave the door open a little bit. When they leave it open you've got to sneak over and try to push it closed and catch their reaction if there is one. You hope there's no reaction.

I went and stood in the bathroom door, just looking at her. She's cleaning away. After she finishes the toilet she bends over to get the floor. She's wearing one of those half-brassieres, and with that button loose, I can see her breasts. I can see everything but the nipples. I can see down her dress to her navel. Needless to say I've got an erection. I move a little closer to her and she bends over the bathtub, and her uniform is all the way up over her ass. It was too much for me. I had my drink in my left hand; I put my right hand inside my robe and started playing with myself. If you can picture this . . . I'm standing in the bathroom right behind this beautiful creature who's bent over so her ass is practically in my face, with those lace panties, with hair sticking out of the panties, and I'm jerking myself off, and I came that way, and as soon as I came I looked down, and she was looking at me through her legs. Her hand was on her cunt, and she was rubbing her cunt.

Hopper appeared to be completely out of it—no one else was home—so I had an excellent opportunity, Cupid and Psyche–like, to scrutinize his penis up close. It was red and big and mottled and poked up weirdly out of the bed sheets. *What a horror show! I hate San Diego! How am I supposed to do my homework! Let's go back to England!* Leaving my books on the kitchen table, I stomped outside and for an hour or two patrolled the little apartment complex playground, brooding resentfully, till my mother came home with my sister. I never mentioned any of it. Forty years later I wonder: Was Hopper pretending to be asleep?

Reading through Art's superprurient adventures—and I find them irresistible—your mind starts going to pot and strange new thoughts crowd in. *Wow! Why not get a big tattoo of a squatting lady in high heels? It might look good!* Or—*How about making friends with that stripper at the gym, the funky Asian chick with the blue hair? (The one who's always doing handstands and practicing the splits!) She might be fun to get drunk with!* It all starts to seem normal—the strange fandance of chicks and booze and sex and looking for a toilet in which to tie on a tourniquet. When we were first dating, Blakey once got querulous about something, really hostile, and informed me rather menacingly that she was "a red-blooded American male." Pepper makes you into one, whether you like it or not. It's like changing all of a sudden into a werewolf.

All the more surprising, then, the pathos the writer achieves when he describes courting Laurie, his last and "greatest love," at Synanon in the seventies. Synanon itself—the most celebrated rehab program of its day—sounds like a Southern California cult nightmare, all rules and regulations and not being able to go to the bathroom without permission. At the Santa Monica "campus," where Pepper lived for two years, there were the usual cult trappings: a charismatic guru (named Chuck) and army of live-in disciples; elaborate rewards and punishments for performing (or neglecting) communal household chores; and daily Khmer Rouge–style group therapy sessions in which the goal was to drive your fragile fellow addicts into a state of mental meltdown.

> You'd be in a game with ten or fifteen people and if somebody, like, pissed on the toilet seat in their dorm or something like that, you'd tell it. You'd accuse him of it in front of the girls. When your covers are pulled in front of women it's really a drag, so there'd be some wild shouting matches. They made up a lot of things, too, just to get you mad, to get you raving. Somebody'd accuse you of farting at night so loud they couldn't sleep, or some chick would accuse some broad of throwing a bloody Kotex in the corner of the bathroom, leaving it laying there. The idea was that ranking you and exposing your bad habits would make you eventually change. And it worked, you know, it worked.

"Innumerable people," Art notes, "were brainwashed like this." Yet some also kicked the drugs. I'm not sure I would have done so well.

But it's waterworks time when Pepper gets to wooing and winning Laurie. After staying sober and drug-free for some time, male and female Synanon residents who wanted to start a sexual relationship could petition the counselors to let them go on "dates" together: little walks around the neighborhood, trips to a nearby shopping mall, chaste bike rides. The formal courtship period accomplished, they might then request permission to spend a couple of hours together in the commune's designated trysting place, a private room known as "the guestroom," upstairs in one of the barracks-like dorms. Pepper was immediately attracted to Laurie, a former college student and music photographer, after meeting her one day on the Synanon bus. But on their first official date, he recalls, he nearly blew it completely. They walked toward the Santa Monica pier. It was a beautiful day. Laurie was wearing a short green dress, "suede, like velvet," and Pepper thought she looked cute.

We walked to the pier and down to the end. On the way back we stopped at the merry-go-round. They have an old, old one there, still working. This old-time organ music was playing.

I felt wonderful. It seemed everything was working out fine. Laurie was very friendly and sweet and she really turned me on. We sat down on a bench and watched the merry-go-round. We made small talk, and I reached over and put my hand on her knee. She seemed to stiffen a bit, but she didn't say anything. I left my hand on her knee, and it really turned me on. I started moving my hand up her thigh under her dress. She let out a roar and jumped up. She said, "I think we'd better go back." We started walking back. I kept trying to put my arm around her, put my hand down her dress. She wouldn't let me. I said, "Look what you do to me." And I looked down to my front, and her eyes followed mine. I was wearing bathing trunks, and my pants were standing all out. I had a hard-on. She said, "Oh!" She really got embarrassed. I said, "Boy, I sure feel comfortable with you. I really feel relaxed." She looked at me and said, "You feel relaxed? I don't feel relaxed. I feel like I'm with some wild animal."

Many apologies later, he convinces Laurie to sign up for the guestroom with him. In the anxious lead-up to this assignation, he worries incessantly about his potency ("I couldn't remember the last time I'd balled without liquor or pills or dope") and wonders if Laurie will be repulsed by his body. (Because of liver cirrhosis and the surgery he'd had to remove his ruptured spleen, his abdomen was permanently scarred and distended and lacked a belly button.

"It was the ugliest thing I'd ever seen . . . It got to the point where I'd never take my shirt off. I hated to take a bath or a shower because I couldn't stand to see myself.") But all *is* well that ends well. After getting past a teasing gaggle of other residents—it's the middle of the day and everyone knows exactly where he and Laurie are going—he finds the very acceptance that he craves:

I said, "Let's go up to the room." She said, "Why don't you go up and I'll follow. Or I'll go up. Please, you go get some coffee and bring it up. I'll have the bed made by the time you get there." I went for coffee. Everybody was saying, "Yeah! Work out, Art!" And, "Boy, I know you're going to enjoy that!" It was really far-out. I liked it. But all the attention got me nervous again. What if I couldn't get a hard-on being sober? I carried the coffee up the stairs, trying not to spill it. Six floors. No elevator. By the time I got there I was just panting. She's got the bed made and the shades pulled. She said, "Look what I got." She'd lit some candles, really pretty. I put the coffee down. We looked at each other for a moment. There was no strangeness at all. All of a sudden we had our clothes off and we were laying on the bed making love, and it was the most beautiful thing in the world. And it was so vivid. There was no numbness from juice or stuff. After we finally separated, we lay there looking at each other and I tried to cover up my stomach. At first I'd had a shirt on, but Laurie'd made me take it off; now I reached for it, but she said, "Oh, please don't. I think it's beautiful. That's you. You look real. I like the marks around your eyes, everything about you. I don't like a pretty man without wrinkles or scars." She stroked my stomach, and she kissed it.

One perhaps can imagine the scene: just listen to "Bewitched, Bothered and Bewildered"—tender, tenebrous, ensorcelling—on *Modern Art*: *The Complete Art Pepper Aladdin Recordings, Volume Two.* Love leads the way.

Now wet blankets everywhere will be saying, *This is all such a load of crap.* The dope, the tattoos, the goofing, the living-without-a-belly-button, the creepy redemption-through-a-good-woman— what a self-destructive (and self-deluding) bastard Art Pepper must have been. *And what's up with you, Terry Castle, that you claim to like this guy?* I admit it: it is strange. And I probably can't keep wiggling out of it by joking about it being a sex thing. Toward the end of *Straight Life* there's a long and absorbing interview with one of Pepper's old Synanon pals, a sixties-style dyke named Karolyn. Despite never having had any interest in men, she reveals, she once considered sleeping with Pepper anyway, mainly because he was funny and intelligent and "a kindred soul somehow." I know what she means. The tenderness between lesbians and straight men is the *real* Love That Dare Not Speak Its Name. (Consider Stein and Hemingway, Bishop and Lowell, k.d. lang and Tony Bennett, or me and my best pal Rob.) But even she acknowledges that Art had a "sadistic streak" and liked to play nasty games with people. She disses poor Laurie (the interviewer-wife) for falling in with Pepper's "egotistical" demands. Like all "macho men," Karolyn complains, "Art needed to have a ma," someone he could "be a baby around."

When I started to do some research on Pepper, as soon as Bev and I returned to San Francisco, I found that a number of prominent jazz writers held similar views. One of the books I'd bought before going home for Christmas was Ben Ratliff's 2002 *The New York Times Essential Library: Jazz: A Critic's Guide to the 100 Most Important Recordings*. I now perused it in detail and was dismayed to discover that Ratliff, the *Times*'s impressive, frighteningly savvy, thirty-something jazz critic, was a pretty major Art basher. True, he listed *Art Pepper Meets the Rhythm Section* in his top 100 CDs, but mainly, it seemed, so he could take youthful swats at certain canonical jazz classics (such as Miles Davis's *Kind of Blue)* that he thought too arty and studio-fied:

> If you're interested in the great unmasterpiece, workmanlike toss-offs of jazz—if you feel like you have to enter a soundproof chamber before you can properly deal with carefully considered concept records like Kind of Blue or A Love Supreme or Take Five—[Art Pepper Meets the Rhythm Section] is a good place to start.

As for *Straight Life* itself, Ratliff seemed irritated by its very existence. Since I was in the throes of instant fandom, having just picked up eight more Pepper CDs at Tower Records in the Castro and begun blabbering about the memoir to everyone I knew, this cool-guy jadedness was disconcerting.

The issue for Ratliff seemed to be Art's honesty—or lack of it. He takes issue, in particular, with a famous passage in *Straight Life* in which the saxophonist describes the taping session for *Meets the Rhythm Section* at a Hollywood studio in early 1957. Pepper hadn't played for half a year at that point, the mouthpiece on his alto had rotted away, and he was completely strung out (he says) on heroin and booze. The hapless Diane had to drag him out of their apartment. ("She said, 'It's time to go.' I called her a few choice words: 'You stinkin' motherfucker, you! I'd like to kill you, you lousy bitch! You'll get yours!' I then went into the bathroom and fixed a huge amount.") At the studio he was too dazed, he claims, even to know what music he was supposed to be recording. But there was no place to hide: "I was going to have to play with Miles Davis's rhythm section."

> They played every single night, all night. I hadn't touched my horn in six months. And being a musician is like being a professional basketball player. If you've been on the bench for six months you can't all of a sudden just go into the game and play, you know. It's almost impossible. And I realized that that's what I had to do, the impossible. No one else could have done it. At all. Unless it was someone as steeped in the genius role as I was. As I am. Was and am. And

will be. And will always be. And have always been. Born, bred, and
raised, nothing but a total genius! Ha! Ahahaha!

You have to hate yourself for quite a while—and then somehow
move beyond it—to get this loose and crazy in print. But Ratliff
seems to dislike both the junkie melodrama and the whole comico-
grandiose Pepper persona. *Art Pepper Meets the Rhythm Section* may
be an "honest record"—or so he grudgingly allows—but "if you believe the story of its making you'd have to conclude that Pepper, unprepared and unarmored, was forced to pull the music out of himself,
since tepid run-throughs and stock licks weren't going to work in
such exalted company." In the end one gets the feeling that Pepper is
just *too much* for Ratliff, that the old guy has to be defended against—
not only for playing the sax, doping up, and balling chicks to startling
excess, but for describing it so unambiguously, with the ludic genius
of a trailer-park Villon. He's an outlandish daddy-o from some time
before *les neiges d'antan*—if Southern California can indeed be said
to have had them.

Against such skepticism I can only counterpose, however naïve
it must sound, my own readerly intuition, the faith developed over a
lifetime of book-worming that even when an autobiographer is prone
to distorting or embellishing the facts, it is still possible to locate
some core emotional truth in the writing. Why read a memoir otherwise? Nobody would bother with Rousseau's *Confessions* if they
didn't believe there was something to "get" about Rousseau by doing
so. Somewhere in *The Interpretation of Dreams*, I seem to recall, Freud
remarks that if a patient in an analytic session tries to deceive the
analyst by concocting a dream for discussion and interpretation, the
fake dream will be just as revealing as a real dream. You can't invent
a dream-story, in other words, without drawing on exactly the same
repressed material present in the "authentic" dream. Your grimy psychic fingerprints will still be all over the steering wheel.

I like this idea, in part because it relates to something I've come to believe more and more about both writing and music making: that in order to succeed at either you have to stop trying to disguise who you are. The veils and pretenses of everyday life won't work; a certain minimum truth-to-self is required. Pepper makes a similar point in his life story when he observes that jazz musicians really only *play themselves*: the greatest and most fertile improvisations are transmissions from within. Describing the impact of John Coltrane on his playing in the late sixties—in emulation of Coltrane he actually took up the tenor for a while after getting out of San Quentin—Pepper acknowledges that the overpowering Coltrane sound was not something, after a while, he could afford to get lost in:

> *It enabled me to be more adventurous, to extend myself notewise and emotionally. It enabled me to break through the inhibitions that for a long time had kept me from growing and developing. But since the day I picked up the alto again I've realized that if you don't play yourself you're nothing. And since that day I've been playing what I felt, what I felt, regardless of what those around me were playing or how they thought I should sound.*

You can hear Art *playing himself* everywhere in his oeuvre; just load up the player and start in any place: with "You and the Night and the Music" or "Tickle Toe" or "All of Me"; with "Surf Ride" or "Nutmeg" or "These Foolish Things"; with "Junior Cat" or "Angel Wings" or "Why Are We Afraid?"; with "Zenobia" or "Chili Pepper" or "I Can't Believe That You're in Love with Me," or (one of my huge favorites) "Long Ago and Far Away." Magical she may be, but Jo Stafford has nothing on Pepper in the truth-and-beauty department.

So, Core Emotional Truth Time: why am I obsessed with Art Pepper? The first reason should be obvious: *because he's dead and*

I don't have to deal with him. He's a safely freeze-dried genius. I can sample him when I like and don't have to clean up the vomit or piss or deal with the discarded works on the bathroom floor. He's as predictable now as a twenty-bit digital transfer. He's always ready to talk—in his own way—but only when I put in a request. (*Hey, Art, let's have "Suzy the Poodle"!*) You can hear him talk—literally and often hilariously—on the four-volume live set, *The Complete Village Vanguard Sessions*, from 1977. But the words never change. He has never asked me yet to get a bouffant or wear shiny pink nail polish. He's the perfect man for me.

The second reason may be less obvious: *because he's not my step-brother Jeff.* I've managed to leave Jeff out of this piece thus far—or almost. (He appeared briefly, like a stowaway, in the first paragraph.) But I've been thinking about him constantly, somewhat wretchedly, as I've been writing. This process of composition, needless to say, has been more protracted than I originally intended. Christmas is now long past; a second Gulf War has begun; I've lost twenty pounds by kicking my chocolate habit; and I'm still here at the keyboard. I've put off finishing for so long, I suspect, because the only ending I can see is not very pretty. Looks to be more like a set of honks, squawks, or bent notes, or one of Art's grubbier self-revelations.

Grubbiness in a moment; first, the uncanny. The uncanny part of my heroin Christmas came as Bev and I were driving back to San Francisco on the morning of the twenty-sixth. We'd decided to take 101 all the way for a change, though it makes the overall journey an hour longer. I'd done Highway 5 so many times over the past few years I couldn't face it again—especially since, as on the trip down, we were going to have to go the whole way with no music other than the radio. At least on 101 you get to drive next to the ocean for longer and at one point pass through Santa Barbara. I've always liked Santa Barbara; even if it's mainly 1920s fake-Spanish, it reminds me of how California used to be when I was a kid, before my parents split up.

You also go up the western rather than eastern side of Los Angeles. That was how we ended up whizzing by the familiar freeway exit (just past Mulholland Drive) for Van Nuys and Burbank Boulevard. Not so far beyond Getty-Land. David Hockney–Land. Isherwood-and-Bachardy–Land. But so different. I thought at once of my stepsister Lee and how I'd stayed with her and Greg for two months in the summer of 1983, just before I took up my job at Stanford. Their house, a pokey little tract home on a cul-de-sac off Van Nuys Boulevard, abutted at the rear onto a huge new car dealership. I used to sleep in the tiny spare room back there, on a fold-out couch next to the gun cabinet and pinball machine. Every night till midnight, while I tried vainly to sleep, a strident female voice, loudly amplified over the car-lot paging system, would regularly summon various salesmen to the white courtesy telephone. The huge fluorescent light towers illuminating the cars bathed the objects in my room in a strange spectral glow.

I'd just come from Harvard, where I'd been lonely out of my mind for three years at the Society of Fellows, and had a summer research fellowship at the Clark Library at UCLA. *I was a scholar of the eighteenth century! I had a job at Stanford! I was writing my second book! Yes, ahem, it's about the masquerades of the period. You know, masquerades.* Each day I trundled off to the Clark in Turk's turquoise Mustang, which he'd loaned me for the summer. I tried to stay at the library each day for as long as I could because being at Lee and Greg's depressed me. Lee never worked and so she was always there, drinking and eating and watching television, with the odd little foray out into the alley now and then to snoop through her neighbors' garbage cans. I didn't know anyone else in Los Angeles, and was still a fairly timid young woman, but even so, I'm not quite sure why I ended up staying there. I hadn't got much money and I guess I wanted to please my mother. My mother had suggested it, maybe as a way of symbolically marking my return to California after twelve years away at school. Back within Hailing Distance and Even Residing (Temporarily) with a Member of the Family! Of course she didn't like Lee much either, although unlike the rest of Turk's offspring—Dee Dee the crack addict, Linda, the put-upon wife of a ne'er do well, and Jeff the sociopath—Lee had at least married someone halfway decent. Greg was actually good-looking in a Tom Selleck–ish way; no one could figure out what he saw in Lee. Lee was fat and smelled bad; her teeth were brown from smoking. She wore big sweat-stained tank tops and stretch pants. Greg's most thrilling moment, he once told me, had been installing Burgess Meredith's telephone system at a house in Beverly Hills.

Jeff had died six months earlier, at their house. He'd been living with them for a few months beforehand, had even—unbelievably—found some sort of pathetic job in Van Nuys, working as a delivery boy for a caterer. (My mother told me later the caterer was an older gay guy who thought he was cute.) All Christmas Day till late, Jeff was out delivering things; Lee and Greg went away somewhere overnight. When they came back on the morning of the twenty-sixth, they found him in the middle of the living room—brains, wet hair, odd gobbets of flesh, scattered around on the furniture and carpeting. He hadn't left a note but had propped up his high school graduation equivalency certificate near where he lay.

By the time I stayed there, of course, the carpet had been replaced. Lee only mentioned Jeff a couple of times. (Greg never did at all.) The first time was to say that he had been "murdered" by some evil black men. She got up in my face as she said it—a female Uriah Heep—and I was disgusted by her. The second was to excoriate a spur-of-the-moment visit my mother paid me in Boston right after Jeff died. (I remember that visit well: we went out of the house one cold sunny Cambridge morning and, without warning, my mother threw up some weird orange stuff in the snow. She laughed and we went on to Harvard Square as if nothing had happened. We ate lunch at Dolphin Seafood, even though it was the middle of winter.) My mother hadn't been able to face Turk's bottomless despair. Lee was foul-mouthed and critical.

As soon as Bev and I passed the exit it struck me: almost twenty years to the minute—10:00 a.m., December 26, 2002—since Jeff killed himself. He had now been dead almost as long as he'd been alive. And I'd had exactly that long, too—two decades—to think about him dead, always with the deepest sense of relief. You have to understand that Jeff was a nightmare: Turk's youngest child and his only son, grotesquely doted on by Turk, though Turk was mostly away at sea on submarines during Jeff's infancy and early childhood. By the time Turk's first wife dropped dead in the yard in front of the kids—a few months before Turk and my mother started dating— Jeff had already started to go to the bad. At the age of eight or nine he was a smoker and heavy drinker, prone to pilfering vodka and mixing it with cough syrup. He took up drugs in junior high. Since Turk came over every evening to see my mother, Jeff and his sisters, nominally under the care of Lee, the eldest, ran wild. I hated it when we had to drive across San Diego to see them, or go along with them on some grisly group excursion; I was already a ghastly prig. But somehow I adjusted. We were (to me) mortifyingly poor—my mother barely kept things going on the $200 a month she got for child support from my father—and after a while Turk started picking up groceries for us at the Navy base. Whenever he came over, plump and tan and amiable in his khaki chief's uniform, he usually brought Tracy and me M&M's. He was hoping my mother would marry him—kids and all—and she ultimately did four years later, in 1971, when I went away on a scholarship to college and the child support from my father abruptly fell to $100 a month. She didn't work; she felt she had no choice.

Granted, Jeff never did heroin—or not that I know of. Even so, my mother and Turk had plenty to cope with throughout the 1970s. The violence started in his early teens. He skipped school whenever possible and one day broke into a house down the street. The owner, a youngish divorcée with two small children, was home; he lurched drunkenly after her with a hunting knife. He reviled her, said she was a bitch and he was going to kill her, chased her round her living room, then slashed her couch wide open in a fury so all the stuffing came out. When he was arrested, he seemed sullen and indifferent, even mute. He never had any explanation for what he did and wouldn't answer questions.

Jeff didn't seem to be motivated by anything sexual. Nothing obvious, anyway. Though by the age of fifteen or so he had grown into a tough, hard, butch-looking young man, he never had a girlfriend or indeed a friend of any sort. He was muscular and short with close-cropped hair. (His head was often shaved in the youth detention camps in which he was periodically incarcerated.) From some angles he looked a bit like Genet, though wasn't like him in any other way. I am tempted to say—knowing how ruthless it must sound—that Jeff had no interiority. He never seemed to be thinking or feeling. He rarely smiled; hardly ever spoke; seldom evinced an interest in anything, at least when at home. He had no humor or fantasy. Whenever he was around, he ignored my mother and Turk and sat balefully on the couch, watching television. I never saw him reading or talking on the phone. One of the first psychiatrists to examine him—Jeff must have only been about twelve at the time—said he had the same psychological profile as Charles Whitman, the guy who shot six or seven people from the clock tower at the University of Texas in the mid-sixties.

I was away at school; I managed to stay mostly out of it. During my five years in graduate school especially I hardly ever went to see my mother. I studied for exams and listened to music. I lived alone and sometimes smoked hashish by myself. I got some of my first jazz LPs: the late Billie Holiday sides on Verve, *The Gentle Side of John Coltrane*, Betty Carter, Ornette's *Dancing in Your Head*. The latter had just come out and I listened to it a lot when I was trying to get over the Professor. I loved *Die Entführung aus dem Serail* and Pergolesi's *La Serva Padrona*. But I heard about Jeff all the time: how he'd drunk up Turk's booze, smashed cars, stolen money, lied compulsively. My mother had an emotional breakdown in the mid-seventies—she and Turk fought constantly over him—and she was in the Navy hospital for a while. I didn't go to see her. Turk usually defended Jeff, and had long fatuous father-son "talks" with him, during which Jeff would not respond. Turk was a kindly man but weak. I developed a private theory that Jeff was brain-damaged, a lobe incorrectly folded somewhere. He seemed mentally defective. He spoke with a strange, slurry, adenoidal sound, as if his throat and nostrils were full of phlegm. For most of the seventies and into the eighties I lived with the recurrent fear that he would kill my mother or Turk or both.

In the late 1970s Turk somehow pulled some strings and got Jeff into the Marines. Jeff learned hand-to-hand combat and sea rescues and pugil stick fighting at Camp Pendleton. Not long after his unit shipped out to Australia, he beat up a prostitute in Sydney so savagely she almost died. He was in the brig for a while, then the Marines tossed him out. Turk, ever hopeful, wangled another billet for him, this time in the Navy reserves. Jeff went to sea again for six months, during which time he got into a bar fight in Hawaii and killed a Samoan man with his bare hands. Throttled the guy till his eyes almost popped out. The military lawyer argued it was self-defense—successfully—but Jeff received a less than honorable discharge. Soon after that, I guess, he went to live with Lee and Greg in L.A. and started working for the gay caterer.

I think of Jeff as someone who had no language, or no language other than brutality. Not that he couldn't read or write, on a primitive level. One of the strangest things about his death were some crude letters—presumably sent back and forth between him and another Marine—that turned up in a closet afterwards. They could only be described as billets-doux—but sick, obscene ones. Full of things like, *I going to fuck you cunt, you fuckin cunt, suck my dick*, scrawled in pencil. My mother told me about them once, how upset Turk had been. Turk himself idolized other men but his homoeroticism was sentimental and unconscious. He was short and diabetic and had soft, bosomy breasts. He didn't like taking his shirt off. He used to say he wanted to kill all the fags. (He politely pretended not to know about me.) The happiest time in his life had been when he was under the North Pole for months in a nuclear submarine. It was so hot and claustrophobic down there, he said, he and the other guys spent most of their time in their skivvies, and sometimes even polished the torpedoes in the nude.

But it was Jeff's fate to stay locked up inside himself. He did not have the genius, the munificent resources, of an Art Pepper. Art has a story in *Straight Life* about almost killing somebody, just before he got out of San Quentin. He'd been put in the prison "adjustment center" for glue sniffing and overdosing on some contraband pills called black and whites:

It had a lot of romance, being in the adjustment center. People look up to you for being there and being cool, not whining. There were guys in there waiting to go to trial for murder or for shanking people, and I was digging this whole scene. I'd hear the others talk, and I started thinking how great it would be to kill someone and really be accepted as a way out guy. All the guys that were really in would know about it. "Man, that cat, Art Pepper, he wasted a cat, cut him to ribbons. Stabbed him and stabbed him, blood pouring all out of the guy. Don't fuck with him, man." I started dreaming about it and thinking about it and seriously planning it. I was all ready to do it and could have done it. I had the nerve. I had the shank, and I was in the process of choosing my victim when I got my date to get out.

Blame it on bureaucracy: somebody's date with the shank was not to be.

In spite of the torments he suffered, Art, you would have to conclude, was blessed by life. This has to be in the end one reason why I'm so drawn to him. Yes, in lots of ways he was just plain lucky: witness the dumb moral luck in the foregoing. It's exhilarating to see people escape disaster in some goofy and arbitrary fashion. But Pepper was also blessed by having a language. Not just *one* language, in fact, but two. He could play and he could talk. He did both things well enough, so gorgeously in fact, that despite all his flaws people came to love him and wish him well. And being loved he somehow managed to survive. On account of his honesty (or brilliant stab at it) he was granted a second life. (Art, writes Laurie Pepper in the afterword to *Straight Life*, "valued honesty above fame, even above art." He was "obsessed with knowing and with being known and believed that a failure of honesty in his life would contaminate his soul and his music.") Jeff had no human utterance and was cut out from the love side of things from the beginning. He was granted only a miserable smidgen of a life. Frail Watteau—not to mention Mozart— outstripped him by quite a bit. Who's to say what's fair or why things turn out the way they do?

I pride myself on having a language, of course, and on being able to put my thoughts into words. It's one of the genteel ways I like to stomp on people: a kind of evil hobby, the downside of taking an interest. I've been going after my mother for some time now; I've been a hard daughter for her to love. She deserves a lot better. For years I cherished (and often recounted to gratified therapists) a disreputable episode I witnessed one Christmas during her marriage to Turk. Jeff was there and about fifteen, so I must have been in my early twenties. Jeff was fooling around on the upstairs landing, on the little balcony overlooking the living room. The rest of us all sat below. Somehow he had hoisted himself up onto the balcony ledge, and was balancing there precariously when suddenly he lost his grip and flipped over the railing about fifteen feet to the ground. I jumped up along with everybody else and saw him on the floor next to the stairs, whimpering bizarrely. He was okay, it turned out, but had fractured his leg in three places. For several months afterwards he had to wear a large plaster cast up to his hip. To my mother's annoyance he had to use her bathroom during that time; it was downstairs and he couldn't get up the stairs on crutches. She used to complain about how he scratched the toilet seat with the top of his cast and left drops of dark brown urine all over the place.

As soon as Jeff fell, I looked over at my mother in amazement and saw a reflexive zany grin flit across her features. She instantly suppressed it and assumed a look of stepmotherly concern; I was the only one to see it. Turk had leapt across the room and was already busy yelling at Jeff for scaring him half to death. Yet to me her smile was fairy gold, the perfect illustration of something that Freud (whom I was avidly reading at the time) was always talking about: how when people try to hide their real feelings, the feelings slip out anyway, in involuntary tics and small, incriminating gestures. It was the kind of thing that characters did in the novels of Richardson and Laclos. What a hypocrite my mother was! As bad as Madame de Merteuil!

Self-satisfaction of this sort wears thin, however, when you get older. I told Blakey the other day that I was designing this piece so the conclusion would be like a heavily laden truck: it would start rolling backwards right at the end, and I would be crushed beneath the wheels. On purpose. All the important stuff rear loaded—then I'd show the brakes failing. *It will seem as though I'm criticizing my mother again but it will really be myself that I'm attacking!* Blakey looked dubious, so I quickly changed my tune—several times. *It's really about music! . . . It's really about California! . . . It's really about addiction! . . . It's really about car trips!. . . . It's really about lesbianism! . . . It's really about why I became an eighteenth-century scholar! . . . It's really about making up wild stories!* It's really about being moronic, like Madame de Pompadour, surrounded by putti and cooing doves, admiring herself in a hand mirror.

The thing *is* rolling to a stop now, I realize, and all that's left for me to do perhaps is to put myself in the way of it and smile. Sometimes in raucous old bebop recordings from the late forties—the grotty straight-ahead bootleg ones with murky nightclub sound, people talking and glasses clinking in the background—the music doesn't end properly, with the usual reprise and nail-it-down final chord. It just breaks off abruptly in the middle of a solo or chorus, as if someone had knocked over the mike. You're left with the sense of a close-packed human chaos, now terminated. Art Pepper is a kind of mannequin or decoy, I guess, the sort of mummified icon that even a person as terrified by mortality and other people as I am can latch onto and worship. It's true: I love his deftness and valor and craziness, and the exorbitant beauty of his playing. I love the quick, creamy sound he gets out of his alto. I love his shame-free storytelling. I love his handsome young male face. But I too was glad when Jeff fell off the landing. I hated the fucking punk—frankly wished him gone from the earth—and would have laughed out loud if I could.

AN ART PEPPER BIBLIOGRAPHY

Balliett, Whitney. *Collected Works: A Journal of Jazz, 1954–2001*. New York: St. Martin's Griffin, 2002.

Dyer, Geoff. *But Beautiful: A Book about Jazz*. New York: Farrar, Straus and Giroux, 1996.

Pepper, Art and Laurie. *Straight Life: The Story of Art Pepper*. New York: Schirmer Books, 1979. Reprint, New York: Da Capo Press, 1994.

Ratliff, Ben. *The New York Times Essential Library: Jazz: A Critic's Guide to the 100 Most Important Recordings*. New York: Henry Holt, 2002.

Selbert, Todd, ed. *The Art Pepper Companion: Writings on a Jazz Original*. New York: Cooper Square Press, 2000.

Sicily Diary

Mummified corpse, Capuchin
catacombs, Palermo
(Photo by Marco Lanza)

DID WE HAVE A GOOD time? Palermo: raucous, sunny, dirty, Fanta cans, car-squashed plastic water bottles, bus exhaust fumes, lots of underemployed young men on rusty Vespas, and me wondering if the panic attacks I'd had the week before Blakey and I left San Francisco were going to come back again. The fill-in shrink I'd gone to see in Margo's absence right before we left said, *Terry, have some compassion for yourself. Take the Klonopin if you need to.* I remained girlish, surly, evil—remarking silently to myself, as a way of not listening, on his absurd brown leather pants; couldn't stop looking at them the whole fifty minutes. A middle-aged psychiatrist's idea of hipsterdom? But who am I to be critical? Writing problems—as always—the trigger for my agitation: my appalling fraudulence and lack of skill. Tears.

We only had one full day in Palermo. I'd planned it as our "recovery day" after the SF-to-Frankfurt-to-Rome-to-Sicily eight-mile-high, Al Qaeda-be-damned holiday marathon. (Labyrinthine airport security everywhere—the two Russian planes had just "mysteriously" gone down.) Blakey, who'd been to Palermo before, insisted that the one thing we *had* to do was go to the Convent of the Capuchins and see the catacombs. Her mother, Late But Punctual, the celebrated archaeologist, had taken her there when B. was seven or eight. Only later did B. confess she'd become hysterical in the place and that LBP (in high dudgeon) had had to drag her out. Late But Punctual was an expert on the ancient Mycenaeans. What you'd call a hard case. Couldn't tolerate crybabies. The Hobbesian ethos runs in the family. B. says she's going to teach her three-year-old Korean niece to repeat the maternal motto: *bellum omnes contra omnem.*

If you type "Palermo catacombs" in on Google you can see a bit of what we saw: hundreds of mummified cadavers, most of them from the late nineteenth century, hung on the walls, set in niches, laid out on grotty catafalques, all in a sort of weird underground city with sidewalks, street lights, and little allées. Most of the corpses are those of wealthy Palermitans and their families; apparently in 1860 it was a great honor to be stuck down there. Nowadays it only costs three euros to get in. A morbid old monk at the door takes your money. No photos allowed, but obviously people sneak their cameras in. We were the only people speaking English.

Almost the first thing you see is the waxy little girl, Rosalia Lombardo, the freshest corpse in the place, embalmed in 1920 at the age of two. The mad doctor who worked on her (*Count Fosco!*) took his secret flesh-preserving formula with him to the grave. (Most of the other dead are preserved with plain old white vinegar.) Rosalia definitely has a peculiar polystyrene look about her. Strange to think that had she lived she could still be alive today. My own mother—still booming around San Diego at seventy-eight in Turk's old Camaro—was born only a few years later than she was, after all, in 1926.

As for the rest: imagine all of Balzac's characters come to life—the whole roiling human comedy—then instantly dead again. Not only dead, but in the skankier stages of dissolution. Skulls that aren't quite skulls yet, Still Too Much Going On. Faces with expressions. Vestigial hair and teeth. Gaping eye sockets, some with dried-up black-currant eyes. Many of the corpses appear to be screaming; their lower jaws have dropped open or come off altogether. Others seem to be laughing (or at least cocking a snook). The Capuchins—quite a lot of them—wear big ropes round their necks signifying penance. Everyone else is in regular nineteenth-century clothing, fairly rotted away of course but enough there to be evocative. The slightly lumpy-looking hand-stitched seams are like those you see on the coats worn by Nadar's sitters. Some of the men even have little crumbly velvet slippers. *The dandy in his study!*

It's all astonishingly well-organized. Professional Men (teachers, lawyers, businessmen) have their own special alley; likewise the Virgins, Babies, Widows, and French Bourbon Military Men. The priests are arranged in rows, heads reverently bowed, like baseball players listening to the national anthem. Whoever looks after all of them—now there's a job—would seem to have a sense of humor. Nonetheless, the place could stand a good vacuuming. Everything a bit musty and fluffy. "THE MOST GHOULISH SIGHT I'VE EVER SEEN," says one of the Google bloggers. The Palermo tourist Web site is cagier: "the exposition of the corpses may arouse admiration" but "can also upset sensitive people." So might *not* be such a good idea to take the kids. Even if they start squawking they want to see Rosalia, just say no.

So was it the gothic dust of the nineteenth century? Or the (slightly "off") shrimp and calamari? By the time we took the ferry to Lipari, twenty-four hours later, it was impossible to ignore: a certain griping, flopping feeling in my stomach, like a lonely goony bird struggling to take off. Strange *ressentiment* at the thought of food. Campari and soda, sadly, no help—even with several beer chasers. B. tried to make me laugh—still worrying, obviously, about my lingering mental problems. At one point she succeeded in channeling Wally, our new miniature dachshund. (Named after the opera, not the duchess.) *Hi, Mommy! Are there baby dachshunds in Sicily? Can I*—wriggle wriggle lick lick—*kiss you on your snout?* Though only eight months old, Wally is as slutty and insouciant as Private Lyndie England. All she needs is a dangling cigarette and a tiny pair of four-legged camouflage pants.

Made it through the first day on Lipari okay, even managed to motor with B. round the island in a little rented rubber *gommini*. Bronzed couples kept vrooming by us in gleaming speedboats, the men, in minuscule bathing trunks, preening and smoking and standing up at the wheel. We could see them laughing at us. Not much to do when we got back, though, unless we were to take in a local theater production, *Topo Gigio e la Montagna di Pumice*. Topo Gigio, as I explained to B., was a talking mouse on the Ed Sullivan show in the 1960s. (B., thirteen years younger, has no memory of that decade.) But did we have enough Italian even for the presumably simple-minded things a mouse might say? Sorry, Topo; no go.

Like a fool I kept trying to eat that night: had some tortellini with Maalox for supper, washed down by a large *bicchierri* of orange-flavored Metamucil, the healthful fiber supplement B. had brought with us from California. Tottering around Lipari town that evening—everyone else in thongs and mini-shorts and see-through beach wraps—we looked pale and Victorian and ridiculously out of place. Lady Hester Stanhope and her Special Friend. Why hadn't we gone to Lesbos instead? Ended up watching Olympics back at the hotel, the women's high jump. Lots of freakishly tall ladies, more like deer than women. I got fixated on their weird leggy movements. Oblique slow-motion start, arms held high and stiff, then the rapid scissoring forward to liftoff. Most of them seemed to be jumping in their underpants: pubic bones quite visible as they sailed backwards over the bar.

Next day's goal, that dream from my 1950s childhood and first cinematic glimpse of Ingrid Bergman: Stromboli! (*Gaslight* actually my favorite, though.) Piled onto the scruffy tour boat filled with voluble Sicilians and assorted squalling offspring, then churned off across the waves. Intestines profoundly restless. A couple of crampy-shivery snorkeling stops in the blue Tyrrhenian sea, then debarked at Panarea for the afternoon. Still in denial, despite rough, gasping, even passionate bout of diarrhea, surrounded by mops and buckets in a little gelateria WC. Trying to persuade myself that I and the stomach bug were having only a brief affair.

A major turn for the worse, however, when we docked at Stromboli. The sun was starting to go down, the fabled volcano smoking in a sinister, belching fashion. I stopped to paw over T-shirts at one of the many souvenir stalls in a pathetic stab at normalcy. Quick addled look-in at the Volcano Education Center: B. said, *what exactly is magma, anyway?* I mumbled. Inward writhing like Laocoön. Signs all along the waterfront telling you, in several languages, where to run to if the warning sirens went off. The permanent population on Stromboli is now only 324. Walked gingerly toward the main pumice beach in desultory search of a swim. But then nothing to do but break for it: bowels suddenly on fire. B. watching in horror. Mad, self-flinging plunge into the waves, followed by Byronic exaltation (*this is something I've never done before; I am breaking every law of God and Man*); then sordid, liquefying release. Catharsis accomplished, I hurried back onto the beach groaning like Mr. Pooter after the umpteenth insult from Lupin, his annoying ne'er-do-well son.

We never made it to the Bergman-Rossellini love nest, somehow missed it altogether by wasting an hour or two in a little cyber-outpost halfway up the volcano. (The latter doubled as a kind of outfitting shop for crater-bound hikers.) Hippy music, love beads, and a single creaky Italian PC with farcically slow Internet connection. B. was undeterred, however; sat amid the helmets and goggles and backpacks catching up on the blogs from the Republican convention. The *Daily Kos*, the loathsome *Drudge*, the online *New York Times*—and me, still a bit queasy, peering at it all over her shoulder. A gloating Dubya on every Web site, looking simian and proud. How had it all gone so wrong? Pliny the Elder, ascending Vesuvius in AD 79, would never have gotten waylaid halfway up in this moronic fashion. But then perhaps he wouldn't have fallen into the lava, either. What lies in store for any of us? Poison gas, or just our eyeballs melting in our heads from the heat?

Stomach never quite that bad again, though even with Bridget and Barbara—they'd flown from London to meet us in Ortigia, our last Sicilian stop before Rome—I had a few residual minor accidents. Had to retire in haste from the Hotel Guttkowski breakfast room one morning, to the obvious displeasure of the seventy-something Polish lady who ran the operation. Some comment on her fare? She wore sunglasses indoors, like a sort of elderly cokehead; and kept saying, "*You arrrrh ?ho kind,*" to everybody but me. (Even tolerated Bridget and Barbara, who in matching golf shirts and vegetarian Doc Martens looked like a butch version of Tweedledum and Tweedledee.) Whenever I saw her coming I hid my head in the day-old *Guardian*, or the gorgeous Electa book of Antonello da Messina paintings I had borrowed—was in fact tempted to steal—from the coffee table in the front lounge.

We'd all arrived in Ortigia on Wednesday; the same day the Russian school siege began. The latter taking a while to register: glimpses of a newspaper photo here and there, an early Reuters image of a woman who'd been let go after some negotiation running out with a baby in her arms. But I didn't pay much heed, more concerned with how-I-am-functioning-in-this new-environment? Was I pushing B. away? (I was reading *The Human Stain* and full of pedantic pronouncements.) Ortigia itself beautiful and strange and dilapidated, a peculiar mixture of briny sea smells, narrow streets, crumbling baroque facades, slums filled with squatters. Televisions blaring from open doorways, Sicilian women hanging out laundry. Obvious poverty, but also (not so subtly) on the way up. Money coming from somewhere. A Max Mara store on the main drag. The Guttkowski itself a new, designer-ish boutique hotel catering to British and French tourists. All very "directional" and *World of Interiors*. None of it stopped me from having a gibbery little panic attack in the back seat of the rental car, though, when Bridget drove us out to swim at the lido south of Syracusa. Blakey taking my hand, like Don Giovanni with Zerlina.

The last day there—the vacation anomie setting in—we sat at a pizzeria on the dock in the sunny midafternoon, while Bridget and Barbara discussed the failings of their employer, the NHS. Both are managers. How to move people through emergency rooms quickly. Speeding up triage, etc. Thumping Europop in the background suddenly giving way to frenetic Italian news broadcast. Got a bit of it. Boldoni, the television journalist kidnapped in Iraq, now dead for sure, it seemed. Then gabble gabble gabble *scuola* gabble gabble *esplosione*. Interrupted Bridget and Barbara: "I think they just said 'school explosion.'" Everyone looking grim and peeved and suddenly worn out. Big thoughtful silence. Don't think Bridget had cared for my histrionics the day before. Then my mind slid away and forward; wondered what it would be like to say goodbye to Blakey—for a fairly long while—in the Frankfurt airport in a few days.

The pictures everywhere, of course, by the time she and I got to Rome: of poor little kids, clad only in their soiled underpants, grasping at plastic water bottles; flopped on the ground amid trucks and jeeps and adults with semi-automatic rifles. Mothers bent in prostration over little forms laid out on the grass. I studied the diagrams of the gymnasium, read all about the shrapnel-stuffed pipe bombs, hung from the basketball nets like Christmas lights. Haunted by the fact it was the first day of school. Everyone marching in to the music, flowers in hand. Flowers later eaten, to get the moisture out of them. The old Pope, drooping in the shadows, sent condolences, condemned the perpetrators.

I've been home a couple of weeks now. Blakey back in Chicago, her fall term having started a week ahead of ours. Beslan (and Putin) seem to have fallen out of the news. It's now all election stuff, all the time. Margo said okay to up the pills for a while: a somewhat spongy return. The most interesting thing I've done since coming back to San Francisco has been to change my opinion—a full 180 degrees—on Nan Goldin. The *Ballad of Sexual Dependency* lady. I never really liked that book. Too many stringy-looking downtown types in psychic disarray. An odd resentment also of Goldin's art world fame. The whole eighties thing. But the new collection of her most recent photographs, *The Devil's Playground*, has left me stunned by its beauty. It came in the mail from Amazon while we were away, a huge heavy Phaidon volume over two inches thick, and I spent the first evening after I got back with it on my lap, turning the pages over slowly, as if they were made of vellum.

As usual, Goldin photographs her friends—Bruno, Valerie, Joana, Clemens, Simon, Guido—doing all sorts of ordinary but vulnerable human things: kissing or fucking, holding babies, sometimes just smoking, or standing in doorways or lying naked on their beds. The intimacy Goldin establishes with her subjects is extraordinary, almost uncanny, as if she were warming them into life with the camera lens. Luscious pink and gold flesh tones, deep reds, deep blues. Painterliness. Everyone in a kind of sensual dream, except you know it is also real life. Astonishing sequence of "Clemens and Jens" making love on Goldin's rumpled bed in Paris, one on top of the other. A man *absolutely* inside another man. A hand pressing down on a back. Open mouths. Lunar light. Two Endymions embracing. You see the mole on Jens's left shoulder blade; Clemens's toes curling in ecstasy.

A few self-portraits, too, including some strange bleak ones Goldin took when she was at the Priory, the London drug rehab place. (She'd had an accident and gotten hooked on the morphine she was given as a painkiller.) But even the pictures without people in them are stupendous. Stopped with a little gasp at "Stromboli at dawn, Italy, 1996," a ravishing experiment in grisaille. Then, too, in the book's final section, another memento mori: "Skulls of monks, Cripta dei Cappuccini, Rome, 2001." Goldin's love of the world, her dauntlessness and intensity, are awe-inspiring. The last picture in the book is a kindly one and a valediction: "Gravestone in a pet cemetery, Lisbon, 1998." Shows a tiny gravestone, with dates "27-5-72 à 12-6-86" and the words (in English) "You Never Did Anything Wrong." Told Wally all about it and she said she felt proud of her species.

Desperately Seeking Susan

Susan Sontag, 1975

A FEW WEEKS AGO I found myself scanning photographs of Susan Sontag into my screen-saver file: a tiny head shot clipped from *Newsweek*; two that had appeared in *The New York Times*; another printed alongside Allan Gurganus's obituary in the *Advocate*, a glossy American gay and lesbian mag usually devoted to pulchritudinous gym bunnies, gay sitcom stars, and treatments for flesh-eating strep. It seemed the least I could do for the bedazzling, now-dead she-eminence. The most beautiful photo I downloaded was one that Peter Hujar took of her in the 1970s, around the time of *I, Et Cetera*. She's wearing a thin gray turtleneck and lies on her back—arms up, head resting on her clasped hands and her gaze fixed impassively on something to the right of the frame. There's a slightly pedantic quality to the whole thing that I like, very true to life. Every few hours now she floats up onscreen in this digitized format, supine, sleek, and smooth.

No doubt hundreds (thousands?) of people knew Susan Sontag better than I did. For ten years ours was an on-again, off-again semi-friendship, constricted by role playing and shot through in the end with mutual irritation. Over the years I labored to hide my growing disillusion, especially during my last ill-fated visit to New York, when she regaled me—for the umpteenth time—about the siege of Sarajevo, the falling bombs, and how the pitiful Joan Baez had been too terrified to come out of her hotel room. Sontag flapped her arms and shook her big mannish hair—inevitably described in the press as a "mane"—contemptuously. *That woman is a fake! She tried to fly back to California the next day! I was there for months. Through all of the bombardment, of course, Terry.* Then she ruminated. Had I ever met Baez? Was she a secret lesbian? I confessed that I'd once waited in line behind the folk singer at my cash machine (Baez lives near Stanford) and had taken the opportunity to inspect the hairs on the back of her neck. Sontag, who sensed a rival, considered this non-event for a moment, but after further inquiries, was reassured that I, her forty-something slave girl from San Francisco, still preferred her to Ms. Diamonds and Rust.

At its best, our relationship was rather like the one between Dame Edna and her feeble sidekick Madge, or possibly Stalin and Malenkov. Sontag was the Supremo and I the obsequious gofer. Whenever she came to San Francisco, usually once or twice a year, I instantly became her female aide-de-camp: a one-woman posse, ready to drop anything at a phone call (including the classes I was supposed to be teaching at Stanford) and drive her around to various Tower Records stores and dim sum restaurants. Most important, I became adept at clucking sympathetically at her constant kvetching: about the stupid-ity and philistinism of whatever local sap was paying for her lecture trip, how no one had yet appreciated the true worth of her novel *The Volcano Lover,* how you couldn't find a decent dry cleaner in downtown San Francisco, etc., etc.

True: from my point of view, it had all begun extraordinarily well. Even now I have to confess that, early on, Sontag gave me a couple of the sweetest (not to mention most amusing) moments of my adult life. The first came one gray magical morning at Stanford in 1996, when after several hours of slogging away on student papers, I opened a strange manila envelope that had come for me, with a New York return address. The contents, a brief fan letter about a piece I'd written on Charlotte Brontë and a flamboyantly inscribed paperback copy of her play, *Alice in Bed* ("from Susan"), made me dizzy with ecstasy. Having idolized Sontag literally for decades—I'd first read "Notes on Camp" as an exceedingly arch nine-year-old—I felt as if Pallas Athena herself had suddenly materialized and offered me a cup of ambrosia. (O great Susan! Most august Goddess of Female Intellect!) I zoomed around, showing the note to various pals. To this day, when I replay it in my mind, I still get a weird toxic jolt of adolescent joy, like taking a big hit of Krazy Glue vapors out of a paper bag.

Things proceeded swiftly in our honeymoon phase. Sontag, it turned out, was coming to Stanford for a writer-in-residence stint that spring and the first morning after her arrival abruptly summoned me to take her out to breakfast. The alacrity with which I drove the forty miles down from San Francisco—trying not to get flustered but panting a bit at the wheel nonetheless—set the pattern of our days. We made the first of several madcap car trips around Palo Alto and the Stanford foothills. While I drove, often somewhat erratically, she would alternate between loud complaints about her faculty club accommodation, the bad food at the Humanities Center, the "dreariness" of my Stanford colleagues (*Terry, don't you loathe academics as much as I do? How can you abide it?*)—and her Considered Views on

Everything (*Yes, Terry, I do know all the lesser-known Handel operas. I told Andrew Porter he was right—they are the greatest of musical masterpieces*). I was rapt, like a hysterical spinster on her first visit to Bayreuth. *Schwärmerei* time for T-Ball.

The Sarajevo obsession revealed itself early on, in fact, inspired the great comic episode in this brief golden period. We were walking down University Avenue, Palo Alto's twee, boutique-crammed main drag, on our way to a bookshop. Sontag was wearing her trademark intellectual-diva outfit: voluminous black top and black silky slacks, accessorized with a number of exotic, billowy scarves. These she constantly adjusted or flung back imperiously over one shoulder, stopping now and then to puff on a cigarette or expel a series of phlegmy coughs. (The famous Sontag "look" always put me in mind of the stage direction in *Blithe Spirit*: "Enter Madame Arcati, wearing barbaric jewellery.") Somewhat incongruously, she had completed her ensemble with a pair of pristine, startlingly white tennis shoes. These made her feet seem comically huge, like Bugs Bunny's. I half-expected her to bounce several feet up and down in the air whenever she took a step, like one of those people who have shoes made of Flubber in the old Fred McMurray movie.

She'd been telling me about the siege and how a Yugoslav woman she had taken shelter with had asked her for her autograph, even as bombs fell around them. She relished the woman's obvious intelligence (*Of course, Terry, she'd read* The Volcano Lover, *and like all Europeans, admired it tremendously*) and her own sangfroid. Then she stopped abruptly and asked, grim-faced, if I'd ever had to evade sniper fire. I said, no, unfortunately not. Lickety-split she was off, dashing in a feverish crouch from one boutique doorway to the next, white tennis shoes a blur, all the way down the street to Restoration Hardware and the Baskin-Robbins store. Five or six perplexed Palo Altans stopped to watch as she bobbed zanily in and out, ducking her head, pointing at imaginary gunmen on rooftops and gesticulating wildly at me to follow. No one, clearly, knew who she was, though several of them looked as if they thought they should know who she was.

In those early days, I felt like an intellectual autodidact facing the greatest challenge of her career: the Autodidact of all Autodidacts. The quizzing was relentless. Had I read Robert Walser? (*Ooooh errrg blush, ahem, little cough, um: No, I'm ashamed to say . . .*) Had I read Thomas Bernhard? (*Yes! Yes, I have!* Wittgenstein's Nephew*! Yay! Yippee! Wow! Phew! dodged the bullet that time!*) It seemed, for a while at least, that I had yet to be contaminated by the shocking intellectual mediocrity surrounding me at Stanford U. This exemption from idiocy was due mainly, I think, to the fact that I could hold my own with her in the music-appreciation department. Trading CDs and recommendations—in a peculiar, masculine, train-spotting fashion—later became a part of our fragile bond. I scored a coup one time with some obscure Busoni arrangements she'd not heard of (though she assured me that *she had, of course, known the pianist*—the late Paul Jacobs—*very well*); but I almost came a cropper when I confessed I had never listened to Janáček's *The Excursions of Mr. Brouček*. She gave me a surprised look, then explained, somewhat loftily, that I owed it to myself, as a "cultivated person," to become acquainted with it. (*I adore Janáček's sound world,* she opined.) A recording of the opera appeared soon after in the mail, so I knew I'd been forgiven, but after listening to it once I couldn't really get anywhere with it. (It *does* tend to go on a bit, in the same somewhat exhausting Central European way I now associate with Sontag herself.) The discs are still on my shelf. Given their exalted provenance I can't bear to unload them at the used CD shop in my neighborhood.

And she also flirted, in a coquettish, discombobulating, yet unmistakable fashion. She told me she had read my book, *The Apparitional Lesbian*, and "agreed with me entirely" about Henry James and *The Bostonians*. She made me describe at length how I'd met my then girlfriend. (*She wrote you a letter! And you answered? Terry,*

*I'm amazed! I get those letters all the time, but I would never answer
one! Of course, Terry, I'm stunned!*) Though I was far too cowed to
ask her directly about her own love life, she would reveal the occasional tidbit from her legendary past, then give me a playful, almost
girlish look. (*Of course, Terry, everyone said Jeanne Moreau and I were
lovers, but you know, we were just good friends.*) My apotheosis as tease
target came the night of her big speech in Kresge Auditorium. She
had begun by reprimanding those in the audience who failed to consider her one of the "essential" modern novelists, then read a seemingly interminable section of what was to become *In America*. (Has
any other major literary figure written such an excruciatingly turgid
book?) At the end, as the audience gave way to enormous, relieved
clapping—thank God that's over—she made a beeline towards me.
Sideswiping the smiling president of Stanford and an eager throng of
autograph-seekers, she elbowed her way towards me, enveloped me
rakishly in her arms and said very loudly, "Terry, we've got to stop
meeting like this." She seemed to think the line hilarious and chortled heartily. I felt at once exalted, dopey, and mortified, like a plump
teenage boy getting a hard-on in front of everybody.

Though otherwise respectful, Allan Gurganus (in the *Advocate*
obit) takes Sontag to task for never having come out publicly as a lesbian: "My only wish about Sontag is that she had bothered to weather
what the rest of us daily endure. The disparity between her professed
fearlessness and her actual self-protective closetedness strikes a questioning footnote that is the one blot on her otherwise brilliant career."

I have to say I could never figure her out on this touchy subject,
though we did talk about it. Her usual line (indignant and aggrieved)
was that she didn't believe in "labels" and that if anything she was
bisexual. She raged about a married couple who were following her
from city to city and would subsequently publish a tell-all biography
of her in 2000. Horrifyingly enough, she'd learned, the despicable

pair were planning to include photographs of her with various celebrated female companions. Obviously, both needed to be consigned to Dante's Inferno, to roast in the flames in perpetuity with the Unbaptized Babies, Usurers, and Makers of False Oaths. I struggled to keep a poker face during these rants, but couldn't help thinking that Dante should have devised a whole circle specifically for such malefactors: the Outers of Sontag.

At other times she was less vehement, and would assume a dreamy, George-Sand-in-the-1840s look. *I've loved men, Terry; I've loved women* . . . she would begin, with a deep sigh. What did the sex of the person matter, after all? Think of Sand herself with Chopin and Marie Dorval. Or Tsvetaeva, perhaps, with Mandelstam and Sophia Parnok. In Paris, all the elegant married ladies had mistresses. And yet in some way I felt the subject of female homosexuality—and whether she owed the world a statement on it—was an unresolved one for her. Later in our friendship, the topic seemed to become an awkward obsession, especially as I came closer to finishing up an anthology of lesbian-themed literature I'd been working on for several years. She frequently suggested things she thought I should include: most interestingly, perhaps, her favorite steamy love scene from Patricia Highsmith's 1952 lesbian romance novel *The Price of Salt.* As far as Sontag was concerned, Highsmith's dykey little potboiler—published originally under a pseudonym—was right up there with *Buddenbrooks* and *The Man Without Qualities.* Something in the story about a gifted (yet insecure) young woman who moves to Manhattan in the early 1950s to become a theater designer and ends up falling rapturously in love with a glamorous, outré older woman must have once struck a chord; Sontag seemed to dote on it.

And invariably she would probe for Sapphic gossip—sometimes about opera singers and pop stars, sometimes about other writers. Was it true what everyone said about the late Tatiana Troyanis? What about Eleanor Steber? And Brigitte Fassbaender? Or Lucia Popp, for that matter? (*Of course, Terry, the perfect Queen of the Night.*) Did I think Iris Murdoch and Brigid Brophy had had an affair? What was Adrienne Rich's girlfriend like? When was somebody ever going to spill the beans on Eudora Welty and Elizabeth Bowen?

Was there some way, I wonder now, that she wanted me to absolve her? Was the fact that she never mentioned, on any of the occasions we talked, her equally prominent female companion (they lived in the same Manhattan building) a sign of grande dame sophistication or some sort of weird test of my character? (Actually I did hear her say her name once; when someone at an otherwise fairly staid farewell dinner gave Sontag a vulgar present at the end of her Stanford visit—a book of glossy photos of the campy 1950s pin-up, Bettie Page—she said: "I'll have to show these to Annie.")

I was never quite sure what she wanted. And besides, whatever it was, after a while she stopped wanting it. I visited her several times in New York City and even got invited to the London Terrace penthouse to see the famous book collection. (*Of course, Terry, mine is the greatest library in private hands in the world.*) I tried not to gape at the Brice Mardens stacked up against the wall and enthused appropriately when she showed me prized items, such as Beckford's own annotated copy of *Vathek*. We would go on little culture jaunts. Once she took me to the Strand bookstore (the clerk said "Hi, Susan" in enviably blasé tones); another time she invited me to a film festival she was curating at the Japan Society. But there were also little danger signals, ominous hints that she was tiring of me. One day in the Village, after having insisted on buying me a double-decker ice cream cone, she suddenly vanished, even as I, tongue moronically extruded, was still licking away. I turned around in bewilderment and saw her black-clad form piling, without farewell, into a yellow cab.

And the last two times I saw her I managed to blow it—horrendously—both times. The first debacle occurred after one of the films at the Japan Society. I'd been hanging nervously around in the lobby, like a groupie, waiting for her; Sontag yanked me into a taxi with her and an art curator she knew named Klaus. (He was hip and bald and dressed in the sort of all-black outfit worn by the fictional German talk-show host, Dieter Sprocket, on the old *Saturday Night Live*.) With great excitement she explained she was taking me out for "a real New York evening," to a dinner party being hosted by Marina Abramovic, the performance artist, at her loft in SoHo. Abramovic had recently been in the news for having lived for twelve days, stark naked, on an exposed wooden platform (fitted with shower and toilet) in the window of the Sean Kelly Gallery. She lived on whatever food spectators donated and never spoke during the entire twelve days. I guess it had all been pretty mesmerizing; my friend Nancy happened to be there once when Abramovic took a shower, and one of Nancy's friends hit the jackpot—she got to watch the artist have a bowel movement.

Abramovic—plus hunky sculptor boyfriend—lived in a huge, virtually empty loft, the sole furnishings being a dining table and chairs in the very center of the room and a spindly old stereo from the 1960s. The space was probably a hundred feet on either side: *major real estate, of course*, as Sontag proudly explained to me. (She loved using *Vanity Fair*–ish clichés.) She and Abramovic smothered one another in hugs and kisses. I meanwhile blanched in fright: I'd just caught sight of two of the other guests who, alarmingly enough, turned out to be Lou Reed and Laurie Anderson. Reed (O great rock god of my twenties) stood morosely by himself, humming, doing little dance steps and playing air guitar. Periodically he glared at everyone—including me—with apparent hatred. Anderson—elfin spikes of hair perfectly gelled—was chatting up an Italian man from the Guggenheim, the man's trophy wife, and the freakish-looking lead singer from the cult art-pop duo Fischerspooner. The last-mentioned had just come back from performing at the Pompidou

Center and wore booties and tights, a psychedelic shawl and a thing like a codpiece. He could have played Osric in a postmodern *Hamlet*. He was accompanied by a bruiser with a goatee—roadie or boyfriend, it wasn't clear—and emitted girlish little squeals when our first course, a foul-smelling durian fruit just shipped in from Malaysia, made its way to the table.

Everyone crowded into their seats: despite the vast size of the room, we were an *intime* gathering. Yet it wouldn't be quite right merely to say that everyone ignored me. As a non-artist and non-celebrity, I was so "not there," it seemed—so cognitively unassimilable—I wasn't even registered enough to be ignored. I sat at one end of the table like a piece of antimatter. I didn't exchange a word the whole night with Lou Reed, who sat kitty-corner across from me. He remained silent and surly. Everyone else gabbled happily on, however, about how they loved to trash hotels when they were younger and how incompetent everybody was at the Pompidou. *At my show I had to explain things to them a thousand times. They just don't know how to do a major retrospective.*

True, Sontag tried briefly to call the group's attention to me (with the soul-destroying words, *Terry is an English professor*); and Abramovic kindly gave me a little place card to write my name on. But otherwise I might as well not have been born. My one conversational gambit failed dismally: when I asked the man from the Guggenheim, to my right, what his books were about, he regarded me disdainfully and began, *I am famous for—*, then caught himself. He decided to be more circumspect—he was the *world's leading expert on Arte Povera*—but then turned his back on me for the next two hours. At one point I thought I saw Laurie Anderson, at the other end of the table, trying to get my attention; she was smiling sweetly in my direction, as if to undo my pathetic isolation. I smiled in gratitude in return and held up my little place card so she would at least know my name. Annoyed, she gestured back impatiently, with a sharp downward flick of her index finger; she wanted me to pass the wine bottle. I was reduced to a pair of disembodied hands, like the ones that come out of the walls and give people drinks in Cocteau's *Beauty and the Beast*.

Sontag gave up trying to include me and after a while seemed herself to recede curiously into the background. Maybe she was already starting to get sick again; she seemed oddly undone. Through much of the conversation (dominated by glammy Osric) she looked tired and bored, almost sleepy. She did not react when I finally decided to leave—on my own—just after coffee had been served. I thanked Marina Abramovic, who led me to the grungy metal staircase that went down to the street and back to the world of the Little People. Turning round one last time, I saw Sontag still slumped in her seat, as if she'd fallen into a trance, or somehow just caved in. She'd clearly forgotten all about me.

A fiasco, to be sure, but my final encounter with Sontag was possibly more disastrous, my Waterloo. I had come to New York with Blakey, and Sontag (to whom I wanted proudly to display her) said we could stop by her apartment one afternoon. When we arrived at the appointed time, clutching a large bouquet of orange roses, Sontag was nowhere to be seen. Her young male assistant, padding delicately around in his socks, showed us in, took the roses away, and whispered to us to wait in the living room. We stood in puzzled silence. Half an hour later, somewhat blowsily, Sontag finally emerged from a back room. I introduced her to Blakey, and said rather nervously that I hoped we hadn't woken her up from a nap. It was as if I had accused her of never having read Proust, or of watching soap operas all day. Her face instantly darkened and she snapped at me violently. *Why on earth did I think she'd been having a nap? Didn't I know she never had naps? Of course she wasn't having a nap! She would never have a nap! Never in a million years! What a stupid remark to make! How had I gotten so stupid? A nap—for God's sake!*

She calmed down after a bit and became vaguely nice to Blakey—

Blakey had just read her latest piece on photography in *The New Yorker* and was complimenting her effusively on it—but it was clear I couldn't repair the damage I'd done. Indeed, I made it worse. Sontag asked B. if she had read *The Volcano Lover* and started in on a monologue (one I'd heard before) about her literary reputation. It had fallen slightly over the past decade, she allowed—foolishly, people had yet to grasp the greatness of her fiction—but of course it would rise again dramatically, *as soon as I am dead*. The same thing had happened, after all, to Virginia Woolf, and didn't we agree Woolf was a great genius? In a weak-minded attempt at levity, I asked her if she "really" thought *Orlando* a work of genius. She then exploded. *Of course not!* she shouted, hands flailing and face white with rage. *Of course not! You don't judge a writer by her worst work! You judge her by her best work!* I reeled backwards as if I'd been struck; Blakey looked embarrassed. The assistant peeked out from another room to see what was going on. Sontag went on muttering for a while, then grimly said she had to go. With awkward thanks, we bundled ourselves hurriedly into the elevator and out onto West 24th Street— Blakey agog, me all nervy and smarting. When I sent Sontag a copy of my lesbian anthology a few months later, a thousand pages long and complete with juicy Highsmith excerpt, I knew she would never acknowledge it, nor did she.

Enfin—la fin. I heard she was dead as Bev and I were driving back from my mother's after Christmas. Blakey called on the cell phone from Chicago to say she had just read about it online; it would be on the front page of *The New York Times* the next day. It was, but news of the Asian tsunami crowded it out. (The catty thing to say here would be that Sontag would have been annoyed at being upstaged; the honest thing to say is that she wouldn't have been.) The *Times* did another piece a few days later, a somewhat dreary set of passages from her books, entitled "No Hard Books, or Easy Deaths." (An odd title: her death wasn't easy, but she was all about hard books.) And in the weeks since, *The New Yorker*, *New York Review of Books*, and various other highbrow mags have kicked in with the predictable tributes.

But I've had the feeling the real reckoning has yet to begin. The reaction, to my mind, has been a bit perfunctory and stilted. A good part of her characteristic "effect"—what one might call her novelistic charm—has not yet been put into words. Among other things, Sontag was a great comic character; Dickens or Flaubert or James would have had a field day with her. The carefully cultivated moral seriousness—strenuousness might be a better word—coexisted with a fantastical, Mrs. Jellyby–like absurdity. Sontag's complicated and charismatic sexuality was part of this comic side of her life. The high-mindedness, the high-handedness, commingled with a love of gossip, drollery, and seductive acting out—and, when she was in a benign and unthreatened mood, a fair amount of ironic self-knowledge.

I think she was fully conscious of, and took great pride and pleasure in, the erotic spell she exerted over other women. I would be curious to know how men found her in this regard; the few times I saw her with men around, they seemed to relate to her as a kind of intellectually supercharged eunuch. The famed "Natalie Wood" looks of her early years notwithstanding, she seemed uninterested in being an object of heterosexual desire, and males responded accordingly. It was not the same with women, and least of all with her lesbian fans. Among the susceptible, she never lost her sexual majesty. She was quite fabulously butch—perhaps the Butchest One of All. She knew it and basked in it, like a big lady she-cat in the sun.

Perhaps at some point there will be, too, a better and less routine accounting of her extraordinary cultural significance. Granted, Great Man (or Great Woman) theories of history have been out of fashion for some time now. No single person, it's usually argued, has that much effect on how things eventually turn out. Yet it is hard for me to think about the history of modern feminism, say—especially as it evolved in the United States in the 1970s—without Sontag in the absolutely central, catalytic role. Simone de Beauvoir was float-ing around too, of course, but for intellectually ambitious American women of my generation, women born in the 1940s and '50s, the Frenchwoman seemed both culturally unfamiliar and emotionally removed. Sontag, on the contrary, was there: on one's own college campus, lecturing on Barthes or Canetti or Benjamin or Tsvetaeva or Leni Riefenstahl. (And who were they? One pretended to know, then scuttled around to find out.) She was our very own Great Man. If there was ever going to be a Smart Woman Team then Sontag would have to be both Captain and Most Valuable Player. She was the one already out there doing the job, even as we were laboring painfully to get up off the floor and match wits with her.

In my own case, Sontag's death brings with it mixed emotions. God, she could be insulting to people. At the end—as I enjoyed blub-bering to friends—she was *weally weally mean to me*! But her death also leaves me now with a profound sense of imploding fantasies, of huge convulsions in the underground psychic plates. Not once, un-fortunately, on any of her California trips did Sontag ever come to my house, though I often sat around scheming how to get her to accept such an invitation. *If only she would come*, I thought, *I would be truly happy*. It's hard to admit how long—and how abjectly, like a Victo-rian monomaniac—I carried this fantasy around. (It long antedated my actual meeting with her.) It is still quite palpable in the rooms in which I spend most of my time. Just about every book, every picture, every object in my living room, for example, I now see all too plainly, has been placed there strategically in the hope of capturing her at-tention, of pleasing her mind and heart, of winning her love, esteem, intellectual respect, etc., etc. It's all baited and set up: a room-sized Venus flytrap, courtesy of T-Ball/Narcissism Productions.

There are her books, of course: the vintage paperbacks of *Against Interpretation*, *Styles of Radical Will*, *Under the Sign of Saturn*, the quite-wonderful-despite-what-everybody-says *The Volcano Lover*.

There's *AIDS and Its Metaphors*, *On Photography*, *Where the Stress Falls*. The now valedictory *Regarding the Pain of Others*. And then there are some of my own productions, to remind her, passive-aggressively I guess, that she's not the only damned person who writes. (*Caveat lector*: Lilliputian on the rampage!) But yet heaps of other things are also on view, I'm embarrassed to say, the sole purpose of which is—was—to impress her or some facsimile version of her. A pile of "tasteful" art books: Popova, *The History of Japanese Photography*, Cy Twombly, Nadar, Bronzino, Hannah Hoch, Jeff Wall, Piranesi, Sol LeWitt and Jasper Johns, the big Bellocq volume (with her introduction). My 1930s picture of Lucienne Boyer. My Valentine Hugo photo of Breton and Aragon. The crammed CD cabinet, with the six different versions of *Pelléas* (will I really listen to any of them all the way through again before I die?). My little nineteenth-century optical toy from Paris: you crank a tiny lever and see a clown head, painted on glass, change expressions as if by magic.

Yet now the longed-for visitor—or victim—is never going to arrive. Who will come in her stead? At the moment it's hard to imagine anyone ever possessing the same symbolic weight, the same adamantine hardness, or having the same casual imperial hold over such a large chunk of my brain. I am starting to think in any case that she was part of a certain neural development that, purely physiologically speaking, can never be repeated. All those years ago one evolved a hallucination about what mental life could be and she was it. She's still in there, enfolded somehow in the deepest layers of the gray matter. Yes: Susan Sontag was sibylline and hokey and often a great bore. She was a troubled and brilliant American and never as good a friend as I wanted her to be. But now the lady's kicked it and I'm trying to keep one of the big lessons in view: judge her by her best work, not her worst.

Home Alone

Elsie de Wolfe, the "First Lady of Interior Decoration," in rococo costume, ca. 1900

THE LATE MARIO PRAZ—DANDY, scholar, eccentric chronicler of interior-decorating styles through the ages—once observed that human beings could be divided into those who cared about such things and those who didn't. An avid, even ensorcelled member of the first group, he confessed to finding people who were indifferent to décor baffling and somewhat sinister. To discover that a friend was content to dwell in "fundamental and systematic ugliness," he wrote in *An Illustrated History of Interior Decoration: From Pompeii to Art Nouveau*, was as disturbing as "turning over one of those ivory figurines carved by the German artificers of the Renaissance, which show a lovely woman on one side and a worm-ridden corpse on the other." All the more macabre was it when the friend was otherwise refined:

A venerated master of mine at the University of Florence used to
say, from his lectern, many learned things about the Provençal
poets. I hung on his every word. But it was a grim day when I first
crossed the threshold of his house. As soon as the door was opened, I
was confronted by a loathsome oleograph of a Neapolitan shepherd-
ess (that same oleograph used to turn up often in the shops where
unclaimed objects from the state pawnshop, the Monte di Pietà, are
sold). The shepherdess, shading her eyes with her hand, affected a
simpering smile, while Vesuvius smoked in the background.

Granted, in place of the "loathsome oleograph" (which now
sounds enchantingly campy) one might want to substitute any
number of contemporary abominations: fur-covered kitty condos
placed nonchalantly in the living room, embroidered sofa pillows
that say things like "She Who Must Be Obeyed" or "Bless This
Mess," Southwestern-style bent-willow furniture (barf), neoclassical
wall sconces made out of glued and gilded polyurethane, monstrous
sleigh beds from Restoration Hardware, Monet water-lily refrigerator magnets, fake "bistro" clocks, and just about any item of domestic
ornament with an angel or a dolphin or a picture of Frida Kahlo on
it. Yet even without a tchotchke update we can all sympathize with
Praz's baffled revulsion: "It's curious, the squalor, the unnecessary
and even deliberate squalor in which people who profess a sensitivity
to the fine arts choose to live, or manage to adapt themselves."

Or at least some of us can. I think Praz is right: you either have
the "interiors" thing going on or you don't. Sherlock Holmes would
have no difficulty determining into which of Praz's categories I fall:
a quick riffle through the contents of my mailbox, engorged each day
to the point of overflowing, makes it comically clear.

The surreal monthly haul, I'm embarrassed to say, includes just
about every shelter magazine known to man or woman, from *House*
and Garden, *Elle Decor* (not to be confused with *Elle Decoration*, a

British mag that I also get), *Metropolitan Home, House Beautiful,* and *Architectural Digest* to *Dwell, Wallpaper, Veranda,* the British *Homes and Gardens,* and—holy of holies—the epicene and intoxicating *World of Interiors,* a UK shelter mag so farcically upscale and eccentric that it might have been conceived by P. G. Wodehouse. (Until its recent demise I also subscribed to *nest.* More on that dark Manhattan cult mag later.) Add to these the innumerable glossy catalogues—from Pottery Barn, Crate & Barrel, Room and Board, Design Within Reach, Ikea, West Elm, Home Decorators Collection, Williams-Sonoma, Wisteria, Ballard Designs, Plow & Hearth, NapaStyle, Eddie Bauer Home, and the like—that regularly deluge anyone who has ever made the mistake (as I have) of ordering a distressed-teak milking stool or a kilim-covered ottoman online, and any residual doubt about my propensities will be removed.

The obsession, I confess, has its autoerotic dimension. At times, despite the ever-renewing bounty on hand, I still mooch down to an insalubrious foreign newsstand near where I live in San Francisco and peruse *Maison Française, Maisons Côté Sud,* or *Résidences Décoration*—just to practice my French, of course. (Though rather more arduous linguistically, the German *Elle Decoration* also sometimes beckons.) Paging through the offerings on display, I am aware of bearing a discomfiting resemblance to various male regulars furtively examining the dirty magazines across the aisle. An ex-girlfriend (we split up in part over closet space) informs me I am a "house-porn addict," and although the term is exactly the sort of metrosexual-hipster cliché, cheeky yet dull, that one finds every Thursday in the *New York Times* Home & Garden section, it does get at the curious feelings of guilt, titillation, and flooding bourgeois pleasure—relief delivered through hands and eyeballs—that such publications provide.

Yet more and more people, I've come to decide, must share my vice to some degree. The sheer ubiquitousness of interiors magazines—

in airport terminals, supermarket checkout lines, big-box bookstores, doctors' offices, and other quintessentially modern (and often stress-ful) locations—suggests I am not the only person, female or male, gay or straight, experiencing such cravings. (Though hardly one of the more soigné publications, *Better Homes and Gardens*, owned by ABC Magazines, has an annual circulation of 7.6 million and gen-erates nearly $173 million in revenue a year.) And lately the oddest people have started to confess to me their shelter-mag obsessions, including, a couple of weeks ago, a scary-looking young 'zine writer with a metal bolt through her tongue and Goth-style tattoos all over her neck, arms, legs, and back. Crystal meth would seem to have nothing on *House Beautiful*—and the latter won't turn your teeth into pulpy little black stumps.

How to understand such collective absorption? One might moral-ize, of course, and simply write off the phenomenon as yet another example of life in obscene America—home of the fat, spoiled, and imbecilic. How dare to broach such a subject when more than 2.6 billion people, or "more than 40 percent of the world's population," according to *The New York Times*, "lack basic sanitation, and more than one billion people lack reliable access to safe drinking water"? Easy enough to say that shelter mags are silly and odious—not worth even talking about—and leave it at that.

Yet while satisfying to the censorious, such judgmentalism in an-other way begs the question. Even the most embarrassing or guilt-inducing features of daily life, Freud famously argued, have their "psychopathology" and can be plumbed for truths about the human condition. One could as easily argue, it seems to me, that house porn, like the billion-dollar business of home improvement itself, is symp-tomatic of a peculiar disquiet now haunting ordinary American life. However callow it may seem to point it out, being middle-class these days means feeling freaky a lot of the time. The heebie-jeebies are definitely a problem. The issues here are deep ones. Home—no less than the cherished "homeland" of dismal fame—seems in desperate need of securing. The precariousness of All We Hold Dear is dinned into our heads daily. It's hardly feckless to feel scared or neurasthenic at times.

Might paging through a shelter mag be seen—in an analytic spirit and with a certain Freudian forbearance—as a middle-class coping mechanism? As a way of calming the spirit in bizarre and parlous times? House porn, I'm beginning to think, could best be understood as a postmodern equivalent of traditional consolation literature— Boethius meets Mitchell Gold. Though shamelessly of this world— and nowhere more so than in the glutted and prodigal United States of America—it's as spiritually fraught, one could argue, as the breviaries of old.

Which isn't to say that certain people aren't, for complex reasons, particularly susceptible to the shelter-mag jones. Décor-fixated individuals (and you know who you are), according to Praz, are usually "neurotic, refined, sad people," prone to "secret melancholy" and "hypersensitive nerves." Quaint language aside (he enlists the "mad, lonely spirit" of Ludwig II of Bavaria as a historical example of the syndrome), the claim is weirdly compelling. Readers with the obsessive-compulsive gene—the twenty-first-century version, perhaps, of "hypersensitive nerves"—will be familiar with the low-level yet troublesome anxiety produced when something in a room seems misplaced, askew, or somehow "wrong." I won't be surprised when brain scientists discover the odd little fold in the cerebral cortex that makes one agitate over slipcovers or jump up and rearrange the furniture.

But along with whatever innate disposition may exist, the typical interiors fanatic almost always has some aesthetic trauma looming up out of the past—a decorative primal scene, so to speak—exacerbating the underlying syndrome. For the legendary American designer Elsie de Wolfe (1865–1950), the so-called First Lady of Interior Decoration, just such a shock awaited her, she recalled in her memoirs, when she returned home one day from school to find that her parents (pious Scottish-Canadian immigrants otherwise deficient in fantasy) had repapered the sitting room of their New York City brownstone in a lurid "[William] Morris design of gray palm-leaves and splotches of bright green and red on a background of dull tan." Something "that cut like a knife came up inside her," de Wolfe recollected. The young Elsie, she writes, "threw herself on the floor, kicking with stiffened legs as she beat her legs on the carpet." The novelette-ish third person is a nice dramatic touch: Freud's Dora had nothing on Elsie in the girlish-hysteria department.

And indeed, there's just such a primal scene in my own childhood: the day my mother, faced with replacing our bedraggled old tweed sofa, decided in a fit of desperate-divorcée economy to spray-paint it instead. (When I succumb to rectal cancer, it will no doubt be the result of having sat on this unwholesome piece of furniture throughout my adolescence.) In a single sunny late-sixties San Diego afternoon—I can still hear the clack-clack of aerosol cans being shaken—our couch went from its normal faded-beige color to a lethal-looking southern California turquoise. That wasn't the end, though: overcome by a sort of decorative frenzy, she then sprayed the flimsy shelf unit separating the "kitchenette" from the living room in our tiny pink-and-green motel-style apartment, and after that, two discarded toys of mine, a hapless pair of plastic palomino ponies. Resplendent in turquoise from forelock to hoof, Trigger and Buttermilk were subsequently elevated to the unlikely role of room-divider ornaments. No doubt my adult hankering after Zuber *papiers peints*, Omega Workshop textiles, and Andre Arbus escritoires germinated at just this moment.

Now, it's worth considering to what degree decorative trauma functions as a mental screen for more troubling kinds of distress. Is the interiors mania rooted in deeper childhood travails? Elsie de Wolfe's Calvinist mother seems to have been gruesome enough: she made de Wolfe wear sack-cloth pinafores and shipped her off at fifteen to a *Jane Eyre*–style boarding school in Edinburgh. In his notes to the elegant new Rizzoli reprint of de Wolfe's so-called design bible, *The House in Good Taste* (1913), Hutton Wilkinson, the president of the Elsie de Wolfe Foundation, suggests that the revolutionary decorating philosophy de Wolfe evolved in the first decade of the twentieth century, one favoring simplicity, creamy-white walls, natural light, informal furniture groupings, bright chintzes, had its psychic roots in juvenile pain and estrangement. (De Wolfe "simply didn't like Victorian," Wilkinson writes, because it was "the high style of her sad childhood.")

Again, no question but that family ructions—notably my parents' nuclear war–style divorce when I was seven—left me, like de Wolfe, with a bit of a shelter neurosis. As soon as the papers were filed, my British-born mother yanked me and my little sister out of the standard-issue suburban West Coast middle-class home we had occupied for as long as I could remember and took us off to a dreary seaside bungalow in the UK. Returning to San Diego three years later—my mother then in flight from British Inland Revenue—we landed in the aforementioned cheesy apartment, the best she could do on the child support she received from my father. I spent my mopey teenage years there like an exiled monarch, dolefully contemplating the spindly 1950s hibiscus-print bamboo armchairs and roll-up window blinds (courtesy of Buena Vista Apartments management) and lamenting the fate that had befallen us.

The real nightmare, however, was a squalid domicile across town that threatened off and on to become our future home: the "snout house" (a boxy SoCal tract house with garage and driveway dominating the frontage) owned by the man my mother would later marry, a hapless submariner named Turk, whose previous wife had dropped dead there of alcohol poisoning a few months before my mother met him. The place was my private House of Usher: an emblem of the hideous life that awaited us should my mother, out of economic desperation, ever accede to one of Turk's frequently proffered marriage proposals. And as if to confirm its baleful role in my imaginative life, it was an abode of surpassing ugliness: dank and malodorous, with fake wood paneling and a tattered Snopes-family screen door at the front admitting numerous flies. The only decorative touches were the grimy ashtrays on every surface, a faded Navy photo of the USS *Roncador* surfacing, and, in one dim corner, a dusty assemblage of bronzed baby shoes, one for each of Turk's five rowdy-urchin children. Luckily, by the time my mother married him I had already left for college, so I—the female Fauntleroy—never had to live there. Staying overnight was bad enough, though: I have dreams to this day in which the mother who dropped dead emerges from the closet— here, now, in my grown-up bedroom in San Francisco—to enfold me in a noxious and crumbly embrace.

Which brings me back, by a somewhat gothic route, to shelter mags and their allure. One essential part of their appeal, it seems to me, lies precisely in the fact that they proffer—even brazenly tout— an escape from the parental. (The step-parental, too, thank God.) They do this in several ways, perhaps most conspicuously through a glib, repetitious, wonderfully brain-deadening "express the inner you" rhetoric. Now, supposedly no one actually "reads" shelter magazines; you just drivel over the pictures. Patently untrue in my experience: I devour all the writing, too—such as it is—no matter how fatuous and formulaic. I take special pleasure in the "editor's welcome"—usually a few brief paragraphs (next to a little picture of said editor) about new decorating trends, the need for beauty in one's life, how to create a private "sanctuary" for yourself, the meaning of "home," etc. It's always the same stupefying tripe, but soothing nonetheless.

Who is this editor? She (rarely he) might best be described as the Un-Mother. She is typically white, middle-aged yet youthful, apparently straight, and seldom much more ethnic-looking than the Polish-American Martha Stewart. She is often divorced, and may (paradoxically) have grown-up children. But her authority is of an oblique, seemingly nontoxic kind—more that of a benevolent older sister or a peppy, stylish aunt than any in-your-face maternal figure. And the therapeutic wisdom she dispenses—almost always in the cozy second person—is precisely that you don't have to do what your mother tells you to do. In fact, your ma can buzz off altogether. You can now buy lots of nice things and make "your own space" from which all signs of the past have been expunged. *Yay! No more USS Roncador!*

If you enter the words "not your mother's" on Google, you'll get nearly 400,000 results, a huge number of which point you immediately toward shelter-mag articles. "Not your mother's [whatever]" turns out to be an established interiors trope, endlessly recycled in titles, pull quotes, advertisements, photo captions, and the like. "Not Your Mother's Tableware" is a typical heading, meant presumably to assure you that if you acquire the featured cutlery you will also, metaphorically speaking, be giving your mom the finger. (Other online items that are not your mother's: wallpaper, mobile homes, Chinette, faucet sponges, slow cookers, backyard orchards, and Tupperware parties. Beyond the realm of interior decoration—it's nice to learn—you can also avoid your mother's menopause, divorce, Internet, hysterectomy, book club, Mormon music, hula dance, antibacterial soap, deviled eggs, and national security. Thank you, Condi.)

"Your House Is You, So Start Reveling in It" is a virtual creed in Shelter-Mag Land, one derived from the holy books of interior design. "You will express yourself in your home, whether you want to or not," proclaimed the prophet Elsie in *The House in Good Taste*—best to "arrange it so that the person who sees [you] in it will be reassured, not disconcerted." In *The Personality of a House*, a rather more florid copycat volume from 1930, Emily Post was no less insistent: "[Your home's] personality should express your personality, just as every gesture you make—or fail to make—expresses your gay animation or your restraint, your old-fashioned conventions, your perplexing mystery, or your emancipated modernism—whichever characteristics are typically yours." Narcissism in a go-cup: the ladies say it's okay.

Now, in 2006, the message is ubiquitous, sloganized, inevitable. "Not Everything in Your Home Is All About You, You, You," reads an ad for flooring in a recent issue of *Elle Decor*. "Oh, Wait. Yes, It Is." Unsurprisingly, it is taken for granted that one's inner life, externalized in décor, will be an improvement on whatever has gone before. "What do you think you want?" asks *Elle Decoration* (September 2005). "A bigger house? A better view? Frette bed linen? A matching set of original Saarinen dining chairs?" It seems that "you" have very expensive tastes. But that's fine too, because shelter literature is all about consumption, luxury goods, and the pipe dreams of upward mobility.

When one has pretensions to taste, such dreams can be hard to resist. Out of necessity my own decorating style has long been fairly down-market and bourgeois: your standard Academic-Shabby-Chic-Wood-Floors-Vaguely-Ethnic-Somewhat-Cluttered-Bohemian-Edith-Sitwell-Crossed-with-Pottery-Barn-Squeaky-Dog-Toys-Everywhere-Eccentric-Anglophile-Lesbian. (The last two elements being signified by various grubby Vita Sackville-West first editions on the shelves. No one else on the Internet seems to want them.) Yet raffishness notwithstanding, the entire visual scheme is as fraught with socioeconomic symbolism as any. Having been plucked out of the (semi-) prosperous middle class as a child, I have spent thirty years or so trying to wiggle my way back in. Indeed, to the degree that such mobility is possible on an academic salary, I've sought fairly relentlessly to upgrade to even higher status; 1920s-Artistic-British-Boho-with-Inherited-Income has usually been the target look, as if Augustus John and Virginia Woolf had mated. (The "British" part has no doubt been a way of renegotiating childhood fiascos on my own terms.) Say the words "Bloomsbury" or "Charleston" and I become quite tremulous with longing.

That the "express yourself" ethos of the shelter mag is both illogical and manipulative should go without saying. While encouraging you to find your "personal style," the Un-Mother also wants to show you how. Even my own fanatically considered décor, I'm forced to admit, may be part of some greedy stranger's business plan, a version of that nostalgic "vintage" or "Paris flea market" style heavily promoted to urban college-educated women of my generation throughout the United States and Western Europe over the past decade or so. (Other incessantly marketed "looks" now vying for dominance in Shelter-Mag Land: "mid-century modern," a variety of Baby Boomer Rat Pack retro distinguished by funky space-age design, Case Study houses, pony skins on the floor, and, if you're lucky, lots of Eames, Mies, and Corbu; and the more minimalist, Asian-inspired W Hotel look, involving wenge wood, stark-white walls, spa bathrooms, dust mite–free bedding, solitary orchids in raku pots, etc. The latter mode, like the frigid minimalism of the British cult architect John Pawson, always strikes me as simply the latest twist on twentieth-century fascist design.) But whether my never-ending quest for antique finials, faded bits of toile de Jouy, old postcards, and other quirky "flea-market finds" is a product of disposition or suggestion, I am, I realize, as much a slave to commodity fetishism as any McMansion-owning reader of *Architectural Digest* (hideous bible of parvenus from the Hamptons to Malibu).

Resentful, matriphobic, pretentious, gullible: could the shelter-lit addict be any less appealing? Unfortunately, yes, as a brief foray into Shelter-Mag Land's heart of darkness, its paranoid psychic core, will reveal. Here the real-world rooms on display—static, pristine, and seemingly uninhabited—are key. To be "at home" in the World of Interiors, one rapidly gathers, is to bask in the privacy of your own space, serene and unabashed, while the rest of the world goes kaboom all around you. Not for nothing does the industry term "shelter magazine" play subliminally on "bomb shelter." Self-fortification is one of the goals here; likewise the psychic eradication of other people.

Some shelter-lit purveyors are tough minded enough to cop to it: that the urge to "project the self" through décor can be deeply allied with misanthropy. "I live inside my head," the decorator Rose Tarlow declares in *The Private House* (2001), "often oblivious to the world outside myself. I see only what I wish to see." In her own home, she acknowledges, other people aren't really part of the scene:

I know there are times when we plan our houses as much for the pleasure of our friends as for ourselves, because we wish for their enjoyment, and rely on their appreciation and praise—especially their praise. Thankfully that stage of my life has passed!

Having now become "interested in a home only for myself," she would like nothing better, she says, than to live in a "nun's cell," a sort of little medieval crypt world. ("I imagine a bed covered in a creamy, heavy hemp fabric in a tiny room that has rough, whitewashed plaster walls, a small Gothic window, a stone sink; outside a bird sings. Peace prevails.") The book's illustrations—chill, austere, and undeniably gorgeous—give form to the tomblike aesthetic: not one of the exquisite rooms shown (all designed by Tarlow) has a human being in it.

Shelter-Mag Land is a place in which other people are edited out, removed from the picture, both literally and metaphorically, so that one is free to project oneself, for ever and a day, into the fantasy spaces on view. In any given interiors piece this "disappearing" of other people is usually a two-part process, beginning retrospectively, as it were, with the ritual exorcism of the last owner before the current one. Former owners invariably have atrocious taste, one discovers, and every trace of them must be removed. When the former owner is also the Mother in Need of Banishment, positively heroic measures are necessary. A 2004 article in the *New York Times Magazine* has a telling item about how Goldie Hawn's daughter, the actress Kate Hudson, bought "the Los Angeles house she grew up in" precisely in order to gut the interior and remodel it in "her own image." No Goldie vestiges will be allowed to remain. "Goldie's taste is more classic," notes a male designer assisting Hudson. "Kate wants to turn everything on its ear." Don't look now, Private Benjamin—the kid's just decoratively cleansed you.

But other people need cleansing, too, most urgently the lucky oinkers now in possession. It is common for interiors magazines—higher-end ones like *World of Interiors* especially—to suppress the names and images of current owners. There are exceptions, of course: *Elle Decor*, for some reason, likes to run pictures of blissed-out property owners—usually Ralph Lauren–ish white people relaxing on patios, cuddling their French bulldogs, or flourishing salad tongs in a gleaming Corian-countertopped kitchen. In some cases, especially when he's gay and humpy, the designer responsible for the new décor will be shown lounging about the premises looking highly pleased with himself, like a porn star who's just delivered big time.

And small children—especially if beautiful, blonde, and under five—sometimes get a pass, though they are liable to appear in curiously fey and stylized ways. For several years now I've been keeping tabs on a shelter-mag cliché I call the Blurred Child Picture: a light-filled shot of some airy urban loft, all-stainless kitchen, or quaint Nantucket cottage, in which the child of the house is shown—barefoot, pink, and perfect—either whizzing by in the background or bouncing joyfully on a bed. The face and limbs are often fuzzy, as if to suggest a sort of generic kidness in motion. These hallucinatory urchins usually turn out to bear excruciatingly hip names—Samantha, Cosmo, Zoe, and Miles are current favorites—and seem as branded and objectified as the furnishings around them. The ongoing reproductive anxieties of young, white middle-class American professional women—a crucial segment of the shelter-magazine demographic—would seem to prompt such wish-fulfillment imagery: here's your new space and a designer child to put in it.

But the ideal room in Shelter-Mag Land is unpeopled—stark, impervious, and preternaturally still. As aficionados know, just about every room shown in a shelter magazine has been meticulously staged by unseen stylists: flowers placed just so; covetable objects illuminated; expensive art books arranged on tables; takeout menus, sex toys, and drug paraphernalia discreetly removed. The place is usually flooded with heavenly light—as if an angel had just descended outside, or a nuclear flash had irradiated the environs. When windows in a room are visible, one typically can't see through them: they remain opaque, like weirdly glowing light boxes. The unearthly illumination from without is mesmerizing. Whether or not one likes the space on view, one finds oneself absorbed, drawn in by the eerie promise of peace and immutability. It's seductive, sanitized, calm-verging-on-dead: mausoleum chic.

The standard interiors shot might be categorized as a degraded form of still life—a kind of iconography distinguished, traditionally, by the absence of human subjects. And as with the painted form, the viewer is faced with puzzles and paradoxes. Confronting the perfectly styled objects before us, are we, the spectators, in the presence of life or death? Where are the human beings? In the traditional *nature morte* (the French name for the mode is telling) the depiction of food and drink—fruit, bread, goblets of wine, limp game birds—alluded to organic processes (here's something good to eat), but a "life" inextricably dependent on the death and decay of other living things. In the most profound and unflinching still-life arrangements (Zurbaran's, say, or those of the seventeenth-century Dutch school) the viewer is suavely implicated in the cycle of mortality. A human skull sometimes appears, Hamlet-style, as an explicit and sobering memento mori.

There's one big problem here, and you don't need to rent old Ingmar Bergman movies to see it. There's a real skeleton at the door, and whoa—looks like he's aiming to get in. He was first spotted in Shelter-Mag Land, scythe in hand, one sunny September morning a few years ago, and recently he's turned up again—in true *Seventh Seal* fashion—in one of its favorite "style destinations." (Two days into the unfolding Katrina disaster, *New Orleans Style: Past and Present*, the most lavish of recent shelter books devoted to the doomed southern city, had sold out on Amazon.com. I know—I was trying to order it.)

It's fair to say that even while seeking to exploit readers' existential fears, the shelter-lit industry has itself been traumatized over the past five years, its Benday-dots dream world cracked open by explosions from without. The first shock to the system was 9/11, an event so cognitively strange, so incomprehensible according to shelter-mag logic, that what to do about it—rhetorically, psychically—remains unresolved in most interiors publications. What sort of high-gloss feature to run when other people not only won't go away but also want to blow your trendy "sanctuary" to bits? "Home," after all, is what terrorists set out to destroy: the everyday illusion of comfort and safety, the rolling-along-as-usual feeling that is bourgeois life. Floods and fire and civic breakdown in the Gulf Coast states put a further grisly spin on the problem. It's hard to focus on window treatments when bodies are floating by outside.

It's true that in the aftermath of 9/11 at least one gallant Un-Mother—to her credit—tried to address the matter as best she could. Dominique Browning, the melancholic editor of Condé Nast's *House and Garden* and a dead ringer for the Lady of Shalott, ran a number of columns in which she wrote awkwardly yet movingly about the effect of the attacks on her mental world.* These columns were painful—I remember starting to cry while reading one—not least because one saw Browning struggling against the banality of the context in which she wrote. Such pathos in Shelter-Mag Land was a shock, like finding a dismembered corpse in a beautiful meadow. *Et in Arcadia ego* indeed.

A similar pathos suffused a *Metropolitan Home* essay by Emily Prager ("Safe as Houses," September 2004), the only interiors article I've come across so far to tackle 9/11 at any length. Prager, a longtime Greenwich Village resident who witnessed the collapse of the South Tower, candidly recounted how the day's events left her "wounded in my sense of home." The piece ended with its author in a state of panicky ambivalence, wanting to flee New York yet unable to follow through on any of the fantastical moving plans she kept devising. Scarcely a comforting endpoint—but at least Prager seemed able to articulate her confusion.

Other responses, however, have been less honest and sometimes freakishly dissociated. For example, the editor of *Elle Decoration* (a publication aimed largely at fashion-conscious working women in their twenties and thirties) recently offered this schizoid hodgepodge of girl talk and carpe diem:

Colour. Pattern. Decoration. Ornamentation. It's all coming back. I think it's to do with celebrating life—perhaps it's because, in these terrorist-aware times, we're more conscious than ever that this life isn't a rehearsal, it's the main event. And what simpler way to add some joy and pattern to your life than with flowers.

---

* Author's note: *House and Garden* folded in 2007—a casualty of a global economic recession, skyrocketing production costs, and intensifying digital competition.

Though priding itself on being hip, even the Home & Garden section of *The New York Times* has gone a bit bipolar lately. Opposite a jaunty piece about co-op residents cat fighting online (December 2, 2004), the editors ran a full-page public service ad for a government disaster-readiness Web site, complete with a huge picture of a grim-faced FDNY firefighter and apocalyptic copy. ("After a terrorist attack your first instinct may be to run. That may be the worst thing you could do.") The emotional dissonance was nerve-jangling, corrosive, surreal. Maybe the best thing, after all, would be to go round to the neighbors and make it up with them.

Yet the most disturbing case of 9/11 schizophrenia involves the now defunct *nest*. Often heralded as the most iconoclastic interiors publication since Fleur Cowles's short-lived *Flair* of the 1950s, *nest* set out to be everything the ordinary shelter magazine was not: louche, sly, sexy, so dark and downtown in sensibility it was funny—an interiors rag for the John Waters set. Typical features had to do with Hitler's decorating tastes, the phallus-studded home of Miss Plaster Caster (she who once made plaster moulds of rock-star penises), Lucy and Ricky's sound-stage "apartment" on *I Love Lucy*, how to arrange kitty boxes when you live with 114 cats, and the joy of clear-plastic sofa covers. My all-time favorite piece was about the Toys "R" Us–style "playrooms" of "adult babies"—men and women who find sexual gratification by wearing diapers and lying in oversized baby cribs. Every now and then amid the camp one would encounter authentic blue-chip writing: Muriel Spark on "Bed Sits I Have Known," John Banville on Gianni Versace's Miami villa (outside which the designer was shot), the poet Eileen Myles on what it was like to sleep on a city sidewalk—as she had done—in a cardboard box for two weeks.

The magazine was quite stupendously mannered—redolent of Ronald Firbank trawling for hunky handymen at Home Depot. Yet manner proved bootless when *nest* fell victim to a grotesque and unfortunate coincidence. Attached to the cover of the fatal thirteenth issue—Summer 2001—was a black silk mourning ribbon, the sort of thing one might find on a Victorian scrapbook or photo album. (*nest* regularly violated ordinary packaging conventions.) On the cover itself was a cleverly Photoshopped image of the U.S. Capitol wrapped in a huge white shroud with black-and-white funeral bunting. It transpired that Rei Kawakubo, the fashion force behind Comme des Garçons, had been asked by *nest*'s editor and presiding genius, Joseph Holtzman, to design a "mourning" dress for the Capitol building, precisely to ready it for "whatever calamity may befall us in the future." The shroud tarp and bunting were the result: Christo meets Edgar Allan Poe. The "national grief" theme was in turn playfully reflected in the issue's editorial content: one item had to do with the planning and decoration of Abraham Lincoln's funeral cortege, another with Sarah Bernhardt's coffin bed.

One can hardly overstate the spookiness of it all—for those morbid enough to notice—when the imagined "tragedy" came to pass a few weeks later. The Summer 2001 *nest* suddenly seemed ghoulishly prescient, akin to the British journalist W. T. Stead's uncanny 1892 short story about a White Star ocean liner's sinking in the ice fields of the North Atlantic (Stead himself would go down on the *Titanic* twenty years later), or "King's Cross," a melancholy Pet Shop Boys song of 1987 that seemed to predict the terrible Underground fire at that ill-starred station a few months later. Odder still, however, was the official *nest* response to the devastation at Ground Zero and the Pentagon.

There wasn't one. No comment on Kawakubo and the shrouded Capitol; no mention of the attacks; no nuttin'. Given *nest*'s Manhattan address and relentless downtown feel, the absence of immediate acknowledgment was creepy, as if the magazine had suffered a brain injury and been rendered selectively mute. The blankness and blockage never went away. *nest* carried on for several more years, through the Fall 2004 issue, but one couldn't help feeling that the debunking zest had gone out of it; the punkish will to provoke seemed tainted and damaged. I lost some of my enthusiasm for the magazine after the 9/11 watershed: *nest,* it seemed, was just too hip to be human.

In retrospect the aphasia seems part of a more pervasive syndrome. Despite the rad profile, *nest* was as knee-deep in bathos and bourgeois denial as any other shelter mag. But who among us isn't? How could anyone reconcile the scarifying truth—all men are mortal—with that illusion of calm and safety to which most of us still regularly aspire in everyday life? Regardless of means, status, or political investment, just about everyone craves warmth, light, four walls, and some bits of furniture—a shelter, in a word, from miseries we know are out there and others still to come. Our vulnerability is too extreme to be "integrated" in any supposedly therapeutic fashion.

So we devise psychic buffers. The habits of bourgeois life—first adumbrated in Northern Europe as early as the sixteenth century—have been for some time the buffer of choice, civilization's all-purpose comfort-and-happiness maximizer. But the bourgeois outlook could hardly be called valiant or hardheaded: it's all about *not* staring death in the face. Under its sway one seeks a world without pain. The search is doomed, of course—the "safe house" a house of cards. But maybe we needn't start thinking about that yet.

I find myself hung up on the predicament: how to strike a balance between the longing for security (that infantile need on which shelter mags batten) and the more grown-up recognition that any "serenity" to be achieved is illusory, or at best fleeting. I'm a dawdler on the road to unhappy consciousness. Yet there are signs—this essay among them, perhaps—that I've started to wean myself of the more brainless aspects of my addiction. I've let some of the crap subscriptions lapse: *Old House Interiors* (too boring-Berkeley-in-the-seventies) and the ludicrous, vamping *Architectural Digest.* *House Beautiful* had started to irk me: its former male editor—odd and smarmy—was always twaddling on in fake-folksy manner about his adorable daughter "Madison." But is he gay or straight? That's what I want to know.

And I'm getting tired of the whole Let's-Pretend-There's-Nothing-Wrong trip; it's become so breathless and false. Death has lately been popping up rather explicitly in Shelter-Mag Land, but hidden in plain sight, as it were, like the purloined letter. Something one might call "taxidermic chic," for example, has become a huge fad: cow skulls, fossils, stuffed rodents in doll clothes, lizards embalmed in varnish or the like—all deployed as "edgy" urban décor. (Trendy rag-and-bone-cum-interiors shops like Evolution in SoHo and Paxton Gate in San Francisco make a bundle out of this strange and desiccated style.)

In the face of such dissociation—dead meat as Addams Family décor?—I've even had bouts of outright revulsion. The worst came not long ago as I was innocently paging through *Homes and Gardens*. I had found a feature—instantly mesmerizing—about a renovated English farmhouse built in 1604. My sort of wattle-and-daub thing exactly! One could just see Vanessa Bell in it, paintbrushes in hand. I was fascinated to read how the current owners, a handsome couple with children, had kept "the carcasses of the original kitchen" in the interest of authenticity. And I also loved the milky gray "period" color chosen for the drawing room: a Jacobean hue named "Silken Flank." But the pièce de résistance was undoubtedly the Vintage Hospital Bed—late-nineteenth-century and loaded with pricey Stieff teddy bears—taking pride of place in their daughter's bedroom.

A lovely white iron bedstead: funky, fresh-looking, impeccable shabby chic. I wanted it immediately. But suddenly I found myself imagining all the people who had slept—and possibly died—in this particular bed over the past hundred years. In fact, the more I looked at it, the more it reminded me of those metal beds you see lined up in haunting photographs of First World War military hospitals, in which a ward full of grievously injured young men—heads bandaged, empty pajama sleeves pinned up—lie propped against pillows and (if they can) glumly regard the camera. Teddy bears notwithstanding, one could almost smell the carbolic. How many blind or limbless soldiers, I wondered, had succumbed in little Scarlett's bed?

From there my thoughts went naturally on to the avian-flu epidemic of 1918–19. That appalling global contagion killed more than 20 million people: surely one or two of them must have expired in this particular bedstead? Bird-to-human influenza viruses have been in the news, of course, so the speculation was not unduly morbid. If the earthquakes, floods, or dirty bombs don't get us, I gather, the Asian poultry will.

In Hardy's *Tess of the d'Urbervilles*, there's an unforgettable passage in which the ill-starred heroine, brooding on mortality, wonders on what "sly and unseen" day she will die. "Of that day, doomed to be her terminus in time through all the ages, she did not know the place in month, week, season or year." Tess could have used www .deathclock.com, where you fill out a health questionnaire and get back your exact date of death. Having discovered when mine will be—January 28, 2038—I've found myself wondering lately where I will die. On a city street? In an overturned car? In some dark and fathomless polar sea into which my plane has crashed? But what about at home, in bed, Evian on the nightstand and Wally the mini dachshund snoring stertorously under the covers? Given my "home" fixation, that would be an especially poetic fate. Will my 400-thread-count Egyptian-cotton bed linens be any comfort to me then? And what about the teak milking stool? If she ever knew—and I doubt she did—the Un-Mother isn't telling.

Travels with My Mother

The artist Agnes Martin (1912–2004)

OFF TO A GREAT START at lunch at the Phoenix airport: Terrorist Threat Level Orange for "high" as usual, women's restrooms jammed, and then the waiter in Aunt Chilada's Cantina—garish faux-Mexican with a jalapeño pepper theme—calls me "sir" when he takes our order. Fume for a second, then descend into bath of elemental shame. *Why does this always happen to me? Do I really look like a guy?* No doubt I will suffer the lonely death of the sexual pervert. Can't get mad about it, though: my mother, thankfully, seems not to have heard the waiter's mistake. She is sitting right across from me in her US Airways wheelchair, peering around inquisitively at the lissome Hispanic busboys, off-duty pilots eating lunch, and our monstrously fat fellow diners. She can't drive anymore and hasn't been out of her house in San Diego for quite a while, so this Santa Fe trip is a huge and somewhat nerve-racking adventure for her. Given the ear-splitting noise around us, I have been spared, though, her usual critiques of my personal appearance; restaurant clatter and the boomy voices of Fox News emanating from the big-screen TV at the bar, thank God, have clearly flooded out her hearing aids. Justice served, too: Paris Hilton dragged shrieking back to jail after three days on the lam.

My mother, eighty-one and widowed for twelve years, is tottery, near-sighted, psoriatic, and deaf, and apart from a residual compulsion to lament her elder daughter's unfeminine appearance, has largely reverted in old age to a state of Blakean innocence and moral simplicity. (Little Lamb—you rackety old thing—who *did* make thee? I have some questions I'd like to ask Him.) True: ravages of macular degeneration notwithstanding, she still spends an hour every morning "putting her face on," with predictably fantastical, Isak Dinesen–like results. (She once had her eyelids tattooed to look like blue-black eyeliner.) She is still in love—in a distant way—with George Clooney, though playing with the Paint program on her computer (adapted for low vision) and writing the news every day to her pals in the Brit Group, a gossipy little chat room for elderly British expatriates, have cut into her movie watching. And she can still plunge a knife—without warning—deep into one's narcissistic wounds. Not long ago, apropos of nothing, she took mournful pleasure in observing that with my whimsical new blue-framed glasses, floppy dyed-blonde locks, and middle-aged paunch, I was beginning to resemble David Hockney. But she has become a lot less dangerous overall. I take advantage of her inattention and quiz Blakey under my breath: *Do you think I look like a MAN?* B. gives me an appraising glance but is noncommittal. Then everything lands on our table in a steaming, salsa-drenched heap: guacamole, sour cream, and

chicken tostadas in huge encephalitic, butterfly-shaped tortillas—
nacho chips on steroids—and a tumbler-sized margarita for me, even
though it's only 11:00 a.m. *Yummyburgers!*

The trip is a belated seventieth birthday present for my mother—
very belated, I'm afraid, given her present advanced age. Previous
Girlfriend nixed it back in 1995 and I caved; my mother is still indignant ("I never liked her or her weird diet"). Said PG was four feet ten
and ninety pounds: a tiny, frail, somewhat eccentric Jewish-Canadian
vegan with gluten allergies who wore rubberized Doc Martens and
played the medieval vielle. We once visited all the Cathar fortresses
together. I miss her a lot sometimes, especially when I'm listening to
the music of the *trobadors* or pondering *l'agonie du Languedoc*. But
I have to admit Blakey is a better fit. B. is solicitous if not saintly
around my mother. Helps her fold up her white metal cane from
the Braille Institute and calls her "Mavis" in a polite, Boston-bred,
upper-middle-class-lesbian-daughter-in-law way—much as Mary
Cheney's lover, one imagines, addresses her in-laws as "Dick" and
"Lyn." B. played squash at Yale—is still v. buff—and has pledged to
help me push the wheelchair around. Neither of us has been to Santa
Fe before but we believe it to be flat.

The trip is also, of course, an Artistic Pilgrimage; we're hoping
to pick up on the celebrated arty-bohemian Santa Fe vibe: adobe
houses with huge ceiling timbers, decorative cow skulls on pure
white walls, chunky turquoise jewelry, high desert air and the famous
Southwestern "light"—indeed, the whole Stieglitz–O'Keeffe–
D. H. Lawrence–Mabel Dodge Luhan–Willa Cather–Pueblo Cliff
Dwellers–*Death Comes for the Archbishop* thing. Maybe we'll even
see Julia Roberts (the sun-dried actress—a forty-something Roma
tomato in disguise?—has a ranch near Taos). Our hotel is right on
the plaza and has the requisite Navajo rugs; the rental car is good to
go; and we've got big museum plans for our next three days.

The O'Keeffe collection is the must-see, of course, though I confess that the prospect of Mavis in tandem with Georgia is a bit worrying. Although unable to take up the art scholarship she won in England in 1941—the Blitz put an end to her formal education—my mother has always been alarmingly "artistic." Through both of her ill-starred marriages—the first to my gloomy-guts father, with whom she emigrated to California, and the second to Turk, the salty old American submariner with five wild children whom she married in the early 1970s to stave off destitution—her hobby no doubt kept her sane. (Apart from a much-loathed teenage stint "in the gasworks" in St. Albans after the war ended, she never worked.) She was a member of the Clairemont Art Guild and did monoprints on weekends with her friend Frances, a wisecracking old dame in Capri pants and Simone de Beauvoir turban. Together they inked rollers, tore newsprint for collages and cut do-it-yourself mats while my mother declaimed on the subject of Turk's husbandly misdeeds. Frances, puffing on mentholated cigarettes, was the raddled and raspy Suzuki; my mother, a much abused Cio-Cio San.

After my stepbrother Jeff killed himself in 1982, my mother made the little upstairs room that had once been his into her creative lair—nine feet square of dense, paint-flecked, Krazy Glue squalor. Francis Bacon's famously naff South Kensington studio (now recreated in a Dublin museum) is a neatnik's in comparison. Tracey Emin's *Bed*? Pristine and fresh-smelling. The mess is still intact; my mother stopped using the room ages ago but never cleared it out. Now, living alone, she can't get up the stairs. True: Ruskin says one should not indulge in the pathetic fallacy, but peeking into this dust-laden *camera abbandonata* during hurried visits to the maternal hearth, I can't help feeling that the crumpled tubes of acrylic paint, pots of dried-up gesso, broken picture frames, old bits of bubble wrap, and rotting cardboard are moping. They yearn for the past, but the past is a dream. They miss their Prime Mover and her passionate ways.

They lie about, higgledy-piggledy and disconsolate. They seem to reproach me silently when I slip in to purloin rubber stamps or the odd box of pastels. My mother once had a museum reproduction of a Calder mobile hanging above the work table. *I love color more than anything else!* she is still wont to exclaim. Turk, in a fit of subaltern rage, went in there one day and smashed it to bits.

The problem—grotesque daughter that I am—is that I could never bring myself to like my mother's work as much as I should. Colorful it is; Matisse the big influence. The aesthetic is relentlessly sunny, cheerful, and pretty: the baleful milieu in which many of the pictures were created—the Mavis-Turk ménage—is never in evidence. My mother's great subjects are flowers and women's faces, with the occasional female nude thrown in. (*I don't want to paint men! Women's bodies are much more beautiful!*) Granted, in her prime she occasionally hit it—made a still life or watercolor portrait of such informal ravishing loveliness one felt one's own complex sort of gratitude. (Jane Freilicher's gorgeous gouaches come to mind.) Beauty *is* Truth. But she seemed not to realize when she had produced a winner. Her pictures hang on the walls indiscriminately, the stunning ones mixed in with a lot of mermaids, dreamy girls in kimonos, elfin-looking flappers in cloche hats, simpering angels, and the like.

To put it as churlishly as possible, I'm a bit nervous about pushing my mother around the Georgia O'Keeffe Museum because I fear being swept back—annihilatingly—into the world of "my mother's taste." My whole life up to now—as even the slow-witted reader may have deduced—has from one angle been a fairly heartless repudiation of maternal sentimentality: all the bright, powerless, feminine things. Now especially, her world is largely one of kitty cats, splashy floral bedspreads and pillow shams, See's peanut brittle, cheap coffee mugs with jokey inscriptions (*Because I'm the MOM—That's Why!*), sympathetic female friends. It's all very Calendar Girls: cute, full of kindness, irretrievably down-market, and—to me at least—weirdly depressing. At this point in her decline, her house has become a hellish Knick-Knack Central, the chaos of the upstairs studio having spread ineluctably downward since Turk's death. The kitchen in particular is a veritable Mavis-midden, overflowing with feathers, beads, glue-sticks, bits of decorative ribbon, tweezers, little embossing guns, and myriad other implements she uses for her main artistic pursuit these days: making strange-looking necklaces out of polymer clay. Not-withstanding the huge magnifying glass she uses to see what she's doing, most of these recent concoctions—alas for those who receive them as gifts—have a pendulous, lopsided, somewhat savage look: the perfect thing for a stylish Aztec to wear to a human sacrifice. But she spends hours creating them and enjoys herself enormously. Who but a monster—or an Yma Sumac–hater—would begrudge her? The surrounding disarray is all part of some sweet yet decisive revenge.

Rightly or wrongly, I can't help associating O'Keeffe's work—colorful, vegetal, Modernist yet compromised, endlessly reproduced on tatty note cards, posters, and datebooks—with my mother's abstracto-feminine creations. Like the beetle-browed Frida—you know the one I mean—O'Keeffe has become a sentimental icon, the culture heroine of a generation of (now increasingly elderly) female amateur artists. After all, it's said, she was a feminist of sorts: earthy and independent; muse to a host of eminent men (Stieglitz, Paul Strand, et al.); lived almost forever. Best of all, she is supposed to have celebrated—fairly unabashedly—something called "female sexuality." Who can contemplate those swelling pink and purple flowers—or the roseate canyon-wombs opening up within them—without thinking of the plush, ding-donging joys of female genitalia? Georgia, by God, must have had orgasms to spare. Until the 1990s, when the Asian-minimalist spa aesthetic finally took over, there was hardly a hippy-dippy hot-tub establishment between Baja and Men-docino that didn't have an O'Keeffe poster (or several) decorating the premises. The fact that the artist seems to have been a frightful old harridan who ended up leaving her entire $50 million estate to an unsavory boy-toy sixty years her junior is seldom allowed to tarnish the legend. Oh, and by the way—to judge by the famous Stieglitz snaps, she looked *just like a man*.

How to cope with it all? I've been imagining the Santa Fe trip as both a fulfillment of daughterly obligation—it's costing me a bundle—and a sort of spiritual Trial of Taste. (It's not just the O'Keeffe, of course; almost as soon as we arrive and begin exploring the town plaza, I realize I shall also have to guard myself against copper bangles, polyester tees adorned with Native American pictographs, pony hide rugs, postcards purporting to show a family of jackalopes squatting in the desert, pimply valet parking attendants in Stetsons and cowboy boots.) Still, I'm not entirely unprepared. I've secretly inoculated myself with what I consider the ultimate Connoisseur's Good Taste Vaccine. Everywhere we go, I tell myself, what I'll really be doing is *looking for the Agnes Martins*. Agnes, I've decided, will be my private talisman, my anti-O'Keeffe. Yea, though I walk through the Valley of Southwestern Style, I will fear no evil. My aesthetic invulnerability assured, I'll be able to enjoy everything else ironically, starting with the jackalopes and the women who love them.

And who, precisely, is Agnes Martin? Her semiobscurity is exactly the point. True, her paintings now reside in all the fabled modern collections and sell for millions of dollars. True, like O'Keeffe she lived near Taos and Santa Fe for much of her life. But she remains a cult figure—an artist's artist—legendary among the cognoscenti for her reclusive style of life and the Zen-like austerity of her vision. I first read about her in the 1970s in a weird stream-of-consciousness piece in *The Village Voice* by the then-radical-lesbian writer Jill Johnston. Johnston—herself once a fixture in the New York art world—described making a kooky pilgrimage to New Mexico to find Martin: a sort of Sapphic Quest for Corvo. I don't remember much about the article, except that Johnston quoted a gnomic comment by Martin on death: *you go out either in terror or in ecstasy.* I recently saw some photos of Martin in her studio just before she died and thought she looked a bit like Gertrude Stein: stocky, impassive, the same Julius Caesar haircut—only dreamier, blue-eyed, more aerated somehow. Her emotional remoteness seemed absolute.

Yet Martin's story has always enthralled me. Born in rural Saskatchewan in 1912, she moved to New York in the 1940s to study art at Columbia. After a spell as a graduate student at the University of New Mexico she moved to Taos, where she supported herself for a number of years—barely—by painting and teaching. In 1957 she was discovered by the Manhattan gallery owner Betty Parsons and moved back to New York. There, alongside Rothko, Barnett Newman, and Ellsworth Kelly—fellow Abstract Expressionists seeking a new way forward after the death of Jackson Pollock—Martin won acclaim for her delicate, somewhat cerebral experiments in geometric form. She was touted by the critics and attracted the attention of wealthy collectors. Success notwithstanding, however, Martin was repulsed by art-world gamesmanship and one day in 1967 simply loaded up a pick-up truck and drove back to New Mexico. There she built a small adobe house with her own hands at the foot of the Sangre de Cristo mountains and began a new life as a hermit. She stopped painting and for seven years wrote poetry and studied Eastern philosophy. (Hatje Cantz published a book of her writings in 1992.) When she began producing work again in the mid-1970s—her prices having escalated astronomically in the meantime—she refused, despite the pleas of dealers, to relinquish either her privacy or the ascetic mode of existence she had embraced.

The modern world left her cold; in the stark New Mexico landscape she found a spiritual clarity unmarred by material entanglements. Daily life was spartan. Though she liked classical music she never owned a stereo; nor did she have a television. She had no pets. One of her obituaries reported that when she died (in 2004 at ninety-two), she had not read a newspaper for fifty years. Two years before her death she allowed a persistent woman filmmaker to shoot a documentary about her: it was entitled *With My Back to the World*. Leaving no survivors, she directed that her estate be used to fund a foundation for artists but insisted that it not bear her name.

The paintings are reticent in turn—pale, spare, barely there. (Martin rejected the term Minimalist in favor of Abstract Expressionist, but if she wasn't a Minimalist, it's not clear who would be.) Her pictures seldom reproduce well, and at first one looks much like another. This similitude is due no doubt to the fact that Martin's basic technique stayed the same for years. She began with a square canvas precisely six feet by six feet, and primed it with plain white gesso. On top of the gesso she then laid down faint horizontal lines in pencil, followed by exacting, ultra thin washes of oil paint or acrylic. Sometimes she added vertical pencil lines, creating delicate grids; at other times, she made simple horizontal stripes. The bands of pigment were usually matte white or off-white, sometimes tinted a pale gray or yellow. Later in her career she added a nearly invisible coral pink and a faint blue pastel to her palette. And that, kids, was that.

It is impossible to overstate their self-effacing beauty. Martin herself wrote that she believed the function of art to be "the renewal of memories of moments of perfection." Making art seems to have been a kind of meditation for her: she meant her paintings as aids to contemplation—"floating abstractions" akin to the art of the ancient Chinese. And it's true, though they are built up line by line, by almost imperceptible increments, that after a while her pictures begin vibrating on the retina with strange energy, flipping gently back and forth between metaphysical registers like one of Wittgenstein's playful visual paradoxes. The sense of calm they evoke in the viewer is similar to the liturgical mood Rothko's work can produce, but Martin is less morbid, theatrical, and self-consciously "profound." Facing down the void, Rothko can at times be downright bombastic. Martin is more humane and in some way stronger: smaller in scale, indifferent to sublimity (though her paintings achieve it), uninterested in making statements. It's the difference, perhaps, between Lowell and Bishop.

Yet there is no doubt that Martin's work will always be caviar—the very palest of pale fish roe—to the general. Who better, then, to serve as my guardian angel? The artist would no doubt be appalled to hear it, but admiring her work aloud is now a fail-safe way for the upwardly mobile poseur to signal intellectual depth and all-round ahead-of-the-curveness—like subscribing to *ArtForum* and actually reading it. Martin is the sort of artist show-offs show off about, know-it-alls know about. I think *I* like her—the whole chaste package—because she was so obviously unlike me, so seemingly unencumbered by envy or the need to strategize. Thinking about her has a soothing effect, like imagining myself reincarnated as a smooth and shiny pebble glinting in sunlight at the bottom of a cold, clear mountain stream.

Meanwhile my mother is emitting plaintive yips. Even as we propel her round Santa Fe, B. and I—wheelchair-pushing novices both—keep rolling her into unexpected cracks in the pavement. Each time she pitches forward melodramatically and gives a little squeal of fright. Is she faking it? Hard to judge—we *are* pretty inept. I make feeble jokes about getting up speed and running her off the top of a Pueblo cliff dwelling to her death. She huffily maintains she can walk a bit, but after one or two arthritic attempts, is happy to plop down in the chair again and gaze about expectantly. B. and I are both reminded of Andy in *Little Britain* (we just got the DVDs)—the dough-faced, lank-haired, supposedly paralyzed invalid who climbs trees, assaults people, swims in the sea at Brighton, and even bounces on a trampoline whenever Lou, his kindly yet moronic caretaker, has his back turned. We try to explain the joke to her and even act little bits out—B. doing Lou, me Andy—but Mavis isn't really paying attention. We're outside a Häagen-Dazs place and she wants one.

I get my first inkling that my daughterly *snobisme* (it sounds even worse in French) is about to be compromised when my mother spots the rubber-stamp store. We've been indecisive so far about what museum to do first; just then Stampa Fe floats into view. One of my mother's polymer clay pals has said it's great and she's instantly psyched. Panting a bit, Blakey and I hoist her and chair up the stairs (it's on an upper floor and there's no elevator) and I wheel her in— unable to suppress my own rapidly growing excitement. For I, too, I'm chagrined to confess, am a rubber-stamp addict. As Bugs Bunny might say: a weal wubber-stamp fweak. I've got hundreds at home; they're taking over all the drawers in the work table in the spare room. Blakey rolls her eyes, sits down, pulls Richard Rorty out of her bag, and prepares to wait for several hours.

I guess I left this part out earlier: that I'm as "arty" as my old mum. Can't help it—it's a mutant gene, like homosexuality. And though I can neither draw nor paint, I'm fairly good at working around my limitations. Like numerous five- and six-year-olds—or Max Ernst and Hannah Höch, as we "creatives" prefer to say—I do collage. Rubber stamps, along with scissors and glue and glossy pages ripped out from *The World of Interiors*, are an essential part of my praxis. (I have the art-world jargon down pat. *Yeah, I work in mixed media. Gagosian's doing my next show.*) It has not escaped my notice that even in London at the very center of the intellectual cosmos—the London Review Bookshop on Bury Place—there's a rubber-stamp shop right next door. Titillating to admit, but as local surveillance cameras would no doubt corroborate, I have sometimes been seen to nip into Blade Rubber ("the biggest range of stamps and accessories in London") even before I go next door—game face on—to peruse the latest tomes on Stalinism or global economics.

What sorts of subject have I tackled? Blakey informs me that it is called "blog whoring" to publicize one's blog in print, so I won't even mention Fevered Brain Productions, my digital art Web site. Oops, it popped out. Let's just say I'm a neo-Surrealist—a bit dark, a bit Goth, a bit grunge—a sort of lady Hans Bellmer. As a child I was enchanted by the Surrealists' Exquisite Cadavers game—the one in which you make comic figures out of mismatched body parts. This love of the grotesque has never gone away; even today, I enjoy putting dog or cat heads on human bodies and vice versa. Always on the lookout for detached torsos, legs, feet, hands, eyeballs, lips, etc.— anything to *dérégler* the senses, if only a teeny bit.

In Stampa Fe my mother and I go on a mad bacchanalian spree. Piling stamp blocks into my basket, I am even less restrained, I'm sorry to say, than she is. (Given her eyesight problem and seated position, she has to struggle and claw a bit to drag things down to her level.) I try to pretend that the stamps I'm grabbing up are "cool," that my choices express my highly evolved if not Firbankian sense of camp. Thus I eschew the ubiquitous Frida K; ditto anything with Day of the Dead skeletons on it. I avert my eyes from a stamp showing Georgia O'Keeffe in her jaunty gaucho hat. But somehow I end up with things just as bad: a Japanese carp; multiple images of the Virgin of Guadalupe; a slightly dazed-looking cormorant; a sumo wrestler kicking one of his fat legs in the air; a woodcut-style picture of little people with sombreros on putting loaves into a mud-baked Mexican oven. Despite a longstanding ban on rubber stamps (or coffee cups) with sayings on them—*Cherish Life's Moments*, *Happy Easter*, *You Make Me Smile*—I succumb to *A New Thrill For The Jaded*. I'll stamp the envelope with it when I send off my next property tax bill.

When we finish our sweep and I'm swaying groggily at the cash register—my mother slumped in her chair behind me like a satisfied pythoness—I'm forced to confront a terrible possibility: that Mavis and I may actually be more alike than I prefer to believe. (B. has sometimes intimated as much.) Even as the little machine regurgitates my Visa card with a malevolent whir, I'm flooded with self-doubt. Whom am I kidding, after all? Is a lurching sumo wrestler in a loincloth really any less vulgar, aesthetically speaking, than my mother's mermaids or kitty cats? Than a frog wearing a top hat? A poodle playing a tuba? An abyss seems to open up for a moment: I see, as if in Pisgah-vision, the appalling triteness of my sensibility. Forget Agnes Martin: I'm as banal and bourgeois as any of the hundreds of thousands of middle-aged ladies who do "scrapbooking." (See Google for the depressing lowdown on this new billion-dollar U.S. leisure industry, the post-modern white-suburban-female equivalent of cyberporn.) And with my mother egging me on, just as she did when I was a child, I clearly can't control myself. When B. finally comes to drag us away from the place, we look like the survivors of a jungle plane crash who have had to resort to cannibalism to survive: the same foam-flecked lips, hollow cheeks, and shifty, demented expressions.

After Stampa Fe I am chastened, subdued. Despite fifty years of walking and talking on my own, I realize I'm already starting to de-volve, to morph back, as if inexorably, into that hungry, unkempt, much-loathed thing: My Mother's Daughter. All the familiar inse-curity is surging back up in me, along with the lower-middle-class family mania—seemingly inbred in both of us—for talking endlessly and anxiously about what things are "nice" or "not nice." Infantiliza-tion hardly encompasses it. Even as we trundle from boutique to bou-tique I find myself reflexively chirping back my mother's aesthetic verdicts, in part (I tell myself) to make her feel secure in a strange place, in part for the simple reason that I am becoming more and more disoriented. We're like a mother-daughter ventriloquist-dummy team, only one in which the ventriloquist, for some odd reason, is sit-ting in the dummy's lap. Delivered trillingly yet forcefully, over the shoulder, Mavis's opinions become my opinions; as I push her along, my wooden jaws—loosely secured by pegs—start clacking up and down in a strange parody of the maternal speech. She's sitting down but leading the way. I'm getting blurry by comparison.

Connoisseurship—the whole fetishistically cultivated power of judging for oneself—goes out the window. Which would look "nicest" in my living room, I hear myself asking: the primitive figure made of wire and bottle caps or the little wooden cross studded with *milagros*? (*Well, you know I don't like religious things. Some of the people in my polymer clay group do crucifixes. I don't like that, do you? Still, I am not an atheist: I'm an agnostic. Maybe there's a God but we can't know. Your little guy is cute but I like this one better. Of course I do pray to your grandmother for help when I've lost my keys or something. I missed her so much after I married your father and went to America. I ask her where they are. Hah! She always points me in the right direction!*) Should I buy two of the Pueblo Indian street vendor's embroidered table runners since they are Both Nice? (*Ooh! Why not? That might be extravagant, though. Your sister's got a horrible lot of credit card debt. I'm so worried about her. The three of us love to shop, don't we! We've got the shopping gene! I think if you really love something you should get it. That one you're holding up is quite nice but I think this one is better. This one is nicer, too. Do you really need two? Why don't you go ahead and splurge?*) Though confidently broached, the sibyl's recommendations are not always compatible with one another; I am filled with mental confusion as well as shame and guilt.

Blakey—who will increasingly leave the pair of us to our own devices over the course of the week—is amused but mostly indifferent. She has the aristocrat's disdain for shopping and no urge to acquire little sentimental knick-knacks. Or even big sentimental knick-knacks. Her own aesthetic preferences are virile, insouciant, unworried—majestically upper-class in the classic down-at-the-heels way. She happily wears ancient sweat pants from her Yale days, moth-eaten pullovers, and frayed Oxford cloth shirts—the last sometimes put on accidentally, with a charming lack of paranoia, inside out. She has no interest whatsoever in home decoration or in what color the dog's leash should be. Her academic specialties notwithstanding (eighteenth-century literature and the theory of mind), the contemporary art form she holds in highest esteem is no doubt the Pixar feature: marooned on a desert island and starved for companionship, she would take Wallace and Gromit over Locke and Hume any day.

We get a brief Mavis-respite the afternoon we drive to see the Taos Pueblo—the "longest continuously inhabited settlement in North America." The pueblo is a strange and dusty desert encampment by a stream, a massing of ancient-looking adobe huts in varying states of dilapidation. Ratty dogs run free everywhere; they don't seem to belong to anyone. The Pueblo Indian residents have developed a highly efficient tourist-processing operation: parking lots, admission booth, regular "walking tours" with native guides. (*No photos of the Elders without their permission. Please remember you are on the sacred land of our ancestors. Do not throw garbage in the stream. At the end of the tour you will have the opportunity to buy authentic handmade pottery and beautiful silver jewelry from the traditional artisans who still live and work here.*) There's no escaping the whole degrading setup, in which everyone—tourist and "native" alike—is forced to play his or her prescribed role: Put-Upon Noble Savage or Sympathetic But Clueless White Person. Even the babbling brook gets roped into it. The foreign tourists, of whom there are a lot (since the dollar's in the toilet), seem to have an easier time of it than we Yanquis do. They obviously don't think of themselves as the spoiled descendants of murderers and thieves. We know we've got some of General Custer's DNA and feel bad about it.

The respite comes when B. and I find we can't maneuver the wheelchair on the dirt paths well enough to take my mother on the walking tour. After much discussion she tells us just to leave her in the shade somewhere—it's hot and windless—and do it without her. We're hesitant but park her under a tree next to a trio of elderly Pueblo ladies who are selling necklaces and rings laid out on an old folding card table. Mavis insists she will be okay but when I look back

I can't help noticing she looks pink and exhausted and a bit frightened of the ladies.

The tour, led by a somewhat zombie-like young Native American woman, turns out to be perfunctory. She recites a canned history of the place in somnambulist fashion, shows us the Indian cemetery and explains that everyone in it is buried upright. We see adobe huts under repair and hear about the bricks used; she points out the mud ovens that the year-round inhabitants—some of whom are gazing suspiciously out of their dirt windows at us as we go by—use to bake bread. Though the Taos Pueblo is without electricity, gas, or running water, she explains, residents are forbidden to use the nearby stream for bathing or cooking or anything else: it belongs to the spirit-ancestors and cannot be sullied. We, the gaping white tourists, all have the same question: *Then where do people go to the bathroom?* Our guide remains impassive and unsmiling: she's obviously heard the question a zillion times before. Either they go to some communal toilets at the little shopping center outside the Pueblo's main gate, she says, or else they use a utensil. Some of us laugh uneasily at the thought; a rake in the group yells out: *Chamber pots!* More awkward tittering. Still as if in a trance, the Indian maiden announces the end of the tour, drops us in front of the souvenir shops, and coolly collects all the tips that the hard-looking woman back at the ticket booth—a fat and somewhat sinister personage with homemade tattoos, pockmarks, and huge brown bloodshot eyes—has instructed us to pay her.

It is with some relief that I spot my mother still under the tree. Alone in her wheelchair she looks vulnerable and dignified. It's starting to hit me that she really can't walk anymore. That her vision is failing and won't come back. I try to imagine such debility but can't. She seems to be okay, though: she's been chatting with the Indian ladies about jewelry-making and spreading the gospel of the Internet and polymer clay. They all wave goodbye as we wheel her off, back through the ancient sawhorse barriers to the car. The late, lazy afternoon scene—turquoise sky, lofty ribbons of high cirrus, distant blue-black mountains on all sides—imparts a kind of tristesse. My mother and I are in some baffling place; I'm with her yet I miss her. I get pissy and crabby loading her back into the car. We eat a huge, overpriced meal in Santa Fe—all those zucchini blossoms really add up—and my mother chatters away through most of it.

Yet at some point during our remaining days, a lot of the daughter-angst starts to drop away. Like some frantic, dusty, overturned bug, I finally stop waving my many legs about and lie still. I will simply wait, I decide, for someone either to turn me right side up or squash me underfoot. (Can the latter indeed be much worse than a very intense massage? *Cr-runch! A-h-h . . . !*) I'm definitely calmer—even starting to enjoy myself. Maybe it's the spirit-ancestors. Or maybe it's Agnes. Because we do catch up with her: we find the small but exquisite room devoted to her at the Harwood Museum in Taos and make a beeline for it.

The space is bijou, only about fifteen feet across: white-walled, octagonal and windowless, with the same low light Tate Britain has in its Blake room. Seven paintings are on display, one on each wall; you go in through the eighth side of the octagon. Though plain and unadorned, the space is the opposite of austere. The pictures seem alive and sentient and even to be regarding one another across the space—enjoying each other's company in a friendly familial way. It's a tiny orgone box of a room, full of faintly pulsing energy currents, but also strangely full of grace, a promise of contact. The prosperous matrons of Santa Fe—major donors—are allowed to hold private yoga sessions in there.

The paintings are from the 1990s, a late period as extraordinary, in its own quiet stone-butch way, as that of Titian, Milton, or Yeats. You'd call it a flowering except there aren't any flowers; just the same old pencil lines and stripes. But the lines and stripes have become positively floral in their glow and poise and breeziness.

Most of the pictures are pink and blue—the same pale hues used to indicate sex in the world of baby clothes and Sippee Cups. The familiar stripes have been laid out precisely and painstakingly, like the military rows of tulips in Uncle Toby's garden in *Tristram Shandy*. Yet far from being insipid—the work of a saccharine or enfeebled talent—these late pastel zips vibrate with joy and renewal and intelligence. Martin never minded repeating titles; she saw nothing wrong with using one she liked over again or giving a new picture a title very similar to that of an earlier one. But in the late work this repetition becomes almost rhapsodic, at times even oddly sexual. Martin's last paintings all have names like *Beautiful Life*, *Lovely Life*, *An Infant's Response to Love*, *A Little Girl's Response to Love*, *I Love Love*, *Loving Love*, *I Love the Whole World*. Though Martin seems to have banished any hint of the erotic from her life—at least in her hermit years—Stein and her work again come to mind: the babyish, burbly and hypnotic love-language, say, of "As a Wife Has a Cow: A Love Story," dedicated to Alice B. Toklas.

To my surprise—my mother and I have gone into the orgone box and I'm spinning her around—she is an Agnes Martin aficionada. (*Oooh, they are nice, aren't they? You know she became a recluse? I think she was strange. I've always liked her, though, more than the other Minimalists. . . .*) My snob-self is frankly stunned at this unexpected display of maternal hip: it's as if Wally and Charlie, my dachshunds, were suddenly to begin discussing Hans-Georg Gadamer. (*They were even using the word* hermeneutic*!*) But it is soon matched by other feats of critical discernment. She and I tour the Ernest Blumenschein Home—Blumenschein being one of the major New Mexico painters of the 1920s and '30s—and she finds his sickly greeny-yellowy paintings of adobe churches and Indian squaws as hideous as I do. Those wretched Fauves have a lot to answer for. We are in ecstasy together at the Museum of International Folk Art; neither of us, we realize, has ever seen an Ikat fabric or a nineteenth-century Punch and

Judy puppet we didn't like. My mother even condescends to admire some of the rusty *retablos* (Mexican religious images painted on tin) that I am slavering over; the colorful naïve style, she agrees, makes the fact that they depict Jesus, the Virgin Mary, St. Francis, and various other creepy individuals far more palatable.

By the time we finally roll into the Georgia O'Keeffe Museum, late on our last afternoon, we are in a state of bizarre, even uncanny amity. The museum is a set of blocky adobe buildings just off the historic Santa Fe Plaza. Predictably it's packed out, almost entirely with women. (The one or two men standing around in their Teva sandals look sheepish if not a bit anxious, like errant hunters in a Renaissance painting who've blundered into a sacred grove and see a troop of maenads coming to rip their guts out.) I get heavily cruised by the butch German number running the ticket counter—something that happens to me now about as frequently as an asteroid strike—and immediately subside into a warm and jolly mood. One can't help noticing that the gallery is crowded with ladies—*ahem*—of a Certain Persuasion. Everywhere you look: big no-nonsense gals in polo shirts and purple fanny packs, all sporting the same grim gray clippered haircuts, like space shuttle astronauts.

Blakey wheels Mavis off to the main rooms and I lose sight of them in the throng. I'm stuck in a sort of antechamber where a huddle of fans are staring reverently at a series of cheesy photographs by Cartier-Bresson or somebody of the artist in her later years. She's a grisly old thing indeed: picking herbs in her Ghost Ranch garden, making the perfect little salad for one, displaying a cow skull, standing (arm theatrically raised) in front of a canvas. What a ham. She's usually dressed in black, in a sort of Medea outfit typically accented with white scarf or blouse and the signature black hat. Everyone coos and chortles in front of one picture especially: O'Keeffe on the back of a motorcycle driven by a comely young man, the parched New Mexico desert in the background. O'Keeffe wears dust-covered dungarees and grins at the camera coquettishly. Georgia's a brand, a franchise, a Gap ad, a sitcom star. *You go, girl! No problem if you look like a man!*

But something odd is also happening. The paintings, when I get to them, are not, I notice, as huge and blowsy as I was expecting. Several in fact are quite small. Not Vermeer small, but definitely smallish. And one or two, I have to admit, are pleasing, especially the pre–New Mexico ones from the 1910s and '20s. *Hmmm.* Addled connoisseur-brain starts gently powering up again, trying to process the unanticipated subtleties of the situation. *Okay, they're all still flowers, but aren't some of them at least as good as ones by those American Modernists you like so much? You know: Marsden Hartley, Arthur Dove, Charles Demuth? If you didn't know they were hers, wouldn't you be impressed? Aren't you being hard on her—as is your perverted wont—because she's a woman?* I keep looking round for more of the expected monstrosities—lewd river basins, vaginal canyons—but have only intermittent success. A few throbbing pink and yellow horrors float in and out of view in the distance, of course, but the worst offenders in the O'Keeffe Anatomical Fixation Department don't seem to be here—that ghastly, fart-in-your-face Jack-in-the-Pulpit picture, for example, in which the gargantuan botanical specimen flaunts what looks like a little purple-black asshole.

Mavis and Blakey roll back into view, then B. slinks off to the museum bookshop to read up on O'Keeffe's financial shenanigans and the punk-gigolo boyfriend. As soon as she's gone, my mother flips into girlish-conspiratorial, faintly passive-aggressive mode. *Blakey is so great. I can see you obviously enjoy each other's company. She's so smart! I am just in awe of her intellect. I guess that's why she's so moody. It's nice how she sometimes wears a* skirt, *isn't it?* Soon unveiled, however, is the fact that B. got bored looking at the pictures and whizzed a certain elderly party round the galleries in careening breakneck fashion. *I couldn't see anything! It was all a terrible* blur!

I know she meant well. I was afraid I would fall out of the chair! Mavis wants to go back and read all the wall labels, me pushing this time.

But the quaint reversion to maternal archetype seems more for old times' sake than anything else. We have a fine time, it turns out, just trundling along from picture to picture. Indeed, were I wearing white rubber-soled shoes and a little nurse hat we'd look exactly like an ad for a light-filled, nicely decorated assisted-living facility. Except we're also eyeballing the paintings, like a pair of regular Bernice Berensons. And amazingly enough, whether through divine grace or telepathy, the complex verdict I've formulated on O'Keeffe—yes, showy and easy (though the works do look better when you see them in a group); early stuff preferable to later; loathe all the famous pictures but sort-of-like some of the more obscure ones (*My Last Door*, from 1954, could almost be a Malevich)—turns out to be identical to my mother's. We have our different semifavorites, but neither of us feels like enforcing our choices on the other; we have arrived at our views independently and now weigh them dispassionately, like grown-ups at a committee meeting. I lose my surly-insecure edge— feel suddenly less tormented by filial *ressentiment* and incipient acid reflux. Mavis is judicious, even stateswoman-like. Harmony spreads to the blighted corners of the earth. We both agree that, like it or not, O'Keeffe really makes you look. I don't say it aloud, but I rue and dread the day when such looking isn't possible.

Blakey likes to point a moral at times and that evening in the hotel—our last in Santa Fe—she outdoes herself. As I maunder on about the day, my mother, and the odd vagaries of taste, she delivers an irresistible challenge: *Name ten female artists of the twentieth century who are better than O'Keeffe and I will clean up all the dog and cat poo in the backyard forever.* I start off confidently enough: Agnes M. (natch), Popova, Goncharova, Sonia Delaunay, Hannah Höch, Eva Hesse, *umm* . . . Living artists aren't permitted, or photographers, so, gosh, Louise Bourgeois and Imogen Cunningham and Berenice

Abbott and Kiki Smith and Cecily Brown and Marlene Dumas and Ida Applebroog and scores of others get knocked out at a stroke. (*Nicole Eisenman: please know I worship you!*) Marie Laurencin seems far too feeble to mention; so too, I'm afraid, does Vanessa Bell. Gwen John? Not exactly a she-titan of the brush. Elaine de Kooning? The canonization of wives has never seemed to me an effective feminist strategy. Dame Laura Knight? I love her, but does anyone else? Joan Mitchell? Marvelous but . . . *uhhh* . . . I peter out at Number Seven or Eight in a welter of anguish and indecision. If only Kandinsky or Andy Warhol had been a woman.

But my moral understanding is also in need of enlargement. Having entirely lost interest in my feckless responses, Blakey is now propped on the bed with her laptop and engrossed in the online *Daily Mail*, her favorite source of celebrity gossip and all-around human drama. By some freak of synchronicity a big double-spread—"My Daughter's a Lesbian and I'm Devastated!"—is the day's leading non-celeb story. There are pained interviews with both mother and daughter (now apparently estranged), complete with dramatic photos. The mum in question is a big, rather trollopy-looking lady with cavernous décolletage—very Edna Turnblad—living some-where dreary like Hove or Eastbourne. Mandy, the twenty-something daughter, sports a pale but noticeable mustache, black T-shirt, studded leather belt, and lip piercings. Mandy's obviously the town fright, eager to terrorize old-age pensioners in the local Tesco. Her un-natural tastes are hardly the worst of it, her mother avers: Mum's greatest fear is that "society" will discriminate against ugly, head-strong Mandy and make her life a living hell: *"I don't want to see my little girl get hurt!"*

I'm hardly surprised by Mandy's Amazonian riposte: that her mother's expression of concern is simply a hypocritical displacement of her own deep maternal homophobia. After all, that's what I used to say (or thought I might say) when I was her age and my mother

made similarly doleful observations. I am entirely unprepared, however, for B.'s thunderous jeremiad, complete with fist-pounding on
the fluffy duvet: *I hate that fucking Mandy! What an idiot! I hate fucking lesbians! She looks like a pooch! I feel sorry for the poor mother! Of
course she's devastated! Anybody normal would be! That Mandy should
go live in the gutter and drink piss!* While I balk slightly at B.'s subsequent suggestion that we cease being lesbians at once and begin an
Internet breast-feeding service, her impassioned moral commentary
leaves me abashed, rather like Emma when Mr. Knightley takes her
to task for her unkind words to harmless old Miss Bates.

How should a Santa Fe Diary end? *Today we set off on the arduous
eight-week stagecoach journey back to California. Though rough and
indelicate in manner—as I learned to my dismay when one of them
was so careless as to miss the spittoon adjacent to where I stood awaiting
our departure—the young gentlemen in Stetsons at our hotel in Santa
Fe were most eager to help us secure our heavy boxes. I wore my pretty
yellow calico dress for the journey; Miss Beaverbrook had chosen her
usual frayed blue gingham suit with the buttons missing. So as not to
delay our embarkation I thought it wisest not to mention that her muslin
petticoat was besmirched with some small unknown foulness.*

*The day was fine and bright and despite an oft-expressed fear of those
savages who might molest us en route, my Venerable Mama proved a delightful travelling companion. Though frequently requiring short stops so
that she might admire the picturesque desert vegetation—scores of them
in fact—she was a constant source of useful and enlivening information.
Miss Beaverbrook and I listened raptly and the hours (and miles) flew
by. Struck by a pithy reflection, Miss Beaverbrook several times registered her pleasure by closing her eyes and breathing deeply and slowly,
as if to cogitate upon my mother's worthy sentiments more thoroughly.*

*When we drove past the sign marking the road to Roswell—a place
where the local Indian tribes, I am told, worship a god who takes the shape
of a large flying disc—Mama observed that my great-aunt O'Keeffe had*

once traveled the old Santa Fe Trail, too. Before, that is, she disgraced herself forever in the eyes of God and man. I boldly enquired as to the precise nature of Aunt Georgia's offences but no doubt out of solicitude for Miss Beaverbrook's youthful sensibilities, Mama refused to expatiate. Our only terror of the day—thankfully brief—came when an enormous jackalope sprang from the mesquite and into the path of our coach, requiring our driver to pull up short in a swirl of dust and neighing horses. The jackalope was at least twelve feet tall and gaped at us menacingly, revealing hideous yellow snaggle-teeth. The men shot at it with their rifles, however, and the monstrous beast bounded away—huge antlers flashing and large white cottontail bobbing—into the sagebrush. We all thanked Providence for our deliverance.

The Professor

Proglomena

The author, 1976

HAVING DROPPED SERIOUS POUNDAGE THIS summer on WeightWatchers and become ever more buff and lissome in the process, Blakey has started me on yet another *régime amaigrissante*. I much prefer the French term, I have to say, to the boring old English "diet." Like all things French, it's elegant—almost neoclassical-sounding, like something from a little shop in the Marais. You can burn up to fifty calories just by pronouncing it. But I also like the way it suggests something rather more austere, even theological, than merely dumping the Mrs. Fields in favor of bok choy. To me it hints, fittingly, at some arduous and refining ordeal—a conversion to Jansenism, perhaps, or some terrible Protestant night-sweat of the soul. *You, pale criminal*, etc. And that's me exactly—pale, criminal, a bit bloated. Exercise turns out to be just as important as eating less. O, Lord, I accept these blue sweatpants and stale-smelling T-shirt, this wafer-thin iPod—so tiny and portable yet so full of song in thy praise. Till death do us part will I follow Blakey on our Daily High-Speed Power Walk through the neighborhood, disagreeable though the hilly bits are. She is the Chosen One. *Gotta get to U-U-U and that booty* . . . Can't help wondering what she's listening to, though. One of her Great Professor lectures on Spinoza? The *Enigma Variations*? Fitty Cent? We both got our headphones on now and we pumpin'.

B. is the Chosen One in another sense, too: we are getting married this month at San Francisco City Hall. Our *nupitals*—or so our pot-smoking mountain-mama dog-sitter mistakenly refers to them—have both a true-love and a civic-duty dimension. (They've also prompted the latest bout of fitness training.) It is time to share the love, with various Castles and Vermeules in attendance. But we also want to pile on before the November election: in an effort to overturn the recent California law legalizing same-sex marriage, dull hordes of the pious and cretinous have managed to stick an antigay referendum on the ballot. Yet even if the wretched thing passes, we figure, the more couples who marry before Election Day, the harder it will be for the courts to nullify the marriages later. So order in those crates of confetti! It's like the Enlightenment all over again.

And so too, historically speaking, the time seems right to begin this piece: a wee reminiscence of my Sapphic salad days (the 1970s) and dire yet life-shaping acquaintance with the Professor. I've had it in mind to write about the Professor for a while, but as B. can attest, have had to do a fair amount of emotionally taxing research first. Some of this research has been archival in nature: a matter of digging through Old Journals of the Time. (These will figure prominently later.) Ghastly to admit it, but I've got a huge groaning boxful of them, the earliest and scruffiest dating back to 1972, several years before the Professor and I met. One of my undergraduate English teachers had made us keep one—a little vade mecum, he called it—in which, Montaigne-like, we were to preserve our thoughts about the books we were assigned that term. It being the "liberated" 1970s, we were free—indeed encouraged—to incorporate personal material into our responses. Alas, reviewing this virgin effusion now, I am embarrassed to see just how obsessively, if also coyly, I managed to relate whatever great work I perused (everything from Homer's *Iliad* to Rosa Luxembourg on the Revolution of Rising Expectations) to the tormented crush I had at the time on Phoebe, the straight hippy-girl roommate with whom I had been painfully infatuated since our freshman year.

> —*Saw P. this afternoon with her ceramics teacher in the cafeteria. They didn't see me. Not again. Felt just like the narrator in* Notes from Underground *when he has to step into the dirty snow on the Nevsky to let the Cossack officer go by. Indeed:* "*I could not even become an insect.*"

Unfortunately for me, the professor in question, a somewhat dissolute character with a beret and a foot-long Mr. Natural Keep-on-Truckin' beard, seemed to intuit the nature of the attraction to P. and relished all the suppressed girl-on-girl hysteria. (My journal always came back with approving "yes's" and "good's"—sometimes even a tiny "whoa"—next to the more suggestive entries.) Thus was a habit ingrained: I kept journals religiously for the next ten years. And no, it hasn't been fun confronting them again; when I finally dragged them down a few weeks ago from the top shelf in the coat closet—the place where they've been lying, dusty and unregarded, all this time, I felt more than a spasm of foreboding. There they all were, in their neat, puerile, incriminating stacks, patiently awaiting some sadder-but-wiser postmodern rediscovery. Reading them through for the first time in twenty-five years was not going to be easy—nor was it.

Along with the journal dredging, however, some serious musical research has also been necessary. Folk music, after all (especially folk music of the more dismal, depraved, and gallows-ridden sort), was a central element in my relationship with the Professor. We had bonded (if ever so briefly) over elf-knights and demon lovers, silver daggers and Little Sir Hugh, the chatty ghosts of maidens drowned at sea— even the odd croaking *corbie* or *twa*. To get into just the right mind-set, therefore—the proper mood for maundering—it has been necessary to immerse myself once more in great aural tidal waves of Joan Baez, Pentangle, Peter, Paul and Mary, Buffy Sainte-Marie, Ewan MacColl, Judy Collins, Fairport Convention, Incredible String Band, John Renbourn, Ian and Sylvia, and countless other folkie-tinged worthies of the late sixties–early seventies era. Dylan too, of course: the Professor claimed to have known him in the fabled days in the Village. *Blood on the Tracks,* possibly my favorite Dylan album ever, came out just pre-Professor, I recall, during my last year in college. When I met her a short time later, a few months into my new Ph.D. program, it was strange to find that despite the putative Bob connection, not only had the Professor not yet heard it, she had not even heard *of* it.

And thus it was the other day—as B. and I bowled along on the now-obligatory Power Walk (me lollygagging a bit, I confess)— that I found, through the music, this essay's starting point: my donnée. I had been listening on my iPod to a true musical relic, a collector's item of such rarified loopiness I had not thought to hear it again, as they say in the *Aeneid*, this side of the Styx. The rara avis in question was Alix Dobkin's 1973 album *Lavender Jane Loves Women*, an eccentric self-produced paean to Sapphism—at once noodly, maudlin, and curiously rousing—that I had recently rediscovered online. Warmed-over folkie, loosely speaking, was indeed the mode: American-lady-singer-with-acoustic-guitar-and-fake-Scottish-accent-croons-archaic-sounding-pseudoballads. The record even included a feminist update of Child ballad No. 223—about a pistol-packing gal named Eppie who "wadna be a bride, a bride." But

Lavender Jane's overriding message, strictly women-only, was 100 percent of its historical moment: *Destroy the Patriarchy! Dykes Rule! Adam was a Rough Draft! Mother Nature Is a Lesbian!* Radical lesbian propaganda in folk-song guise, in other words—enough to make an erstwhile Mytilinean proud.

Now, it's true I still owned my original *Lavender Jane* LP. It's in the garage even now—complete with worn yet striking hand-drawn purple cover, vaguely floral in design, with an arabesque blob meant (I think) to look like the mons veneris. Along with its handsome sister album from 1975, *Living with Lesbians*—the latter graced by a picture of crop-headed Alix and some hard-boiled mates hoeing dirt in a communal field and glowering suspiciously at the camera— I've hung on to it for decades, hoping that it might one day become valuable. (Note to Smithsonian: I also have a pristine Patty Hearst "Wanted" poster from the same era, deftly snatched off the wall of a post office in Tacoma, Washington during my SLA-wannabe phase.) But I hadn't actually heard any of Dobkin's music for a long time; I'd jettisoned my last turntable ages ago and no longer had the equipment to play it on.

Thus when the morbid desire to listen to her again came over me recently—for hadn't Dobkin's deep singing voice, though plusher, borne an uncanny similarity to the Professor's?—I found myself Googling her. I doubted I would unearth much, though; given the esoteric nature of her recording career, I assumed Dobkin had been sucked down a cultural memory hole more abyssal even than the one that had engulfed the ukulele-strumming Tiny Tim—the dim falsetto-voiced singer (purportedly male yet oddly reminiscent in looks of the older Vita Sackville-West) who had once been a regular on *Rowan and Martin's Laugh-In*. Yet such was not the case. Not only did I find Alix's Wikipedia entry in a nanosecond, I soon hit upon *Lavender Jane* itself, freshly pirated and all ready for clicking and downloading at ten cents a song (!), on—of all things—a dodgy

Russian Web site specializing in Beatles and Bee Gees bootlegs. Now, how exactly had the digital entrepreneurs of Smolensk and Novgorod obtained this freakish memento of 1970s radical lesbian feminism? Had the globe-trotting Condoleezza Rice had something to do with it? I didn't know. It was definitely iffy, even sinister. But I went ahead and clicked away anyway. Here's hoping that Ludmilla and Svetlana —or indeed any other lesbo-Russki cybergangsters who may now be using my credit card number—got a chance to play some of the songs while they hacked into my account; I suspect they might have enjoyed them.

So what was *Lavender Jane* like after thirty years? It has a claim, after all, to a certain minor historical importance: it was one of the first-ever recordings of what subsequently came to be known as "women's music"—music written by or performed by lesbians, usually exclusively for other lesbians. In the 1970s the sanitary euphemism seemed necessary: many of the form's early proponents were closeted, or half-closeted, and still hoping, one presumes, for mainstream careers. (Perhaps on some distant purple planet: except for maybe Melissa Etheridge or k.d. lang, few such careers ever materialized.) Nor could you find an album like *Lavender Jane* in a record store: I had to order my copy through the mail, like contraband plutonium, after seeing a tiny ad for it in the classified ads section of *Ms.* magazine. All this, in the end, for a fairly anodyne (and soon-to-become formulaic) product. Hard to believe in an era of Chicks on Speed, Vaginal Cream Davis, and Le Tigre, but "women's music" disks are still occasionally manufactured, like reproduction Bakelite rotary-dial telephones, with all the time-honored generic features preserved intact: plaintive warbling on the part of the female singer-songwriter, ultrasaccharine lyrics about waterfalls, women's hair, and kindly gym teachers— the occasional quasi-clitoral image or (*gasp*) female pronoun folded in here and there to insinuate, ever so delicately, the same-sex erotic setup. Funkadelic and potty-mouthed it is not.

And indeed, as soon as the first notes of "The Woman in Your Life"—the lead-off cut and Dobkin's signature piece—came plink-plonking over my headphones the other day, I was immediately reminded of the genre's gauzy inanities. The lyrics—a paean to a sort of *Our Bodies, Ourselves*–like self-concern—would no doubt work well in a sales pitch for vibrators:

> *The Woman in Your Life*   [plink]
> *Will do what she must do*   [plonk]
> *To comfort you and calm you down*
> *And let you rest now;*   [plink plonk]
> *The Woman in Your Life,*   [plink]
> *She can re-e-e-st so easily*—   [plonk]
> [decisive STRUM and dramatic pause—]
> *She knows everything you do,*   [plink]
> *Because the Woman in Your Life is You.*   [plonk]

The basic conceit established, it doesn't take long for the creamy goo to start seeping in—not least because The Woman in Your Life (aka You) knows a "way to touch" to make you, *um*, whole:

> *She can t-o-o—u-ch so easily*—
> *She knows everything you do,*
> *Because the Woman in Your Life is You.*

Ladies, start your labia!

Other songs broached similarly delicious themes. In "A Woman's Love"—a slightly boomy treaclefest (apparently recorded inside a cistern) in which Alix was accompanied, uncertainly, by an (alas) fairly pitch-impaired cellist and flute player—she celebrated her discovery of her passion for, yes, a Woman. Why had she been attracted to her? Because said woman—or so one learned amid gallons of sloshy reverb—*was a Woman*. Ah, mystery solved!

Elsewhere, in a fatally perky folk-song medley of "Handsome Molly," "Sweet Betsy from Pike," "Goodnight, Irene," and "Darling Clementine," the singer offered a down-home dollop of Sapphic Americana. Such songs—she explained in her chatty liner notes (*so glad I kept that LP*)—were part of "Lavender Jane's great Dyke HERitage": lesbian love songs that needed reclaiming as such. And sure enough, as Alix jogged brightly from one tune to the next, the kinky world of one's pioneer foremothers—of gal–gal bundling, quilting bees, and little women-only houses on the prairie—came vividly to mind.

All easy enough to lampoon, of course, and I hadn't even gotten yet to the album's blockbuster final number—one that I fully expected, based on what I could remember of it, to reveal itself definitively, now and for the ages, as The Worst Song Ever Written. To borrow a canny phrase from a hipster colleague: seemed like Alix was about to rip Nana Mouskouri a new one. Indeed, when the ditty in question, the unfortunately named "View from Gay Head," started coming in over the 'phones, I was already tittering quietly in cynical forepleasure.

As the first couple of verses unfurled I felt a malicious urge to share the merriment. Blakey, it's true, was about ten or twelve paces ahead of me, but I'd been managing quite nicely (I thought) cardio-wise, and had even surmounted my bête noire, the infarction-inducing Sanchez Hill, in fairly good time. Surely Blakey wouldn't object to stopping the onerous Power Walk for just a sec to exchange headphones and exult in the ludicrousness of it all? Nor did she. After I had explained who Alix Dobkin was—B. having been maybe six or seven, I guess, when the original *Lavender Jane Loves Women* album came out—she listened in wide-eyed horror and disbelief, then began emitting great girlish war-whoops of laughter. These eructations became so insistent that she was soon quite breathless with guffawing and had to bend over at the waist, hands on hips, gasping all the while, like someone who had just finished running the 400-meter high hurdles at the Olympics.

Reasons for mirth—as I well knew myself—were not hard to find. According to Dobkin's liner notes, the song had apparently had a kind of mystical, magical, jubilant birthing, its chorus having come to its creator, "Ode to Joy"–like, while she was driving with her girl-friend to Gay Head on Martha's Vineyard in the summer of 1973. (*Wow, 1973! They could have seen Lillian Hellman! Maybe even've run her over!*) Pretty great, too, some of the other compositional details. "After we arrived," Dobkin explained, "I wrote the verses and very carefully lifted the tune from the Balkan song, 'Savo Vodo,' which I had recently learned at my Balkan singing class." Ah, yes: how well we remember rocking out to "Savo Vodo"—not to mention those air-guitar favorites "Pobjednicki Cocek" and "Vai, Ce Rau Ma Simi Acuma."

And from one angle, the lyrics of "View from Gay Head" no doubt offered glorious satiric fodder. Each verse was a potted parable of sorts, designed to expose the vileness with which the greedy pa-triarchal brutes who ruled the world (men) drove women, shrieking and tremulous, into the arms of their own sex. Luckily for the poor battered gals, though, this abrupt exit from the not-so Edenic Garden of Heterosexuality was really a Fortunate Fall: once one lady-refugee met up with another, awesome dyke-dacious ecstasy ensued, accom-panied by huge bursts of shared cleansing revolutionary anger. Thus in the song's opening verses—oddly ornamented with wobbly little eighteenth-century trills by the flute-cello backup team—Alix sang of one "Cheryl" and new squeeze "Molly," the blissful beneficiaries of just such an eroto-political awakening. "There are two kinds of people in the world today," the pair had realized:

One or the other, a Person must be;
The Men are Them and the Women are WEEE—EEEE!

This key insight, laid bare with the analytic clarity of Marx and Engels, led ineluctably to boogie-oogie-oogie Woman-Love. Now "both agree-ee-ee-ee-ee-ee," crowed Alix, "It's a pleasure to *bee-ee* a *LES-BEE-ENNE*!"

Cue loud and lusty chorus, sung by Dobkin and ragtag but euphoric female choir, several of whose members sounded as if they might be age six or under:

LES-BEE-ENNE! LES-BEE-ENNE!
LES-BEE-ENNE in No Man's Land!
LES-BEE-ENNE! LES-BEE-ENNE!
ANY WOMAN CAN BE A LES-BEE-ENNE!
[dainty flourish by flute player]

And so it went: the incendiary Cheryl and Molly succeeded by literary-lez "Liza," who "wishes the librar-eee/Had men and women placed separate-leee"—all the way to "Louise" (grousing at "a million second places in the Master's Games") and right-on Alix herself, who in the course of decrying the sexual warfare waged on women by men, absolutely *nails* my favorite internal rhyme in all of English poetry:

I'll return to the bosom,
Where my journey ends—
Where there's no penis
Between us friends!

I feel faint just typing it.

But faint—whether with joy, pleasure, or involuntary glandular stimulation—was hardly the state in which I found myself as I continued to observe the rippling laugh-bomb "View from Gay Head" had set off in Blakey. Quite the opposite: I suddenly felt uneasy, a little spooked, as if I'd had a scary dream the night before—some grisly vision crowded with frights—but now couldn't remember anything about it. A chill passed over me and I smiled wanly even as B. launched into some of her cherished satiric themes: the idiocies of the old hard-line feminism, the embarrassing travesty that Women's Studies had become in American universities, the aggravating failure of our lesbian friends to acknowledge the sheer hottitude of Daniel Craig, Cristiano Ronaldo, or various other brawny baby-daddies now gracing the covers of *People* magazine and the *National Enquirer.*

Ordinarily I would have been seconding these delightful sentiments, even suggesting other neglected hotties from history. (*I* know *Rupert Brooke is dead, but—o-h-h, what a studmuffin . . . Did you know that he and Virginia Woolf went nude swimming in a Sussex duck pond in 1913?*) But today something was different. Suddenly conscious— somewhat painfully—of the age difference between myself and my boisterous bride-to-be, I felt a stab of pure seventies-nostalgia, at once perverse, plaintive, and self-righteous. *You have no idea what it was like to be gay then. Nobody ever talked about it. There weren't any other lesbians. At least where I was. It wasn't like being at Yale with Maia and Sylvia and Jodie Foster in 1987.* Did I actually say such dreary things? Something along this lines, I confess, even as B. pulled a droopy-sad Pagliaccio-face—her usual gambit during my more pathetic sermons—and pretended to play an invisible two-inch violin, holding it delicately between thumb and forefinger and mooning tragically as she did so.

But I was increasingly piqued, too, by less comfortable feelings: a certain shamefacedness, above all. Who was I to make fun of Alix Dobkin? I worried I had been unjust, even disloyal—not only to the spunky songsmith, who by now is probably an entirely inoffensive lesbian grandmother and fully paid-up member of the AARP, but also to my confused, somewhat impressionable twenty-year-old self. Yes, granted: even thirty years ago, I found some of the numbers on *Lavender Jane Loves Women* wanting. (Warning from the U.S. Surgeon General: Do Not Play "Hug-Ee-Boo Song" While Operating Heavy Machinery.) But on the whole, hadn't I been right in there with Alix from the start? An admirer? An acolyte? Maybe even the Biggest Fan She Ever Had?

With the rap of a gavel, the Judge Judy tribunal in my brain, permanently empowered, was at once in session and I found myself under harsh DIY cross-examination. The first time I heard "The Woman in Your Life," three decades ago, the court wished to know, had I not become desperately eager to find a recording of it? (*Yes, your Honor. It was the theme song on a feminist talk show on the Seattle public-access radio station to which I had become fanatically devoted.*) Had I not also *adored* Alix's superb cover version of Dusty Springfield's "I Only Want to Be with You"—so far unmentioned in this all-too-strategic and shifty prologue? (*Um . . . er . . . yes, your Honor.*) Was it not a million billion tons better than the one Annie Lennox did when she was in The Tourists? (*Uh . . . yes . . .*) And indeed all the more poignant, given Springfield's own long-unacknowledged lesbianism? (Slight catch in voice: *Um, well, um . . . yes, your Honor. I guess. . . .*) And what *about* that "View from Gay Head"? Hadn't every line of the lyrics come rushing back as soon as I heard it again? Hadn't I found myself humming along, even mouthing the words of the chorus with a certain bemused if not rakish enjoyment? (Head bent in mortification, quiet sniffling sounds: *yeah, um . . . your Honor . . . I . . . uhhh . . . snuffle snuffle . . .*)

Finally, and most damningly, was it not the case—or perhaps one should say *is* it not the case—that I have been playing Dobkin's songs nonstop since I retrieved them online? That they make me feel strangely happy-go-lucky, as if—despite much evidence to the contrary—all were right with the world? That sometimes, amid the inanity, Alix hits the thirty-year-old emotional love-spot with such warmth and precision, reaches back so deeply and surely to the lonely, naïve, damaged-yet-hopeful young listener I once was, she makes me want to cry? That her singing is beautiful? That she makes me reflect, with gratitude, on the great kindness and understanding that I have received from people, gay and straight, over the course of my life? That when you get right down to it, a certain Terry Castle *loves* Alix Dobkin?

Guilty as charged, your Honor.

And thus my donnée, the question that now haunts me: What happened to that other T-Ball? The kinder, gentler T-Ball? The acoustic T-Ball, so to speak? Where did she go? She who was once, *in illo tempore*, as soft and pattable as a much-loved old flannel shirt or the consoling suede puppy-skin on the tummy of Wally? Putting it more bluntly: How had I become the japing, nay-saying, emotionally stunted creature I now felt myself to be? A veritable devil when it came to making fun of people but, oh, so much harder on myself?

The Dobkin rencontre suggested, obviously, that I had not, in fact, always been "that way"—that there had been a time of illusions and (relative) simplicity, a Bambi-time. How then had I morphed from doe-eyed little forest creature into the Thersites of Noe Valley? That my long-ago relationship with the Professor might be involved seemed most likely—a personally tailored Intro to Savage Irony 101—but beyond that, mental confusion reigned. How, precisely, had the rot set in? What did it have to do with my sexual orientation? And perhaps most important, what attitude to adopt toward it now? For even as I wallowed in wistful compassion for my younger self, I could also see in retrospect that some tempering—a certain steeling—had been necessary. Little T-Ball, poor shatter-brained mite, *had* had it coming, after all. The Bambi lifestyle is a dangerous one: one moment of baby-deer myopia, one dainty-hoofed gambol into freeway traffic, and you're road kill. What I saw now as the ineluctable corrosion of my character, in other words, might have been adaptive: a way of surviving.

But was that the good news or the bad news? Or was it just what it was? Did the concepts of good and bad even apply? Here indeed was a mystery worth plumbing: I was fat; I was mean; but I was alive.

The Gods Tried to Warn Me

SO WHO EXACTLY WAS Terry Castle—now Spoiled Avocado Professor of English at Silicon Valley University—way back in 1975? An embarrassing incident in the spring of my senior year in college will demonstrate just how deep the baby-fawn syndrome went, and how troublesome it would turn out to be, even as I was about to launch myself, purblind and gullible, into graduate school, a new life, and the cold Professorial embrace. Precocious one was, but also foolishly unguarded.

The kindest way of explaining it? Put it this way: I was so avid a Student in those days—so ardently devoted to the intellectualization of my world, so confident about my fledgling powers of analysis, so scholastic in my aspirations, so serious and chaste and idealistic— *such a twatty little Simone Weil wannabe in fact*—that I had somehow managed mostly to avoid acknowledging the real world and its inhabitants. Emotionally speaking, I was dim and unschooled, a sort of very low-grade idiot savant. (As—at a far more exalted level, I now realize—was Simone herself.) My undergraduate years, spent at a tiny then-barely accredited private school in the Pacific Northwest, had been a somewhat soggy, inconclusive affair, but apart from having to endure a plethora of fir trees, dark precipitation-filled days, and the sulfurous smells that wafted up from the lumber mills down by the Sound, I had not found my sojourn there particularly challenging. In some of my literature classes I was better informed than my professors. It was easy to be snobbish about the place, to feel superior. Compared with the apocalyptic urgency and difficulty of my high school years—during which I had been compelled by such frenzied longing to get away from San Diego and the worsening emotional chaos associated with the Mavis-Turk ménage (not to mention the crew of new and piratical stepsiblings) that I frequently ended up weeping at the dinner table over my chemistry homework, fearful I wouldn't win a scholarship . . . *ack ack ack* . . . —well, after all *that*, college was a pretty much bound to be a cinch. It was easy to do well and I nailed it.

Adding to the general hubris: my social life, though still sheltered, had likewise improved somewhat over the course of my undergraduate career. In high school I had been almost freakishly solitary and skittish, with no idea how to comport myself in ordinary-teenager fashion. A certain embryonic yet disabling class discomfort was involved: I was mortified by the fact that my parents were divorced (something still fairly unusual in the middle sixties) and that "home" during my adolescence was a tiny flat in the Buena Vista Garden Apartments, the somewhat rackety low-rent complex where we lived for the eight years before my mother finally married Turk. Bizarre as it sounds, by the time I left for college I had never once called anyone on the telephone or invited a classmate over after school. Nor had I myself been so called or invited. Not once had I sat on the bedroom floor with a set of girl-chums, gossiping about boys and teachers, "ratting" our hair Shirelles-style (still a preferred SoCal mode as late as 1970), listening to the radio, or having long metaphysical conversations about *Jesus Christ Superstar*. On the contrary: I'd been reclusive, a regular *Secret-Garden*-Frances-Hodgson-Burnett-Girl-Hysteric-in-Training. At seventeen, I remained passionately (if uneasily) mother devoted; frighteningly watchful, in school and out;

abnormally well read in Dumas novels, G.K. Chesterton's Father Brown stories, H.P. Lovecraft, and the lives of the poets (Keats being the huge sentimental favorite); but in all other respects mostly shy, quiet, lumpish, and dead.

In contrast, by the time I was a senior in college I felt I had "lived"—especially in what I imagined to be an erotic sense. Not that I'd been completely in the dark earlier: again, several achy-yet-pleasurable crushes on female teachers in high school had suggested the direction things were tending. In fact, if only abstractly, I was already half-cognizant even then of my budding sexual orientation and took a precocious scholarly interest in it. Various "grown-up" literary discoveries helped to shape it. With a forwardness and frankness rare at the time, for example, my tenth-grade French teacher had been inspired one day to tell us the checkered story of Rimbaud and Verlaine—the tumult, the buggery, the absinthe, all of it—and I had been riveted. Not a surprise, I suppose, that said French teacher, a *gamine* yet severe young woman we addressed as "Madame Moller," was one of the main crushes. Though hailing from Omaha, she refused to speak English, played Brel and Juliette Greco songs for us, and seemed unimaginably cosmopolitan, having once been an exchange student in Nice. Her Navy ensign husband was on a river boat in Vietnam.

I began devouring certain louche modern authors in secret: Gide, Wilde, Thomas Mann, Hermann Hesse, even Yukio Mishima, then at the height of his celebrity in the West. Sexual deviance, or at least what I conceived it to be, began to exert a certain unhallowed, even gothic allure—a glamorous, decayed, half-Satanic romance. (Hesse's *Demian*, one of the now-forgotten cult books of the era, was for some time my dark anti-Bible.) Not least among the attractions that such literary homosexuality proffered: some drastic psychic deliverance from familial dreariness and the general SoCal strip-mall stupor. In *Death in Venice*, after all, Aschenbach never had to go out to eat at a Carl's Jr. with Turk and the squalling stepsibs, let alone shout his fries-and-shake order through the tinny speaker at the drive-through window.

As for "homosexual practices"—and I confess I wasn't exactly sure, mechanically speaking, what they were—they sounded sterile and demonic but also madly titillating. Well I remember when Mishima, in uniform and at the head of a crazy little band of gay right-wing militarists, had himself decapitated by his homosexual lover on the balcony of the Japanese Defense Command in Tokyo in 1970: I'd read all about it—bug-eyed and agog—in my mother's *Time* magazine. Anything could happen, it seemed, in the fascinating world of sexual inverts. Lesbianism didn't figure much, if at all, in these early reveries: one of the oddest parts of the fantasy, I guess, was that I was male, dandified, and in some sort of filial relationship to various 1890s Decadents. I knew more about green carnations, the Brompton Oratory, *The Ballad of Reading Gaol,* and the curious charms of Italian gondoliers than I did about Willa Cather or Gertrude Stein—not to mention Garbo or Stanwyck or Dusty Springfield. Some of the obliviousness was due to the times: lesbianism was seldom mentioned—ever—in those days and the sparse information one did come across left more questions than it answered. I was vaguely conscious of *The Killing of Sister George*, the notorious lesbian stage play made into an X-rated film starring Beryl Reid and Susannah York in 1968, but also bewildered by what I read about it (again in *Time* magazine); it didn't seem to involve pining surreptitiously after a blond fellow schoolboy in some oppressive yet romantic Prussian military academy. Even today after repeated viewings—requisite because I suffer, alas, from a never-to-be-requited crush on the deceased but still superhot Coral Browne—I'm still not *entirely* sure I understand the bit with the cigar.

Needless to say, all this inward high-school posturing went undisclosed: as noted, I kept no journal then, nor had I any confidante or sidekick. I wouldn't have dreamed of bringing up intimate subjects with my somewhat addled and uncomprehending mother. Though we never discussed it, I know that she was already worried—when she had the time to think about it, that was—by my balky ungirlish demeanor and the fact that for some reason my period hadn't started. Nor would it, mortifyingly, until I was almost eighteen. (One's hormones were plainly on strike: talking tough to management and holding out for a better deal.) At the time I left for college I had never slept with anybody or even kissed anyone; nor, when you got right down to it, could I really imagine doing so. The idea of sex with a woman, of "having a lesbian lover," was simply unthinkable, like living alone at the North Pole or deciding to become a lycanthrope. If the thought existed at all, it was as a mote, a sweet nothing—a little "feather on the breath of God," barely sensed now and then, but mostly hidden away (*pace* Donald Rumsfeld) in some dastardly psychic dossier labeled "Unknown Unknowns." I was innocent—gruesomely so—or that was how it seemed.

All this changed in college, as if someone had flipped a switch. Within a day or two of arriving at my new dormitory, I'd already met the aforementioned Phoebe, whose bare feet, Joni Mitchell LPs, elaborately macraméd jeans bottoms, and well-thumbed volumes of Anaïs Nin's diary proclaimed her—thrillingly—a Free Spirit. She was a sort of apprentice-Earth Mother in fact: a Northern California hippy-girl of a kind altogether unknown in right-wing San Diego, home of gray steel battleships and the myrmidons of the Pacific Fleet. Her dorm room, a short trek from mine, was a little temple to dreamy Marin County bohemianism. On her dresser, for example, next to a weird yet intriguing arrangement of pine cones, dandelion fluff, and dried seedpods, she had placed an ancient-looking copy of *Leaves of Grass*, several poetry books by Gary Snyder, and Kenneth Rexroth's translations from the Chinese. Her clothes were rustic, homespun, hand-sewn, nothing like the matching stretchy-polyester top-and-pants outfit, hideously enlivened by orange and white stripes, that my mother had bought me—along with a towel set and a little study lamp—at the Fed-Mart just before I left for college. (My mother cannot be blamed for this eye-slitting ensemble: I'd coveted the stripey top especially and had implored her to buy it for me. Didn't realize it then, of course, but the whole look was distinctly baby-butch jock *avant la lettre*: the perfect thing—in another world—for the annual "Dyke-A Shore" ladies' golf tournament in Palm Springs.) Phoebe was the first person I'd ever met who'd been to the People's Park in Berkeley, had sat on the grass there in fact, and wore huarache sandals made out of old tires.

I was mesmerized, and Phoebe in turn took a pensive, if ponderous, interest in me. We bonded at once over our snobbish disdain for our female dorm-mates, especially the idiotic Pi Phi's, a giggly, geese-like set of sorority sisters who occupied one wing of the dorm and constantly ran shrieking up and down the hall with large plastic curlers in their hair. We preferred deeper mysteries—things shamanistic. We became inseparable: P. took me on long spontaneous nocturnal walks in the rain, showed me how to do the I Ching (the slow, old-fashioned way with yarrow stalks) and gave me one of her precious embroidered shirts from Guatemala. Proud of our outsider status, we ate every meal alone together at a little table upstairs from the main college dining room, even as hordes of our uncouth classmates happily stuffed themselves on industrial meatloaf and mashed potatoes under a large WPA-style mural featuring Paul Bunyan and his comely pet ox, Blue Babe.

As it happened we were in the same introductory humanities course that fall: a weird class on myth and religion in which we read Jung, Bachofen, Malinowski, and a truly dispiriting pile of "existential theology" tomes, including Rudolf Bultmann's less-than-scintillating *Kerygma and Myth*. I know I described my college curriculum earlier as somewhat less than rigorous, but in the light of this scary

Tübingen-style booklist I should perhaps amend that slightly. Having originated as a Christian teaching college, the school had still a number of professors who were ordained Protestant ministers, mostly of a severe, if not Ingmar Bergman–ish, intellectual stripe. Our religion professor was one of these men of the cloth: blond, handsome, and chillingly ascetical in steel-rimmed glasses. Seated at the end of a seminar table, he looked just like the young Max von Sydow.

Now Phoebe was a rebel—or fancied herself one—and I, in turn, viewed her as my oracle in all things. One dank night that term, having scornfully agreed that Bultmann was too irksome to be endured a moment longer, we decided to renounce him forever and so tossed our paperback copies of *Kerygma*, etc. into the thick undergrowth beneath the dripping Douglas fir trees near the dorm. We were cackling away like a pair of *Macbeth* witches after this unholy sacrifice when suddenly Phoebe turned, embraced me, and kissed me—thoroughly, warmly, wet raincoat and all— and said she loved me. That was the first time that *that* had happened. I declared in turn, somewhat squeakily, that I would throw myself under a truck for her. Would in fact be eager to do so. I guess I meant it—at least to the extent that an emotionally retarded eighteen-year-old *can* mean such a declaration. In any case, my heart leapt up in the event: the bolts-in-the-neck Frankenstein-loneliness of teenagerhood was now presumably at an end. I went to bed that night in ecstasy and although I crept out early the next morning, I confess, to retrieve poor Rudolf, soggy and grubby and limp with the dew, from the bushes (I had started to worry about needing him to study for the final exam), the feeling of dizzy exaltation lasted for some time.

It lasted for almost three years, in fact; but three years also imbued with so much angst and frustration, one could hardly have called the relationship—my first *coup de foudre*—a particularly wholesome one. For all her moody artist charm Phoebe turned out to be a

coquette—a veritable Zuleika Dobson of the Pacific Northwest—
and ultimately heterosexual in a curiously leaden way. She excelled
at a sort of dreamy, noncommittal, D.T. Suzuki–Zen-and-the-Art-
of-Archery seductiveness. The first year I knew her, for example, she
would often tut-tut, with a long-drawn-out sigh, over the fact that
her middle-aged high school English teacher, a shy misfit bachelor
named Mr. Smith, had been besotted with her all through her school
days and indeed still was. (He was the person, I later learned, responsible for her interest in Eastern religions; along with the I Ching, she
was always going on about *saddhus* and *bodhisattvas*.) It was true:
occasionally she would even let me see some of his plaintive letters.
These were often accompanied by sad little koan-like love poems executed in black ink with Chinese brushes on homemade brown paper
scrolls. One of Mr. Smith's more lugubrious poetic efforts, I recall,
was an effusion entitled "Handicappèdness":

HANDICAPPÈD!
Yes, I am HANDICAPPÈD!
HANDICAPPÈD!

HANDICAPPÈD!
The Buddha laughs—
By the cold snow-stream in the mountains!

Liberally blotted with odd accent marks, ink splotches, and jokey
Zen-master exclamation points, these little poem-scrolls seemed to me
to indicate a woefully unbalanced mind. Yet they struck a chord, too,
somehow. Pleased by his attentions, Phoebe kept the hapless Mr. Smith
dangling on the line by writing back to him, long poetic missives in
which she made a point of never once acknowledging his lovestruck
appeals. She'd expatiate for pages instead on rain forests, the beauty
of the Sound, mysterious bearded men she'd met while hitchhiking

(possibly *bodhisattvas* in disguise?), peyote visions she had read about, or whatever other West Coast woo-woo was preoccupying her that week. (Sweat lodges? Carlos Castaneda? The Book of Thoth?) Like the cryptic notes she would leave for me in my dorm room when I wasn't there—one consisted of the whole of Matthew Arnold's "The Buried Life," transcribed without explanation—P.'s sibylline messages were typically embellished, Art Nouveau–style, with luxuriant, strangely accomplished doodles: alchemical signs, vines with curly tendrils, elongated damsels, star-forms, and the like. I was ravished by it all.

But though ultimately consummated (farcically) the relationship was hardly a joyous initiation into Sapphic life. Over the three years of our folie à deux, I had become ever more self-conscious and chatty about what I called my "inversion." (I'd discovered *The Well of Loneliness* by this point—not to mention D. H. Lawrence and the kinky early novels of Iris Murdoch. It was perversion full speed ahead.) Meanwhile Phoebe became ever more the not-so-unconscious tease. With what seemed to me distressing calculation she lost her virginity during our freshman year to a rail-thin boy in a neighboring dorm who wore a Pendleton jacket and was seven feet tall. I was distraught and promptly followed suit, losing mine a month or two later to a nerdy youth in my poetry class who still lived at home with his parents and while hardly seven feet tall—more like five-eight—had a ten-inch-long penis. I was too ill-informed at the time to know there was anything out of the ordinary about this astonishing pink saber, or the explosive clumsiness with which its inexperienced owner wielded it. (A similar cluelessness would beset me again, many years later, when friends tried to teach me to play bridge. Through some freak of cosmic probability—similar no doubt to the one said to have produced the Big Bang—I drew all thirteen clubs on my first hand.) Yes, I now felt "experienced," but the act itself—nerve-wracking, pointless, and seriously yucky-poo—also seemed inconsequential. My ardor for Phoebe raged unabated.

She, in turn, played the role of Isadora Duncan will-o-the-wisp. At her urging—I was somewhat frightened by the idea—we went hiking and camping in British Columbia one spring break, not long after the virginity-breaching business. Unbelievably to me now, we walked and hitchhiked all the way, hundreds of miles, with towering backpacks replete with dangling metal cups, tent stakes, plastic bags of granola, and paperback copies of Chuang Tze and Basho. We had virtually no money. When a heavy rainstorm forced us to stay overnight in a rat-trap little motel in Port Angeles, Phoebe, clutching a blanket and with nary a word, shuffled in at one point from the other room in which she had supposedly settled for the night and crawled into my puffy mummy bag with me. She was stark naked. I too was starkers, except for a pair of *echt*-utilitarian underpants, now admittedly somewhat grotty after the day's hike. Apparently at her ease, P. fell at once into a deep and complacent slumber. I was a ravaged, silent wreck the next morning—a bit like the goggle-eyed creature from Munch's *The Scream*—and desperate to leave Port Angeles.

Later, for about a year and a half, we shared an off-campus apartment—and again, a bed. As before it was utterly chaste: indeed, Phoebe often lamented that she could never reciprocate my yearnings, of which she was quite aware. I was "unconventional," she declared, whereas she was perfectly normal. Given that she was often in bed with her arms draped around me when she said such things, it was all perfectly agonizing, too. And the end, when it came, was outlandish. She'd suddenly acquired a second boyfriend and demanded that I move out of our apartment, presumably so she could sleep with him without me glooming around in the background. (As Blakey would say—no doubt with a cruel snort—*harshin' on everybody's buzz.*) Though mortified, as Phoebe's official slave for life, I complied at once and rented a flea-infested studio apartment a few blocks away for $65 a month.

Yet no sooner had I vacated the premises than she abruptly

canned the boyfriend and dropped out of school—for good, as it happened—and moved back to California. Shocked and bewildered by these ructions, I was even more astounded a month or two later when she began sending me odd, rambling, but unmistakably erotic letters from her parents' trailer camp in the Sierra Nevada, the rustic redoubt to which she had retreated. She regretted our untried intimacy, she said, and wanted to see me again. Might we meet at my mother and Turk's house over the upcoming spring break? Mavis, she said, was all for it. (P. had met my mother once and, both being artistic, they'd hit it off famously.) Needless to say, I flew to San Diego two days later, heart in mouth, and in a whirl of demented lust Phoebe and I had sex five nights in a row—incompetently enough, I see now, but also at such a flailing and histrionic pitch it was bizarre that my mother and Turk (asleep in the big room downstairs) remained, like characters put under a sorceress's spell in some medieval romance, oblivious to the activity above them.

This brief bacchanal, it must be said, had its imperfections, including one spectacularly ill-starred evening when P. and I went to visit Gus—a nice, hippy-dippy, none-too-bright acquaintance of mine from high school whom we'd run into at the beach—and got colossally stoned on his waterbed. Whether due to the waterbed or to Puff the Magic Dragon, the scene—to my horror—suddenly took an all too intimate turn. Emergency measures were called for. In a state of some panic I hurriedly frog-marched Phoebe—now mumbling and near-comatose but clearly loath to leave—out the door and into Turk's old Pinto, which I'd borrowed for the evening. Brain on fire, I then leadfooted it at once back to my mother's house. (I shudder now to recall this deranged freeway flight, my own faculties having likewise been considerably impaired by our debauch.) When we pulled up outside the house, Phoebe—who was very drunk as well as stoned—promptly vomited up her Spaghetti Factory dinner all over the floor of the Pinto, then flopped about flirtatiously on the front seat, slurpy and slurry and simpering like Dean Martin after six or ten double Scotches.

As we struggled into the house and up the stairs—me cursing inside, trying not to wake anyone up (it was around 2:00 a.m.) and grimly fretting over what on earth I would use to clean up Turk's car—Phoebe was amiably burbling away to herself, the drunken gist being (as I heard with some dismay) that despite my sincerest amorous efforts I would never be able to *give her what Gus could*. Now Everybody Loves Somebody Sometime, I guess. Or is it that People Who Need People Are the Luckiest People in the World? Either way, Phoebe's blunt assessment was not exactly a confidence booster. I absorbed it as best I could under the circumstances and by the time we bade our sober, shy farewells at the airport a day or two later—neither one of us really wanting to look the other in the eye—I had in my own mind transformed the whole evening (of which P. seemed to have no recollection) into something Wild and Fun and Oh-So Grown-Up. I returned to college in a state of maudlin tristesse—proud of every fleeting, fumbled caress, brimful still with dumb-beast adoration, and with all my half-slaked desires of three years morbidly intensified. They had nowhere to go. I often wonder what extraordinary dismay I might have felt had I known there and then that thanks to the capricious turns of Fate (a complex myriad of them, in fact) I would neither see nor hear from Phoebe again for almost twenty-nine years, until I ran into her by accident, along with her fourteen-year-old daughter, at a crafts fair in San Francisco when we were both too old to care.

But onward to the Bambi-event. With Phoebe gone, my last year as an undergraduate began dolefully enough: I studied, rode my bike in the rain, and wallowed in my romantic solitude. I had a little job working nights in the school library. This last activity, though dull in many respects, nonetheless played a substantial role in my on-going sex education. Even as I whiled away the hours every Friday and Saturday evening in the morgue-like precincts of the reserve desk, I would explore the library's X-rated holdings, all of which were kept off-limits to the general student body in a nearby locked cupboard to which I had a key. *Erotic Art from Around the World* was a favorite, likewise *Tropic of Cancer*, and an old illustrated edition of Casanova published, I think, by the Fortune Press in the 1920s. But I also found things pertinent to my own case: *Diana: A Strange Autobiography*, a dated but illuminating anonymous memoir from the 1950s (full of curious facts about the hothouse life in women's colleges and secret lesbian bars in Paris); Dr. George Weinberg's *Society and the Healthy Homosexual* (1972), one of the first books to argue (successfully) that the American Psychiatric Association drop its classification of homosexuality as a mental illness; and—most exciting of all—a near-pristine copy of Sidney Abbott and Barbara Love's recently published *Sappho Was a Right-On Woman!* (1972), a moral and political defense of lesbian civil rights far more tough, judicious, and emotionally à propos than the goofy title might suggest. Along with the *Village Voice*, whose back issues I now burned through over the course of several weeks (not that I had ever been to New York), these books were to jumpstart my radical-dyke phase. With roaring girls such as Jill Johnston, Robin Morgan, Kate Millett, Ti-Grace Atkinson, Mary Daly, and Monique Wittig for inspiration, could Alix Dobkin [*annunciatory flute trill*] be far behind?

And even as I ruminated endlessly over how and when Phoebe would be restored to me, I fell into a handful of relationships, as if by accident, that served to pass the time till graduation. One was with a classmate and fellow oddball named Davy, from Pocatello, whose curly brown hair and Peter Pan–like company appealed to me. (I somehow excluded him from my general indictment of the male sex.) He'd made a suicide attempt the previous year, he told me, but was now over his depression. He played chess competitively (not a Master but near it); and idolized Nijinsky. We rode around town on his puttering Honda 90 while he regaled me with strange or touching facts he'd absorbed from his reading. He'd just read the memoirs of Dorothy Caruso and been much struck by her declaration that she loved Caruso because "he had *a great soul*." (*Was this true of all great artists?* We debated the question at length.) The reason the faun-god Nijinsky was able to leap so high in the air, he explained on another occasion, was because the bones in his feet, freakishly, *were those of a bird, not a man*. Davy often made me laugh by reciting, wide-eyed, his favorite sentence from *Ulysses*: "For *him*, for *Raoul*!" (a quote from the trashy romance novel Molly Bloom is reading on the day of Bloom's wanderings). The line became a comic catch-phrase for us, to be uttered at any incongruous moment. With Davy's assistance I made a second half-hearted attempt at normal sexual intercourse, but to no very pleasing end. He later went on to live in a series of unlikely places (Tonga, Japan, Montana, Caracas) and would write me scribbly letters with big, odd-looking postage stamps, but never settled anywhere or found a vocation. Maybe he has now but we've lost touch.

Engaging me further was also a more complex friendship: with a blonde woman who sat behind me in my 9:00 a.m. class on the History of Literary Criticism. My private nickname for her was the Daring Divorcée: she was an intelligent, petite, extremely attractive woman named Karen. She was in her early thirties, had two small children, lived in the suburbs in a sixties ranch house with a carport, was a firm and vocal ex-Catholic. Having recently divorced an Irish-American Weyerhauser exec, she had come back to school to get an M.A. in Comparative Literature. She was intrigued by me, she later explained, because in class my hair, seen from behind, was always *confused*, a regular topological tangle. I guess it looked as if I had gone to bed with it wet, lain on it in some untoward fashion, and then—like a female Strewelpeter—neglected to smooth it down before I left the house. Unfortunately, Karen was correct: I'm afraid I still sometimes do this.

We fell into bed one evening: she'd put Laura Nyro and Labelle's *Gonna Take a Miracle* on the record player, and though basically straight as a one-dollar bill, was obviously in an experimental mood. The same thing happened a few times more and so I moved into her house—"to save on rent"—that last spring and early summer before I left for the Midwest. To my dismay—and I rarely seem to have been in any other state of mind in those days—she lost interest in the sex part almost at once, though we went on sleeping in the California King marital bed together. I remember being unsettled indeed when her six-year-old daughter Polly—as dark-haired and fey as Flora or Miles in *The Turn of the Screw*—would come into the bedroom in the morning and give us an eerie, impervious, reproving glance. I began to regress a bit in the odd situation; started to act in fact like one of the children. I wrote mysterious, droogy love sonnets, usually about P., but some about someone else known (enigmatically) only as "K."

Granted, in the intellectual realm I was able to maintain—albeit feebly—a quasi adult demeanor. Karen and I shared an enthusiasm for Renaissance literary arcana and were much fired up that spring about alchemy, the Metaphysical poets, Sir Thomas Browne, and Hermes Trismegistus. Good old Hermes T.: *wacky but cool*. Karen's specialty was Spanish literature of the Golden Age and with her long blonde hair illumined in the lamplight she would sometimes read Góngora poems to me, in the soft, lisping Spanish accents (or so I imagined) of a seventeenth-century infanta. But at the same time she was also a fledgling satirist and freethinker: embittered by her failed marriage, ferociously anticlerical, droll, caustic, and self-protective. This side of her, I have to say, appealed to me less than the infanta side. At the time I met her she was recovering from a brief and disastrous affair with a morose male undergrad named Richard (I knew him by sight) who'd dumped her in a painful and inexplicable fashion. His pink boy-skin, she would lament, had been that of an Adonis—the most delicious downy fuzz. But now she detested him. She had hatched an idea, she said, for a short story: a divorced woman in her thirties, having fallen madly in love with a college student and been rejected by him, hits a pedestrian while driving. The pedestrian turns out to be the student. Karen confessed to being undecided about the story's ending: whether the accident would kill him or just leave him horrifyingly maimed—the Adonis features scarified, the beautiful fuzz caked with blood. It was the sort of technical question, we agreed, that a writer like Doris Lessing would know how to resolve.

When the Embarrassing Episode began to unfold that spring, Karen had by far the most jaded—and accurate—view of things. I had been nominated by my college for a fancy graduate scholarship sponsored by one of the great American dog food families. Given that in the greater world of higher education my college was regarded as distinctly subpar—the place wouldn't be granted a Phi Beta Kappa chapter until the late 1980s—the fact that I made it into the regional semifinals was considered a marvelous coup for the school. In anticipation of my interview—to be conducted, somewhat peculiarly, everyone thought, in the early evening at the newly refurbished Sea-Tac airport—I was "prepped" incessantly by a crack team of withered male professors. The group included a temporizing, semicretinous sociology prof whose main contribution was to observe I had "attractive hands" (unlike the Strewelpeter rest of me, presumably) and that I should accentuate all my answers to questions with graceful hand movements. (He demonstrated to loathsome effect.) They were worried, obviously, that I was eccentric—no doubt a bit troubled—and that given my well-known man-hating propensities would bomb out without some kind of last-minute makeover. My feminism in full spate, I was obliged to rail to friends afterward about what disgusting patriarchal pigs they all were.

They were right to be worried, though not in the way one might have expected. A day or two before the event, my interviewer, a humanities professor at one of the regional state universities, phoned me to arrange logistical details. His name was Keith, he said, and he was responsible for meeting with all the Dog Food Fellowship candidates of Oregon, Washington, Idaho, Utah, and Montana over the next week—hence the evening date at Sea-Tac. Having decided where we would wait for one another, he asked me what I'd be wearing so he would recognize me. I made some remark about our conversation being like that of two spies arranging an exchange of secret dossiers. We both laughed. Already I liked him. He would be in a blue work shirt, corduroy pants, and cowboy boots, he said: such informality suited him. I responded by saying I'd probably be wearing an Indian cotton ethnic-looking turquoise dress. The latter garment was in fact the only dress I owned, and while hardly appropriate by present-day standards, was the only thing I had that remotely approximated an interview outfit. Although so short, hemline-wise, one had to wonder if it was really meant to be some sort of tunic or long shirt (a peplum, perhaps?)—it had, nonetheless, a certain Pier One Imports *je ne sais quoi*. I used to wear it with a pair of baggy-kneed mushroom-colored tights I'd bought under Phoebe's tutelage, and thus arrayed, imagined myself the very cynosure of hippy-chick chic. (If one *had* to be female, after all, one might as well be Janis Joplin.) On the afternoon before the interview I made an unusual concession to decorum by deciding *not* to wear my usual red print bandanna tied around my brow Apache-style, a countercultural fashion I had recently adopted with enthusiasm.

Karen drove me up to Sea-Tac in her rusty yellow Datsun: the plan was for her to pass the time reading in the airport while I had the interview, then we'd drive back. Keith, my interviewer, turned out to be instantly spottable: he was in his early forties, loose and lanky and boyishly handsome, with wavy brown hair and airy blue eyes that matched his work shirt. Unlike most professors I'd ever seen, he seemed vital, friendly, up-to-date. Had the hair been a little bit longer or less kempt, he might indeed have passed as an unusually good-looking member of a rock group—someone in Creedence Clearwater Revival, say, or maybe Country Joe and the Fish. And now that I think about him again, thirty years later, I realize he also bore some resemblance to George Plimpton: the same lazy-eyed, WASPy, good-sport affability. He was popping gum and smiling whimsically at everyone around him. Later on he would smoke a yellow corn-cob pipe. Once I'd identified myself to him, Karen wandered off—looking slightly ill at ease, I descried—and he and I sat down for our interview in one of the airport's spiffy new lounge areas.

For reasons that will become clear in a moment, it is difficult for me to remember much of this first phase of the evening. Keith's opening gambit has stayed with me, nonetheless, for three decades. The Dog Food people had asked that fellowship candidates give evidence of a religious/ethical commitment of one sort or another—not necessarily Christian, but something to indicate a thoughtful engagement with the spiritual life. I must have concocted some suitable white noise on the subject for my application essay—but whether I had declared myself a Taoist, a Gnostic, or a worshipper of Kali the Destroyer, I can't recollect. Keith, however, went straight to it—my personal cosmology. Subjects more numinous than Ph.D. programs and research projects, it seemed, were to be our focus.

Keith prefaced everything by saying that he was going to ask me some "odd" questions about my life and beliefs, but that if any query troubled me, I might *choose not to go down that road*. He gave me a glowing look when he said this last; he didn't want to be "oppressive," he assured me, or take advantage of his apparent position of power and authority. Nor would he get too far into my "personal head space" if I didn't want him to. That said, his first question was still ultrabizarre. It took the form of a Sufi parable to which I was to respond, as if on the analyst's couch, with "whatever came to mind."

A man is looking for a lost key. Another man comes to help him look. They can't find it. The other man says, where did you lose it? The

first says in the house. The other man asks, why then are we look-
ing for it here in the garden? Because the light is better here, says
the first.

Now it's true, under normal circumstances, being asked to embellish ("without censorship") on a kooky little wisdom-tale like
this one should have been right up my alley. (*Ooh . . . yeah . . . I get*
it . . . Wow. The LIGHT *is better* here. . . . .) But I was dumbstruck.
All I could think of was that Keith, still smiling beatifically at me,
was amazing—warm, trippy, charming, colloquial, nothing like the
person I had imagined or (*hah*) that my evil, square, and desiccated
team of mock-interviewers had prepared me for. A Sufi parable? The
real riddle, perhaps, was who was the stunning "Keith"? A shaman?
A helper from another realm? Some sort of magus figure—like the
one in the John Fowles novel or Hesse's *Glass Bead Game?* He obviously possessed some refined and uncanny magic. For a man of his
age, I noted, he had smooth well-preserved skin and fantastic wet
dark eyelashes. I was frankly astonished, yet at the same time felt
relaxed with him, in an almost metaphysical sense. As he continued
looking deeply into my eyes I experienced a hot rush of gratitude: he
acted as if he *knew* me—down to the squalid core—and was nonetheless prepared to cherish everything about me.

Granted, when it came, my answer was girlish and muzzy—some
not very good made-up thing about how the light was "like life"
and the house was "death." I was trying to sound spiritual and deep.
No doubt he sensed the spuriousness, however, for with what I immediately took to be yogic omniscience he told me that I had not
yet brought all of my intuitive "power" to bear on the situation—I
wasn't really opening up to him. My psychic energy, usually febrile,
was somehow *blocked.*

Me? Not using my intuitive power? Not opening up? *Blocked?*
However gently proffered, this criticism of my visionary faculties

could not go unmet. Though dimly aware I still wasn't exactly re-
sponding to the Sufi thing, I began blathering away fairly wildly on
the theme of "blockage" itself—how it reminded me of the radical
psychiatrist Wilhelm Reich's concept of *armoring*: the harmful binding of orgasm energy—"orgone," in Reichian lingo—that modern
society supposedly produced in human beings, resulting in war, destruction, neurosis, and Having-a-Pole-Up-One's-Ass on a global
scale. I had recently seen *WR: Mysteries of the Organism*, Dusan
Makaveyev's X-rated 1970 documentary about Reich, and had been
much impressed. As far as I was concerned, WR was a martyr in the
struggle for sexual enlightenment. (*The Food and Drug Administration
imprisoned him for quackery in 1956! He died in prison! How grotesque!
How sadly typical of our fucked-up country!*) To channel the precious
orgone in a healthful manner (or so I seemed to recall from several
eye-popping scenes in the movie), you either had to sit in the nude
in an orgone box—a sort of copper-lined Porta-Potty that somehow
attracted cosmic rays—or else set off cascading multiple orgasms in
yourself by lying supine, arching your back, and hyperventilating
with the aid of a half-undressed Reichian massage therapist.

Yet these disjoint comments were all it took. In what was clearly a
mind-boggling instance of Jungian synchronicity, it turned out that
Keith—who had been listening to my WR divagation with a wry
little buddha-grin on his face—knew all about orgone boxes: he had
even *sat in one* while undergoing a course of Reichian therapy with his
"lover, Jan." (No one said *partner* in those days, but his frank word
for her was still startling.) I must have seemed curious or else simply
gaped in amazement, for he then began to elaborate in increasingly
vivid terms. He enthused about the liberated Jan; their relationship, he said, just like those Wilhelm Reich advocated, was at once
open, free, and deeply erotic. He was missing her greatly while he
was on the road. No, they weren't into sexual possessiveness, he said;
the best relationships were uncoercive—self-actualizing for both

members of the couple. Both he and Jan had other lovers. Yet thanks to the orgone therapy and similar ventures he and Jan were now sexual "equals." He especially had evolved under the aegis of feminism and realized that the clitoris was as important, "spiritually and every other way," as the penis. He had become far more nurturing. In several respects, he noted winsomely, he was now even more "female" than Jan was.

Needless to say, the Sufi parable—not to mention the Dog Food Fellowship—had been forgotten. But Keith now wanted to know more of *my* thoughts—on eros, feminism, penises, and the like—and I in turn, animated by his example, had become as eager to reveal myself as any boa-shedding exhibitionist. It was as if, beautiful eyelashes fluttering, he had given me a vial of truth serum.

While ponderous, elliptical, and half-mad, the epic journal entry I composed the day after our meeting shows frame-by-frame, Zapruder-style, how bad things quickly became. I began it with a blowsy endorsement of my companion, followed by some woozy metaphysical speculation and the obligatory I Chingiana:

> *I met him last night as a sorcerer, yet who was all good. Like the idea of God I had been thinking about—that God contained both good and evil, yet chose to be good, in the same way that mortals must choose that. When he talked about alpha waves, he said you know that I won't do anything to fuck you over. I knew that, and I knew he had chosen the path of benevolence. The Helper.*
>
> *He said the airport was unreal.*
>
> *When he began to come across—it reminded me of that hexagram I got last week, 48, Yî, Augmenting. Yî indicates that (in the state which it denotes) there will be advantage in every movement which shall be undertaken, that it will be advantageous (even) to cross the great stream.*
>
> *The wall made out of water? You pass through it?*

(No answer possible to these last, self-posed rhetorical queries, I guess—so on to a description of some of Keith's other questions.)

Did I think, he asked, I would have to support a lover, ever?——

(I can't recall why this bizarre question came up; nor—to Blakey's exasperation—what I said in reply. B. remains curious: What if she wants to take early retirement and live out her days at a spa-ranch in Arizona? Do I promise to *shell out?*)

Then—how many of my teachers in college had I fallen in love with? I gulped, thought for a long time. I thought about H., and said one, and he said only one? Puzzlement. Then I said why did you ask me that question—he said Far Out, because I'm trying to get a sense of you on sex and teaching, and where your erotic dispensation is. I said there won't be much for you to pick up because I am consciously blocking it—then I told him I was homosexual; right away he understood all that had gone before, it all came clear. He wanted to know if I was out of the closet, and I said I hadn't told my mother. . . . He said how good it would feel to come out. He felt like he understood gayness. He had several gay friends. He himself loved women—indeed worshipped the female genitals especially— but with Jan's expert help, he had realized that some time in his life he would like to make love to a cock. He thought he might quite enjoy giving another man head.

If I'd had any residual doubts about Keith's bona fides, I suppressed them forthwith.

I told him I was surprised by how much I had revealed about myself, but he said Christ Terry that's where we live. He didn't seemed surprised by my telling him I was gay, had instead been waiting for it.

Prospero > alpha waves. The strangest thing—that his face kept changing; when I first saw him I thought that can't be him he is far too young; later at the table when he smoked his corncob pipe and the light shone up from the bowl of his pipe to his face he seemed old, older than anyone. Inca-land. Ally, bodhisattva, animus, Jungian shadow, hero with a thousand faces.

Plus, one had to admit it: for a man, he was flattering and super-nice:

He described myself to me—he said I had an incredible, overwhelming amount of power, but that I had not decided how to use it yet and was not using it. He said that when I did everything was just going to take off.

My momentary depression (still in the old world of success/failure) but as we walked onto the drawbridge to get stoned, he told me I did not have to worry about surviving.

The reference here to a "drawbridge" and getting stoned? A key part of the evening, I'm afraid. At a certain point any pretence we were having an interview dissolved and with a disarming giggle Keith asked me if I would like to go smoke hashish with him. I assented as if in a trance and the next thing I knew found myself drifting out with him, like the eponymous heroine of *La Sonnambula*, onto the pedestrian bridge that connected the terminal with the upper level of the new multistory airport parking lot. (All this took place, of course, in those long-lost innocent days before antiterrorist bollards, no-go zones, closed-circuit video cameras, and endless security checks.) Once we'd found a secluded spot, behind a massive concrete pillar, Keith brought out a honking great spliff, stogie-sized in fact, which we then proceeded to smoke, furtively, right down to the roach.

The effects were instantaneous and phantasmagoric. Already, on our way back into the terminal, we were goofing happily: he looked at me with puckish pride and said, *I perceive that your mind is somewhat blown*. I found this hilarious, a *bon mot* worthy of Voltaire. He seemed delighted by the way everything was working out and asked me to join him for a delicious dope-enhanced supper in the airport VIP restaurant, courtesy of the Dog Food Foundation. This invitation too I dreamily accepted. (I had forgotten all about Karen and the drive back; she might as well have been sucked flailing and screaming into a black hole.) She later said she'd seen us, an hour or so after the interview was supposed to have ended, walking apparently aimlessly around the airport together, looking flushed and dazed.

We had entered a new and somewhat spongiform reality. And thus we dallied, on the way to supper, taking it all in: the brand-new plastic seats and pristine industrial carpeting, the businessmen carrying garment bags, the See's chocolate kiosk. At a certain point, as if yielding to yet another King-of-the-Fairies fancy, Keith took me by the arm and plopped me down in a row of seats in front of a large wall panel composed of randomly pulsing colored lights. The panel was the size of a small billboard and the lights, several hundred of them, flashed on and off like bulbs blinking on an old-fashioned switchboard. The thing appeared to be a high-tech artwork of some kind. *Whatever.* (As one's students are wont to say.) The light patterns were psychedelic and I was soon mesmerized. Keith sat down next to me and, as always, smiling agreeably, began watching, too.

After a while (five minutes? fifteen minutes? an hour?) he leaned over, took hold of both my arms, and placed them carefully and symmetrically on the armrests of my seat. Almost as soon as he touched them, the appendages in question began to feel more like flippers than arms: floppy, uncanny, and still at least a million years away from evolving anything useful like hands, let alone fingernails or opposable thumbs. Getting a manicure would have been impossible. The lights went on blinking hypnotically. He was now going to do something amazing, Keith said—if I trusted him, that was, and he thought by this point I did. The amazing "something," it turned out, would involve the all-important alpha waves—mine and his, mysteriously working together. Once he counted down from ten, he said, I would no longer be able to lift my arms up from the armrests or my feet up from the floor. It would be as if *the world's strongest glue were holding them down. I would not be able to* BUDGE. I couldn't wait; it sounded fantastic.

And in turn, hardly had the promised countdown begun than I felt myself yield, as much to the magical aura Keith seemed to diffuse around him as to the hypnotic suggestion (utterly irresistible) in his voice. By the time he reached "one" I was thoroughly petrified: stiff, euphoric, arms stuck to the armrests, my feet grafted to the floor. I resembled an Egyptian tomb effigy, some butch lady-pharoah immobilized on her massive throne. I had that total Hatshepsut thing going on. The only items missing were the square headdress and false beard.

The sensation of paralysis was dizzyingly pleasurable. Millennia seemed to pass. Yet like a cosmic hum the pleasure continued. Periodically, Keith and I gazed down together at my motionless hands and feet and giggled conspiratorially. Every now and then I'd try to wiggle a digit—unsuccessfully—and we'd giggle some more. As the hung-over dharma-diarist would put it the next day:

> *We were doing it as one impulse, one concern, and we rejoiced in that unity. . . . He was giving an instruction to me, about my own body, but I was agreeing to, consenting to, the instruction, AT THE SAME TIME, simultaneously with its offering. Terms, manipulation and passivity did not apply to our activity.*

Take that, boring dodos. In the end Keith must have released me from my position and helped me up; for my next memory is of the two of us in the restaurant, drinking wine and gobbling down huge forkfuls of orange Coho salmon and baked potato over candlelight. I remember marveling to myself—as if I'd entered the realm of Heideggerian *Dasein—this is the most exquisite baked potato I have ever eaten.* The butter pat, the sour cream, the freeze-dried chives: every luscious explosion on the palate seemed a new ontological token, a guarantor of Absolute Being.

At the same time, as a student of shamanistic encounters, I knew I had been absorbed into Baked Potato–ness—interpolated into the Absolute—for a reason. Shortly after we had finished and our plates had been whisked away, I was hardly surprised when my wizard-companion, now rakishly sucking on his corncob pipe, articulated the Deeper Purpose of Everything with a charming, half-playful grin. *Would I like to go back with him to his hotel room for more wine and pot? He liked me oh so much; he was getting off on imagining how it all was being in my shoes. It would be such a great honor for him; he cared for me—me Terry—so very much.* For a moment I was jubilant. I loved his gentle Brother Sun–Sister Moon face, his curls, and his pinkness—everything in fact about him. I felt I had known him forever, as if he had given birth to me in some primal act of couvade, like one of those tender androgynous male mothers in Ursula K. Le Guin's *Left Hand of Darkness.* A great singing began. He was beautiful—as rich and miraculous and fruit-bearing as a woman. I was tempted.

Yet at the same time, in some odd reflexive fashion, I also knew that I had to decline. I knew he would be kind about it. He was a Loving not a Savage God. He looked rueful for a second then gave me a big smile and didn't press me further. And I, with my usual stunned-ox oblivi-ousness—the certainty that I had to refuse being unrelieved, in the moment, by any real understanding of why I was doing it—was happy enough to shrink politely back into my lovely, lonely, calcareous shell:

I said I'm sorry it's hard for me to do these eye-contact things, and he smiled and crinkled up his face saying he understood, folded his hands on the table, and looked up at me now and again like a funny animal, a cat or a dog, making me laugh in spite of myself. I felt a depth of love in myself that was tremendous, like a great cleansing, and a deep beauty.

A deep enema, I should perhaps have written, for though we parted soon enough—regretfully on both sides—this was hardly the end of the story. With a courtly wave Keith vanished back into the alternative dimension from which he'd come. In a trice Karen had suddenly rematerialized and as if rounding up a lost sheep, began walking me back to the parking garage. I told her what had happened in a sort of glossolaliac loon-burst. (I was still fairly druggy.) I'm sure I must have sounded completely insane, as if I'd been chloroformed and stuffed in a car trunk for two hours and yet claimed to have found the experience more delightful than anything that had ever happened to me. Karen was plainly disturbed—both by my story and my strange gabby-glorified state. She tut-tutted audibly, looked suspiciously around in the back seat before unlocking either of the car doors, and to my dismay, said she found it "terrifying" that someone with Keith's "mystical power" was wandering around incognito in the Sea-Tac airport. It reminded her, she said, of those archdevils, the Jesuits. Was I sure he'd been a wholly benign presence? I remonstrated indignantly until I beat her down and made her change her tune. Okay, she said— well, maybe he *was* a good spirit, after all, a version perhaps of the Alchemical Androgyne, like that character in Cocteau's *Euridice*? Eutebus? Some name like that. It was possible, anyway. Placated for the time being by this hypothesis, I continued to rave about Keith and his marvelous doings almost all the way home, until I finally conked out, there in the passenger seat—mushroom tights askew and head lolling forward, like that of a Hogarthian wastrel after a debauch.

The denouement was swift and crushing, though again I didn't grasp the finer points for some time. Various people wanted to know how the Dog Food Fellowship interview had gone and I was happy to tell them—including one of my fellow students, a poufy-haired, platform-heeled gay guy named Arthur, who, as it happened, was also competing for graduate fellowships. The personal situation, as I should have seen, was potentially flammable: Arthur was a moody disco-queen in the making (though none of us knew it at the time; *Saturday Night Fever* was not to be released until 1977) and I was clearly the more successful young scholar. Yet blind to the possibility that Arthur might be less than pleased by my visionary adventures, I had babbled on excitedly about Keith and the airport and the dope, the Sufi parable, the blinking lights, and the sheer sublimity of it all. The treacherous Arthur—but who on earth could blame him?—at once told one of our professors, a decent, upright, uptight fellow named Fred, who promptly summoned me into his office for interrogation.

At this point the whole affair seemed to morph into one of those sinister varsity "coming of age" dramas in which everyone ends up getting betrayed, committing suicide, or joining a nunnery: *The Prime of Miss Jean Brodie*, or *A Separate Peace*, perhaps, or better yet, Donna Tartt's scabrous *Secret History*. Fred wasted no time: he asked me point blank about the hash-smoking and the hypnosis business. Had Keith *handed me a marijuana cigarette*? I was as stunningly forthright in response as I was about everything in those days. For what had I to be ashamed of? It had been an Utterly Transcendent Experience. Keith was totally cool—Fred wouldn't know about *that*, obviously—and besides what was the fuss about? It was 1975, after all.

Fred was clearly still worried, however, and asked me if I wanted him to follow up in some way with the Dog Food Foundation. The whole thing remained highly irregular. Absolutely not: I was fairly squittering with self-righteousness by this point. *But what if I didn't get a fellowship because of the way Keith had handled things?* Whether I got a Dog Food Fellowship didn't matter, I replied in a huff; the point had been the encounter itself. *That's fine for you*, Fred persisted, *but what about other candidates, any of whom might have gone in your stead and had a more conventional, possibly fellowship-winning experience?* I didn't care: Fate had not ordained it thus. Outraged by his tired old busybody ways I demanded that Fred definitely *not* pursue the matter officially—a demand to which he reluctantly acceded. I was stern—like a Pope with intellectual leanings, laying down a particularly blood-chilling encyclical.

I didn't get a Dog Food Fellowship. A letter informing me came a few weeks after the talk with Fred. While I sometimes wondered what Keith had said about me in his report—for I found that even though no prize was to be mine I had been "named to the Honorable Mention List of Applicants"—I was not especially upset. I figured that Keith, no-bullshit ace-guy that he was, had probably told the Dog Food Foundation about my lesbianism—maybe even said that I'd announced it during the interview. (*Very courageously*, I now thought.) The fellowship committee—no doubt a bastion of prejudice and hypocrisy—had likely repulsed my application for that reason. *Pfah!* When Fred and my other professors tried, gingerly, to commiserate with me over my lack of success, I was scornful; all I would say was I had revealed a piece of possibly incriminating "personal" information during the interview and that it had obviously been used against me by some hostile and primitive moron.

But it was true I didn't really care. My own weird little projects, like the now-chaste affair with Karen, went on afoot; my graduate school plans seemed unaffected. For no particular reason other than I was curious about a part of the country I had never seen (though in truth I hadn't actually seen *any* part of the country besides the West Coast at that point) I had decided to go to one of the big Midwestern state schools for my Ph.D. I was alone in this somewhat whimsical decision: neither of my divorced parents, British expatriates both, had gone to college; nor had either of them any knowledge of American universities. I hardly saw them, anyway. I hadn't been back to San Diego for over a year. (I wouldn't go back for another year either.) Through all of this period my mother was largely immersed in her own concerns (depressive-fractious husband, sociopath stepson); my ever-distant father, now married to his third wife, remained conspicuously aloof whenever the question of my educational career came up. To judge by his few, and grudging, comments on the matter, he seemed to resent the fact I had academic ambitions at all. When I'd graduated from high school, he had wanted me to get a secretarial job and take night classes at the local junior college. Though presumably well off—he was a highly skilled aeronautical engineer—he had seen fit not to fund any part of my higher education. It wasn't part of the divorce settlement.

So that was the lay of the land, parent-wise. I was used to it, though, and even more used to winning grants and scholarships—which I proceeded to do in short order. The Dog Food decision was moot in the end: when it came time to decide *which* big Midwestern school—and they all seemed pretty interchangeable to me—I had my choice of fellowships and funding packages. It was simply a matter of pinning the tail on the donkey. I opted for the one that offered me the best stipend. Reinforcing my decision: One of the radical feminist magazines I doted on was published in the city in which the school was located; that too, seemed a promising augury. Between the financial aid I was to receive and the fact I knew I would still be able to get food stamps—I had drawn them all through college (*thank you, Lyndon Baines Johnson!*)—I believed I was indeed pretty well set up. A month or so after my college graduation—a ceremony ungraced, apart from Karen, by friend or family member—I left for the heartland and the unseen institution, selected more or less at random, on my way to what seemed to me a delightfully cushy berth in another universe entirely.

Yet though I'd left the scene, the fellowship imbroglio continued to sputter on. Someone wrote to me later that fall (Karen? Davy?) to say everybody was talking about it: amid a swirl of rumors, the Dog Food Foundation had abruptly relieved Keith, my quondam interviewer, of his position as its regional representative. He was in official disgrace. I too was in some sort of disgrace-by-association, it seemed; the story now was I hadn't received a fellowship because the people in charge thought I had shown appalling bad judgment. Arthur was apparently exultant. I was horrified: someone higher up than Arthur—some malicious *professor*, I feared—had obviously snitched in turn.

My first urge was to apologize—in a sort of abject panic—to Keith himself. Admittedly, I wanted to exculpate myself; given all the embarrassment, I figured he must be infuriated with me. But far more important, I remember thinking, I *cared* about him. At the first news of his humiliation, my feelings for Keith had become as tender and protective as Joan of Arc's for her feeble Dauphin. I wanted to kneel before him in my chain mail, pledge undying troth, and stanchions unfurled, lead his troops to victory once again—all in the name of God, Holy France, dope, and blinking lights.

Not knowing how to contact Keith—such things were unfathomable in those pre-Google days and besides, I wasn't altogether sure of his last name—I had to make do with Fred, whom I strongly suspected of being the Vile Snitch. I still have in my possession copies of two long typewritten screeds I sent Fred that fall and winter, my first in the Midwest. They are fluent, principled, full of aggrieved expostulation, and as pompous and callow as one might imagine. In the first, written soon after I heard that Keith had been dismissed, I blasted Fred for his deception: he had tricked me that past spring, I complained, into revealing incriminating details about the Dog Food interview; then, against my wishes, had used the confidential information to calumniate my pot-smoking, orgone-channeling hero:

The incident [i.e., the hash-smoking interlude] in no way represented part of an intellectual seduction or Mephistophelian maneuver—it came at a time when we were just two people relating in a certain way to each other, unofficially and completely privately. I explained all this to you, and reiterated my absolute confidence in [K.]. I noted . . . that I felt he had accommodated his interviewing techniques very effectively (and professionally) to my own personality and needs at the time.

Once I was launched, it became hard to stop. "What grieves me most of all is to think that there has been a horrendous mix-up of values in the whole business," I railed:

I thought, over-idealistically perhaps, the point of the Dog Food enterprise was to make for a more humanistic and humane spirit in the academic world by aiding those people who expressed concern for such values. [K.] embodies this "Dog Food effort" in his whole approach: he was above all a humane interviewer, concerned for me as a person (which is more than I can say for my college "trainers"). His courtesy and compassion were evident to me; and my judgment in this is neither naïve or "schoolgirlish."

While I am glad to see that in classic anxious-autodidact fashion, I had learned enough at this stage in my scholarly life to know that "judgment" was spelled with only one *e* (or that that, at least, was the more *elegant* spelling), it is not clear I possessed any great portion of the faculty in question.

My second letter—composed after the turn of the year—was worse. Fred had replied to my first one, I see from my journal, with a heated (now unfortunately lost) "philosophical cannonade." I was full of self-pity and world weariness by this time, discouraged by the fact that he and the other teachers had ignored my all too justified plaints. I thought of myself as officially sadder but wiser. And though I conceded that the whole experience was one I would "probably have to think about more," I claimed to be determined, in martyr-like fashion, not to hold a grudge against rank double dealers like Fred. ("*What am I supposed to do now—kick myself for being grotesquely naïve? shut up entirely from now on? stop trusting people?*") At the end of this second missive—to which I don't believe Fred, sensibly enough, ever replied—I gave a bemused, quasi-valedictory account of my doings, now that I found myself, in the flat dead of winter, amid "the miles of snow plains." Ominously—or so it appears in retrospect—I see I was still "reading up on Sir Thomas Browne, alchemy, Jung, and Neumann." The Great Mother still had me gripped, blind and mewling, in her cavernous inner spaces. Yet there were other elements to freeze the spirit—if only, again, in hindsight. "*I am also finding an outlet and support for my poems in* Your Mama Wears Army Boots, *a local feminist magazine*," I wrote proudly. And yes, though I didn't record the fact anywhere other than in my journal, between the first letter to Fred and the second I had met Her: my smiling and savage Professor.

The Professor

AFTER ALL THE BUILDUP, I confess I find it a struggle to recapture, amid the glints and wipes and warp zones of memory, every aspect of the Professor's supercharged allure. I had to work so hard to forget her—to escort her out of the building, so to speak—that it is difficult to go back now and take note of her magnetism: to allow her her rightful nimbus, her full, devastating share of importance in my life. No doubt certain once-charmed memories were banished long ago out of psychic necessity; telling details have blown out to sea. The Professor seems at times curiously effigy-like to me now:

straw filled, hypothetical, more mannequin or puppet-form than real woman. And when it comes to the quotidian details that impart life and breath and romance, it is safe to say I know my cat Theo far better than I ever knew her. Easy enough, were this essay called *The Kitty Cat*, to vamp at length about the latter's digestive likes and dislikes, fey psychic quirks, and the usual breathtaking feline heartlessness. I have enough dope on Theo, moral and otherwise, to plot future trends. Should I suffer a fatal collapse one day and my corpse lie undiscovered for weeks, decomposing on the kitchen floor, she's exactly the sort of kitty, I realize—dainty and impervious—who would happily feed off it for the duration. Not much sentiment there. I've had Theo for fourteen years (long before B. and I got the dogs); I knew the Professor for barely six months.

And six months, of course, is no time at all. I have no idea what the Professor's favorite color was; if she had lots of aunts and uncles and cousins or just one or two; if she suffered from any allergies. I would be curious, now, to know what she thought of assorted events and people from the intervening years—the Clintons or the Bushes, say, or the 9/11 hijackers. That creepy Mohammed Atta. True, I still recall the Professor's birthday. It fell in late April; she even celebrated one (her forty-first or forty-second?) toward the end of our debacle. I remember going to her office that slushy spring day to give her a present (the McGarrigle Sisters' first LP) and just how awkwardly she took it from me, as if I'd handed her a dead rat by its tail. The damage by that point had been done. The Professor was nearly twenty years older than I was—of an age to be my mother; or perhaps, given the deep voice and salt-and-pepper hair—silver in places—my father. She died of stomach cancer a couple of years ago, I heard, in her early seventies.

Regarding what might be called her *soul*, I had no time to collect much more than the most rudimentary data. And what material I did gather I had little way of comprehending. I received the signals all right: indeed, there I sat, rapt in my headphones, in front of the radar screen, recording all the blips and squeaks. But I had no means of decoding them intelligibly. Perhaps Alan Turing or some other Bletchley Park wizard might have been up to the job, but I—shy, feral, and still emotionally frozen at twenty-two—was not. So claggy and baggy and unexamined my own needs then, the needs of other people (as should be clear by now) remained largely invisible to me. I saw through a glass darkly. And besides, how could a being as wondrous as the Professor even *have* needs? She was a sun-god, a sort of lady-Phoebus Apollo. She flooded out all one's somewhat fragile circuits. When she withdrew, leaving me in pitch blackness, I found myself as close to snuffed out as it is possible to be. Easy enough to turn melodramatic and Curse the Night. Yet the *soul* was indisputably there: it was, I realize now, what I loved about her. But it got lost very soon in the shuffle.

And easy enough, too, to deliver, like a volley of shellfire, the caricature version: the Professor as Hoary Mean Thing, camp, supersized and frightful, with all the glaring, eyeball-popping, Joan-Crawford-as-Mildred-Pierce mannerisms intact. I've delivered such blasts many times over the past thirty years. The Professor was my very own bespoke *monstre sacrée* for so long—so long the resident she-Minotaur in my private psychic labyrinth—that I developed, fairly early in the game, what might be called a Professorial *shtick:* a narrative, often comic, in which the more Grand Guignol aspects of our relationship became fodder, in the presence of others, for a catharsis at once reviving and entertaining. The Professor, I had to admit, made great copy. There were enough details—Flaubertian or Freudian—to make one feel marvelously suave and blasé after the fact: the Very Weird Long Grey Braid; the Withered Leg, the Loaded Pistol in the Bedside Drawer (often to be taken out and examined during lovemaking); the Room in Her House One Was Never Allowed to Enter; the Gruesome Crime-Scene Photos, Bloody and Horrific, she once showed me (again after sex) from a murder trial she had been involved in once as an expert witness.

All zany enough, to be sure. Yet far more intriguing to me now is a rather more mysterious issue: how the Professor and I came to collide so disastrously in the first place. Who was responsible? Which of us was more to blame? No way around it: the Professor precipitated a series of near-ruinous events in my life. Not fatal, but close enough. It would be disingenuous—especially having written paragraphs like some of the above—for me to say I have never yearned for revenge. Writing, I'm convinced, is often nothing *but* revenge—a way of twirling one's mustache, donning buckler and sword and feathery hat, shaking one's gauntleted fist at the gods. You get to be Puss-in-Boots-on-a-Tear. And why shouldn't you? What other feeling is one supposed to have after one gets clobbered? Okay: Jesus Christ left some notes in the Suggestion Box. Yet few people ever seem to heed them while tangled in this mortal coil.

Equally disingenuous would it be, however, for me to suggest the Professor intended every aspect of my unhappiness or that I was not already in a fairly perilous emotional state when I met her. Perhaps because I find myself advancing with such disturbing rapidity through middle age—and have indeed been a professor myself for some twenty-plus years—I feel able to be rather more thoughtful now about the whole business. Coolly diagnostic, even. With the advantage of years I've started pondering again just what it was about her that drew me to her: what peculiar pathos she evinced, and why I was so vulnerable to it. For pathos it surely was.

Some of it, yes, was plainly visible: the Professor had suffered from polio at the age of twelve or thirteen; one leg was shorter than the other and noticeably atrophied. She had a herky-jerky way of walking and was unable to run (if you could even call it that) other than in a halting and chaotic fashion. The infirmity did not prevent her from taking intense pride in her athleticism; she relished the challenge of her handicap and the sympathetic attention (mostly from young women like myself) that it brought her. Having become adept at a sort of crab-like sideways scuttling and lunging, she managed to play badminton and tennis with some success (doubles especially) and even threw herself into a game of softball now and then—butch and hearty and gym teacher–ish in nylon windbreaker and stretch pants—if, that is, some fleet of foot surrogate were allowed to run the bases for her. This buoyant response to misfortune, her sheer gaiety and éclat under the circumstances, epitomized for me gallantry of an absolute sort. It was as if she bore a fencing scar: some ancient and noble wound suffered in an affair of honor.

But many things about the Professor drew my sympathy—drew, indeed, my lonely and passionate love. Some of them, I see now, had more to do with me than with her. Or with something deranging that happened when the two of us were together. I'm hoping here, obviously, to make some sense of my obsession with her, though I hasten to add I don't expect to "make sense" of the Professor herself. I'm becoming less sure one *can* make sense of certain individuals. The Professor's kindness and brutality offset one another so perfectly—were so freakishly counterbalanced, one against the other—it would be foolish to try to make her personality "cohere" in retrospect. It didn't. There was no way it could. The Professor was a hybrid, a sort of unicorn. And besides, I'm now well aware of a similar, if less severe, incoherence in myself. No matter what one does, it seems, certain warring parts of the psyche never really get reconciled. The much-touted "integration" never happens. The least one can hope for, then—? That at some point my mixed-up memories of her and much else might simply *expire*: like coupons for a defunct rug-cleaning service or an old take-out menu lying in the dry leaves on my porch. Then might a lesson be said to be learned: *I'll be expiring myself, of course—no doubt soon enough. After a while no one will remember either of us.*

So on to the new Scene of Life. I noted earlier that a certain scary precocity as a Student was one of the factors that made me so susceptible to the Professor. To that might be added the frightening isolation I felt upon arriving in my new (and strange) Grain Belt home. The alien corn, indeed. I might as well have landed on Mars: so thoroughly lost was I, I didn't realize *how* lost. I'd arrived, it's true, somewhat unpropitiously: an acquaintance at my former college had a friend in the new city, a woman named Mindy, the scion of a wealthy department store family. My schoolmate had arranged for me to stay with Mindy for a few days while I searched for an apartment. Yet when I arrived, that hot and airless August morning, and called my putative hostess, she immediately disclaimed all knowledge of the arrangement. (*Fie, thou still-unknown Mindy! What a cruel minx thou wert! Perhaps thou shalt send me thy overdue apology now?*) At the taxi driver's suggestion I ended up—though carless—staying in a shabby motor inn downtown, seemingly untenanted apart from me, from whence I immediately began the quest for more permanent lodging by perusing all the local bus maps and classified ads.

As I climbed into the first of many buses later that day, I confronted a ruddy, blue-eyed, pink-cheeked older man, happily perched, like a bouncy six-year-old, on the plastic banquette seat behind the driver. As soon as I'd paid my fare and taken the seat across from him, he gave me an enchanting smile and held out his arms in greeting. He wore a pair of ancient high-top sneakers and despite the heat, a long, flowing muffler. These sartorial accoutrements gave him a certain resemblance to the eccentric tapir-like protagonist of Edward Gorey's *The Doubtful Guest*—a mysterious furry creature who arrives inexplicably at one's front door, politely takes a seat on the living room sofa, and then, without ever saying a word, proceeds to stay on forever.

With the swift unerring friendliness of the truly mad, the smiling man got right to the point: *would I be his* PEN PAL? I must have appeared startled because he suddenly looked mournful and frightened and said being pen pals would actually be *wonderful*: his name was Dick, after all. I was even more disconcerted by this last statement and still wondering what to say when he broke into an excited and chummy gabble. *What's your name/who are you/where are you going?* He was feeling so so happy, he squeaked: *You remind me so much of my daughter!* He had a poem by Edgar Guest he wanted me to read, he exclaimed, and here he actually started to pull a piece of grubby paper from his pocket. By this time, however, I had already lurched off down the aisle and found another seat as far from him as possible. I watched him warily for several blocks. He got off soon enough, though not without a last wistful look in my direction. Yes, disbelieving readers: Dick *is* my father's name. (*Oh, THAT explains everything!*) Oh, shut up.

To judge by the diary entries I kept those first months I went a bit cuckoo myself. I wrote in my journal, indeed, with the enthusiasm of a Victorian onanist—usually no fewer than five or six times a day. My solitariness—in the new place, and more broadly, in the world— seemed absolute and intractable, the sort of thing one can't shake even when one somehow *does*, miraculously enough, get to know a few people. It's true that on one level I was functioning more or less adequately: I found an apartment (a somewhat dilapidated one) in an ugly yellow brick building near the campus. And though the term had yet to start, I met some of my fellow graduate students in the English department and recorded my impressions of them. (Rather censoriously, I'm afraid, in a sort of warmed-over Mitford-Sister idiom: "*Last night I attended the grad student beer bust, and it was quite dreadful. Full of young men with beards, older sullen professors. Revolting scenes.*")

One piece of good fortune (though not one I would really be able to cash in on for a while): my first week in the new place, I met a young woman of my own age—now my oldest and truest friend. (Elsbet's coming out for the B & T Wedding Party later this month.) We met by a fluke. A few days after my arrival the couple across the hall in my building invited me to the movies with them and their friends. Elsbet was there—the just-tagging-along roommate of one of the friends. I gave her a splashy journal write-up right away: "*Elsbet: large humorous person in a leaf-green suede coat, whom I met last night. Takes voice lessons and sings opera and Tammy Wynette songs. From Eau Claire, wherever that is, and about to start an M.F.A. in Sculpture at the University*." She was bosomy, robust, comically Norwegian American, and oddly determined to befriend me. I was shy and a bit nonplussed but I liked her at once.

And to the extent that anyone could that autumn, Elsbet managed to lift my spirits in the midst of my disorientation. I reveled (as did she) in her broad Wisconsin accent; she was a gifted raconteuse. I heard all about her crazy old Norwegian aunties and what growing up in Eau Claire was like. So many Bengts, Eriks, Sigrids, and Ingrids: it was like an Old Norse saga. She taught me how to say "you bag of shit" in Norwegian: *Du Drittseck*. Everyone in her family was cultivated, musical, and high achieving; Elsbet, the decidedly non-academic baby. She'd fixed on an art degree, she told me, in part to distinguish herself from her annoyingly talented older siblings. She enjoyed music too, though, and one weekend we drove out of town to see a bearded Garrison Keillor, then still in his twenties and a local radio announcer, do his new live show, *A Prairie Home Companion*. The Red Clay Ramblers were his guests, I think—plus some primitive-looking Viking types (from Tröndheim?) who played Hardanger fiddle. Elsbet kindly explained all the local jokes to me— Powdermilk Biscuits, Norwegian bachelor-farmers, the Chatterbox Café, and all the rest of it. It was corny and fun, but also, like the rather alarming Snow Plow Emergency signs on every street, somewhat alienating to a San Diego girl. *A Prairie Homeless Companion* might have been more appropriate.

And there were limits to what even Elsbet could do. (That our own relationship would not be a romantic one was somehow clear from the start.) You would not have guessed it from her unflappable demeanor, nor indeed the immense good humor, but the very month I met her she had been dumped—somewhat summarily—by her college girlfriend, a tall and gloomy cellist named Amelia. Amelia—vegan and woodswoman—was earnest, judgmental, and reeked of garlic. She was about to decamp for Cremona to learn violin making in the celebrated Guarneri workshop. I met her a couple of times and thought Elsbet well rid of her. (Amelia's notion of bacchanalian excess: to light a candle, brew a mug of chamomile tea, and eat a single square of organic dark chocolate very slowly.) But she'd undoubtedly left grief in her wake—Elsbet seemed pained and put off by Sapphic romance. One result was that when the chaos with the Professor began, I was hesitant to tell Elsbet about it for some time, partly out of a sense of delicacy, shame, embarrassment.

Looking back at my journal entries from those first months I am struck above all by their tone: dismal, tedious, curiously deadened. So Terry-versus-the-Conqueror-Worm. At first it was simply the shock of a drastically new place—one so stark and flat, as I noted for posterity, "you can see everything in a straight line from wherever you are standing"—all the way out to the "pale silver water towers and grain elevators." I missed the blue promise of the Pacific Ocean somewhere over the next hill. (I missed hills, period.) Not to say my sense of geography was any less vague than it had been: Elsbet went away to Chicago one fall weekend and I realized that I didn't know in what direction it lay. (Though the city's magnificent skyscrapers and adjoining natural bathtub, Lake Michigan, would later provide a dramatic backdrop for my checkered romance with the Blakester, I never visited the place until the mid-1990s.) I felt islanded. Meanwhile the late summer heat bore down and my apartment became dank, close, and oppressive. *Wizard of Oz*–style thunderclaps startled me on muggy afternoons; and the resulting cloudbursts, while fierce and cooling, never lasted long enough. Everybody had warned me my new home would be cold; no one had told me it would also be unbearably hot. The Midwestern mosquitoes were another novelty. They viewed me with undisguised glee and took to feasting indoors and out on my pale, easily irritated, all too Anglo-Saxon flesh. Sometimes they came in pairs or trios: well-padded mosquito-matrons lunching at the Four Seasons.

I tried to keep a lifeline going to Karen and the mist-shrouded Pacific Northwest with letters and phone calls, but these on the whole failed to satisfy. The phone calls were expensive, and besides that, Karen, now in her own Ph.D. program in Seattle, had already begun to morph into someone about whom I knew less and less. She seemed to be dating an mysterious unnamed man; I had a creepy suspicion it was my friend Davy—he of Nijinsky and the bird feet. *Arghh!!!* The Invert's Lot Is Not a Happy One. (I had introduced them.) And even at a distance Karen remained dry and intransigent in her refusal to mother. I see from one journal entry—characteristically maudlin—that I asked her over the phone if she "loved me" and her Wittgensteinian reply was *I love this salami I'm eating.* Yes, true enough—sometimes she added a brief, mollifying comment or two, and I, in my fallen-angel exile, made mopey attempts to cultivate a more mature philosophical outlook:

> *Karen refuses to provide pity: I demand it in my letters and she returns with impersonal replies, or at least detached replies. We talked about this a bit: she said one's twenties were awful but even though things were bad now I was "not necessarily doomed to be miserable."*

Yet in the only sense that mattered to me, she had vanished forever. That I might have some misery-free future in store struck me as highly unlikely, and her willingness to imagine one for me as a hollow (and hardly palliative) fare-thee-well.

Nor, needless to say, could my real mother bolster me across the miles. We talked every week or so but she and I were entering a lengthy period during which we would see one another for perhaps two or three days every *other* year. (I saw my father even less often.) My teenaged stepbrother Jeff had begun his stupefying spiral into chaos and brutality, and Dee Dee, one of my stepsisters, barely out of high school, had become seriously addicted to coke and pills. The prissy aesthete in me shuddered even to hear about these step-relations—so tacky, macabre, and fantastical their doings. Nor would the problems end anytime soon. Later, after moving to Wyoming, Dee Dee would have three babies in quick succession—all, according to my mother, born crack-addicted. Her boyfriend, Frankie, weedy and feckless, was a supermarket bag boy, and once after Dee Dee kicked him out, tried to set their mobile home on fire with kerosene and old rags. (She and the kids were asleep inside.) Luckily this homicidal scheme came to naught: Dee Dee woke up, and she and Frankie got back together soon after. Not long ago, my mother told me Frankie had died fairly horribly. While driving around drunk—a quaint Wyoming custom— he had careened into the back of a parked big rig. As in a sick John Waters sight gag, his head was found some distance from the wreck.

Whenever I spoke to my mother, she and Turk were at war, usually about his kids. From my distant and secretive perch I would urge her to divorce him. She would cry over the phone in the heartrending way I remembered from my early childhood. Her health was poor, she would say; she didn't know how she would ever support herself; she was afraid to leave. So on it all went. Even after Turk stopped drinking in the late seventies (cold turkey, so as to feel less of a bad example to Jeff), the doom-laden atmosphere never lifted. He abruptly lost whatever minimal relief and *joie de vivre* the booze had once granted him.

Granted, I dreamed about Mavis fairly often—zany, running-amok dreams, filled with Daliesque, sometimes alarming details:

Crazy dreams last night—Bing Crosby fondling my breasts under my red tee shirt. Paralyzed with horror. My mother in a place I have just realized was the house on Valley Road in Sandgate [the English seaside village where we had lived when I was a child]; said a man had burst in, and had stabbed her a lot of times in the kitchen. But we looked and she had no marks on her. Then the people—the man and his family—came back in a station wagon. Alors, the man's children jumped out of the car, even though I was yelling obscenities at everyone. The kids turned out to be "Maoris." Later, went out to dinner at a place like a Denny's with my mother, Turk, and my sister.

Bing Crosby? Maoris? Denny's? *Alors?* Thirty years on I have no memory of this dream or what—don't ask—it might have betokened.

I counted on the start of the new school year to stabilize me and to some extent it did. However confused I might feel inside, I knew that I could still study—that I Was Now Getting My Ph.D. Homework might be burdensome, but it was a familiar, even cherishable, yoke. I couldn't wait to *have some*, in fact, even if it turned out to be harder than anything I'd faced before. In a neurotic frenzy of overpreparation, I had already bought all the books for my upcoming courses (a Chaucer survey, An Introduction to Irish Literature, and Literary Research Techniques) a good month ahead of the first week of classes. When that week finally arrived I'd ploughed through huge great wodges of the stuff—a cultural history of medieval England, Wellek's *Theory of Literature*, the complete essays of W. K. ("Mr. Intentional Fallacy") Wimsatt, the entire *Táin Bó Cúailnge* in Thomas Kinsella's translation, and enough Lady Gregory poems to last several lifetimes. I was already plotting out possible seminar papers. Thus the Crazed Good Student in me revved up to warp speed: she whose deepest, maddest wish was to astound her teachers with her unprecedented brilliance (and thus win their love) and stun fellow students into a state of admiring, if not joyful, subordination. Why I thought trouncing my classmates in every academic task set before us would prompt affection in them for me is beyond me. (*True or False? The delusion that doing well in school will win me love has disfigured my life. Discuss in 5–7 pages.*) Yet throughout my graduate career I made a habit of writing at least one of my "final" research papers the very first week of the quarter, and then announced the feat to all and sundry. I was ferocious—and to my contemporaries no doubt a particular horror.

Which is not to say I found much pleasure in these torrid bouts of cerebration. On the contrary, once classes began I became a quivering ball of school-related anxieties. I worked hours at a stretch; I fretted; I found it difficult to sleep. Perhaps from sitting at my desk so much, I developed, humiliatingly, a painful rectal fissure. (That Auden suffered from the same affliction has always been of curious comfort.) True, as the new term unfolded, I managed to learn my way around, made my first foray to the library, and got to know several of my fellow grad students, if only to say "Hi" to. Yet compared with what I had been used to at my tiny undergraduate college, my courses were huge and impersonal. The campus itself was vast, gray, and anonymous, the trees increasingly bare, and the blank looming presence of the prairies all around hardly a visual or imaginative solace. How I would make myself known to my lofty-seeming professors was unclear to me, and by the time the piles of dead leaves began to disintegrate, a subtle polar nip made itself felt in the air, and the first tentative snowflakes drifted down, my days had become clouded with self-doubt.

Ah—the psychopathology of everyday life:

I have to review Chaucer today, Christ the difficulties of forcing myself to concentrate. My anal problem still seems to be here. Anal,

banal. I dreamed last night I was in my class expounding on the dif-
ference between the witches in the "Merchant's Tale" and the witches
in Macbeth. *Except there aren't any witches in the "Merchant's*
Tale." Excruciating embarrassment when I realized my mistake. At
first I was standing in front of the class, then I was standing on one
side of a street and they (my classmates) were all on the other side.
I was trying to balance on a heaped-up pile of slush and lecture.
Switched to somebody's home—a strange woman there, gave me a
kitten, which I gave to a little girl. Then I was in a place that seemed
to be where Ted lived [the teaching assistant in my Chaucer class].
I was trying, hopelessly, to lace up some high boots. Later part of
the dream: with my mother walking through some kind of tree-lined
place. Odd clothing. Dreadful gloom.

I frequently consulted the I Ching for guidance but got the same
result, Jian, or Hexagram 39, over and over again. This singu-
larly dreary conglomerate of yin and yang—or so Wikipedia now
informs me (I long ago forgot whatever I once knew about any of
it)—signifies "LIMPING"—with "other variations being 'ob-
struction' and 'afoot.'" "Its inner trigram is *bound=mountain*"—the
Wikster continues, "and its outer trigram is *gorge=water*." Hardly a
prediction of fun and frolic. I had yet to visit the scenic campus of
Cornell University in hilly upstate New York: but might I, even then,
have nonetheless been familiar with the concept of *gorging out*—
throwing oneself into one of the famous local abysses? Hard to say,
but it's possible.

Of course, I wasn't totally inert in the face of depression; I'm
sitting here today, after all, perky and plummy, like the proof in
the pudding. And it's true: I made various attempts to find extra-
mural activities in those first months that I thought might help to
ground me in my new life. Music was, as always, a mood elevator. True, it was difficult to listen to records from my recent West

Coast past: Alix D.'s *Lavender Jane Loves Women* must have mi-grated into my Records-I-Never-Play-but-Can't-Bear-to-Throw-Out Pile somewhere around this time. Other music from the spring before (Baez, Bonnie Raitt, Nyro, and a shameful yet rav-ishing item called *Puccini's Greatest Hits* full of very, very early, pre-obese Pavarotti, recorded just after he'd given up professional football and sang like a hunky angel) was too fraught with remind-ers of Karen. (She used to sing "Vissi d'arte" every morning in a tiny but perfectly pitched soprano.) I needed, I knew, to lay down some new associations—start building up a soundtrack for the *vita nuova*. The McGarrigles' debut album—later to be the Professor's ill-omened birthday present—was one pleasing early purchase: I adored Anna's spectral, superb, Emily-Dickinson-on-Vicodin ver-sion of "Heart Like a Wheel" especially. I'd also found some good budget reissues in the local record store: a *Rigoletto* from the 1950s with Kraus, Merrill, Moffo; Bach cello sonatas; Schubert's C Major String Quintet. Who knew that soon enough the last mentioned would prove more sinister than inspiriting? It still hurts to listen to it. You can almost *hear* the syphilis pinging in the notes, the bacte-rial catastrophe.

Thanks to Elsbet, country-western music—mainly associated in my mind up till then with Turk, his gambling-addict first wife (the one who dropped dead), and his hillbilly in-laws in Ohio, "Mammy and Pappy Root" (Root pronounced always to rhyme with *mutt*)—became a new enthusiasm and source of campy delight. Elsbet had recently seen Waylon Jennings in concert and did a marvelous satiric impression of him—ramrod-stiff, guitar thrust forward, whamming and bamming through his pile-driver theme-tune, "Are You Ready for the Country?" (No one could accuse Waylon of too many lilting or samba-like polyrhythms.) I got the LP of the same name and was enchanted, both by the honkin' bar-band sound and Waylon's scary-skanky machismo: the greasy black leather "Outlaw" hat, huge belt buckles, the ugly-wispy Hells Angels beard. Morbidly fascinating, too: how one freezing winter night in 1959, just after he'd been hired as Buddy Holly's new bass player, Jennings had narrowly escaped death by foregoing his seat on the doomed chartered Beechcraft that was to take Holly and his fellow musicians to the next stop on their Midwestern concert tour. Hung over from partying, Waylon elected to stay behind and take the bus the next day; Holly, Ritchie "La Bamba" Valens, and the "Big Bopper" all died when the tiny airplane subsequently crashed in a snowfield in Iowa. Chillingly, several pilots in the vicinity of the crash that starry, starry night reported briefly picking up a faint and quavery chorus of "Nearer My God to Thee" on their cockpit radios.

But the lady singers were the big draw for me—Tammy, Patsy, Kitty, Loretta, and most of all Dolly Parton, just then beginning to parlay a huge musical talent and engaging personality (not to mention Daisy Mae–like bazoombas) into glorious worldwide fame. "Jolene"—her masterpiece—led off my first and still-favorite Parton record, *The Best of Dolly Parton* (1975), and to this day I still find the skittery, throbbing, furiously up-tempo minor-chord guitar vamp at the start of the song the most enthralling opening gambit in all of recorded music. Yes, better than the Prologue to *Das Rheingold*, Furtwängler conducting. Nor was the potent Sapphic depth-charge in Dolly's lyrics lost on me. When the overwrought speaker, terrified that the rapacious Jolene will poach her man, veers off into a lofting, near-hysterical paean to her rival's attractions—

Your beauty is beyond compare
With flaming locks of auburn hair,
With ivory skin and eyes of emerald green;
Your smile is like a breath of spring,
Your voice is soft like summer rain,
And I cannot compete with you, Jolene.

—you didn't need to be one of the Ladies of Llangollen to figure out the supersexy subtext: *Dolly is really into this gal!* The eerie mountain fiddle soaring up behind Parton was yet another dizzying lamia-touch.

A few months later—the night the Professor and I began our affair, in fact—I remember how we listened to this song and laughed at the album's awe-inspiring back cover photo: a full-length picture of Dolly, in red bell-bottoms and a low-cut sequin-studded top so tight, sharp-angled, and geometrically enhanced she resembled a sort of freakishly endowed Demoiselle of Avignon. The stupendous Dolly bosoms—here pointing up and out like a pair of massive triangular battering rams—were so stylized and Brobdingnagian, they seemed indeed to inhabit their own perspectival system, one different, volumetrically speaking, from the one in which the rest of her was located. Confronting this alarming cleavage, the Professor had grinned and mugged and feigned girlish fright, then given me one of her lewd-yet-charming signature smiles. *God,* said she, *I wouldn't want to bump into* THAT *from any angle!* Our eyes locked and it was fantastic.

Of course, even in my new and unfamiliar milieu, I had hardly abandoned my radical politics or the ongoing Struggle Against Patriarchy. Were said patriarchal structures to be eradicated, I figured, it might make it easier for me to find a girlfriend. I was still pretty psyched about it, in fact. I continued to follow the more inflammatory feminist publications—*Off Our Backs, Heresies,* and the like—though, it was true, I often ended up devoting most of my time to the personals ads, sparse and uninviting though they usually were. But I also knew that I needed to make contact pronto with the local version of what was often referred to, in those pious-pawky days, as the "Women's Community." (The "Wimmin's Community," I guess I should say: as certain readers may recall, in the hardline lesbian-feminist subculture of the 1970s, the words *woman* and *women* were frequently spelled in new and eccentric ways for sanitary reasons—anything to avoid the odious suffix "-man" or "-men." Thus *womyn*, *wimmin*, *womon*, *wymmin*, and like oddities.) So eager was I to meet new *wimmin-lovin' wimmin*—or even just some *womyn-lovin' womyn*—one didn't need a Ouija board to figure out that I would fling myself forthwith into the world of regional Amazonia.

And despite my poor track record in the love-and-romance department, I was quite gormlessly optimistic—rather like a young hero in Balzac or Flaubert, just arrived in Paris from the provinces and eager to attend his first salon. The city in which I now resided was undoubtedly bigger and less backward than the small town in which I had gone to college; and given what appeared to be a sizeable "Women's Community," seemed likely to offer a cornucopia of new social and erotic possibilities. There was a women's bookstore (later to become famous in lesbian circles as the model for "Madwimmin Books" in Alison Bechdel's satirical comic strip *Dykes to Watch Out For*); a newly established "Lesbian Resource Center" in a nice, leafy suburb; a feminist health-food co-op with women-owned bakery attached (*yum! carob brownies that taste like cardboard!*); and last but not least, *Your Mama Wears Army Boots*—the community's flimsily stapled, ardently revolutionary, cosmically silly literary magazine.

It did not take long, however, for a certain disillusionment to set in. My initial foray—to a weekly support group at the new Lesbian Resource Center—was hardly inspiriting. The first meeting I attended was a sort of one-woman bitchfest in which a strange monomaniacal lady (not even a lesbian, it seemed) described at length the various atrocities committed against her by her ex-husband and numerous trashy boyfriends. (*He made me strip and crawl round the house wearing a dish rack on my head!*) She looked just like one of Charcot's bug-eyed patients: you could see places on her temples where primitive electrical probes might be connected. Not much for anyone else to do but endure the dramatic monologue and cluck in bewildered sympathy. Sisterhood was Powerful but in this case the Sisters were at a loss.

Perhaps because of the maniacal lady—though she never came back—subsequent sessions followed a less "talky" format and focused instead on 1970s encounter group–style activities: humming together while lying on the floor, visualizing pleasant ambles on some idyllic tropical beach, meditating about the place we felt "safest," that sort of thing. At the last meeting I remember attending, the frizzy-haired woman who "facilitated" the weekly session had us do a Fruit Ritual. The latter began alarmingly enough: she gave us each an orange out of a big brown shopping bag and told us to spend ten minutes getting to "know" our orange as *fully as possible* without peeling or consuming it. *Look at it, sniff it, touch it, roll it around in your hand!*—she exhorted. *Feel its skin! Touch its navel! Make sweet sweet love to your fruit!* Thankfully, one wasn't required to put said orange up to one's ear to hear if it was saying anything. Mine was no doubt screaming with rage—in a tiny yet shrill citrus-voice—if only at being forced to take part in such a farcical ordeal.

After ten minutes, in a surprising interpersonal twist, we had to choose another member of the group and present our orange to her as a sort of woman-woman love-gift. Each of us had formed an *intimate bond* with our fruit; now, it seemed, we would *share the feeling*. This part of the activity was a horror story straight out of junior high school. *Would the "cool" girl across the room give you her orange? Would you hold yours out to the attractive lady with the buzz cut, only to have her spurn the tenderly proffered offering?* Nor was that the end of it, either. Having selected your partner—that is to say, having flung yourself in desperation on some equally unpopular, still-unchosen member of the group—you were then obliged to stand there, open-mouthed and arms hanging loose at your sides, while she fed you her orange piece by piece. The roles—natch—were then reversed and you did the same for her. (I have no memory of my partner in these higher primate-like exchanges, having clearly suffered PTSD as a result of the whole experience.) Such inanity combined with sadism was too disagreeable even for me and I hightailed it out of there shortly afterwards.

My second letdown, alas, had to do with *Your Mama Wears Army Boots*. Because I wrote poetry, I'd hoped to get involved in the magazine and so had volunteered my eager services. Yet the small collective of women who put the thing together—five or six flannel-shirted, incorrigibly middle-class young women, all of whom bore self-perpetrated names like Artemis Longstocking, Sarah Margaretchild, and Pokey Donnerparty—was rather less dynamic, creatively speaking, than one might have hoped. The ringleader was an off-putting gal in army fatigues named Labyris. (Labyris Snakegoddess was her striking *nom de plume*.) She was not especially bright, and though still only twenty-three or twenty-four, so dogmatic on the topic of female oppression as to seem brainwashed—as if she'd been abducted by Sapphic aliens and programmed with phrases from the Redstocking Manifesto. Her small talk was a bizarre mishmash of matriarchal fantasy and Pol Pot—evocative indeed of those edicts and prohibitions one found so often laid down in the lesbian radical press and at consciousness-raising sessions:

Wimmin Who Sleep With Men Are the Slaves of Patriarchy.
Testosterone: The Root of All Evil.
Wearing Perfume or Deodorant or Makeup is Counter-Revolutionary—a Sign of Pathetic Surrender to Oppressive Patriarchal Standards of Beauty. (Allergenic too.)
If Only Men Had Periods. Then They Would Find Out What Suffering We Amazonian Warriors Go Through Every Month.
[A] Is Not Behaving in a Sisterly Fashion. We Need to Confront Her On It.

*[B] Is Not a Real Lesbian—Even If She Is Sleeping With [C].
She Has No Dyke Consciousness At All.*

Bisexuals Are Traitors to Lesbian-Feminism.

Male-to-Female Transsexuals: Never to Be Allowed into Wimmin's Space. They're Still Men, After All.

Same Goes For Boy-Babies and Male Children. Even Ones with Lesbian Mothers.

At the same time, because she was a radical feminist, and thus Womanly and Empathic and Deeply In Touch With Herself, Labyris also had her sensitive side. Once I happened to ask her how she was doing, and received a soulful, if also diffident, reply:

Well, I'm Feeling Really Centered Now?

But I'm Really Getting Burned Out On All the Politics in the Community?

I Really Need to Work On Myself Now?

(Confusingly, it was *de rigueur* in those days to affect a tentative, questioning tone when discussing serious personal things—an annoying tic that subsequently infected the general American female population in the 1980s and '90s.) A short time later Labyris would publish an eloquent poem about her need for private time in *Your Mama*: "My Primary Relation to Me." I see I noted the title in my journal with a spate of horrified exclamation points.

A strange puritanism held sway everywhere. We were not a very pretty bunch. In the brave new world of radical dykery, the call for collective action and an end to male domination had resulted (only temporarily, as it turned out) in the suspension of traditional lesbian role playing: the bad old 1950s duck-ass-and-hairspray world of butch and femme. Like old-style bar culture generally, butch and femme were seen as *unfeminist*—a pathetic and reactionary imitation of out-of-date sex roles. By contrast, members of the "Women's Community" rejected *oppressive heterosexist models*—with the consequence that everyone sought to look as neutered and ugly as possible. No dressing up, on the one hand, like a sort of midget Elvis Presley, or on the other, like Brenda Lee in a 1950s chiffon party dress. Most gals wore the same basic uniform—turtleneck, T-shirt, or flannel shirt; jeans or possibly lumpish-looking corduroys; hiking boots or grubby running shoes. As the weather got colder the whole enticing ensemble might be supplemented with a moth-eaten man's suit coat from Goodwill or one of the drearier unisex squall jackets available from L.L. Bean. Unshaven legs and armpits?—a misogynist cliché of the time, of course, but definitely part of the Sappho-Spartan aesthetic.

I was more or less amenable to the prevailing style (or nonstyle)—anything so long as I didn't have to wear makeup. My "look" at the time? Not hugely different, I guess, from what it has always been. Apart from a brief bleached and gelled flat-top phase in the late eighties, I've always favored uncoiffured short hair, jeans or pants (never a dress), and anything tailored or vaguely military in cut. Jaeger jackets. Navy blue bell-bottom sailor pants. Men's shirts, for sure. I remember a friend once looking into my closet and saying, *You can tell a lesbian lives here. Why?* I asked. *Too Many Shirts.* Army surplus stores, I admit, have played an embarrassingly large part in my sartorial life. Only recently did it dawn on me, for example, that especially given present-day midriff-bulge issues, multipocket camouflage pants (not to mention those thick olive-green webbed belts with little tabs on them on which to hang grenades) just don't look very good on me.

Since no one was ever to be sexually *objectified*—i.e., evaluated on physical appeal—revealing outfits, overtly erotic gestures, indeed flirting of any sort, were pretty much verboten. Which isn't to say a confusing kind of subliminal tease didn't go on. Labyris, for example, was a compulsive giver and taker of what in later and more satirical times would come to be called "lesbian hugs." (My ex, Bev, calls them "dyke specials.") These were those soulful, interminably held embraces—usually performed to mark somebody's arrival or departure—in which you closed your eyes, buried your head deep in the warm place between the other woman's neck and shoulder, rocked slowly back and forth on your heels, and made susurrating goo-goo sounds while also moving one or both of your hands around on her back or waist. If her shirt was not tucked in at the back and you could make roving, small-of-the-back flesh contact, so much the better. Then you might twiddle delicately with her belt loops or even investigate the waistband on her jeans.

Such ritual fondlings, oddly enough, were universally understood, not as amorous overtures, but rather more militantly, as a sign of one's advanced feminist consciousness and egalitarian commitment to sisterhood. Labyris and other embrace addicts like her were truly the foot soldiers of lesbian liberation. No one was to be excluded from the collective hugfest—except, of course, any shy newcomer who might suddenly arrive on the scene. In that case it was important to demonstrate to her that she was definitely *not* part of the existing circle of love, and would have to wait, possibly forever, before gaining admittance to it. In the presence of a New Girl, everyone's hugs took on a peculiarly self-congratulatory warmth and fervor, as if to signal the primal Hobbesian law that underlay so much of the era's either-you're-in-or-you're-out Sapphic culture: *we are very very popular and you are not!* Think about it: isn't falling into a soul-clinch with some gal even more fun when the two of you have an onlooker—a polite, possibly lonely person, anxious to be welcomed, whom you don't know and already suspect you don't want to know? *That'll show her!*

And yes, no matter how humpy, bumpy, and involved these embraces became, it was nonetheless borne in upon one that they were never to be interpreted—Isis forbid—as *sexual* in implication:

DID YOU GET THAT? UNDER NO CIRCUMSTANCES!
NOT SEXUAL AT ALL! NEVER EVER! NO WAY!
IF YOU THINK IT'S MEANT TO BE SEXUAL
THERE'S SOMETHING WRONG WITH YOU.

The successful gal-radical was thus as adept at sending out mixed messages as any Mozartean coquette. Labyris, for example, knew precisely how to play it: the exact moment when drawing back, breaking contact, might leave an emotionally susceptible hugmate sick with erotic confusion. I found the ritual (and all its unspoken rules) both good and bad. Good, in that being sisterly and nonsexual felt safe to me; I had zero rakish charm and little concept indeed how one went about flirting with someone. Bad, if not excruciating, because I longed to be touched in some unconditional way. I had suffered—forever, it seemed—from an appalling case of skin hunger. Like most English people of their class and generation, my parents had been cold and physically skittish—my mother all the more so after the divorce. I was the proverbial *ours mal léché*. And as for my two abortive love affairs up to that point: *never, never, never enough*. The result: crippling ambivalence toward hugs in general and lesbian hugs in particular. It didn't matter, paradoxically, whether the hug was given or withheld—both situations were hard. And the larger problem would be around for a long time: I consciously avoided ever having a professional massage until my forties, precisely because the thought of such purposeful and pleasurable contact released in me such a chaos of painful and conflicting emotions.

My private difficulties apart, a pervasive fear of sensuality in the world of *wimmin-lovin' wimmin* made for a peculiarly convent-like atmosphere. No one dared critique it thus at the time, of course, but as weird little enclaves like the *Your Mama Wears Army Boots* collective demonstrated, the lesbian-separatist movement of the 1970s was no less neurasthenic, sexually warped, or passive-aggressive than any other utopian venture one might name. Indeed, it may have been worse. The fact that we were all young women—overgrown girls, really—merely intensified the atmosphere of underlying hysteria. Things, to be sure, would change drastically enough a decade or two later—witness dildos, drag kings, and *The L-Word*. Even as early as 1981 or '82 attitudes had begun to budge a bit: I remember attending a raucous feminist conference at Barnard in one of those years at which a rebellious horde of self-described "sex-positive" lesbians of all stripes—hardcore S&Mers, unrepentant butches and femmes, Sapphic maenads favoring fetish wear, bondage, and the like—descended on the event and proclaimed the coming era of strap-ons, nipple clamps, and black silk negligees. *No more prudish granola dykes! Girl-on-girl porn for all!* But in 1975 such things remained undreamt of. *Off Our Backs* had yet to be supplanted by *On Our Backs*. The typical "women's community" of the seventies was in consequence as kooky, prim, and repressive as the Massachusetts Bay Colony. Maypoles, lewd dancing, flagrant obscene mirth: all unthinkable.

True: I worked as a member of the *Your Mama* collective for a little while that fall—mostly stapling copies of the mag together on weekends. I also contributed poems to one or two issues, though in a style rather more Ogden Nash or Hilaire Belloc, perhaps, than Adrienne Rich. (Rich, to the shock of the American poetry establishment, had recently come out in the press and was regarded as saintly—if not semidivine—by the *Your Mama* gang.) While the collective tolerated my comings and goings, it was becoming clearer and clearer that my sensibility did not exactly harmonize with prevailing rad-lez attitudes. Yes, *Your Mama* published "Mucous Jungle," a jaunty little piece of doggerel I'd written about having a dreadful head cold—full of droll references to snot, jungle foliage, the brackish Amazon, oral sex, etc.—but I was obviously an oddball. And after a while, I in turn felt myself becoming frustrated with the frumpy-ideological house style. Labyris, Pokey, Artemis, and the rest began to seem a bit tiresome. I was even starting to suspect that my interest in Lesbian Nation—at least its official political and aesthetic manifestations—might be on the wane.

The feeling was intensified by encounters that fall with a celebrated professor at the university—not *the* Professor, but a woman who might be characterized, retrospectively, as the Professor's mirror opposite: the *Anti-Professor*, so to speak. Jo was from the Deep South: a short, surly, crop-headed professor in the history department. She was in her mid-forties, built like an old-fashioned fireplug, and butch and mercurial beyond measure. Academically speaking, she had come up in the bad old days and had been in the closet for many years before undergoing a Damascene conversion to radical feminism. As the university's then-sole self-professed "dyke" professor, she was bluff, pugnacious, and histrionic, a charismatic teacher and speaker, but also intellectually plodding and hopelessly sentimental about women and the feminist cause. Humor-wise, she made Olive Chancellor, the dour spinster-suffragette in Henry James's *The Bostonians*, seem like Milton Berle. I never did take a course from Jo: she was a scholar of the American labor movement and I confess I found factory reform and shirtwaist makers somewhat dull in comparison with various dotty Brontës and the flagellation poems of A. C. Swinburne. But I saw Jo often enough at women's events: she migrated back and forth (as I did on a much smaller scale) between the world of the University and the "community." And after I began attending a weekly feminist reading group that she facilitated, we were regularly in one another's sights.

I can't say we hit it off. Jo would have detested the metaphor, but she was unquestionably the Queen Bee of the local lesbian hive. *What does Jo think?*—such was the question whenever some new call to action or political scheme was hatched. She had her own little loyal entourage: a set of doting female worker-drones (many of them graduate students in English like me), as well as an apparently inexhaustible supply of temporary love mates: brawny lady-carpenters, vegan poets, Tarot card readers, food co-op workers. (She wasn't particularly successful, it seemed, at maintaining actual relationships.) She did not appear to use deodorant. She was also—as I see so much more clearly now—generous, brave, truthful, and decent.

While I admired her warmth and even, sometimes, her strength of character, I also found her slightly ridiculous. Jo was especially revered by the "community" on account of several well-known personal struggles. Besides having Heroically Endured a Hellish Existence as a Lesbian in the Dark Ages (the 1950s), she was also, very volubly, a recovered alcoholic and (in her own doleful phrase) a Chronic Overeater. Within five minutes of meeting her you were likely to hear about these life-trials in some detail. The second affliction was one on which she particularly liked to expatiate—usually when everyone around her (as at the feminist reading group, say, after a lively discussion) was grabbing paper plates and about to launch, innocently enough, into a cheerful potluck meal at someone's house. Given Jo's deep, baritonal Southern drawl and melodramatic tendencies, these sorrowful admissions of frailty and struggle, like Dickens's account of the death of Little Nell, were almost impossible to listen to with a straight face. Indeed the phrase *"Ah-m uh crawnic ovuh-eaduh"*—piteously enunciated, diphthongs lengthened into absurdity—remains a running joke for me and Blakey thirty years later. It was considered the purest sadism, obviously, to drink a glass of wine or appear to enjoy your food in front of Jo: her strong unstable features would screw up in an anguished rictus and her expression become that of a Sad Clown, a sort of lesbian Red Skelton, on the verge (terribly enough) of starting to cry.

Jo realized, I think, that her power over me was limited and thought me cold and priggish. (I was.) She was ambivalent about the academic world and often fantasized about leaving it. Perhaps because I was a new Ph.D. student and had already begun to cultivate

a minor reputation as "smart"—or at least ruthlessly competitive—
she seemed to associate me with the very life she wished to abandon. I remember having a chat with her once in her office that fall,
in which she revealed with some pride (and more than a little hostil-
ity) a dramatic plan, indeed, to leave the cosseted life of the scholar
behind and join the proletariat. She was going to get a uniformed job,
she announced—maybe even "*drahv buus*." Now "*drahvin' buus*" was
clearly another Jo-ism for the ages. She made the activity in question—tootling gently down the avenue, halting every block or so to
take on elderly passengers—sound like some primitive yet cathar-
tic physical function: something one might perform in private, with
deep shame, but also with an enormous, juddering sense of relief.
I admit it, I probably simpered. I deserved whatever dirty look she
gave me. An effete little twit like I was could not be expected to understand such urgency, such ecstasy, such authenticity.

Not surprisingly, Jo's pronouncements seemed only to strengthen
in me a yearning for the academic life. If I had been ambivalent about
my Ph.D. studies at the beginning of the school year, I ceased to
be so. So what if Jo didn't want to be a professor anymore? Fine: I
did. I wanted to read Edith Wharton novels, own a nice middle-class
house with hardwood floors, have lots of bookshelves, kilim rugs,
and a Krups coffee grinder, drive a sporty little lesbo-prof car. A
year or two later, when Jo took a leave of absence to start a lesbian-
separatist commune with some cronies out on the prairie, I remember
thinking she had finally gone birthday-suit bonkers. Life at My Án-
tonia's Farm (named thus in honor of the sacred Willa) was grueling,
one heard, and seemed mainly to consist of shifting hay-bales, split-
ting very unfriendly rocks, steaming up huge vats of bulgur wheat,
and having endless late-night bouts of ideological self-criticism with
one's comrades. Hardly enticing. (What would Garbo or Tallulah
have thought? Or Elizabeth Bishop, for that matter?) The colony
later petered out, one heard, after fights and bickering and cash-flow

problems. The land was sold off, and the grizzled Jo—now somewhat subdued but also at last in a stable relationship—was soon enough back at the university, where she would remain, in harness, for the next twenty-five years. The girlfriend was known as Skydancer and I think they ended up staying together.

Jo—and the aristocratic disdain we felt for her—would prove to be an instant bond between me and the Professor. The Professor and Jo knew one another well; the latter had somehow been involved in the hiring process which had brought the Professor to the University some seven or eight years earlier. (Linguistics, the Professor's specialty, fell between disciplinary stools, and English, Sociology, and Psychology were all involved.) Not only had Jo been on a one-woman crusade then to bring more female professors to the university, she had also sussed out, one gathered, the P.'s not-so-mysterious sexual orientation. But whatever sympathy might have existed between them had long ago dissolved. Above all, Jo resented the Professor's secrecy about her sex life. And deeply closeted as the Professor was (though of course as I would later discover, every lesbian within 250 miles except me knew all about her), she in turn was bound to find Jo vulgar and down-market. To the extent she was willing to talk about it, the Professor's own attitude toward being "queer" (her term, used in the old-fashioned, apolitical sense) was haughty—almost regal. Sleeping with women was about sex, plain and simple, and had nothing to do with politics. Parading around as a "radical feminist" or some other thing was childish. Jo was nothing but a loudmouthed dolt. The Professor seemed to view herself, by contrast, as a sort of Ancien Régime lady-libertine, a subtle and inscrutable woman of the old school. She was a connoisseur, a sensualist, skilled in the arts of homosexual love; Jo was like a seagull at the dump, squawking and flapping her wings over an old potato-chip bag. Disenchanted as I had become with Amazon Nation, I found such moral refinement—for such the Professor's nihilism seemed to me at the time—intoxicating.

So how *did* I and the Professor meet? She was a sort of Christmas present—one filled with cordite, nails, and bits of broken carnival glass. As fall turned into winter I was, by hook or by crook, doing okay—even managing well in some areas. My studies had started to engage me and to my great satisfaction I had begun to attract some of the professorial attention I'd so relentlessly sought. I'd done pretty well in Chaucer—not least of all when I'd met with the instructor in his office, as all the new Ph.D. students did, to recite from memory a lengthy passage of Middle English from the General Prologue. Professor Hooley (for such was his comical name) was about my father's age, in his middle fifties, though hardly like my father in looks or temperament. Bald and jovial, he seemed, by contrast, the very model of Chaucer's own Friar. Easy enough to picture him in coarse wool monk's habit—a loose piece of rope round his waist—drinking and wenching and palming off fake relics and indulgences. He was distinctly flirtatious: he remembered having read my Ph.D. file, he leered, and could now *put a name to the pretty face*. My application essay had been *outstanding*. He had a daughter, he confided, an English major in the department, only a year or two younger than I, but she was *hopelessly dumb*, he was afraid, and would never be as accomplished as I was. A Problem Daughter (about whom more is to come). She apparently wanted to join the Air Force. Rueful laughter followed—though whether it was at his, her, or my expense was not clear.

My Irish lit professor, one Larson by name, was another jolly old dog—white-haired and goofy, though in an even more infantile way than Hooley. He was fond of silly jokes and bawling out Clancy Brothers songs during lectures. He was Scandinavian, stereotypically so in looks, yet nonetheless affected a loud and insistent Irish brogue: your typical Boorish-Swedish-Stage-Irishman. He'd enjoyed my final paper, he said—on satire and magic and Celtic poetry—and thought I should try to get it published. I was amused by his propensity to burst into "Kevin Barry" at any provocation but viewed him, too, with mild superciliousness. (He would later prove a mentor both singular and kind.) In class Professor Larson habitually referred to Ireland's ancestral enemies—i.e., one's own cutthroat kinsmen and kinswomen—as "Brits." Not having heard the term before, I wondered if I should consider it an ethnic slur and reprimand him for it. I didn't, though, and that was probably a good thing. History, public and private, has its moral tangles. Little did I know that at that very moment, my long-lost cousin Bridget—whom I would meet again in 1987 after thirty years of noncontact—was a sergeant in the Women's Royal Army in Belfast, performing, among other duties, strip searches on Catholic women suspected of smuggling contraband to IRA men held in the Maze prison. Somewhat recklessly, too, given the British Army's position then on homosexuality, she was also involved in a clandestine love affair with a fellow soldier—a tough lady in the Military Police named Roni. Roni later got slung out during one of her unit's periodic witchhunts.

Elsbet was around too, of course—a new friend to be valued—though much preoccupied with her M.F.A. program and family doings. I felt I couldn't impose on her too much. She invited me home with her that Thanksgiving and I met her parents and siblings, which was nice, though I felt sorely abashed around the aged and imposing Norwegian aunties. (My ordinary social skills remained pretty abysmal.) For the holiday meal, the whole family, young and old, all put on boiled-wool hats and skirts and reindeer jackets and toasted one another with aquavit and alcoholic punch. The table centerpiece of holly and pine cones was topped with a festive little Norwegian paper flag.

But in other ways I still felt lost. The scene in Eau Claire might as well have taken place on Pluto, so foreign, at bottom, did it seem to me. (Family life to me still meant one mother, one sister, no money, palm trees and crabgrass and canned-soup meals at a folding card table.) True, my sex life was momentarily quickened: I actually went out on a couple of dates that December with a scrawny, sallow-faced, thirtyish woman I had met at the Lesbian Resource Center. Celeste was half-Scottish and half-Sinhalese—not a particularly attractive combination in her case—and worked as a freelance German translator. She followed a fanatical macrobiotic diet and lived in a dark and dirty one-room basement apartment near one of the lakes. The walls were decorated with photos of Dietrich, Conrad Veidt, and other louche celebrities of the Weimar era; the floors were cold bare linoleum. Celeste nurtured a number of paranoid theories: that heavy metals in deodorant went straight up from your armpits into your brain within seconds; also, that if you stirred anything you were cooking on the top of the stove in the wrong direction (clockwise? counterclockwise?) the resulting meal would give you cancer.

We slept together a couple of times—once, nightmarishly enough, after she'd dragged me to see Rainer Fassbinder's lesbian-psycho film, *The Bitter Tears of Petra von Kant*. As Celeste's cinematic tastes might have hinted, our love trysts were neither romantic nor particularly wholesome. True, I was pleased, in a statistical sense, to have had the experience: Celeste was still only the third woman I'd gone to bed with, and I was definitely counting. Three seemed to make it official, Sapphic love–wise. I could now say I was an old hand at the business—almost like Colette or Janet Flanner or somebody. I attempted to cultivate what I took to be a cynical, devil-may-care attitude: one didn't have to "fall in love" to have sex with someone; one just did it. That was what being grown-up and sophisticated was all about.

Yet however detached I tried to be, my brief affairette left me feeling empty. *The Bitter Tears of Terence von T-Ball*. The first time we embraced I had been shocked to discover that not only was Celeste's body bonier and pimplier than any I had encountered before, she also seemed to have a sort of gingery red fuzz all over her. To move a hand up her knobbly spine was to brush this curious she-pelt in the wrong direction—almost as if one were caressing an orangutan. (Something I've never done, I hasten to add—but believe myself capable of imagining.) The touch thing was there but nowhere close to being right. In combination with Celeste's unusually wet, self-involved, and aggressive way of kissing, the overall erotic package was in fact fairly sick-making. (*Who knew that sex might be revolting?*) You could see why some people took vows of celibacy.

But I was also frightened by Celeste's somewhat dank personality. After our first sexual encounter—and despite the fact that we were in my bed, in my apartment—she had insisted that I get out of bed and sleep in the front room like an errant hubby. She couldn't tolerate anybody next to her at night, she declared, couldn't bear to feel someone else's arm or foot. Not even a king-sized bed could satisfy this need for *Lebensraum*. No explanation. I had no real couch to speak of, just a sort of truncated love seat thingy that had come with the apartment, so I ended up sleeping on the floor that night, on a small remnant of olive green shag carpeting about three feet by three feet that I had found on the street one day and used as a primitive living room "rug." I immediately convinced myself that being ejected thus from my own bed was fine—possibly even kind of cool. When it came to meeting the demands of mixed-up women, I was as eager to please as ever—Nora Flood in *Nightwood*, carrying her betrayal money "in her own pocket."

As it happened, the Irish Lit course led me to the Professor. Just after Thanksgiving, during the last week of the term, one of my classmates, a tall, blonde, somewhat suburban-looking woman in her thirties named Alice, a local community college instructor who had come back to school to finish a Ph.D. on Burns, approached me with an invitation. She had overheard me saying to someone in the class I would be staying in town over the Christmas holiday. Would I like to come to her house on Christmas Eve and spend the evening with her and her husband and a very good friend of theirs? There would be roast beef and mulled wine, said Alice; she was also going to put together little Christmas stockings for everybody.

Now, I had never really spoken to Alice, except in the fitful artificial way one does while sitting at one's desk in the front row, waiting for the teacher to arrive. She was older and very straight-looking—neat and ladylike in an Our-Miss-Brooks way. Not my style at all, I'd judged, but nonetheless I'd been curious about her. She was from a devout if chilly Presbyterian family—she told me later—but had lost her faith as a result of reading Thomas Carlyle's *Sartor Resartus*. (She must have been the last person on whom the work had had that devastating effect since 1858.) This weird Victorian spiritual crisis—for such it had been—had not, however, divested her of an intensely serious, indeed Christian, sense of moral duty. Kind to a fault, she had the ability to make one suddenly aware, without spite or voyeurism, of the gaping emotional gulf that existed between oneself and others. Awfully enough, when I realized what it was she was offering, a little cache of tears—hot, involuntary, and no doubt stored up behind my eyeballs for several months—started up in my eyes. I accepted at once with an embarrassing mixture of gratitude and self-pity.

But I must I confess: I felt slightly uncomfortable, too. Alice was obviously a Very Good Person but had not, it seemed, picked up on the Fact of all Facts—that I was G-A-Y. (I was preoccupied, in those days, of course, with who knew and who didn't. Paradoxically enough, being a "radical lesbian" and dressing like a Special Forces commando did not necessarily mean you wanted anyone from the Real World ever to twig on the fact. That would have been *too scary* by far.) I assumed the knowledge would repel someone as straitlaced as Alice. I determined therefore to be circumspect. I was right about her naïveté; nor would I be candid myself until circumstances later made it painfully necessary.

The Professor, perhaps needless to say, was the "very good

friend." Now, this was exciting news indeed. The relation between linguistics (the Professor's subject) and literature was one of the areas I was hoping to pursue in my Ph.D. work. Having taken, among other ultra-nerdy things, a History of the English Language course as an undergraduate, I was eager to hear more about labio-dental fricatives, glottal stops, and the Great Vowel Shift. Who knew? Despite a vague plan to study Cruelly Oppressed Women Writers, maybe I would do some linguistics too. I'd noticed the Professor's classes in the course catalogue (Poetry and Phonetics, The History of Slang) and heard she was a big shot in the field. And when Alice came to pick me up late in the afternoon that snowy Christmas Eve, she confirmed it: yes, the Professor was a renowned scholar of regional dialects. A major contributor to the *Linguistic Atlas of the United States*. She traveled high and low across the United States collecting folk idioms, samples of local speech, regional pronunciation patterns. She had even—very famously—found some of those putative vestiges of Elizabethan English in Southern Appalachia.

But equally dazzling (and not entirely unrelated): while doing her Ph.D. research at Columbia in the early sixties, she'd also had another life—a brief yet glamorous career as a folk singer in Greenwich Village. (*Amazing.*) She had even made a few records. (*Records!*) Alice sounded a bit starstruck—*wait till you hear the Professor sing.* She had known the Professor, it seemed, for three or four years; Alice's husband, Tom—a handsome, mustachioed fellow who taught in the medical school—had served with the Professor on some faculty council a while back. Now not only was the Professor one of Alice's dissertation advisors—she knew a lot about Burns's dialect poems, it turned out—she'd become a good friend. She and Alice went to the movies, played tennis several times a month. (*Astounding how quick on the court the Professor could be, even with her bad leg. Yes, she had polio as a kid.*) The Professor, I would see, was fantastic. *So witty and down-to-earth. Not snobbish or pedantic at all. Always had students for friends. So charismatic and fun.*

Yet though clearly so wonderful (and still only in her early forties)—and here Alice's brow furrowed slightly—the Professor, alas, remained *unmarried*. Alice hoped her friend wasn't going to end up a *lonely spinster*. She and Tom were trying to find the Professor a nice boyfriend; it must be so awful being single over the holidays. Given that the Professor was also Jewish, Alice had concluded, she no doubt felt doubly isolated around Christmas time.

I listened to this intriguing description raptly—especially the folk singer part. (I would ponder the spinster part a bit later.) Back in my teens, folk music had been a hobby and an escape for me—yet another of my private dream worlds. It was partly the era, of course: the Great Post-Sixties Aftermath. I'd imbibed any number of songs, second-hand, from old Joan Baez and Judy Collins albums, and even taught myself to play (however crudely) several Child ballads on the guitar. And as with all of my solitary enthusiasms, I got pretty studious about the whole business.

Folk melodies delighted me—the modal harmonies, the minor chords, the raw, archaic, stripped-down simplicity of it all. The Ye-Olde-England aspect added a pleasantly narcissistic element: however far the old songs and ballads had migrated over the centuries (to every part of North America and beyond), they nonetheless alluded to the world of my own family forebears. Lord Bateman, Fair Annie, the Wife of Usher's Well: they pointed one back to some fabled yet familiar "English" past—magical, medieval, even premedieval at times. (My feudal-sounding name, *Castle*, had also no doubt disposed me to Green Men and elf-knights and maidens on milk white steeds.) Something oddly English, too, in the strange emotional reticence in folk performance: the way traditional songs so often turned on the grisliest events and situations—murders, drownings, hangings, children dropped down wells, girls smothered in their beds or whose breast bones had been made into harps—yet the mode of delivery was typically impassive, deadpan (almost comically so at times), as if the singer were entirely disconnected from the frightening mayhem he or she described.

There was the American side of things too, of course, and yet more musical romance to conjure with—the world of blues, gospel, work songs, and mountain music, and the heroic, ever-present link, by way of Dylan, Baez, and Woody Guthrie, between folk music and social protest. (Alix Dobkin and "women's music" were simply the latest twist, one realized, in a long-unfolding story.) Thanks again to early imprinting, I was instantly agog to hear about the Professor's sixties singing career in Greenwich Village. Back when I was a kid, in far-off San Diego, the little music store at our local shopping center, weirdly enough, had not only stocked the usual goods—guitar strings and harmonicas and cheap instruction books such as *Teach Yourself the Ukulele*—but also occasional back issues of *Sing Out!*, the legendary magazine of the 1960s East Coast folk music scene. There they were, discreetly tucked away in the sheet music section, next to chord charts for "I Get Around" and Jan and Dean's "Little Old Lady from Pasadena," and a plethora of surf guitar fake-it-books.

These intriguing little booklets—the same size and format as *TV Guide,* but published, it seemed, in some other universe—had captivated me at once. They too seemed to allude to a seductive alternate world—one more contemporary, perhaps, than that of Lord Bateman and his ilk, but one chock-full nonetheless of music, passion, and partisanship. The politics of *Sing Out!* were decidedly left-wing, if not flagrantly Commie-Pinko, so along with the sea shanties and logging songs, one couldn't help learning a great deal also about Trotskyism, Sacco and Vanzetti, the Abraham Lincoln Brigade, and any number of brave and illustrious Wobblies. Marooned in a right-wing navy town, with a bigoted stepfather to boot, 1 was in love with the subversiveness of it all. Yet it was precisely this legendary world—that of bohemian New-York-Jewish-Leftie intellectual culture no less—in which the Professor, it seemed, had come of age. Thus was one primed to adore. The ardent life intimated in *Sing Out!* had cast its spell over me and I was ready to be enchanted with anyone who'd lived it.

And enchant she did. For despite Alice's concern about the Professor's encroaching lonely-spinsterdom, the lady in question—first glimpsed from ten or twelve feet away in Alice and Tom's dining room—hardly seemed in need of emotional rescue. On the contrary: she looked radiant—almost theatrically so. The radiance was in one sense actual. Comfortably perched on a tall breakfast stool, the Professor sat bathed in a sort of halo of hot unnatural light. I had walked in on a photo shoot, I realized: chairs and tables had been pushed aside and with the aid of tripod, lamps, and light umbrellas, Tom—an expert amateur photographer—was taking a set of what turned out to be publicity shots of her. The Professor cracked jokes and smiled happily at the camera while Tom clicked away.

My overheated brain, meanwhile, was taking its own pictures—trying to absorb all the luminous details. Handsome Older Woman. No, make that *Stunning* Older Woman. Amazing Silver-Grey Hair. (*Gorgeous in this light!*) Red Cashmere Sweater. Dark Tailored Slacks. Butch? (*One would think.*) A Few Small Beads of Sweat Glinting on Her Upper Lip. (*From heat of lights, no doubt.*) Acoustic Guitar Cocked Upward in Jaunty Fashion. (*Comical and lovely!*) A Certain (Virile) Sensuousness. (*Understated, but there.*) Tanned Wrists. (*So beautiful.*) Warmth. Glowing Smiles. That *Joy* in Being Looked At. All the brightness made of her a *numen*; one could not turn away.

And indeed, as soon as introductions were made, one heard all about it: the Professor's life in the Village in the glory days of Baez, Mimi Farina, Peter, Paul, and Mary, Judy and Bob. (*All old friends, of course.*) And yes, she had made one or two records then, now long out of print, but still, there they were: a part of American history. Her specialty had been grisly Appalachian murder ballads—the lyrics, she quipped, were always good for a laugh. She strummed brightly, then sang a snatch of "Silver Dagger" in a bold and resonant contralto. Lately, it seemed, she had begun performing again on a modest scale, at the University and around town. The local paper was going to do a little feature on her—the Folk-Singing College Professor. She chortled gleefully and fairly basked in the glow of the soft box. I've still got one of the wallet-sized black-and-white head shots taken at this historic session. The Professor looks beatific, free.

In the flesh the Professor was at once seductive and bizarre. She wore her hair, striking and lustrous, swept back severely and away from her face above her ears—so much so that if one saw her only from the front, one might mistake her for a man, thin-faced and beautiful, albeit with a strange pompadour hairstyle. In the back the long strands of hair were gathered together into a single thick rope-braid, nearly two feet in length. She later told me that in the Village, circa 1958, all the beatnik gals wore such braids, but I've never seen anybody—in pictures from that time or any other—sporting this peculiar Elvis-Crossed-with-Pippi-Longstocking look. The voice, as before: thrillingly low and unfeminine. As Alice and I approached, the Professor's eyes lit up with pleasure. I felt myself being thoroughly vetted. I guess I passed muster because she kept a light sardonic gaze trained on me for most of the evening. Even more than Alice or Tom, I seemed to be her *beneficiary*, the one designated to receive the stored-up prize of her attention. I was a new and appreciative audience of one for whom she might demonstrate, like a series of card tricks, her various winning (and subtly flirtatious) ways. Neither Alice nor Tom seemed to notice what she was up to. She had registered their myopia—their obliviousness to the wordless greeting that had taken place between us—and on some level I must have, too.

Did I—in this fatal period—ever *really* read any of the many books that I claimed, in daily jottings, to be perusing? Only the day before meeting the Professor, I find now, I copied into my journal a florid passage from Colette's 1937 erotic memoir *The Pure and the Impure*—another of my sacred texts at the time. In the excerpt in question Colette is describing the woman who became her lover and patron during her post-Willy, harum-scarum vaudeville days (1905–12): Mathilde de Morny, the rich, eccentric, and perverse Marquise de Belboeuf. Colette's nickname for her girlfriend was Missy; lesbian friends such as Natalie Barney and Liane de Pougy called her Uncle Max. To judge by the surviving photographs, Missy was portly, uxorious, and vulnerable-looking; a stone butch and lifelong cross-dresser, with a sentimental preference for gentlemen's evening dress. (Imagine a somewhat tubbier, even gloomier Radclyffe Hall type—complete with lorgnette, cummerbund, and cigarette holder.) Although Colette, teasingly, never mentions her own liaison with the Marquise in her memoir (she refers to her former lover only as "La Chevalière"), she captures Missy's melancholia—and sexual neurosis—with a certain off-the-cuff yet intimate precision:

> As I write this I am thinking of La Chevalière. It was she who most often bruised herself in a collision with a woman—a woman, that whispering guide, presumptuous, strangely explicit, who took her by the hand and said, "Come, I will help you find yourself. . . ." "I am neither that nor anything else, alas," said La Chevalière, dropping the vicious little hand. "What I look for cannot be found by searching for it."

Now, were such a passage copied into a journal by a character in a novel—the protagonist, say, in some not-very-good 1970s lesbian bildungsroman, about to fall catastrophically in love with Ms. Wrong, it would no doubt register as "foreshadowing" of a comically pretentious and ham-fisted nature. But there it is, in my own minuscule, still-adolescent handwriting: a glaring affront to both taste and plausibility.

I guess in the moment of writing I must have felt some emotional identification with the mopey Marquise—or enough of one, at least, to want to preserve Colette's account of her. Yet at the same time I seemed not to want to register what I had written down. Even La Chevalière's rudimentary self-awareness was beyond me. If "vicious" hands existed—and I still very much wished to believe they did not—I was not myself in the business of dropping them. Dropping hands, vicious or otherwise, just *wasn't me*. Abandon the Love Quest? Give over the cherished search for "it"? A psychic nonstarter, I'm afraid. The thing I looked for, I'd persuaded myself—*could* be found by searching. It had to be. If it wasn't—well, I would just have to kill myself. So why bother writing the Colette passage down? I may have done so, it occurs to me now, for some sort of weird *future reference*. For the uncanny benefit of myself *now*—in this instant—a reader some three decades on, a different person, conscious of, *ahem*, life's little ironies. For I was in fact about to fall off the earth.

It took a few weeks, still, to spin into darkness. The evening at Alice's (need one say?) was enthralling. Alice and Tom cosseted and fed me; we drank Bristol Cream sherry and feasted on cheery holiday fare. Alice's Christmas stockings, filled with useful things like Q-Tips and sugarless gum and those little astrology books you get for $1.99 at the supermarket checkout, made us all laugh. We consumed a Yule log of sociopathic deliciousness. An hour or so into the meal, I was flying—enjoying a first-class ride on a magic carpet. It turned out the Professor, like Hooley, my Chaucer prof, had also been on the department graduate admissions committee the previous year, and remembered my application very well indeed. (*I thought, wow—Terry Castle—what a great name! And what fantastic recommendation letters! Who IS this woman?*) I blushed in a virginal way, embarrassed but enormously pleased. The Professor was inquisitive, and amid smiles, asked a host of delightfully intimate questions. Alice and Tom joined in. I became an object of general interest and concern. I ended up—shyly at first—telling all about my mother and father, their divorce, why I wasn't at home for Christmas, my English background, the situation in San Diego.

Such adult attention was dizzying. I fairly tumbled out of my shell. At one point I even brought out one of my most-cherished pieces of private Terry-lore—that I was somehow distantly related to the late-Victorian actress Ellen Terry. (*Was named after her in fact. Some sort of great-great-great-auntie, my cousin-twelve-times-removed or something.*) Thoughtful wows all round. Alice said something about the John Singer Sargent portrait of Ellen Terry as Lady Macbeth, and hamming it up, I instantly assumed my putative auntie's pose in said picture: arms comically upflung, the glittering crown of Scotland held aloft in my hands, a crazed and maniacal gleam in my eyes. The Professor was enchanted. And not only *that*, I proudly explained: because of various theatrical marriages afterwards, the connection meant I was also related (*gasp*) to both Charlie Chaplin and John Gielgud. By then I was euphoric, as if all three—Ellen T., Gielgud, and the Little Tramp—hovered above me in thespian spirit-form, rapturously applauding. Yes: their tragicomic blood coursed in my veins.

The evening culminated in a tipsy late-night walk through the snow and the Bestowing of the Guitar. Apparently wishing to prolong the festivities, the Professor had invited us round to her house, a few blocks away, for a hot toddy. We all put on clumpy, salt-rimmed snow boots; the Professor, I noticed, donned a mannish red-checked Woolrich jacket and what looked like a fur trapper's hat. We scrambled happily down the quiet snowbound streets. I was still high on having been (unusually for me) a chatty and dynamic guest. My favorite holiday carol was "Good King Wenceslas," I announced to everyone apropos of nothing: I especially loved the phrase "deep and crisp and even." Someone said it was now officially Christmas, a minute after midnight.

The Professor's house then loomed up majestically in the moonlight: a perfect example, she joked—of Midwestern Stockbroker's Tudor. (Another phrase I'd never heard before: I had been thinking the fake half-timbering magnificent.) Could an evening become yet more magical? Yes, it could. The Professor got us our nightcaps and while Alice and Tom built up a fire in the living room, she took me around to see everything: upstairs, downstairs, the bedroom, the guest room, the lovely studio space, the Native American rugs, the state-of-the-art stereo system (artfully disguised under pieces of antique ethnic textiles), the huge record collection, even the windowless little utility room in the basement in which, with the aid of an elaborate Rube Goldberg–ish system of stakes and string and purply-white fluorescent lights, the Professor had cultivated a flourishing stock of marijuana plants. I was agog. She noted my reaction with pleasure. *Hey, Terry—you'll have to come over again sometime soon*, she chuckled, *and we'll smoke some*.

I was exhilarated, almost delirious. Both house and owner were perfect. And even as the party began to wind down—Alice, Tom, and the Professor having decided to drive me back to my apartment across town together—there came the coup de grâce: the Professor insisted that I borrow one of her several guitars. It would be mine on a sort of indefinite loan, she said. She didn't need it at the moment; I'd said I played, but didn't have an instrument. And besides, surely we would be getting together again soon to play some songs, no? It would mean—and here she gave me a dazzling smile—that we would *have* to see each again. Such persuasion was irresistible. I took the instrument into my hands like a precious relic. Beautiful it was, with modest-yet-charming caramel-colored top, woven strap with little red and blue and yellow woolly bobbles, and some nice mother-of-pearl inlay around the sound hole. It gave forth a loose, open, sweet-natured tone. A regular Instrument of Joy. When I got up the next day and saw it, propped up against the book-filled orange crates in my little living room, I had to confront it all—the insane bewitching Cinderella-truth. Everything I remembered from the previous night had really *happened*—the whole miraculous encounter. The Professor wasn't a figment; I hadn't dreamed her up. I felt clobbered—positively *brained*—with happiness.

Yet over the succeeding days, and despite the violent onrush of ecstasy I felt whenever I let myself think about her, it was not clear to me what—if anything—could now transpire between the Professor and myself. The thing was frankly so unprecedented: *she was a distinguished professor at the University, for God's sake*. Affable she might be, but how could we even really be friends? She was far too exalted. One pondered the emotional signage: *Don't Even* Think *of Parking Here!*

In the awkward journal entry I made later that first morning—for it was now a sunny and cold, knife-sharp Christmas day—I was garrulous, trying to stay calm, feigning matter-of-factness:

> *I had a lovely evening last night with Alice and Tom and [The Professor]. Alice, a totally sweet person—had made peanut brittle, cookies, and a stocking for me. Drank sherry and then Cabernet—I felt pretty drunk by the time dinner was over. [The Professor]— totally phenomenal, she seemed so utterly a figure of perfection for me, I felt like one of the mortals visiting Olympus. She plays the guitar and sings, knows everyone in folk music, has a fantastic house, huge tape deck and stereo speakers—I sound like some kind of gaga groupie. But God! Hiker, marijuana plants (also larger than life) growing in the basement, beautiful person. Realize she is what I would like to be—or think I would. She was nice to me, lent me one of her guitars. Taurus. I guessed successfully, to my own surprise, that she was an earth sign. Wow—so out of my reach, as one might say.*

One *might* say, but clearly I didn't want to. The hyperbole here—not to mention the stupefying envy—now makes me want to squirm. Could I really have been so threadbare and exposed? Even so I was trying, hope against hope, not to fall into the usual greedy desperation.

And indeed I stayed safe for a little while. Oddly absent in the foregoing, I see now, is any speculation about the Professor's sexuality. I think I was shielding myself on that front as best I could. However much the evidence had pointed toward it—and virtually all of it had—the possibility that the Professor might be homosexual was simply too staggering, too blinding, too refulgent a prospect even to contemplate. A *mysterium tremendum* she would—and should—perforce remain. As long as one didn't *know*, one was not obliged to *yearn*—to hanker after her (no doubt agonizingly) in the flesh-and-blood world. It was so much easier to hanker over phantoms, after all—you didn't have to worry about being rejected by them. You could sit tight for a very long time.

Yet like Our First Parents reaching blindly for the fruit, I was fated to know. True, the new year brought its distractions. Classes started again (Victorian Poetry this time and Larson's Joyce seminar); and I reconnected with Alice, who was auditing the Joyce. I ran into the grunting Jo several times too and even had a snarky little chat with her over coffee one afternoon about Christina Rossetti. (*"Jo had on odd stretchy clothes, a sort of Avon-lady pantsuit. She has no sense of self-adornment."*) I attended my feminist reading group. But the potion was about to be decanted, the Tristan chord to sound.

Once classes had commenced, I began mooching around the hallway near the Professor's office, in a shady way, rather like a police informer. One afternoon I actually hung out there for an hour or so, hoping to see the Professor in her office, but without any luck. I mentioned this futile little patrol ever so casually to Alice. *Had she seen the Professor? I just wanted to say hi.* Like an unwitting Pandarus,

Alice must have transmitted this information-mote on at once; for no sooner had I arrived home that evening than the Professor called—the first time ever. She'd tried me several times before, she said. She'd had a cold, she said: that was why she hadn't been around. She wanted to know *what I'd been up to.*

I was startled—both by the call and her question—and devolved at once into clammy self-consciousness.

> *Talked for about ten minutes, I was nervous, trying not to be a drip. Her self-possession awes me. Deep voice. I have those ancient feelings of worthlessness—"why is this person bothering to speak to me"—the sense of myself as "uninteresting," boring. Results in real ineptitude.*

Yet however nerve-wracking in reality—*what a stupid idiot I am ugh why couldn't I speak to her in a normal way*—the call was hardly displeasing in principle. The Professor had obviously been thinking about me. The adult attention, again, was overwhelmingly pleasurable; her inquiries, so personal, an odd mixture of soothing and arousing. Indeed when I'd picked up the phone and first heard her voice, I'd had that split-second grandiose flash of triumph known to erotic fantasists everywhere—the giddy sense that I had somehow *willed* her into calling me. Why else had she telephoned? My banal attempts at small talk didn't matter: I was clearly omnipotent. She was under my spell. She couldn't *not* call.

Ironically, a member of the women's "community"—Labyris, no less—provided the necessary, if perverse, turn of the screw to our courtship. Some of the *Your Mama* women were going to see Patti Smith, Labyris phoned to say, and did I want to go? Now along with Dolly and Waylon, Patti—then making her first Dionysian splash on the scene—had been one of the musical epiphanies of the winter: perhaps the most charged, sexy, and momentous of all. Music unheard, I'd bought *Horses* almost as soon as it came out—having been instantly ravished by the stark, now-iconic Mapplethorpe photo of Smith on the cover. I loved the stunning freak-out of it all: Patti's gaunt visage, punk dishevelment, the sullen unrepentant expression on her face. She looked like a sort of spooky elf-boy. I immediately acquired an oversized white cotton man's shirt like hers at a thrift shop and slouched around my stuffy apartment in it. The tight modernist black pants (ah, one was slim then) were soon to follow.

And then—holy shit—there were the *songs*: wild, outer-spacey, steamy orgone-boxy things with that visionary Land-of-a-Thousand-Dances-Let's-Make-Love-with-Two-Headed-Aliens-T.S.-Eliot-on-Acid feel. The glorious vamps on *Horses* seemed tailor-made for me in particular: Hermaphroditic-English-Major-Punk of a Transcendent Order. It spoke well of Labyris, usually so dumb and doctrinaire, that she was open to it. And wasn't it incredible, she and I marveled: *all that mind-blowing lesbian stuff. Yeah, totally fantastic! I can't believe she sings "Gloria"! Like Gloria's her girlfriend! Like they're having sex!* As if simultaneously invaded by the Patti-spirit, Labyris and I then burst into her delirious love-yawp:

GLOO-OOR-EE-AH!! JEEE—EL—OH—ARR—I—A!!

Of course I wanted to see Patti. Life was suddenly thrilling. *She's comin' up my stairs!*

The excitement I felt about Smith—jiggy, hormonal, somewhat demented—was more than a little bound up, I knew even then, with the Professor and the strange erotic lurch *she* provided. Granted, one could hardly relate the two musically—they were from different eras, different centuries almost. Never the twain, etc. But the brusque, unselfconscious, even flagrant rejection of femininity was the same. Ditto the hiding-in-plain-sight homo-tease. (Was Patti a dyke? Bi? Was the mysterious Robert Mapplethorpe her boyfriend?

Despite "Gloria" no one seemed to know for sure.) So perhaps it was fitting, after all, that it was Labyris, oblivious to the shock waves she was about to set off, who should now spill the beans about the Professor and her legendary menace.

Yeah, said Labyris, *she's a big ole dyke.* I was stunned. I had met the Professor over the break, I had said: what did Labyris know about her? *Well, you know Jo doesn't like her at all 'cause she's too chicken to come out; she's superclosety and uptight. But everybody knows about her. Basically everybody in the world. She has affairs with students. Stuff like that. 'Member that tall woman Elaine who came to the LRC once and was a basketball coach? Well, she had an affair with [the P.] when she worked at the U. last year; and she says she's totally nuts. Really, a total creep. Notorious.*

I was instantly stupid with desire. The scales were lifted, the handwriting on the wall apprehended, the frontal lobes removed. An awe-inspiring charge had suddenly been laid upon me: *SHE* had arrived in my life and I had to do something about it at once. Labyris's mean stories were obviously untrue. That whiney, oafish Elaine: what a moron! The nay-saying Jo: another idiot. The sanctimonious Labyris and her ilk: dull middle-class prudes, all of them. Alice and Tom clearly liked the Professor, and They, One Knew, Were Unimpeachably Good People. Besides, I had the Professor's guitar. She sang folk songs. She knew who Ellen Terry was. She had looked breathtaking in that fur-trapper's hat. Only one conclusion could possibly be drawn. *Of all the lesbians in the world, I alone was smart enough and free enough and passionate enough to adore this sensitive, sophisticated, and beautiful woman as she deserved! No one understood her but me! EE-EEEEH!*

Not one in this crowd of thoughts could I reveal to Labyris in the moment, of course: for part of my charge, I understood already, was to be vault-like discretion. This relationship would be for the ages—an ecstatic fusion of body and soul—and I needed to cultivate in myself the proper spiritual exaltation. Phantom couples arose, as if to spur me on: Sappho and Anactoria; Radclyffe and Una, Gertrude and Alice; Lady of Llangollen No. 1 and Lady of Llangollen No. 2; Garbo and Mercedes; Vita and Violet, Rita Mae and Ms. Rubyfruit. The Professor, so Fate had decreed, was available. She was friendly. She was gorgeous. She'd given me the glad eye. Anything was possible. I had to *get* to her before anyone else did. I had to figure out a way to Ask Her Out.

I began a campaign—the fervor and folly of which can only be judged by the fact that I was willing to adjust my otherwise obsessional studying in order to implement it. I didn't exactly neglect my schoolwork—even at the best and the worst moments I never missed a lecture—but it was as if I were now emitting two enormous parallel streams of energy. I'd ramped up the adrenalin flow, quickened every reflex, called upon every bit of Red-Baron daring, endurance, and stealth I could muster, so as to manage the simultaneous pursuit of scholarship and eros. But I was confused and heedless, too. For precisely what effect a relationship of the transgressive sort I now envisioned might have on my budding academic career, I didn't stop to consider. This sudden recklessness should have been a warning. But there was no one around to challenge me on it. (While aware of my sudden crush, Elsbet didn't know me well enough, she said later, to question its wisdom.) A sort of mad grasshopper gaiety—itself the work of loneliness—drove me on. Thus even as I crammed with eye-crossing intensity—at one point barnstorming through *The Pickwick Papers*, *In Memoriam*, and *Ulysses* all in the same week—I brooded about the Professor. I stayed up late, got up early and consumed cup after cup of coffee, wrote endlessly in my journal about sightings (real and imagined), and planned the stages of my assault.

I had help, it must be said. The Professor was a good sport—in fact did all one might reasonably do in the way of encouragement. As soon as she "got" what I was up to, and it didn't take long, she returned every ball sent her way with amused, languorous, eminently masterful strokes. She fairly twinkled when she saw me: *oh, here I was, strolling the halls again, what a coincidence!* (I had by this time memorized all her usual comings and goings—not to mention her car license plate number and the section of the faculty parking lot in which she was wont to park. She drove a red Honda hatchback.) If we bumped into one another (*by accident of course*) on stairwell or sidewalk, she would shoot me a quick knowing glance, full of glinting, subtle merriment. The effect of it would persist even as she shifted up into her normal "in public" mode of bluff manly heartiness.

And enigmatic though they were, she had her own forms of semaphore. Once she spied me lurking in the hallway outside her office, and laughing gaily (*Terry, come look at these, they're really funny*) ushered me in to see some slides of herself undergoing acupuncture treatment. The window shades had been closed and the room darkened: she was preparing for a guest lecture, she said, in a friend's anthropology course on traditional healing practices. (Acupuncture remained exotic if not esoteric to most non-Asian people in the mid-seventies; the Professor clearly relished the fact that she—daringly enough—had undergone it.) Projected onto the wall at exceedingly close range were huge surreal fleshy close-ups of her back, neck, stomach, and upper arms, all stuck about with gleaming silver pins, some delicately listing to one side or another. Blown up to ten or twelve times their normal size, the body parts on display looked like those of a giantess. One saw vast moles and freckles and, now and then, a vestigial tan line. A humungous white bra strap—almost two feet long—was visible in one picture; in another, the vast, crinkly top of her underpants. Presumably to obscure her identity, the Professor had masked her face wherever it was visible with little pieces of black electrical tape. The masking had not been particularly successful, however—the snaky silver braid being always the dead giveaway—and the overall effect was both comic and vaguely pornographic. Nowadays I can't help thinking, weirdly enough, of Bellocq's turn-of-the-century portraits of New Orleans prostitutes, in which the anonymous subjects—working girls all—pose for the camera, naked but for their black masks, slippers, and smiles.

Granted, I was often somewhat tongue-tied in the Professor's presence—at times agonizingly so. One of our staircase encounters had been the purest torture. Numb as a zombie, my dead flesh flaking off, I hadn't been able to think of anything to say our whole way down three flights of stairs. My heart had been thumping chaotically. The Professor had been smooth enough in the impasse, had filled the dead air with pleasantries, but by the time we got to the bottom and she prepared to leave the building, even she looked a bit nonplussed. She shrugged in wry farewell, and said, *Well, bonne merde, ma petite.* Something about the vulgarity triggered in me a sort of galvanic reflex. I suddenly jerked to life: a fairy-tale frog, exasperated with myself for being so inarticulate. *I always feel so glad when I see you*, I croaked out in a rush; *but I never know what to say.* To my acute shame she heard this appalling revelation and for a second stared through my eyes into my cranium. She reached the soft jelly at once. *Well*, she replied, with a chuckle, *I feel just the same.* And then as quickly as that, she was gone.

The ley lines proved to be the big breakthrough. Having finished early with my classes one day, I'd lingered near the Professor's office for most of a late gray winter afternoon. She was holding her office hours; her door was open and the light was on, casting a warm glow on the scuffed linoleum at the threshold. I wanted her to finish with the long lineup of students ahead of me before I made my presence known; I didn't want to seem like one of them, just another tedious supplicant. I wanted her to feel relief and maybe even excitement when she saw me. For I was now getting desperate: I couldn't go on, I told myself, without making some decisive move. I needed to shed my passivity; flirt, beguile, and disarm with my charm and intelligence. *Setting one's cap at somebody* is how they might have phrased it in the eighteenth century. To fascinate thus I would of course have to disguise all of my monster-sized insecurities. Likewise block out the absurd and painful truth: that I was a first-year graduate student blatantly pursuing a distinguished (and closeted) senior scholar in my own department. Yet *faint heart never won fair lady*! The Ellen Terry DNA would somehow have to carry me through.

At last the coast was clear. Perfect timing: no gun in her pocket, but she *did* seem glad to see me.

Smiles and laughter. I said I was feeling good and indeed she said I was "radiating." It was lovely. Discussion of graduate school, dowsing, the ley lines and Michell's book, then films. Found we share the same favorite Bergman. Persona, of course.

A fair amount of this banter I can't recall—what we said about graduate school, for example. (Something best abolished?) But I remember the "ley lines" part well enough. Ley lines, for those unfamiliar with them, are those primal "energy tracks" along which—according to certain occultists and New Age archaeology buffs—the various monoliths, barrows, and earthworks of ancient Britain (Stonehenge, Glastonbury Tor, Avebury, Thornborough Henge, and the like) can be mysteriously aligned with one another. I'd been reading all about them in a slightly crackpot book by one John Michell—*A View of Atlantis*. According to Michell, the ancient Britons believed that these and other sites were connected by unseen occult "lines of force"—the so-called ley lines. The result was a telepathic network, crisscrossing the Neolithic world like a sort of cosmic Underground. Sites like Stonehenge were "stops" on the line, so to speak—magical hot spots, where the ley lines intersected and sacred rituals might be performed. Or something like that, anyway.

I was infatuated with the ley line idea and described it to the

Professor with half-ironic, half-credulous glee. From there it was a short step to Blake's myth of Albion, dowsing rods, magic wells, chalk figures, crop circles, and the eerie bottomless tarns of folklore. The Professor talked about Native American burial mounds: fascinating stuff, we agreed, and *definitely* related. I was "good for her," she joked, because I was reminding her of all these "things she had forgotten about." My nervousness vanished. I became more and more daring and free. Out of sheer boyish enthusiasm I found myself reading aloud a nugget from the ley line book I'd copied into my journal: "Old stones, barrows, and other ancient sites have a natural attraction for cattle." *Very cool!* Cows and sheep, it seemed, wanted to plug into the same cosmic energy socket everybody else did. The Professor was impressed.

It was a primitive sort of grafting exercise, of course. I was more confident than usual in part because the focus was putatively on "scholarship"—however dubious or half-cocked. I could show off what I knew—twaddle on and play the familiar role of World's Most Intriguing Student. But the Professor and I were both aroused, too (I think now), by the magical adhesiveness implicit in our topic. That a subliminal stream of energy might somehow conjoin two disparate places—possibly even two disparate people?—was exciting. It seemed to grant a license. Outlaw connections became possible. We were like a couple of standing stones buzzing away at each another along some very zippy ley line. And the archaic word "ley" was so suggestive, too. It was hard not to snicker whenever one said it. *Ley, Lady, Ley?* Heh, heh, heh.

That we shared the same favorite film, *Persona*, was simply more dextrose to mainline—the sugary icing on the all too sugary cake. A Sapphic cliché, of course, though neither of us said so: no less a figure than the great Sontag had declared the film Bergman's "masterpiece" and she'd definitely been around the block a few times. Bibi Andersson—could one do anything but sigh? *Ja*, sure, the nurse was *obviously* in love with Elisabet. And yes, wasn't the most fabulous part when Liv Ullmann and Bibi were naked and in close-up and their faces seemed to merge? From such giddy chitchat—a sort of mad secret code by which we made our desires both known and not known—the journey to full-on ecstasy looked like a straight shot.

> *Finally I asked her if she wanted to go out with me—she did, said she was glad I was making the "first move." I said I hoped it was not inappropriate. She demurred admirably—said she had thought of calling me up the other day, but then had started to worry about it being "inappropriate." Laughed again. Later she gave me a ride home. I was so excited afterwards I could barely eat.*

She indeed called me the next day with a plan. (Somehow our roles from the day before had reversed.) We would go downtown that Friday to see a film, the Professor said—the new Truffaut. Before-hand she would take me to one of her favorite "seedy" restaurants, a little Japanese place near the theater. She would probably just honk when she picked me up: I should listen out for her. This last part of the plan was a tiny disappointment: I had wanted her to see me in my place, shabby though it was. (*"Momentarily nonplussed—but now: a resolution that I will not to attempt to 'organize.' My old solipsistic move, desire to impress—the arranging of one's belongings in order to create a studied disorder, a creative persona."*) But who could complain at such otherwise fabulous decisiveness?

By this time I had done the I Ching and gotten, of course, a tran-scendental go-ahead for the whole business: Hexagram 34, aka The Power of the Great:

> *Movement in Accord with That of Heaven. Perseverance brings good fortune. The gates of success are beginning to open. Resistance gives*

*way and we forge ahead. The relations of heaven and earth are never
other than great and right.*

Pretty damn good. Okay, there *were* a couple of tiny worrying bits
in the extended commentary: "Danger of overexuberance; persever-
ance in inner equilibrium necessary." And a sentence or two, way
down in the fine print, that seemed downright contradictory: "the
meaning of The Power of the Great shows itself in the fact that one
pauses. Strength makes it possible to master the egotism of the sensual drives." *Hmmm.* What was that supposed to mean? Of course,
not every part of the ancient oracle-text was reliable: one had to use
one's intuition to determine what was relevant in any situation. All
right, I decided: I'll be "exuberant" and not "overexuberant." But I
ain't gonna *pause.*

The date went as planned: Too Good To Be True. Any less-than-
luminous aspects of the evening were quickly disavowed, so in the
end it was as if one hadn't registered them at all. Yes: I *had* been a bit
gauche and awkward, still. (According to my journal, over dinner
I seem to have made some terribly embarrassing "blooper" about a
heating pad.) Yes: the restaurant was small and seedy as promised,
a cheap noodle place with sticky plastic tables and vaguely unsavory
smells emanating from the kitchen. (*It was rough*, I lied in my account
the next day, *but I loved it.*) Actually, I'd found it frightening: at one
point several men careened in off the street, drunk and foul-mouthed,
and began taunting everyone. The Professor, though instantly grim
and alert, appeared to take it in her stride: when the wizened Asian
owner came out with a huge old-fashioned camera and began flashing the flash attachment repeatedly in the eyes of the interlopers, a
defensive gambit that in fact drove them cursing out the door and
back into the slushy street outside, her only comment (delivered with
cold smile) was, *Oh, things like that are always happening in here.*

The Truffaut film, *The Story of Adèle H.*, was yet another of those idiotic portents that, I see now, shadowed my relationship with the Professor from the start. It was based on a true story: the eponymous Adèle, it turned out, was the second daughter of the great French novelist Victor Hugo. Toward the end of her father's long political exile on the island of Guernsey (1855–1870), where she and her siblings had grown up, she had encountered a rakish British naval officer, one Lieutenant Pinson, and become infatuated with him. That Pinson—a nautical bad boy to rival his operatic counterpart, Lieutenant Pinkerton, USN—did not return her passion seems to have escaped her notice. Horrifying her family, she chased Pinson across the sea—first to Nova Scotia, then to Barbados in the West Indies. In Barbados, she finally twigged on the fact he couldn't stand her and went totally bananas. She was taken back to Europe and committed to an asylum where she died in 1915, one of the bleaker years of the new century.

All I can remember of this turgid flick are endless shots of Isabelle Adjani, the besotted Adèle, stalking around, wild-eyed, in costume-drama misery against a garish backdrop of bougainvillea and colorful tropical birdies. Now has anyone ever noticed that Victorian women's hairstyles are the ugliest in the entire history of the world? Think of George Eliot: those ringlets and vile center part. *Acck!* George Sand and the matching greasy curls: *merde!* Florence Nightingale?—*don't even go there.* One of Blakey's greatest vices is to sneak up behind when I'm not looking, pin my arms to my sides, and using a kind of Death-Comb maneuver, give me an enforced center part. I am then press-ganged into the bathroom and made to look at the nasty result in the mirror.

Well, Adjani had one of those ghastly 'dos—Dreadlocks à la Balmoral, 1875. Plus she's a dreadful actress. (Or was then.) The Professor, I recorded the next day, had "fidgeted" noticeably through the entire film. Conscious of my companion's slightest twitch, I in turn had been unable to concentrate on anything and thus remained oblivious to the film's ominous, even Sophoclean, relevance—so glaring thirty years later—to my own case. As Truffaut said of the film afterwards, "It was [Adèle's] solitary aspect which attracted me most to this project; having produced love stories involving two and three people, I wanted to attempt to create a passionate experience involving a character where the passion was one-way only." The first of Four Hundred Blows.

Still, as far as I was concerned the evening had been exquisite. It had had a positively gob-smacking finish—as if the Professor had sensed my fleeting disappointment over the *I'll just honk* directive earlier and was now definitely on the case:

> *Got back to my apartment; [the Professor] came up and had some wine. Played the guitar and looked around, said it wasn't so bad (my apartment). I felt embarrassed, somewhat ashamed—a hangover from my initial insecurity. But I realize deep down she sees me clearly for myself. She even went in the bedroom & looked at my books, saw my lesbian literature I'm sure. I know she knows. This is a relief. One gets over it without saying it at all.*

Thrillingly, she'd stayed quite a while, loosened up, and let fall some marvelous snippets of inside information. How absurd she found the blowsy Jo, for example, who'd "gone so far from her discipline" she had lost all "mental equilibrium." How she, the Professor, had disappointed all the feminist nutcases at the University by refusing to bend to a party line. Because, you know, *all those people really do is cheapen one's suffering. It's the universal stuff that matters: the shared fact of human mortality.* She had had her own grave trials—with real pain, real melancholia. *She had a hysterectomy two years ago,* I noted later, with Boswellian fascination; her hair had gone silver overnight.

> *Joked to her mother afterwards she had given birth to an 8-pound uterus. Engaged in 62 (?) to a "son of a bitch who ran off with the*

parson's daughter." So never got married. Her mother unforgiving,
wanted grandchildren. Tough tits, Ma. Her mother had collected all
the things she had ever said that had hurt her and played them back
to her. Her [The Professor's] amazement: "she always wanted me to
say that I loved her."

Such pathos was contagious. I felt as if I too had suffered at
the hands of this unkind parent—even then still alive and eighty-
something, brooding away somewhere on the East Coast. We kept on
with the maternal topic. When the Professor learned my own mother
was only forty-eight, she started noticeably, but quickly recovered:
Ha, she snorted, *I don't believe in age.* Our own relationship, said
the Professor, transcended petty chronological distinctions; in fact,
though twenty years younger than she, I had, she noted, a *strange*
ageless quality. Just a fairy-tale changeling, I guess.

Other remarks were yet more revealing. The Professor had obviously suffered deeply: she'd been in analysis for eight years when she
was young, one gathered, and had had to go three, four, or five times
a week.

She talked about dreams, transference, her emergence from a "sui-
cidal" state. Jung was a drip; Freud the real thing. She laughed and
said that with the help of her psychiatrist she'd discovered her long braid
was her "missing piece." Said she didn't talk about her past to many
people. "You don't talk to Alice and Tom about things like this."

Granted, listening to such recollections, occasional uncertainties
regarding the Professor's sexuality did creep in—with the mention
of the wayward fiancé, for instance. But then again, what narrative
ambiguities could not be quickly resolved? The *suicidal state?* The
missing piece? Such remarks hinted at some profound and arduous
confrontation with self: exactly the sort of struggle a young and brave

lesbian coming of age in the lobotomy-happy fifties might well be thought to have experienced. Those were indeed still the *Well of Loneliness* days. Tons of lesbians and gay men even got married then—often to one another—simply out of fear of exposure. (Witness Paul and Jane Bowles.) I shuddered over the repressive circumstances that no doubt prevailed. Plus in some curious way the Professor's heterosexual asides—more of which were to come later—felt almost titillating, part of some droll and enticing *go-away-a-little-closer* routine. For the subject of homosexuality had yet to be broached, amazingly, between us—even as we blasphemed right and left about Jo and the "radical feminist" gang. Key words went unmentioned; key sentences unsaid. We were perfectly at one in this giddy dance-around. With such a taboo on the obvious in place, the references to mysterious straight affairs merely lent an additional frisson to the situation. The unnamed same-sex thing felt even hotter, sweeter—more fraught with *diablerie*.

None of which is to say that the Professor's conversation was in any way gloomy or grandiose. Alluding to past struggles, she preserved a Jimmy Stewart–like delicacy. She was affable, modest: the very opposite, it seemed, of self-absorbed. And happy enough to leaven any darker revelations with what I took to be charming, if not gallant and self-deprecating, humor. *Aw, shucks, babe.* One of her proudest achievements in life, she chuckled, had been receiving a C-minus in a lit class at Wellesley taught by Vladimir Nabokov. I laughed heartily at this shocking admission, no doubt out of nervous hysteria. The very idea of suffering, let alone surviving, such terrifying scholastic ignominy seemed unthinkable to me. Wasn't 98 out of 100 a miserable failure? And the professor was *Nabokov?* The reader will not be surprised to learn that ladies willing to make light of their academic fiascos have often proved perversely irresistible to me. One of my all-time favorite girlfriends of the 1980s—the cocky and hilarious Robin—managed to get a D in a poetry class at B.U. from Helen Vendler. One wanted to swoon at the very thought.

And as she'd left, the Professor had given me the perfect gift—an A-*plus-plus-plus-plus*. We'd been talking about Janis Joplin, then not so long deceased, and needless to say, one of my many dead heroines. The Professor had played some Janis in a class recently and been overcome, she said, by emotion. Her face filled with melancholy. *I almost had to leave the room.* I must have looked stricken myself, because she instantly fixed on me a breath-stopping gaze:

> *She referred back to that day when we'd met on the stairs, when I'd said I was glad to see her but never knew what to say—she said she had felt the same, and that it had "taken a lot of courage" for me to say that. She had written about that stairway meeting in her journal. This gave me a lurching feeling for some reason.*

But before I could exhale in any normal manner, an even sharper bolt from Cupid's quiver lodged itself in my breast. *She said anytime I just needed a place "to be," to come and stay with her. "I don't say that to many people."* O but, alas, poor Yorick, she'd said it to me.

Today Is the Last Day of the Rest of Your Life

DADDY WAS EXTRATERRESTRIAL, OH DADDY take me up, take me up. The Professor and I first made love the day after I'd gone with Labyris and Co. to see Patti Smith. Smith had not disappointed. The concert took place downtown, in an auditorium filled to the rafters with arty would-be head-bangers. We got our wish: the event was as crazed and cacophonous as any *Ubu Roi–iste* might have wished. Glorious indeed Smith's Babel-babble lyrics, the blasting, nerve-jangling sounds emitted by the band, the rivers of sweat dripping off everyone, the transporting spectacle of the singer twirling and chanting and ranting in the flesh. There she was, a human gyro— resplendent (as I put in my follow-up journal entry) in *tee shirt with a Union Jack, combat fatigues tucked into boots, mop of black stringy hair, crawling round the stage, twisting spastically, fucking the amps, beating her chest while she sang*. That Smith was a transcendent dervish-genius was now confirmed, not least by the fact that afterwards the insufferable Jo (there too, incongruously) was holding forth in the lobby and loudly broadcasting her disapproval. Patti was just like Janis, Jo declared; her lyrics were degrading to women. (*"Ah hayd to pluug mah ee-yuhs."*) One was entirely on Patti's side, of course—that of Baudelaire and Rimbaud and Lautréamont and all the other mad dark angels—now and forever. *Les fleurs du mal? Un bouleversement de tous les sens?* Mais, oui, monsieur.

No sooner said than done. Time flies when you are having crazy fun and all hell can break loose in a split second or two. The Professor went into overdrive in that week after the Adjani-evening. She became the man; I took on the deeply defective role of princess. Though sick inside with hope and lust, aquiver with excitement, I also felt weirdly fatuous, almost paralyzed—like someone in a jumbo jet when it begins its insane, mind-scrambling acceleration down the runway. All of a sudden everything starts to race by and it's all you can do to squeeze out some last morbid good-byes: *bye-bye terminal; bye-bye little fuel trucks, bye-bye control tower (hope someone's in there), bye-bye scrubby trees and outlying cargo bays; bye-bye long-term parking lot; bye-bye ground (I'm hearing those strange shaking noises now and one of the overhead bins has popped open)—please don't forget that I love you*. The Professor did it all. I was now both inert and traveling at incalculable speed.

She started calling me every day. She drove me out to see some local Indian mounds, on a little cliff over the Mississippi. She took me to watch her play racquetball. (I gazed down from a glass-encased gallery above the court, like a guest in the royal box at Wimbledon.) At school, in her office with the door closed, she would challenge me to gleeful arm-wrestling bouts: some, the regular elbows-on-the-table variety, others, a rather more elaborate lying-on-the-floor kind of her own invention. One evening she came over and like a Jewish grandmother boiled up a giant pot of corned beef for me. (We ate huge slabs of it, sat on the floor, got loaded, and listened to records.) She described various oddly suggestive dreams she seemed to be having about me. She stared into my eyes, then looked away. She talked about a student, female, who'd had a "crush" on her a few years earlier—her T.A. when she'd been a visiting prof at a large university on the West Coast. She chuckled warmly at the reminiscence. She harped again on my agelessness. *What did I think about this? What did I think about that?* One day she called simply to tell me she had been trying not to call me. *We are skipping all the steps.*

Neither of us—we discovered during one particularly long and involved phone call—was sleeping very well; our patterns of insomnia, the Professor joked, must be mysteriously related. One day, with some hoopla, she invited me to a little mid-morning performance she was giving in front of the TV cameras at a community college: the lady-reporter doing the feature on her wanted some footage of her singing. The Professor wore thick disconcerting geisha-makeup for the occasion and a butch turquoise pantsuit à la Billie Jean King around the time she clobbered Bobby Riggs. She carried her guitar in a vintage black case and had taped a list of songs on the side of her instrument, just like all the old-time folk singers did. I was her one-girl claque and yayed vigorously after every number: "The Maid of Glenshee," "(That's What You Get) for Lovin' Me," even the ludicrous "Froggie Goes A-Courtin.'" However virile the delivery, the Professor's musical repertoire sometimes verged on the Burl Ives–ish.

The Professor flirted with me that day, of course, but also a little bit, somewhat confusingly, with the TV reporter. The latter—a leggy blonde who later became a well-known CBS correspondent—appeared in some odd way to discombobulate the Professor. At one point the Professor forgot the lyrics to one of her gruesome ballads and froze mid-verse while cameras rolled. Afterwards she told me she had "clutched." *That's not happened in years.* She'd like to get to know that reporter better, she said: she would ask her out to lunch; she was way more intelligent than the *usual dumb bunnies* on local TV news. Earlier that morning, when the Professor had picked me up, she'd said we might take a joyride out of town after she'd performed—a scenic jaunt just the two of us—but after this slightly agitating taping session she apparently changed her mind and dropped me off back at my place, saying she needed to be alone. I felt let down, a bit mystified, and all the more out of my mind with love, love, love.

At the very end of this abbreviated courtship we returned to the site of our first meeting. Alice and Tom had invited me over that week: Tom would make dinner and then we'd watch *How Green Was My Valley* on television. Pot roast and coal dust—a pleasant evening with friends. I wouldn't have to go back home late at night in the snow, Alice had added: I could stay overnight and drive back in to the U. with them the following day. I mentioned the invitation to the Professor in one of our phone calls—in part because I wanted her to know and in part because I half-realized I was becoming all too addicted to the heady stimulation she provided. (*Yikes I won't be able to call you,* she said at once.) It might be good to let her know—that is, if one could summon the smoothness and daring—that one still had other things going on. Sweet-natured Alice and Tom: the perfect duck blind. Alice picked me up as planned and drove me to her house just as she'd done on Christmas Eve. Yet barely had we finished supper and hunkered down on the sofa in front of the television with Emlyn Williams and the Welsh miners (me already swathed in one of my hostess's shapeless crocheted Afghans and a pair of bed socks), than a sharp knock was heard at the door. It was the Professor, of course, and, hey, she'd brought her *pajamas!* She happened to be driving by and thought she'd just see if anyone was home.

Yet while deliriously exciting (*oh-my-god-this-is-more-thrilling-than-anything-that-has-ever-happened-my-god-Alice-and-Tom-have-no-idea-oh-my-god etc., etc., etc.*) the Professor's sudden appearance was not entirely gratifying. Her silvery hair was wet because she had just come, she announced, from playing volleyball at her gym with a kid from the English department. *Hooley's daughter, the medieval guy—an undergrad, a really delightful young woman. Eighteen or nineteen—did we know her? You know how you meet someone and realize right away you're going to be friends for a very long time? She's phenomenal.* The Professor looked so radiant and pleased with herself I felt as if I had been impaled—riven by a stab of pain so shocking and exquisite I fairly convulsed inside. (*A jealousy so pure,* I wrote the next day, *it was like a silver beam of light piercing me. Christ who the fucking hell St. Theresa.*) After shooting merry glances all round (she barely met my eye while speaking), the Professor then snuggled up next to Alice on the sofa and asked her to give her a little neck rub; she was sore from all the activity. Even as Alice obligingly rubbed away—*How Green Was My Valley* burbling on in the background—the Professor fell asleep, her still-damp head ultimately resting, somewhat puppyishly, on Alice's shoulder.

It was a shattering display of power. The first but not the last. A blatant riposte to my own wimp's gambit—that of thinking I could play hard to get for a few hours. Not that the Professor ever lost sight of her immediate end: when the movie was over and Alice went upstairs to make up the beds in the guestrooms—yes, there were two rooms, side by side—the Professor finally looked at me full-on:

archly, inquiringly, almost cruelly. I felt crumply and ill with love, messed up in the head, and again, couldn't think of anything to say.

Burning physical attraction coming over me then—I wanted to look at her all night, her hair, her face, her arms when she rolled up her blue jacket sleeves. Her Beloit T-shirt. Oh Christ. Inarticulate shapes, dancing shapes. Too much. . . .

It is now a question of will—if I can will myself to remain integral to myself, whole, serene. Yet my soul is half out of my body and this is scaring me sick.

We went up to our rooms with Alice and Tom; everyone uttered a cheery good-night. All went quiet and then . . . nothing happened. Nothing at all. Unable to sleep I listened for what seemed like hours for any muffled sounds that might come from the other side of the wall. *Watchman, what of the night*, and all that. I lay there like a bewildered Thisbe—avid, on tenterhooks, wondering what Pyramus was up to—but had no way to make a spy-hole. It was both wonderful and the purest agony.

The next day I tried to put the previous night's disquiet out of my mind and to some degree succeeded: though she'd said and done some odd things, the Professor's amorous juggernaut was no doubt unlikely to end any time soon. (*The goblin men not here yet*—my diary entry from that day somewhat eerily began.) At breakfast with Alice and Tom, there had been the usual furtive eyeballing, followed by some awkward but unmistakable semiflirtation at the sink when the Professor and I washed the dishes. Now, it's true I devolved into uneasiness later that day once I was home and she didn't call me. And when the silence continued overnight and into the next morning, I started to panic. Before, she'd been ringing me at least twice a day. I put the silence down at first to her busy schedule: the winter term was now approaching its chaotic end. I myself was writing several papers. Or trying to. I couldn't concentrate on them. Finally I broke down and called her.

She picked up the phone immediately, as if she'd been sitting just inches away from it, and said in stiff formal tones that she was *delighted to hear from me*. We chatted amiably about nothing in particular. After a while, unprompted, she suddenly began to explain in some detail why, on the movie night—unmentioned by either of us till now—she had asked Alice for a neck massage. The episode meant nothing, she said; they always did that, gave each other massages after tennis, etc., etc. She sounded peeved, as if I had been complaining about it. Which I hadn't been. Indeed, the Professor seemed to go off into a little phone-tunnel—a conversational wormhole, so to speak: some private world of Irritation-with-Alice, of whom she now spoke—with unexpected bitterness and sarcasm—as a bit of a prude. I was perplexed. *But don't you think she and Tom are nice?* I cheeped uncertainly. Yeah, Alice and Tom were okay, she sighed, as if now bored by the whole business; but they were sometimes *dull. Kinda uptight.* There was a whole lot of *stuff* they just didn't get. Never would. You couldn't expect them to. The point of this untoward critique wasn't exactly clear, but no problem. I was desperate to hear the Professor's voice. It didn't really matter what she said.

And yes, the following night at my apartment, we finally Made It Into Bed—literally, into the skanky old box-spring that had come as part of my "furnished suite." Everything began as it had on the corned beef evening: with music and drinking and lollygagging on the floor, gossiping about people we knew at the university. Then it was on to smirky looks, awkward pauses, slightly hysterical guffaws, arm-wrestling that went a bit too far, my very own private back rub, and before I knew it, the Professor had dragged me down the little hall to the bedroom, the nearest available Bower of Bliss, and was already stripping down to a pair of unusually voluminous and high-waisted white cotton underpants. (*More like bloomers*—the pedant in me couldn't help observing—*something Dame Ethel Smyth might have worn.*) I struggled and flopped into the bed, like a baby walrus trying to get on a rock. I was being battered every which way by big waves. So tell me, friends: why *do* storytellers use the phrase "before I knew it"? In my experience you only use that phrase when in fact you *did* know it. It's like signing *cordially* at the end of a note: that's the word you employ when you hate the person's guts.

No real memory of the sex—zero, I'm afraid—only of the Professor saying, once we'd gotten underway, *I feel a bit overdressed*, just like when the pilot comes on after take-off to announce you've reached your cruising altitude and what the weather is like where you're going. *You're free to get up and walk around the cabin.* Prompt service from the underlings in response: drink carts rolled out from the galley; all remaining underpants off. And later: the braid at last being ceremonially unfurled and brushed out for sleep. Oh, and that through everything the Professor kept her watch on—a big macho affair, like a scuba diver's, with a host of luminescent dials. It sometimes rubbed against one's skin abrasively, though whether by accident or some libidinous design on the part of the Professor, it wasn't clear. Her grip was fierce and strong. I don't think I slept much afterward—after a certain point, the whole night seemed to get permanently stuck around 4:00 a.m. Nor could I tell if the Professor slept, or only pretended to sleep. I didn't know her, after all. My eyes felt dried out and sandpapery from the close and incessant heat; the ancient radiator in my bedroom had never, through all our rough sport, stopped its tedious clunking and clinking. Otherwise, the apartment seemed dead—indifferent to what was going on, and to me, its latest inhabitant.

And now for the faster-than-a-speeding-bullet part. After (what shall I call it?) this first *consummation*, events unfolded with such brain-compressing rapidity, such neutrino-busting force, that even now I find myself astonished by the violence of it all. The Profes-

sor set the timetable, went in, did some quick, economical bludgeon-
ing, went out. So efficient and merciless her powers of execution one
never saw it coming. But who indeed *could* have foreseen it? Not the
stunned-ox bludgeonee. Yet there the proof is on the page: a few
claustral weeks of implosion and despair—all logged and dated, in
however shaky a hand—by the desolate diarist of thirty years ago.
One felt positively guillotined by the end of it. If only the guys
remodeling one's kitchen could work with such head-removing
alacrity.

To give the short form: the Professor went off on what can only be
called—pardon the just-invented vulgarism—a fuck-fugue. Within
three weeks of seducing me, the Professor had seduced yet another
juicy young maiden: Professor Hooley's eighteen-year-old daughter,
of course—the hunky volleyball player. *Wudda surpriʒe!* (Her name
turned out to be Molly.) And three weeks after that, the P. seduced
yet *another* young 'un—a tall, blonde, lanky, somewhat dimwitted
twenty-year-old named Tina, likewise an undergrad in English.
(*Hey, no fair! She's never even been mentioned before!*) I was the Methu-
selah now at twenty-two: at least I could lord it over everybody that I
was a first-year graduate student. But none of it mattered in the end.
The *Hindenburg* caught fire anyway and the gig was up—my part
at least—almost as quickly as it had begun. If you managed to jump
clear—or even if you were pushed—you just had to run like hell,
though shattered in every part of you you might be.

Okay, okay—I get ahead of myself. How exactly *did* one get from
Point A to Point B? *Rewind, please, and go slowly.* Well, all right—
though I should confess I never really got much further than *A-Point-
One*, or even worse, only *A-Point-Zero-One*. Nor did I know the half
of it. Nonetheless, like the Rat Man or Anna O., I shall do my best to
narrate my undoing.

In its exalted opening phase—and notwithstanding some of the
enigmas of our first night together—my new intimacy with the

Professor brought me instantly and perilously close to ecstasy. Which is to say, before the great airship caught fire, life aboard the *Hindenburg* seemed nothing less than unrivaled bliss—a brief euphoric succession of love-drenched days and nights, during which one floated, high above the world, on golden and pillowy clouds—exultant, ravished, lighter than the air itself. For a week or two at least one could persuade oneself that life had nothing more exquisite to offer. Every desire was gratified; endless new vistas were to be enjoyed. One was slung there, after all—really, quite wondrously *suspended*—from the belly of the colossal mother ship, in every sense dependent. It was heaven trying to absorb it all—the sublime views and splendid accommodations, the throbbing hum of the engines, the barman in his white jacket smiling and mixing cocktails every evening in the Grand Salon.

Undeniable: that some considerable portion of the intoxication arose simply from the need for total secrecy, the doubly, triply, quadruply, clandestine nature of the thing. For the Professor made it clear both by her words and by the speed with which she had cleared out that first morning we woke up together—the braid had gotten whipped back together in about five seconds flat—that there was to be no announcing to the world of anything, ever. Since I had no friends, really, apart from Elsbet and (sort of) Alice, the directive to remain silent seemed easy enough to comply with. I took to the practice of covert action as if I had been born to it—and come to think of it, perhaps I had. Two decades later, when my stepfather Turk was dying in a nursing home in El Cajon and pretty far gone in his dementia, he said to me one day, amid a babble of otherwise crazy loon-talk, *You ran away so many times, they gave you a medal.*

The Professor and I graduated soon enough from meeting at my shabby little flat to having sex at her house: I would take the bus across town and stay over. But there were now various security protocols to be followed. Yes, on those weekdays when we both had to go in to school for classes, the Professor drove us. But she was jumpy during these morning-after commutes: preoccupied, even a bit nervy. No one was ever to see us, so she would hurriedly deposit me by the side of the road a quarter-mile or so away from the English department. My woolly winter hat pulled anonymously down over my brows, I had to tumble out pronto, like an army parachutist, then scramble up and over the dirty curbside piles of rotting snow, while the Professor sped away without a glance back.

This undignified ejection didn't bother me especially: the vulgar truth be told, I relished the sheer outlawry of it all. I got at once into the mad spirit of the thing. I was enough of a bandit (as she was) to enjoy *épater*-ing some notional unseen bourgeoisie. The Closet, all of a sudden, turned out to be fantastically exciting—far more so in fact than Destroying the Patriarchy or even Performing the Fruit Ritual. We reveled in cocking a snook at all the *dull old straight people*: the other professors, one's tedious fellow students, the presumably respectable citizens of the Upper Midwest. (And even some of the *dull old gay people* too: poor Jo!) It was ours alone—a secret at once thrilling and obscene. Life was delicious. It was sick and it was fun. And it has to be said, for all its banality the illicit nature of our connection was also the most potent aphrodisiac I had ever experienced. It sent my physical desire for her—and hers for me, at least at the start—through the roof. We couldn't even stop to chat when we met up those first days; we just had to *do it*. The Professor must care for me greatly, I concluded—as much as I did for her in fact—to risk so much, to play so close to the edge.

I've often wondered why this deception felt so gratifying—for indeed I took a strange, rapt sort of pride in it. The breaching of the teacher-student barrier, coupled with the homosexuality, was obviously a flagrant offence against the System—a sort of double whammy, in fact. We'd smashed two taboos at once. As a Southern friend of mine would say, it was like *getting the cash and the credit, too*.

Thirty years on, in a different world, I remain ambivalent about this aspect of our transgression—what you might call its conjoined, two-headed nature. Worth remembering: the Professor and I violated no laws or codes or University policies; the concept of sexual harassment remained embryonic in academia in those days, laughably unworked-through. Academic culture was mostly unreconstructed—like Sodom and Gomorrah before the pelting rain of fire. Today, of course, official antiharassment policies exist at virtually all American colleges and universities (including my own) and various kinds of professor-student intimacy are now expressly forbidden. Everyone knows instructors who've been disciplined, about whom complaints have been lodged, questions raised, lawsuits filed. Many of the longtime abusers have been punished. All to the good, people seem to agree: *about time, too.* And of course one finds oneself chiming in: *Yeah! Huzzah! I'm down with that. The power disparity is always so great, after all.* As assuredly it is. Damaged men and women can (and do) exploit their authority over others in abominable ways—for wicked, selfish, self-deluding ends. Evil Never Sleeps and It's Working for Management.

Yet at the same time some mad little antic part of me still wants to rebel (if only rhetorically) against the wholesome official template. I don't rebel in actuality, of course, but every once in a while I *do* have the odd impeachable thought or two. This urge persists in spite of (because of?) the fact that my own experience might appear to provide irrefutable evidence of the painful folly of teacher-student love affairs. Indeed, it has to be said: however local and abbreviated and misleading, I have never forgotten, in some long-submerged baby-Sapphist part of me, the sheer euphoria—the release, relief, and vaulting transport—I experienced with the Professor. There was a huge kick in it all. Especially after the confusing love-episodes of my undergraduate years—Phoebe, Karen—the Professor's lust was a kind of instant education. Another woman besides me craved sex with women. A beautiful and distinguished woman, no less. A grown-up woman. An older woman. A noble woman—almost chivalric—with silver-grey hair. For a single iridescent moment, the affirmation of same-sex love seemed to outshine the glaring inequalities of age, money, authority, power, prestige.

In wishful (or maybe just intransigent) moods I sometimes find myself wondering if the same-sex element doesn't ameliorate the teacher-student situation in some degree—make the damnable slightly *less* damnable. For when you get right down to it, doesn't just about every interesting and (dare one say?) *intelligent* older lesbian have lurking in her misspent youth some erotically charged relationship with a female teacher? The woman in question wasn't always literally a teacher, of course: sometimes she merely occupied an analogous position of authority—i.e., was an athletic coach, camp counselor, kindly nun, or the like. She is often recollected, nostalgically, as the First Love. One woman I know was initiated into Sapphism by her high school tennis coach; another by the married Sunday School teacher at her church—there in the empty rec room, amid the little kids' chairs and pictures of Jesus. Another young lady well known to me but who shall remain nameless had a wild affair in her teens with her English teacher at a famous prep school. (They would meet late at night in a deserted Wendy's parking lot for urgent trysts in the teacher's car.) That homosexual men of a certain age can tell similar stories I don't doubt; a comical pal of mine was deflowered by his high school French teacher and to this day recalls the event (and the teacher) with great fondness. *'ello, mon cheri. Deed you zhee me weenking at you? Zut, alors.*

Hard not to feel, if you're gay, the hot, old-timey romance in some of these tales. But it's also arguable, I've come to think, that whenever same-sex love is illegal, unmentionable, or outright taboo—exists only under the Sign of the Closet, so to speak—teacher-student eros can serve a socializing, even genealogical, function across the generations. Think of *Claudine at School*, *Mädchen in Uniform*, *The Prime of Miss Jean Brodie*, or indeed any number of turgid lesbian school novels in which an adolescent heroine becomes infatuated with a charismatic *pédagogue*. (There's even a super-hot depiction of such a liaison, of all places, in D. H. Lawrence's *The Rainbow*.) It's part of the life, part of one's own little heritage. And for better or worse, the Affair with the Teacher still stands as an archetypal rite of passage into the Sapphic world. Shouldn't the role such relationships have played in individual lives be acknowledged and their functions explored? Maybe there could be a museum or even a theme park.

Hard to ignore, of course: the age-old charge that homosexual teachers are predators, eager to "recruit" students and by their devilish lessons convert them to sex deviance. It's one of the oldest antigay canards on the books. The irony here is that the homophobes get things partly right: the teacher-pupil relationship can be a powerfully erotic one. The Greeks knew all about it; witness Socrates and Co. Or even more to the point, the great Sappho herself. One of the surviving legends about the poet holds that she ran a sort of female academy on Lesbos and that the various lovers mentioned in her poems (Atthis, Anactoria, Gyrinna) were her favorite students: teacher's pets in thongs and chitons.

Which isn't necessarily to say that same-sex love can be taught—even were there such a thing as a University of Sappho at Lesbos. (Otherwise known as USL: *transfer students accepted*.) In my own experience the desire preceded any curriculum. The lesbian pedagogue may crystallize or refine what is there, of course, but under the Sign of the Closet her most useful function may be simply to externalize the desire: to demonstrate to the junior partner that homoerotic fantasies can in fact be realized, given weight and heft and carnal life in an otherwise inhospitable grown-up world. She offers a kind of adult recognition and endorsement: a fleshly validation across time zones. If the teacher is a benign, unscrewed-up sort of person (a big

If, I know) she can offer a sense of lineage and belonging. Even as she intimates the emotional viability of a life thus lived, the teacher is often the first to confer on homosexuality both a historic dimension and epistemological gravitas.

Or at least that's one (exceedingly) rosy way of looking at it. Maybe far *too* rosy. Icky-rosy. Pukey-rosy. I may be utterly mistaken. Maybe I'm a blithering idiot. An irresponsible fantasist. Maybe the theme park should be a jail after all. Maybe, indeed, I am eager to place the whole business in such a sanguine light precisely because my own surrender to the Professor was so complete, so abject, and so devastating.

For surrender it was. I was happy to be dominated, to defer to her majesty. Given the differences between us, I reflexively assumed the Professor to be the wiser, the more sophisticated, of the two of us. She was prominent in her field, after all, admired by colleagues and students, and had achieved precisely the kind of success I longed for. (One of her favorite boasts had to do with having attained the rank of full professor at the relatively precocious age of thirty-five. I later became obsessed with outdoing her in this respect.) She was an expert, an eminence, a sort of lady-comet, flashing across the heavens. She zipped round the country giving lectures and performances; had her own letterhead and business cards; toted a briefcase, glossy and magnificent, around with her—no doubt full of important stuff. Yet one's deference, to say the least, was ill-advised. The Professor had problems of her own, it would turn out—manifest above all in a steely, seemingly insatiable appetite for emotional control. Combined with my own equally insatiable desire—to be taken care of—the result was near-instant psychic mayhem. The Professor became cruel; I succumbed to a kind of Sapphic Stockholm syndrome. One joined the cult of Dear Leader. Easy enough to let myself be washed away by the sheer disorderly force of her personality.

In my impaired state it became a positive pleasure—an honor—to yield to the Professor's paranoia. (I didn't understand the paranoia as such.) In addition to the make-yourself-scarce protocol now in place when she drove us into school, there were numerous other imperatives to absorb. They kicked in immediately. Some of these took the form of odd prohibitions and constraints—a sort of behavioral hobbling. Several involved the Professor's house. The place was as delightful as I remembered it on Christmas Eve (why *couldn't* it be mine?). The marijuana plants still flourished. The Oriental rugs still lay about in elegant profusion. The Bose speakers stood ready to serve. In the kitchen the refrigerator was big and white and gleaming and now I was allowed to look inside it and even take things out. I loved it all. But the Professor also had some stipulations. Among the most draconian: that I never set foot—*literally* never set foot—in one room in the house, the one directly across from her bedroom. Here she kept various notes and files and tapes that had to do with her linguistic researches. These files were Top Secret: her duty to her sources and informants—all those aged speakers of Smoky Mountain Speech, Gullah, and the like—demanded the most rigorous confidentiality. Plus, there were sinister people everywhere who would be *very eager* to see into those files. She had to watch her back.

Why she thought I would be interested in these strange but tedious-sounding memoranda was never clear. When it came to the audio files, I would have had no clue, moreover, how to work the elaborate reel-to-reel tape equipment piled up everywhere like something out of *2001: A Space Odyssey*. Still, for me it was *'Nuff said, ma'am*. As instructed, I never did go in there, though I easily might have. In the first flush of passion the Professor had given me a key to her house and so for the month or so we slept together I often found myself hanging around the place on my own—rather like a concubine in a seraglio, waiting for the Professor to come back from wherever. (The Professor sometimes required me to do housework during these solitary vigils: I remember dragging a huge and unwieldy old

canister vacuum around one afternoon and even did the stairs, labo-
riously, with a highly aggravating little sucker attachment.) About
the only good thing to be said about this ultradocility, or indeed my
brief spell of huswifery, is that, yes, *the figure of Bluebeard did cross my
mind*. Later, bless him, he would become, if only allegorically, one of
one's psychic liberators.

My compliance with other taboos was likewise absolute. One night
(I'd come over a few hours earlier), the Professor went out to a play
with Peggy, her current T.A.—a crusty, overweight hippy lady who
posed no romantic threat to me, I figured, and with whom, in fact, I
later became friends. The Professor had planned it out: Peggy might
want to come in afterwards for a drink, she told me, so if I heard
them entering together, I was to remain sequestered in the bedroom
upstairs and not make a sound. No creaking the floorboards or odd
little thuds. Peggy did come in, as it happened, and so for more than
an hour, even as peals of bibulous laughter wafted up from below, I
hid out, Anne Frank–style—afraid to make the bedsprings creak,
hardly daring to turn the pages of the book I was reading for fear of
causing some stray little riffling noise. The situation brought to mind
what one always heard about EST seminars: that hours passed but
you weren't allowed to go to the bathroom. When the door slammed
and she finally came up, the Professor was chortling heartily—*she'd
really pulled the wool over Peggy's eyes*. Peggy, she announced, had
always had a big crush on her. *It was sad but also touching*. The P. was
churned up and a bit drunk and wanted to have sex right away.

The Professor reveled in knowing the score when other people
didn't. Other people often included me. Granted, almost as soon
as we became lovers, she dispensed a modicum of uncensored
information—often melodramatic—about her own parti-colored
past: college loves, this girlfriend and that one, the T.A. girl on
the West Coast, a lady in Puerto Rico, even a plumpish young assistant professor from another department, putatively straight, with

whom she'd had—only a year or two before, it seemed—a tumultuous affair. This other woman was a *hysteric*, I learned; *a real sicko*. The Professor had once had to fire off a warning shot in bed—the loaded pistol was kept in the bedside drawer—to keep said lady in line. (That the Professor was as magnificent a shot as Wyatt Earp I had no doubt: with great pride she once showed me a weird warped quarter that she had supposedly dinged mid-flight when somebody had thrown it up in the air.) Whenever the Professor now saw this Detestable Former Love at faculty convocations or the like, she felt panicky and enraged and had to take a tranquillizer.

But there were many other things I wasn't to know and I was made to know I wasn't to know. Oh, yes, said the Professor, of course she slept with men as well as women; having taken me in her arms, she frequently hinted she was even then simultaneously romancing some agreeable stud or other. (Who no doubt favored women with long silver braids and missing pieces.) *She did what lesbians did, but she refused to be called one.* I was not to ask questions, especially when I didn't hear from her for a day or two. Regarding this purported taste in men I knew nothing, save a little tidbit of 411 that she dropped one evening while we lay in bed, drunk and already bickery, in front of the TV. The Bionic Man (a pumped-up Lee Majors)—just then bending some pieces of rebar onscreen in front of us—was, she allowed, exactly the sort of guy she liked. *You know, athletic—a good physique.* Bionic in fact. The comment—I daresay—expressed one of the very few forward-looking aspects of her sensibility: she was straight; she was gay; she was cyborg-friendly too.

Unnamed women everywhere were in love with her—especially straight ones. They were all over the country, apparently: professors, students, media people, folksingers, sportswomen of various sorts. Some of her exasperation with Alice, it turned out, was due to her belief that Alice harbored repressed homosexual feelings for her but was too stiff and dumb and straitlaced to realize it. *When I was younger I could have really gotten messed up over her.* . . . But luckily, there were women enough with yearnings similar to one's own who *were* prepared to act on them: that made up for it. The well would never run dry. She'd let me know, in good time, the Professor chuckled, if I ever had anything to worry about. But, of course, I never would. She was *crazy* about me; *we'd be together for a very long time.* Probably forever.

Thus even when Tweedledee and Tweedledum, Molly and Tina, came along a few weeks later—the three of us becoming for a brief spell rival boinkees—it was supposedly no sweat. They didn't know about me, the Professor insisted; nor were they aware of each other's involvement with her. They were just two *dumb kids* she was helping out. Teaching them, as it were—Molly, the little baby dyke especially—that it was totally normal and okay to have sex with women. I was the one whom she had graced with a full accounting, the Professor explained, because I was tough enough, grown-up enough, and the one she *really* wanted. She owed it to me. Indeed, I should feel very special. It was precisely because she loved me so passionately—already, she declared—that she was screwing around. *I'm testing you, I guess.* The infidelities (*aw, honey, if you can even call them that*) were simply proof of her feeling for me. I should wait it all out: she'd slough off the other two soon enough. I would be hers and she would be mine because I was *so goddamned smart* and *so goddamned substantial*, such a *fine and superior person—so funny too*—but even more than that because *I understood despair.*

I'll come back to the despair part in a moment. What is most difficult to convey here, of course, is why I remained so feverishly in thrall to the Professor, even as various unpleasant quirks and peculiarities in her began to reveal themselves. The Bluebeard business alone, I realize, suggests a certain monstrosity. Yet the Professor, I swear, was deeply lovable, too; lovable enough, in fact, to balance out whatever misgivings even a harsher judge than I might have entertained. True—the split in her nature was extreme: Ripley's Believe It or Not could have done a feature on her. *Good and Bad Amazingly Combined! Two People in One! The Famous Lady Jekyll-and-Hyde!* She fooled even those, it seemed, far more subtle and streetwise than I. At the university and out in the world, after all, she was managing to function at an extremely high professional level without raising undue suspicion. Yes, I was a needy and overawed twenty-two-year-old. But jumbled up as everything was in my beloved's psyche, I had legitimate as well as pathetic reasons for being smitten with her. She was a menace, it transpired, but a captivating one.

First, of course: the sheer seduction of her personality. She could love-bomb you. In social settings the Professor had a shining, attentive, fresh-faced quality to her—a sort of openness and kindness and unaffected curiosity about the world. She seemed more *alive* in the moment than most people ever became over their entire lives. When she was relaxed, not freaked out about something or someone, she could exhibit an enormous, infectious social charm, a charm almost impossible to delineate after the fact. It was fully embodied yet also somehow philosophical. The Professor was an accomplished winker, among other things, and when she winked at you from across the room you felt an immediate and delicious contact and acceptance. You couldn't keep yourself from smiling back. No doubt, the wink suggested, there was something *funny*, as well as tragic, about being alive and you and she both knew it. *What a farce, eh?*

The sense of the comic was rich and well-developed in her; the lack of pretentiousness genuine. An early, deep-voiced kind of geniality had no doubt been a part of her professional success—had helped to make her a successful teacher and collector of data. She had a way with an audience: got people talking, made people open up in intimate ways. (It was also what made her such an effective manipulator of those who didn't see through it.) She wasn't afraid to play the jester in public. She enjoyed singing little bits of grossly ribald song, for example—especially some favorite lines from a smutty sailor ditty about *frigging in the rigging*. She approved of the silliness, the way lewdness got overtaken by slapstick. In fact, she seemed to relish silliness in any form. She admired dachshunds for the palpably absurd way they waddled through life. She had an iron doorstop in one of the rooms upstairs in the shape of a dachshund. (Was his name *Alexei*? Like the doomed Tsarevitch?) The ridiculous combination of preening amour propre with the Chaplinesque short legs never failed to delight her.

She was likewise drawn, in endearing fashion, to buoyant, fruity-voiced, full-figured *comedienne* types of the sort popular in classic Hollywood films in the 1930s and '40s. Larger-than-life female clowns like Margaret Dumont, say, as Mrs. Gloria Teasdale in *Duck Soup* or Mrs. Claypool in *A Night at the Opera*. Margaret Rutherford in anything. (Or her panto-dame equivalent: Alastair Sim, in bosomy drag, as Millicent Fritton, the girls' school headmistress in *The Bells of St. Trinian's*.) The Professor greatly enjoyed hammy old burlesque queens like Tessie O'Shea and Sophie Tucker; likewise, the glorious Ruth Draper—famed for her arch comic monologues in Edith Wharton–ish *grande dame* persona. Anna Russell, the Canadian opera singer and comedian of the 1950s and '60s was another special favorite: I first heard Russell's (now classic) plummy-ludicrous retelling of the story of Wagner's *Ring of the Nibelungen* one night at the Professor's house. She'd dug the record out from her stack of favorite LPs and insisted that I listen.

The Professor's favorite star of all time, though, was Marie Dressler—she of *Dinner at Eight*, *Tugboat Annie*, and *Min and Bill*. She seemed in fact to have a huge crush on her. Dressler was then just a name to me—a symptom of the seemingly vast age difference between myself and the Professor, so I didn't pay much attention. I know more now. (Was Dressler *too* a big ole dyke? She definitely looks like one in photos.) You can see lots of Dressler today on

YouTube—going all the way back to her 1914 silent film with Chaplin, *Tillie's Punctured Romance*. She's utterly marvelous. One could hardly say that she and the Professor looked alike—the P. being lean and athletic, almost sinewy, when I knew her, and Dressler like a giant washerwoman—but there's something in the theatricality and warmth, the comic mobility of expression, that carries over. A certain bizarre sexiness. After thirty years it's hard for me to retrieve more than a weak-signal, evanescent sense of the Professor's presence *in the flesh*—her distinctive carnal magic—but I've felt closest to her, and her closest to me, while watching Dressler mug and dance and carry on in these flickery, droll, now-ancient video clips. I can imagine the Professor and I laughing at them together, in some life we never had.

Yet even more attractive to me than the Professor's comic side was her melancholia. The two things were related, of course: the comedy, like her sexual promiscuity, bore the traces of, seemed to grow out of, some deep and unfathomable undercurrent of pain. This pain, I suspect, was both what bound us, at first, then sent us careening off in opposite directions with such violence. We saw reflected in one another the same need—ancient, tactile, immense—for succor. I'm tempted to call it a need for mothering, except I'm English and hate the reductive and humiliating cliché sound of *that*. Mother's milk and such. Yuck. *So let's look round for another way of saying it, shall we? Hmmm . . .*

Too bad, fatso. *Mothering*, goddamn it, is the only word for it.

Mothering. The Professor had been right, in one of her seduction speeches, to speak of a universe of human suffering: everyone needed this *mothering*, it seemed, but not everyone got it. Or not enough. The Professor knew the bitter reality—inside and out, apparently—and was able to express it better than anyone I had ever met. In moments of intimacy, this dark knowledge—somehow enthroned in her—gave the Professor what can only be called an overwhelming emotional depth and moral pathos. Overwhelming to me especially because I felt I responded to it in every cell of my being. I recognized it. She seemed to describe me to myself. And to listen to her—especially the pillow talk—was to experience a devastating wish to console. Devastating because the pain was as much one's own as it was hers and one knew that consolation was impossible. One had not the power. One tried to clutch at her anyway, to pat her chest, or lay one's hand or head against her breastbone. But everything was so terribly unstable, like a nightmare.

To return to the world of fairy tales: if the Professor was in one sense Bluebeard-like, she was also, at other times, like the Beast in *Beauty and the Beast*. Her beastliness, like the latter's, was of that achy, endearing, human-all-too-human sort that makes one want to weep. One could imagine her crouching down, like the Beast in Cocteau's film, to lap water from some clear crystal pool. Because the Beast is yet an *animal*—though also a noble and stately one and soon to metamorphose, ever so feelingly, into Jean Marais—he has, one realizes, no other way of doing it. The vulnerability in the movement, the enactment of frailty and mortality, of embodied need and suffering, is heartrending. Yet the Professor too conveyed such vulnerability. She seemed to grasp the nature of things in a way I had yet to understand. I remember once asking her if she would like to live forever. *Wouldn't it be* great *if we never had to die?* No, she responded, *because then nothing would ever mean anything.* Not the answer I wanted, of course, but I've never forgotten it.

The childhood polio—grotesque curse of the American mid-century—was one eminent source of pain; a historic sadness that kept on giving. Even for me at the time it was easy to see that the psychic consequences of the Professor's illness had been deep and disordering. She had had the disease when she was around twelve or thirteen. Though never confined to an iron lung (or at least I don't recollect her ever saying she was) the Professor was clearly still haunted by the mechanical 1940s–'50s sci-fi nightmare of it all. Big metal mummy-tubes. People locked inside what looked like cyclotrons. Her restlessness, her athleticism, her twitchy, quick-to-surface aggression and agitation—all suggested a massive compensatory effort of self-mobilization. The point was not to get *paralyzed*. To *keep moving*. Such willfulness and strength at times made her seem ineffably brave and wise.

One night as we lay in bed she showed me an old black and white photograph of herself. She was on the cusp of adolescence in the picture and posing outdoors, tennis team–style, with a group of ten or fifteen other girls. The girls were all smiling: they seemed in fact to be a sports team or summer camp group of some sort. Everyone had on shorts and white middy blouses and kerchiefs. The Professor was in the middle of the back row, her then-dark hair in pigtails, looking out at the camera with dread and dismay. *That was the day I got sick. I was already feeling sick when they took that picture. That was when it started, right then. I remember feeling sick.*

I didn't know what to say, nor indeed what to do—that night or any other—when the Professor's withered leg began *acting up*. At times she got a tormenting sensation in her calf and hamstring akin to "restless legs" phenomenon. Some sort of neuropathy? She jerked around and groaned briefly and told me that the only thing that helped was *quinine* and she didn't have any. I was fascinated and appalled. I'd been born in 1953, soon after Jonas Salk had tested the first polio vaccine. I was so much younger—a Baby Boomer: safe forever. Quinine sounded like something from the nineteenth century. Such suffering was exotic to me, like the word "poliomyelitis" itself. My goggle-eyed concern during these episodes in turn seemed to exasperate the Professor. She became irritable and nasty. Things were definitely starting to go south the last time it happened—I was fretting incessantly about how to *be* around her—and this strange pain threw her bad luck, and my good luck, into relief. There was nothing I *could* do but look stricken and dumb and far too young to cope with any of it.

That the Professor's disability meant something, inalterable and profound, in the gestalt of our relationship seems clear, though I still can't say exactly what it was. Even now a sort of aphasia comes over me. To be sure, she had developed a certain assertion and bravura in response to it. Yet it had also instilled in her a generalized anxiety and hypochondria. She was obsessed with dread diseases, and cancer in particular. These fears were in turn ineluctably bound up with sex and death. Not long after we'd begun sleeping together, we were again in her bed—the place where almost all of the important conversations I remember having with her seem to have occurred—and she told me she was worried about her breast lumps. They were *all over the place.* She took my hand and guided me to some of them and wanted me to palpate them. (I did so gently, though not without a sickening wave of disquiet.) *Would I stay with her if she had to have a mastectomy?* Oh, yes, yes. *Of course. Yes.* Would love her even *more*, in fact. It was clear one had to demonstrate more equanimity under the circumstances than the reviled Colleague-Lover of a few years back had shown—the lady, that was, whose apparent dastardliness had obliged the Professor to fire a bullet into the bedroom floor. One night when she and the Professor had been making love—or so the Professor scathingly related it—this feeble excuse for a girlfriend had brushed against a particularly hard nodule by accident and instantly become nauseous. Freaked out. Unable to continue with the business at hand. All the more proof, said the P., she was a complete *psycho.* Didn't matter then that she was a former child figure-skating star and a blond cutie-pie and they'd been going to buy a house together. *Fucking cow.*

I remember—again—listening in on such anguish, scared but

mesmerized. *So far, so bad*. One lay on one's side, head raised and resting on one hand, and gazed down into the Professor's unseeing eyes as she talked. (Oddly, despite her Jewishness, her eyes were a stark gray-blue.) As she emerged from her pain-reverie, she would gradually return the gaze, focusing increasingly intently, as if searching one's features for something resembling strength. One tried to look pensive, tough—courageous. But what did one really feel about any of it? This terrifying fragility in things? I couldn't tell you.

A year or two after getting dumped I had a bizarre reminder of the Professor—the polio, the withered leg, and everything else I didn't understand about her. My feminist reading group was having its biweekly get-together. (What were we reading? Eudora Welty? Carson McCullers? Flannery O'Connor? Something corny and 1940s but wonderful like that.) Jo was there, and by some odd coincidence reminiscing vividly about the polio epidemic. She too had lived through it—obviously without succumbing—but as a child had been terrorized by the thought of the disease. She'd been too young to understand about viruses and their transmission and had somehow concluded that "Polio" was a monster who would pursue you and kill you if he saw you having fun at a swimming pool. Polio was his name—a name like Popeye or Bluto. (*"Ah wuʒ tahr-ri-faahd that PO-LEE-OH wuʒ gawna git me."*) It was a gripping account—Jo's eyes had gotten huge and everyone else in the room seemed to have stopped breathing. Just so: at the thought of little Jo and Polio, *that nightmarish monster*, I was instantly overcome with hysteria, an urge to giggle and guffaw as mad and gay and preemptive—as *sexual* in fact—as any I've ever felt. It was hideous: I had to contort my face gargoyle-fashion—grit my teeth and somehow try to keep my lips from moving, so as not to explode. But the image in turn just wouldn't stop being hilarious. The whole dreadful fit went on for what seemed like ten minutes—a sort of multiple orgasm of wanting-to-laugh. I just had to shut my eyes tight—contain the feeling even if it killed me—and somehow I guess I did.

But lodged in the Professor too were other even more archaic fears. She often spoke with some anguish about being Jewish, which she seemed to regard as a sort of primeval curse. Jewishness was not so much a bequest as a kind of doom, the dire and definitive mark of Cain. Perhaps not so unusual for an American woman of her generation, I guess: the Professor had lived through the discovery and first documentation of the Holocaust, after all. News of that inassimilable disaster had coincided exactly with her coming of age. True: I didn't know her long enough to acquire many intimate details about her parents or early life—I can't recall what her father did for a living, for instance, or anything about siblings, except that she had a brother. But one gathered that the family unit (huddled up together somewhere in a middle-class Long Island suburb) was dreary and unhappy—rather like the one Art Spiegelman depicts in *Maus*. The Professor's parents, unlike Spiegelman's, were not survivors, as far as I know, except in the most displaced and psychological sense. Yet the atmosphere of unease—a pervasive feeling of oppressiveness and precariousness—seems to have been similar. There'd been a sort of crazy-suicidal vibe in the air: that *Maus*-vibe.

And thus it was, grimly enough, that our postcoital conversations so often turned on extermination camps, the hideous arbitrariness of fate, *the children who never should have been born*. On the latter topic the Professor's usual steely manner would give way to tremulousness and she would fall into a sort of maudlin schoolgirl reverie. I've said she was a hypochondriac; she could also be morbid and histrionic—a sort of sorrowing death-junkie. Her inner world was dark and sad and full of dangers, constantly flooding out with anxiety. At such moments she exuded a strange mixture of panic, fierceness, and despondency. So labile, in fact, was her emotional state over the period

I knew her, she was having to pop "tranquilizers" fairly often. (I don't know what they were. Maybe Valium? This was all long before Prozac.) No doubt these angst-spells would have become exhausting over the long run, but in the moment I found them stirring and seductive.

The children who never should have been born, I soon learned, had their melancholy counterparts elsewhere in my lover's troubled soul: namely, *the children who should have been born, but weren't*. Which is to say the children that the Professor herself might have had—had she ever married; had she not turned to homosexuality; had she not had the hysterectomy of several years before, had she not delivered (as she put it) a *healthy eight-pound uterus* to the world. This infertility, this regret, this anger at Nature's cruelty, was another part of her I never understood very well at the time—to my sorrow. But I was miles from ever getting it. (And in some way I'm not sure I even get it now, having seldom had more than the most fleeting desire either to bear or raise a child.) It was unlucky too, perhaps, that I was young enough, indeed, for her to have given birth to me. In the early fifties she would have been eighteen or nineteen.

And not so very hard to perceive now: that when the Professor spoke of children—born or unborn—she was also talking about herself. *The children who should not have been born* had been victims of a catastrophic failure of *mothering*. They had gone unprotected into the night, had been starved and clubbed and frightened to death, had been helpless in the face of adult cruelty and betrayal. Not the fault of anyone's real mother, of course, but the effect was the same as if it had been. One intuited as much: that the Professor likewise felt unmothered—implacably so, in fact—and that her Jewishness, not to mention her homosexuality, were bound up with this intractable sensation of neglect. The terrible imperative to self-destruction she claimed to have faced down in analysis in her twenties had no doubt arisen from some deep wound of this sort—some conviction, indeed, that she herself should not have been born. To put herself to death would have been to put things right.

Yet the child who *hadn't* been born—Kid-Zero, in other words, the kid the Professor herself might have had—was also a kind of self-projection. Had she had this child, the fantasy seemed to go, she would have *mothered it almost to death*—loved it and cared for it with a devotion at once totalizing, sumptuous, and unconditional. She would have cherished it in precisely the way that she herself had not been—which is to say, for eternity. After all, someone needed *to damn well repair things. Do some fucking good in the world*. The damage everywhere was ghastly and gross. She had to make it up to some-one—to the poor *little baby,* to herself. And because of her disability she had to be especially heroic. Yes, there was a risk in such love that one might smother or be smothered, but wasn't that preferable to being tortured and starved in a cellar or thrown into some frozen pit to die?

Such wishfulness and dread combined to produce in her an urge to treat me—whom she often seemed to perceive as a sort of youth-ful alter ego—with a crazy-making mixture of compassion and con-tempt. The Professor held a deep belief, among other things, that I had "seen" something utterly monstrous—experienced some kind of Freudian primal scene—before I could ever speak. This scarifying infant vision, made immeasurably worse by the fact that in my word-less state I had not been able to signal my distress, had left me, she declared, emotionally crippled. She was sorry for me on that count. At certain times I became caressable for just that reason. Pathetic but charming. In need of her sexual services. And I believed her—believed the whole tyrannical crackpot story of my infantile past. I was almost proud to have been traumatized thus; the mystery and melodrama seemed to make me more like *her*. And doubtless this

Primal Scene, once rediscovered, would explain my weird personality—my stupid silences, for example, when the Professor snapped at me on the phone and I became mortified or speechless in reply. On some level I was remembering *IT*.

Swept up in this disastrous fiction, I would strain to recall precisely *what* it was I could have seen—as if I could summon it up, say, like the color of my first baby blanket, through an act of pure mentation. Other questions, too, required cogitation. Were certain later moments of childhood uncanniness—the ones that I *could* remember—some sort of hysterical repetition of the original terror? Like the time I opened up the linen closet—pre-parental divorce—and saw that our pretty Siamese cat had given birth in a pile of towels to a mewling and bloody little heap of kittens? I'd jumped back at once, breathless with shock. A few days later my father put all the kittens in a pillowcase and drowned them in a bucket of water in the garage.

Perhaps I should have seen that being cast thus—as messed-up Junior Sad Sack in the Professor's gloomy mental pageant—hardly boded well for our relationship. Perhaps I should have noticed that it was the very quality for which she had praised me when we met and which was supposedly to link us forever—my putative familiarity with despair—that made the whole business untenable. For as soon as Molly and Tina appeared on the scene, my expressions of pain—muted and impaired though they were—seemed only to intensify the Professor's scorn and condescension. Oh, so I was feeling *abandoned*, was I? Just because she was now sleeping with two other young women in addition to myself? I had obviously failed to understand something *really basic. My unconscious was the problem.* I was a *hysteric.* I needed an analysis like hers—and fast. Maybe after, say, some eight or nine years of intense introspection I might then evolve into a viable girlfriend—someone with whom she might like, indeed, to be associated. The Professor felt more and more obliged to harangue me on this last subject, as if I'd broken into her house and left a pile of dirty laundry in the middle of the living room. You had to realize, she often lectured me, that nobody else was going *to clothe and feed you.* You had to do it yourself. Lift up your little baby arms. Grab that baby cup and bring it to your mouth. Indeed, you couldn't trust anyone to do it *but* yourself. I needed to learn this lesson soon, she'd decided: I was so *immature* in many ways. *Whiney, too.* I battened on such insults and implored her forgiveness.

Our erotic relations quickly came to mimic the lopsided dynamic the Professor had delineated—became, indeed, a sort of cartoon version of it. In the beginning, that is, when we barely knew one another, our couplings had been almost comically egalitarian: a matter of untutored yet reciprocal lust. Though both of us, as I've noted, were inflamed by the teacher-student divide—the *de-haut-en-bas* titillation of it all—the initial flood of relief and release gave a deceptively utopian cast to our activities in the moment. Nobody was boss. On the contrary, we were zany sidekicks in some sweaty Sapphic comedy: a sort of lesbian *Some Like It Hot.* We shared marquee billing: our names both up in lights, but neither twinkling more brightly than the other.

But soon enough an asymmetry became discernible. The larkish, happy-go-lucky element started to wear off. From several elliptical asides in my journal I surmise now that from fairly early in our romance the Professor had trouble achieving a climax, but I don't remember what the issue was or if indeed it ever went away. I'm guessing not: I have no memory of being particularly adroit or funky in those days. I was still embarrassingly inexperienced. The Professor in turn was wont to dismiss any experimental forays on my part with chilling abruptness. *Naw, honey, I don't need that.* I became ever more spooked and passive as a result—the *fuckee* more often than not, though never (more fool I) less than responsive. As a bedmate I remained lively and excitable to the bitter end. Imagine, if you will, a fancy banquet table set for thirty—grandly appointed, heavily laden with floral arrangements, silver candlesticks, fine dishes and glassware and cutlery of every description. One was oneself *set* in just such a fashion: eager, if not desperate, for some darling mischief maker to come along, grab a corner of the tablecloth, and yank the whole arrangement onto the floor with carnivalesque flair. Quite the mad clatter. According to the Professor I was a refreshing change, in particular after the West Coast girlfriend, who, while apparently lovely in all other respects, had been entirely dead to her touch.

In turn the Professor became ever more butch and seignorial. She could be rough, even savage, when she was about it, a true ravisher of innocent maidens, though here, admittedly, one's rather pitted and pockmarked memories come partly mediated by a vivid conversation that took place a while later. A year or so after my debacle, an acquaintance of mine, knowing my sad history, brought a friend of hers round to see me one day: a married Ph.D. student in her thirties from Anthropology. The latter had likewise been seduced by the Professor—likewise summarily dumped—and wished to revile the P. with some other local Ancient Marineress who might lend a sympathetic ear. The Married Lady was a hard, glozing, stupid sort of woman—definitely Jenny Petherbridge from *Nightwood*—and I remember not liking her much. Nor did I particularly resonate to her somewhat repetitious invective on the subject of our mutual tormentor. I listened politely, however, as the woman unfolded what was to me an all too familiar tale of woe.

Admittedly, I took ascetic (and uncharitable) satisfaction in realizing that Tweedledum (Tina), of whom I had once been so pathetically jealous, had now suffered her own erotic humiliation. In sleeping with this bitchy gal—and God knows whom else—the piratical P. was apparently treating Tina as shabbily as she had me. It was all so pleasingly ironic. Back when the three of us—Molly, Tina, and I—had all been vying for the Professor's attentions, it was the tall blonde Tina who seemed to have won the sexual jackpot hands down.

The Last One Standing. (Or, as the case may be, the Last One Lying Supine.) As a reward, the Professor had invited Tina to move in with her almost as soon as the victory was decided. There, at the Professor's house, Tina resided for several years—the rest of her undergraduate career, I guess—serving as lover, protégée, chauffeur, dogsbody, mysterious kept creature. (One recognized the P.'s fell hand at work in Tina's subsequent listing in the English Department directory: for "local address," the poor thing now had only a discreet P.O. box and no phone number.) The relationship later ended badly—with Tina, now in graduate school in another state and in debt to the Professor for a considerable sum, having to endure her former chatelaine's long-distance harassment. For in order to reclaim her money, the Professor had set a detective on Tina's trail and in the end succeeded in driving her into bankruptcy. I know about all this stuff—even the detective and bankruptcy part—because I heard about it a decade or so later *from the Professor herself*. The last time I ever saw her, the Professor was boasting about the episode with crazy pride, as if it were a sign of her business acumen, or indeed something to feel warm and fuzzy about.

Beyond the Tina update, however, little in the Married Lady's kvetching diverted me. Yet seared into my brain forever is one of her parting utterances: a cool assessment—delivered with ghoulish panache as she and my friend were about to leave—of the Professor in the sack.

I've been fucked by lots of guys, but no guy ever fucked me like SHE did.

Blunt to be sure, and perhaps a teeny bit on the coarse side? You might not want to get it printed on a T-shirt, let alone have it embroidered it on a sofa pillow. But it was true nonetheless. One bore the Professorial stigmata, if only brainular, for years.

And, as I have to remind myself: my surrender, again, was total. There was always an element of truth, confusingly enough, in the mean things the Professor said about me. (Possibly at times a great deal.) I had received my Orders From On High, so like an obedient aide-de-camp I immediately regressed in the way the brutal logic of our relationship seemed to demand. I became ever more infantile. Sexually speaking, I devolved into an overgrown erotic baby: hungry, enfeebled, emotionally incontinent—a gaping maw of need. My need for soothing became vast, blithery, peckish. It was as if I suffered from some sort of existential colic. And so it is, perhaps, that whenever I try to calibrate now the pleasure to be taken in the Professor's lovemaking, I find myself fixing, not on any putative fireworks moments—they seem to have vanished from recall as if they never happened at all—but on the primitive feeling of quiescence she could produce in every part of me: the voluptuous sensation of being lulled, cosseted, calmly supported—at rest, so to speak, on a soft and buoyant cushion of water. For all her brusqueness, the Professor could induce this state in me with ease—a sort of floaty, cataleptic feeling. *Amniotic*, one might say. Thirty years later I can still summon up various dreamy visual cues I associate with the feeling: the pale, pale blue walls of her bedroom; the Midwestern winter morning sunlight streaming in at the window; bright silvery droplets of water forming and falling from the icicles outside; the soft, lofting white cotton sheets (like those in a wonderful hotel) on her bed. The sensation was delectable—warmth and comfort of the most disabling kind imaginable—and nearly killed me when it was taken away.

Just so: one got very close to the heart of things with the Professor. Yet such self-abandon came at a fearsome cost: for in delivering oneself up thus, one had to let oneself *go limp* in an almost metaphysical sense. Give up all one's skittery will to power. Go loose and floppy and half-dead. Become a flatliner. A rag doll. A rag doll, moreover, suddenly susceptible to hitherto unknown (or at least unrecognized) sources of panic. Preeminent among them: the realization that the bliss one felt was terminable and insuperably linked to the whim of another, seemingly stronger person. One's tutor in ecstasy—the Teacher of One's Dreams—might gather up her notes and papers and depart at any time.

Grief was the tariff one would then have to pay (one half-knew it from the start), and sooner rather than later. The more time the Professor and I spent together after our affair began, the more things seemed "off" between us. Awkward. Bilious. Out of whack. Unpleasant. Anna with her now-dyspeptic Vronsky on the Riviera. And through it all, even as I struggled to disguise it, I was becoming increasingly overwrought—soon to become toweringly so. I worried incessantly (more every day it seemed) about the inexplicable turn the affair with the Professor was taking; and about my ongoing schoolwork, which now stared me in the face. Careening lust had for a while tamped down the obsessive-compulsive seventh-grader in me, but had not by any means expelled the baleful junior daemon from my psyche. The rat-faced little monster was starting to make itself known again. Now not only had spring quarter classes begun, I also needed to start cramming, I'd decided, for my prelims at the end of the summer, the big, bad, banal qualifying exam one had to pass to go on to one's main Ph.D. work. Yet I couldn't fix my scrambled brains on anything. I was losing my self-discipline, I feared, my sense of purpose—my intellectual grip.

I uttered these apprehensions aloud once or twice. The Professor did not like such tedious fretting one bit and expressed herself on the subject with cutting asperity. So I struggled thenceforth to appear wry and carefree. Yet I couldn't ignore it: I was sleeping poorly and becoming more and more uneasy. Making everything worse (one's Primal Scene notwithstanding) the inner turmoil felt terrifyingly unmotivated to me. I chastised myself over the senselessness of it. I had found my Great Love. She was beautiful and wonderful. We were even fucking. I was having regular moments of ecstasy. The Problem of Homosexuality had been solved—Forever. A fantastic new world had opened up. But all I could do was worry about getting through the next book of *The Faerie Queene*. Our sexual relationship was not yet a month old. Why was I so jittery? Why so *stupidly* agitated?

As difficulties multiplied, the Professor and I took refuge in joint intoxication—which only made the anxiety worse. The Professor usually required a Scotch or two in the evening and though never before or since a drinker of hard liquor, I joined in. We slurped whiskey, often assiduously, out of big paper cups in bed. We would frequently top everything off with great cool sucking hits off the Professor's large blue bong—now permanently stationed, along with her gun, on the bedside table next to her pillow. She often needed a lungful or two of pot to get to sleep. So potent and stunning this homegrown marijuana, even the most lascivious bedtime episodes were liable to end quickly, with one or both of us sinking first into sot-like inebriation, followed by a drooling and fitful slumber.

To one degree or another in fact we were stoned for the whole duration of our affair. No wonder that struggling through Spenser's *Faerie Queene* was proving difficult: I was blotto upside the head. I still have my old paperback copy of Spenser's poem and just looking at it—the pages and pages of bewildering verse in tiny print, the demented little crib notes I've scribbled in the margins—can induce in me a sort of mental seasickness. After enough angst and pot and lack of sleep the poet's romance-world—so dense with weird archaisms and arcane symbols, bizarre characters, confusing plots and subplots—seemed more and more to allegorize the scary mental maze in which I found myself. The traces of my anguish are still to be seen. Like a doomed swain—or else some crushed-out girl in high school—I have inscribed the Professor's initials, I find, next to certain especially excruciating passages. (*"As when a Beare hath seiz'd her cruell clawes/Vppon the carkasse of some beast too weake,/Proudly stands ouer. . . .)* And at the end of one of Spenser's more gloomy and sententious stanzas—

> *The ioyes of loue, if they should euer last,*
> *Without affliction or disquietnesse,*
> *That worldly chaunces doe amongst them cast,*
> *Would be on earth too great a blessednesse,*
> *Liker to heauen, then mortall wretchednesse.*
> *Therefore the winged God, to let men weet,*
> *That here on earth is no sure happinesse,*
> *A thousand sowres hath tempred with one sweet,*
> *To make it seeme more deare and dainty, as is meet.*

—I have written *how true* in a microscopic hand and underlined the last two lines.

When the fatal unwinding began I was therefore fuddled enough. The mental chaos would only get worse. Within two or three weeks of our first tryst, my panic level abruptly sky-rocketed: the Professor began hanging out with Molly Hooley. She was taking Molly under her wing, the P. explained, because M. had sought her *advice about a personal problem*. Scads of troubled eighteen-year-olds, the Professor boasted, were wont to solicit her aid in this fashion: compared with other adults, she was "cool," they seemed to believe—someone who could be trusted. Molly's father, Professor Hooley—Mr. Jolly Friar from the *Canterbury Tales*—was evidently the problem under discussion: he'd been making cruel jokes about Molly's appearance at the family dinner table and had reportedly accused her in front of everyone of *looking like a dyke*. However unfeeling this paternal jest, no doubt there was some truth in it: Molly was wide-bodied and husky —had a sort of strapping, third-baseman's build—and did nothing by way of clothing or makeup to obviate that fact. Nonetheless she was blue and upset: the Professor was *very* concerned. To cheer her

up, the Professor had carried her off a couple of times to play racquetball with her; afterwards they'd gone out for beers and shot the
shit. The Professor would roll in on the late side after these charitable
ministrations, full of boisterous chatter and lady-jock *aperçus*. It was
obvious, she told me with a delighted grin, that Molly had a monster
crush on her. But again I shouldn't worry: *that girl still has her baby
fat!* She was just a *mixed-up kid*. A *big galoot*. Could you believe it?
She's even a goddamned virgin! I'm helping her.

   After two or three of these big-sister forays, the Professor decided
that she might have to sleep with Molly after all—just once. You
know: be the can-opener. Better that she—a responsible adult—
initiate the innocent young person than some ugly white-trash gal
Molly might encounter when she joined the Air Force—still her
stated goal upon graduation. The Professor was sure she could keep
it all *contained*; she knew what she was doing; she'd been involved in
lots of situations like this one. That Molly was her department colleague's teenage daughter seemed only to make matters more urgent
and necessary. And while the logic here may have been faulty, the
Professor's unusual frankness was, I dare say, in a perverse way comforting. Looking back on it, I suspect that even at this nutty juncture
the Professor *did* wish to continue her affair with me—or at least had
convinced herself she did. Such uncharacteristic full disclosure—for
she thoughtfully warned me in advance precisely when the deflora-
tion of Molly was to take place—was her upside-down, Reynard-
the-Fox way of demonstrating her troth.

   Yet if the Professor could contain it, I could not—especially
when she invited me over to her house shortly after said hymen-
busting had been accomplished. I arrived around 10:00 a.m. Molly
had left just a little while before; the bed sheets were still rumpled
and gritty. Clearly it was going to be my great and groovy honor
to have Sick Morning Sex with the Professor—now pink-faced

and smiling sheepishly—in the scurfy unmade bed. *C'mon, honey. That kid has no clue—it was all a big anticlimax. You're It.* I confess I yielded. Afterwards the Professor said she felt reborn. Cleansed. She loved me and respected me so much. We would be together forever. But the squalor of it sank into my soul, adding not a little to the septic murk within.

Boggling to me now, that not once during this first trial of my affection did I fume or shriek or expostulate; nor did I ever disparage the Professor's actions—not even in my journal. So great my demoralization, so pedantic my masochism, it would not have occurred to me to do so. Though floored by her behavior—frankly, I was *beyond* floored—was in fact hurtling forward on the way toward breaking the Pain Sound Barrier—I nevertheless had various rationalizations for remaining in a state of doltish passivity. Above all, I felt, it was my duty as an intelligent person to try to *understand* the Professor and give her the benefit of any doubt. My sweet, distinguished, and charming lover, singer of lovely folksongs, friend of the kindly Alice and Tom, popular teacher and respected colleague, *nice person*—the Professor *must* know what she was doing. Besides, with her and Molly it was only sex, after all, and what did *that* matter? (I was still abiding by the illusion that touching other people's bodies and being touched in return was no big deal—*nothing to get worked up about.*) Yes: I am sure I looked mortified when the Professor reprimanded me over my burgeoning neurasthenia, as she now began to do with some frequency. And yes, I'm equally sure that a certain deep-lodged passive-aggressiveness in my character (such as I had indeed often directed toward my mother) was at times detectable in my not-so-sprightly conversation. And once or twice I couldn't help it: I blurted out that I felt bad when the Professor slept with Molly. *My own failing, of course, but yes, okay—I do feel a tiny bit hurt. . . .* Such dazed admissions typically prompted indignation in her, followed by self-recrimination on my part. (*I'm sorry I'm sorry I'm so so sorry, etc. etc.*) To be sure, things felt very odd—but then again, maybe they weren't as bad as they seemed.

Thus I made no big speeches, no operatic gestures. I had been morally flattened—trodden on to the point of two-dimensionality. I was like a piece of old gum on the sidewalk. Hanging up on the Professor, stalking off mid-conversation, refusing to see her again— any of these tried-and-true lovers' gambits would have been impossible for me, as bad as playing truant. Anger (not that I would ever have named it as such) had to be suppressed and reformulated as self-contempt. *I deserved everything I got. The Professor was right, I was acting like a head case over my school stuff. Over this weird thing with Molly. Over the fact I couldn't sleep. I was tiresome; I would have to be better. I was behaving really unpleasantly.* Oh, hell, hell, hell.

My frequent nightmares intimated a somewhat less placid state of affairs. One from around this time—immediately shared with the Professor—was sufficiently grotesque and primal, I see from my journal, to capture her analytic interest. She was even moved to propound an interpretation of it—one that reflected, of course, her own superior wisdom and understanding of my psyche:

> *Told [the Professor] about the awful dream I had last night. Though she thought it a "positive" one. Me caught inside a taxiing air-craft—a man was there who wouldn't let me out. I finally slid open a tiny window and went out head first, landed on the runway. Then the man in the plane tried to run me over with it. I rolled out of the way, ran to the side of the field, next had to crawl through barbed wire. Ambulances all around then, there had been a crash somewhere close by, it seemed, bodies lying everywhere. Corpses laid out on a huge tarp. Pieces of limbs: a horrible scene. [The Professor] was one of the contused bodies—I had a momentary flash of seeing her, then I woke up. Today she said it was a "rebirth dream," that I was*

beginning a new relationship with her. She says I have finally real-
ized I have no power over her. Dead and gone: my image of her as
"someone I could control."

In other words, look on the bright side, T-Ball. Gory though it
no doubt was, the dream indicated that I was finally starting to confront my infantile neurosis. Maybe someday I would cease burdening
people—her especially—with my callow attempts at emotional ma-
nipulation. And what a relief *that* would be! One truly had to rejoice.
The fact—unflagged by either of us—that I seemed to harbor a wish
to see her dead and eviscerated and lying on a bloody tarp meant next
to nothing, apparently, analytically speaking. On the contrary: it was
merely one of several signs (*even a promising one!*) that I was now beginning to Love Her in a New and Healthy Way.

It couldn't go on and it didn't. A week or so after the Molly business cranked up I had a midterm scheduled in Victorian Fiction—
the other class, along with Spenser, for which I had registered that
spring. Work-wise, I had managed to stay abreast in it, largely because I'd read all the assigned novels for the course long before, in
high school, once if not twice. Cathy and Heathcliff were like old
acquaintances—my weird second cousins or something. The midterm format in turn looked to be straightforward: we would be given
several essay questions to take home and ponder; the next day in class
we were to write a theme on the question of our choice. The topics,
when we got them, were predictable if uninspiring: I picked out one
on *Vanity Fair*. And as was my mad-bomber habit with previous tests
of this nature, I drafted my full essay the night before—a polished
disquisition of nine or ten pages—then memorized it. The memori-
zation was an Ayn Rand–like feat of will under the circumstances;
somehow I forced myself to do it.

Next day, all systems go. I could have recited my essay with ease.

All that remained was to sit down and disgorge it onto the page. I'd glimpsed the Professor briefly on my way to the exam room—she was smiling and chatting with someone, on her way back from her morning class. Yet the sighting had depressed me. She either hadn't seen me or was pretending not to. I couldn't tell. Was I driving her away with my dreadful babyishness? Terrifying thought. *She looked so beautiful and friendly, smiling like that at that person. I will die if I lose her. I have to grow up. I have to keep a clear head, keep the lid on.* I entered the examination room and sat down. As it happened, the exam was taking place in an airy lecture hall directly across from the Professor's office. Only ten or fifteen feet away: Her Door, with sign-up sheets and various notes about her classes posted thereon. One quivered. Magic space. The place where all ley lines intersected. She didn't seem to be in there, though; at least the light wasn't on. Maybe I would catch a glimpse of her later. *I hope not with that stupid clod Molly.* Ah, here was the T.A.—the blue books were being distributed. *But why don't things feel right with us? She's become so harsh—so critical, as if she doesn't really like me anymore.* A shuffle of papers and clicking ballpoints—then silence in the room as I and some thirty classmates settled down to write. *Who is she, really? I feel so awful but I don't know why.*

Almost as soon as I opened my examination book, the blackness closed in. Something shocking and discreditable, first of all, had happened to my right hand, the one holding the pen. I was trying to start—yes, trying to indite the first of my memorized sentences, *In Thackeray's novel* Vanity Fair . . . But my hand had gone all stiff: palsied and wonky, as if I were having a stroke. *Hey, you jerk, what's up. Time to start, it's the exam, come on, get going.* My fingers, however, remained frozen. My gorge began rising slowly and heavily, like a cobra uncoiling and lifting itself up, irrationally enough, by its own head. My arms, my neck, began to seize up. I shuddered involuntarily. My recalcitrant digits, terrifyingly, still weren't gripping the pen properly. I couldn't write without trembling. I began to pant and perspire a little. Looking down at my blue book made my vision go spotty and bleary. So far, I could see, I had made only jittery spastic marks. The floor tilted oddly and swam up at me from below.

What on earth is happening. Take a deep breath, calm down. Just think about the essay, just write it. Stop fucking around, just write—I CAN'T—the Professor will be furious. I CAN'T HELP IT. She'll hear you've had a freak-out. IT WON'T STOP. Goddamn it, just start. I CAN'T. She'll say you're a hysteric. Need help. She'll drop you. Look! everybody is way ahead of you—they're filling up their first pages and going on to the second. You're fucked. This can't be HAPPENING. You'll fail. It's fatal. This right now—this thing happening right now—it's FATAL. So stop gasping and stay calm. You'll die if you don't stop shaking. She'll dump you. Just WRITE your fucking exam goddamn it—

But by now the panic had shot through my arms, chest, viscera, bowels, all the way down to my feet and into my shoes. My shirt was sodden and cold; my whole body shaking. The helmsman had collapsed and the horizon—nauseatingly—was lurching up and down. I had to get out of there. I had to duck. I had to knock a few things over. Kick myself. Hit somebody. *Couldn't breathe.* Huge tears of fright and horror and self-hatred were now sliding out of my eyes, like eels. *This is terrible.* I waved frantically to the T.A.—quietly reading a book now at a desk up front—and rushed from the room. A few students looked up curiously and saw me careening out. The T.A. followed.

Outside the classroom—even as we stood a few feet from the Professor's office—the T.A. (a fellow graduate student, though a couple of years ahead of me) watched in consternation as I dissolved into great, gurgling teary heaves. I sobbed out wild apologies and begged his forgiveness. *This has never ever happened to me before, I swear—I've been under a lot of stress—I feel ill—it's really bad—I don't know what went wrong—I couldn't . . . I can't . . . I'm sorry . . .* I gulped for air and wrung my hands piteously; I had crumpled my now-soggy blue book into a sort of foul, screwed-up wedge. A thick and disgusting gray thread of mucous emerged from one of my nostrils and dangled there between us, lengthening slowly. (The T.A. and I both struggled in vain to find some Kleenex.) He was kind; looked almost apologetic, as if he himself were to blame. *Of course, of course—how awful—but no harm done, really, these things happened to everybody. You mustn't feel bad. Not at all. The professor would understand too—really—everything was going to be okay . . . Why didn't I take my blue book home and write out my exam essay later when I felt better? I could hand it back in tomorrow.* I mumbled some grief-stricken thanks. While no longer at risk of choking on gobbets of my own phlegm, I continued to weep unceasingly, as if inconsolable. At least my instinct for self-immolation was unimpaired: I rushed downstairs and ran into the street in search of the Professor.

Pavane for a Defunct Infanta

THE PROFESSOR HAD BEEN PULLING her car out of the faculty lot when I staggered up, palpably distraught, my face white and tear-streaked. She listened while I told her, very quickly, what had happened. Said *get in* and drove me grimly back to my apartment. On the way I was silent—aghast at what I'd done. I had needed desperately to be with her, or so it had seemed when I'd fled the exam room. Yet being with her now, I realized, wasn't actually making me feel any better. *This is all going wrong.* She in turn said little and lay down and fell asleep on my bed when we got to my apartment. Ashen-faced, I sat quietly at my desk for the next hour, writing out my aborted exam essay. I was cold and competent now, even scientific: an exiled Bolshevik, in threadbare coat and tiny old-fashioned spectacles, laying out the mechanics of the dialectic with steely clarity. Becky Sharp, Waterloo, Napoleon, blah, blah. A great arc of necessity animated the lives of men, blah blah. My hands and fingers functioned perfectly now; the sentences of my essay rolled out in a voluble stream, like happy workers leaving a factory. *So what was all that goddamned fuss about.* The Professor went home after while; said she'd call me later, and I think she did. But things from that point on were never really the same.

My life over the next seven or eight weeks? Fractured, forlorn days, catastrophic nights. Chaos, wailing, and darkness. Imprecations. Despairing appeals for mercy. The muffled sound of dead-carts rumbling past at 4:00 a.m. Crude chalk crosses on the doors. Dancing, hip-waggling skeletons everywhere, some beckoning, others simply grinning in hideous triumph. Ashen, serrated, almost numb with disbelief, I struggled after equilibrium by writing daily in my Plague-Journal:

Last night at [the Professor's] Molly called up, was drinking some-where, wanted to come over. [The Professor] came back and told me M. was in love with her. Now tonight they're out together. [The Professor] asked me this morning in bed if I minded if she "held onto" M. I said, No then, but later on the phone I said, Yes I would be upset by it. [The Professor] said she had a feeling she would end up "being affection-ate" to M. "Poor kid." Weird: she seemed almost proud: "I think one of my colleagues' daughters is in love with me." At the same time—continually affirms her love for me, said the feeling was not merely the result of the fact that "you got here first." "You're timeless."

Home alone after two days at [the Professor's]. I feel extremely depressed, not sure why. She is with M. again, though tells me re-peatedly not to worry. Still do, of course. She hurt me quite badly last night when we made love; I actually bled a little. Oh God. Then I tried this morning; she was there briefly, but I was inept. I feel I am losing confidence, wish I knew what to do about that.

Once after we made love she said if we can weather this one, we've won. Want to believe her, but it's hard though.

Didn't write yesterday—one of the more intense days of my paltry existence. [The Professor] called in the morning, remote, depressed. Came over soon after and told me she and Molly had ended up making love again. The night I couldn't sleep and sat talking to myself in the bathtub. The sex with M. apparently "unsatisfying." I felt at one point like I was going to have a case of dry heaves. Have to make a leap of faith and trust her. She says if she "has to choose," no question but I am the one. We went into the bedroom then and made love for the rest of the afternoon. Afterwards [the Professor] said she felt reborn. I'm trying to control evil feelings about M.—who apparently said to [the Professor] the other day, Think what I could do to your career.

Saw [the Professor] at school and we sat on the grass in the sun. She saying I should try to figure out why I was attracted to her. "If it is because you're looking for a mother, the person you are relating to should get you into analysis and say goodbye." Later: "What would you do if suddenly a whole lot of people decided they liked you." She is afraid that even if I do get "socialized," as she puts it, I will end up leaving her. "I'm just trying to arrange it so I don't die alone— but everybody dies alone anyway."

She said she didn't feel she was doing anything "morally wrong" by sleeping with M. I have to accept her perception of the situation, trust to her goodness.

Brain-bedeviling above all: the Professor's crazy changeability—
her constantly shifting moods and modalities. Yer-But-No-But-Yer-
But. No-But-Yer-But-No-But. With regard to me, she flipped insanely
from vilification to ardor and back again. At times, to be sure, she was
just plain old vicious—full of harsh, spouting criticisms, like a foun-
tain. A human acid-bath. I was always watching her, she complained
one evening; it was creeping her out. *Don't you even realize how it dis-
turbs and* UPSETS ME *to see you watching me like that?* I guess I had
a particular Moron-Girl look that especially rankled her. One day I
made the mistake, I see from my journal, of telling her that I felt good
about a talk we'd had the night before: it had renewed my hope that
things were going to work out for us. The Molly element was awkward,
but I'd been thinking about it, I said; I knew I could be philosophical.
I could be patient; I understood. These weak-sister comments were
instantly cut off. No, the talk had been pointless and stupid. I'd just
stressed her out with more whining. Not only that: I had had a *childish expression* on my face all through it that had *greatly annoyed her.* She
looked down and away and frowned darkly at the very thought of me.

In public situations—*like when that nice Tina came over to talk to us
in the English office the other day*—my behavior was *appalling.* Obviously out of control. *Boring and irritating like a tic. Did I want people to
realize what was going on? That we'd been sleeping together?* Plus I was
always so *devious* and *sly.* From the very first, it seemed, I had used
various sneaky intellectual wiles to gain power over her: *Tarot cards,
the I Ching, all your literary allusions.* I was always making references
that were *purposely obscure,* she said. This unattractive habit merely
demonstrated my *anger and insecurity.* Tough shit if now I was getting too upset to concentrate on my homework. Or write my fucking
exams. The sole journal entry I made that week was the transcription
of a gruesome Professorial one-liner:

I don't care if you fail out of school.

Yet at other times, perfectly counterweighting the reproaches—
in fact deftly inserted at precisely those points in the situation at
which one seemed about to recover one's long-submerged critical
faculties—were the psycho-bonbons, the mental milkshakes, the
sweet promises of futurity. Bluebeard wasn't Bluebeard, after all; I
had my adorable Beast back again. Thus even after Tina appeared,
inducing more inward torment in me than I had thought it possible for a single human being (me) to bear, there were just enough
of these Beast-moments to keep me entranced, if also racked with
uncertainty:

*[The Professor] just called up—said she was drunk, then said, "I
just wanted to say that if you want me you can have me, because
I think you're the only one who really understands what is going on
with this affair."*

*She called me before dinner tonight. It was okay. She wanted to
know if I thought she was a "together" person. I didn't really know
what to say. Then said yes of course. She also said you know I'm not
cruel don't you. Again, me nonplussed, but I said yes.*

*[The Professor] running out of her office today to buttonhole me.
"I guess I'd better tell you what I've been doing, but don't let it
make you upset. I'm doing things with other people." She said it was
nothing for me to worry about—said all the time, she realized, she
kept "wondering how I was." Her description (dismissive) of Tina:
"gracious, charming, attractive, vacuous." Dull. A sort of empty
version of me.*

*Last night; we had our best phone talk for a while. She was laugh-
ing—"I'm in love with three people." Went on about Molly and*

Tina, how "fond" she was of both of them, but I, she insisted, was
going to be "one of the central people in her life." Told me again:
"you understand despair." Ended with: "will you hang on if I fool
around for a while?"

Even after the Professor decreed that she and I were going to have a
moratorium on a certain element—for by this time, with three gals on the
go, she was presumably running somewhat short on love-gas as well
as time—the verbal lucubrations, followed by some Sudden-Wild-
Sex-After-All, could always be counted on to keep me in thrall.

Today on the phone I managed to bring up wanting to sleep with her;
she said she did not want that "intensity" right now. Sex was "an
easy answer"—didn't address the real problem. I apologized and
thanked her afterwards for talking with me about it. She is such a
good person. Said at one point, "Terry, you're a damn fine person
in spite of all your shit." When I asked about the no-sex-right-now
thing she said Christ I'm not going into a nunnery.

[Next day.] I am going to [the Professor's] house for dinner tonight.
Trepidation. Feel like I am on some kind of probation. Dinner would
be it, she said: said she didn't want me staying over.

[Next day.] Back home this morning. Last night when I got there
she was teasing—immediately led me upstairs for a "backrub." Ex-
plained that just because she had stipulated no sex, it didn't mean
we weren't allowed to lie down on the bed and get close. Drank a lot
over dinner, she got more and more drunk, rubbed my leg, said she
didn't want the "other me" to come back when the "me" she loved
was present. It felt crazy. We went to bed afterwards and all the joy
and insanity instantly returned.

But as I became more distraught the Professor also withdrew. I recall going to her office one morning—the ill-fated day I took her her birthday present?—and she said I was making her so anxious, just my presence, there in the moment, that I had to get out. *She hadn't felt so anxious* (and here she looked at me wildly) *since J.* She was starting to hyperventilate, she said, was going to have to take a tranquilizer. *So go away. Leave. Fuck off.* I did so.

And not long after—on what would be one of the very worst nights of my life—her brutality took an especially freakish turn:

Hell, hell, hell. Asked her if I could see her tonight; she said she was busy, wouldn't say with what. Came home desolate. Called Elsbet, finally told her all about it. E. came over right away—I cried for about an hour, my head on her breast. E. spent the night at my apartment—slept in the bed, just held on to me. Saved me somehow from myself. Incredibly enough [the Professor] called around midnight. No point to the call. Except to let me know she too was in bed and someone was with her. She kept talking to her in the background. Glasses clinking. Muffled laughter. [The Professor] was chuckling and told me we were lucky—we had avoided something "potentially hideous." Oh Christ but what exactly. Then she hung up. Elsbet enraged. Kept saying I hate her, I hate her.

Had one's dear friend not been there? No trouble whatsoever, Madam—*indeed it would be our pleasure*—to totter down to the freeway bridge a few blocks away and fling oneself, Berryman-style, over the icy railing into the dark.

The endgame had finally begun. The corpse was still twitching a bit, and there were indeed a couple of pieces of Grand Guignol still to endure—one entirely self-inflicted, the other not. The self-inflicted one was laughable—in the way the sinking of the *Titanic* might be considered laughable. As a bit of black existential farce, during which one did not show oneself to advantage. Rather, like J. Bruce Ismay, lily-livered owner of the White Star Line, who when the great ship began to list disguised himself as a woman so as to sneak onto one of the doomed liner's few remaining lifeboats (thus disgracing himself forever), one simply gave up and wallowed and begged one's executioner for a last-minute reprieve. Lesbian readers, I'm afraid, all too familiar with the clichéd subcultural dynamics of the situation described here, will no doubt be especially inclined to groan. But it's true: so desperate was I still to see the Professor, even after her defection had become obvious, I continued to play each week on a ghastly little all-woman softball team that one of the English department secretaries had organized on campus that spring. Ghastly because there on the roster with me, smirking and mugging like costars in some dire lesbian sitcom, were *all three* of them: Molly, Tina, and the brimming, bountiful Professor. No joy in Mudville—any idiot could see that—but one sat there in the mud anyway: red-eyed, gibbering quietly, unable to raise even a hideous rictus of a smile. A situation so awful it demanded a laugh-track.

Plus one could hardly have wished for a more perfect allegory of the Professor's devilish charisma—or of one's own torment. Elegant Tina was the team's agile, golden-gloved first baseman. Baby butch Molly H.—best all-round athlete in our little trio of Professor-lovers—played a skillful Bucky Dent–style shortstop. I was the Designated Zombie: an inept, strangely cadaverous presence at second base. The Professor herself was at the center of things— cock of the walk, a squatting, crowing Chanticleer presiding over his hens—in the position of catcher. She couldn't run, of course (the polio leg); but she could bob up and down, yell out instructions to the defense, pick runners off, and block the plate with the best of them. On top of it all, she was a disgustingly good sport—full of friendly compliments and warm manly butt-taps for the members of the opposite team. And as it happened, whenever the Professor got a hit, the lanky Tina, Atalanta-like, would run the bases for her. One still-awful memory from that green and hostile spring: watching the Professor, eyes aglitter, laughingly toss her tennis shoes to Tina, after she [the Professor] had hit safely to center. (Having come to the game in flip-flops Tina had no base-running shoes.) Somehow the rangy Tina managed to slip into the Professor's Adidas on the fly, even as she sloped off, commandingly, in the direction of first base. Not only was she impossibly tall, lithe, and graceful—for so one was forced to register—she seemed to share the Professor's shoe size. They were obviously fated to be together. One could just see them: in a clinch on the floor in a Foot Locker store, making love amid the racks of the latest Nikes and tube socks.

I played in five or six games before I cratered—hollow-eyed, brain-dead, emotionally gutted. (Though chatty and jokey with the others, the Professor breezily ignored me during our games.) The second and final bit of Grand Guignol came soon after. True: already a couple of weeks before, as soon as it became clear our relationship was starting to implode, the Professor had demanded that I yield up the house key she had so impulsively given me at the outset of our little idyll. I was tractable enough and one terrible sunny morning she had appeared at my flat to reclaim it. I gave it up without protest—her visit lasting all of perhaps thirty seconds—but even so, the Professor stood in the hallway and glared at me suspiciously, as if I were about to pull a fast one.

Then in turn, just after I'd quit the softball team (it was now a week or two before the end of the school year), she called to say she was coming over again: this time to repossess the pretty little guitar she'd loaned me at Christmas. She gave me advance instructions. As with the key, there was to be no whingeing on my part. Now elevated to the role of official consort, the resplendent Tina—or so I was duly informed—played the guitar and sang beautifully. In musical as in other respects, it seemed, Tina left me quite in the shade. She was *just plain old fun to be with,* the Professor observed. The two of them were so *well-suited;* they loved *singing together.* I should *never have taken that guitar in the first place, you know:* it was time for me to be a good little nobody and relinquish it. She and Tina, I gathered, were about to embark on some romantic old-fashioned car trip—presumably in search of hoedowns and hootenannies and cans of Nehi soda.

It was wrenching, of course: for brief and disharmonious as our liaison had been, the guitar was its emblem. Even the Professor seemed a bit embarrassed in the role of Repo Man. When she called that morning to say she was on her way, you could hear disquiet in her otherwise deep and mellifluous voice: an awkward awareness of time's compression, and of the brute suddenness of her about-face. Not so long before, after all, we'd been wriggling around ecstatically on the very piece of green shag carpet remnant on which we were now to face one another. *Things were so different now.* Back then, she'd talked excitedly about driving to New York with me (just as she and Tina were now doing) during the summer vacation. (The prospect thrilled me: I'd still never been to New York, nor indeed anywhere east of Wisconsin.) She was going to introduce me to Judy Collins, she said, and one of the guys in Peter, Paul, and Mary, I forget which one. Then we'd come back and I would move into her house and we'd work on projects together. I was to become a sort of girl-linguist under her tutelage. At some point we'd definitely have to go visit Little Willie McSomebody, a withered, 100-year-old speaker of the Smoky Mountain dialect who'd once been her prize informant, at his (her?) ancient shack in Appalachia. The Professor had been *waiting all her life for me,* she'd said then. Finally, I had come. And I was perfect. So where had all the flowers gone?

Yet while undeniably foul—toxic in fact—the Picking-Up-of-the-Guitar Day nonetheless marked a turning point of sorts for me.

My nadir, perhaps, but also the beginning of the struggle against the death sentence I had received. A tiny *Eureka!* moment. The point at which I first felt stirring within some of that deep unnameable *fury*— later to become howling protest—the Professor had engendered in me. After weeks in a daze I was suddenly coming alive again—beginning to crackle and spark a bit, like a dangerously frayed electrical cord. True, I still pined miserably for the Professor's sexual love. Every hour without her was like traversing a desert. But at last I was starting to grasp—with however parched and cheerless a clarity— that despite the fact I loved her (and I couldn't get the love to stop), the Professor was also fairly unspeakable. Treacherous. Mean. Dishonest. Cowardly. A Sadist. A Sociopath. All of the above. Or at least in the kooky crucible of our relationship, enough of any one of these things for me to feel more than a little ill used.

And in fact, the first, fine fantasy of vengeance loomed up that day: the novel idea that one might take the gloves off. (Before, I hadn't even realized I was wearing any. Nor indeed that I had possibly useful appendages underneath.) Now I freely admit to having become moody and mean-spirited in middle age. I know I have a horrible attitude. Towards *people*, especially. But I've never actually punched anybody out. I've never tripped anybody up or tried to poke their eyes out. I keep the dogs from mauling small children. Nor indeed, not even on some pitch-black moonless night, have I ever TP'd anybody's house—gratifying though that would be in certain cases. Yet as soon as I heard the Professor's car pull up on the morning of my final trial, I was suddenly overtaken—after *how* many weeks of pure hell?—by a wild urge to Clobber Her. *Clock Her. Really Ding Her. Smack Her Down Once and For All.* I lived on the third floor of my building, overlooking a godforsaken little front courtyard, and as I stood at my window watching the faithless Professor scamper up the main steps—while Tina, in the driver's seat, sat coolly idling the Professor's car at the curb—I had a sudden murderous fantasy of flinging the guitar out the window onto her, my wretched abuser's, head.

T-W-A-N-G-G-G!!

[*Sickening sound of splintering wood and bone, the harsh thrum of untuned guitar strings, faint groans, an ambulance in the distance, a discreet death-rattle.*] Death by concussion, woolly bobbles, and mother-of-pearl. Then an old-fashioned undertaker might have come along, closed the Professor's eyes, and laid matching plastic guitar picks on them.

True, I didn't carry out my revenge: it was satisfaction enough just to picture it. It would be like a Road Runner cartoon, I figured, or the Laurel and Hardy movie when the grand piano falls out the window. *Ka-boing!* And for the first time in a month or two I discerned—yes—a small light twinkling in the darkness. Indeed, as the light grew stronger, I was even moved to refine on, to embellish, my concept. To sing a little aria. If only the Professor had lent me—instead of that stupid guitar—*some lead weights. An anvil, maybe. Or a set of bowling balls. A refrigerator even.* (The P. had, in the meantime, come and gone, taking her purloined property with her.) And thus—amid dark and bloodthirsty visions—my first year of graduate school came to an end.

I survived, of course. The summer was long and the Midwestern heat furnace-like. I had a little part-time research assistant job, after which I swam every day in the pool at the University gym. I resumed my Ph.D. work and subsequently passed my qualifying exams that fall. The test-taking heebie-jeebies of the previous spring did not return; I did as well as people expected me to. And there I remained at the

University—working more or less doggedly for the next four years, even as the Professor pranced and preened, took on (so one heard) various new paramours, and cut a rakish, merry swath. She was like a carousel horse. Always coming round again. Impossible to avoid in fact. (And still—fantastically enough, after everything—in the closet.) One had to encase oneself fairly rigidly in order to prevail. Trade in the Sapphism for stoicism. Wear an artificial carapace. No more Rubyfruit Jungle. Marcus Aurelius wuz da Man.

Most of that first year I cultivated an air of cool disconnection when I saw her—a sort of nonseeing, lost-in-the-stars look. But after a while we began to acknowledge one another in the halls again—I, extremely gingerly; the Professor, more often than not, with a big, psycho smile and jovial hello. It was inevitable; I saw her—literally—several days a week. Once, improbably enough, she stopped me in front of the Social Science building to tell me she was "really getting into" the music of Adam and the Ants. I reciprocated on these occasions with vague pleasantries and sought to maintain what I hoped was a mild, manly, dignified mien—Dobbin, indeed, in *Vanity Fair*. Sometimes I even asked politely after Tina. Granted, I was still quite ferociously obsessed. I watched the Professor from afar and kept spooky-morbid tabs on her comings and goings. Not the healthiest response, I realize, under the circumstances, yet also perhaps inevitable. One's eye had indeed offended, but plucking it out seemed far too painful to bear. One loved one's grief too much. Ordinary life thus required that one give in to regular little crying jags—off and on, it turned out, for the entire four years. Special anniversaries—Christmas Eve, the first date, the first disrobing—were always noted and produced the purest, most pungent, agony.

Yet over the long haul it became easier *not* to know—not to hear about, not even to fantasize about, whatever it was she was up to. True, at one point I couldn't help noticing she'd traded in the Honda for a large, high-off-the-ground Jeep-thingy: I'd see her tooling round campus in it, cheeky and exalted in the driver's seat, beaming with self-regard and thuggish warmth for all. The silver braid gleamed and glinted in the sunshine. She was definitely a guy's guy. (Oh, yeah: something about driving around the back country looking for the last speakers of Ozark English or Okracoke justified the gas guzzling: you *had* to have the four-wheel drive.) In my second year in graduate school I got my own car—an ancient VW bought for $200—and that helped, fortunately, to even things out a bit for me psychologically. Yes: I had to spend five or six greasy weekends that summer with Alice's husband, Tom, crawling around with tar and rivet-gun under the chassis, repairing (with his help) the rotted-out metal struts that ostensibly held the whole thing together. But once my frail chariot was semidrivable, I enjoyed a new sense of freedom. One of the first things I did after it rattled back to life was to drive across the city late at night and park in a dark spot across the street from the Professor's house. There I sat—a brooding crazy—for two or three hours. One was doing one's best: this sinister little stakeout, punctuated by sobs, did in the end lay something to rest.

And after a long and ill-timed absence, Lady Luck, too, came back into my life. Several kindly bystanders, witnesses to the train wreck, came to my assistance. Elsbet had been a rock once I had started slipping and spiraling downward, of course, and as the summer unfolded, she took me off for therapeutic weekends at her family's rustic cottage on Lake Chetek. There she cooked me sustaining little high-protein Nordic meals and remained stalwart and kind during the monotonous bouts of keening that often overtook me. Stalwart was she, too, during more alarming flights—whenever I said I was going to kill myself, for example (this would go on for a while), or when I suddenly lolled forward at the dinner table and flopped my head down, tragicomically, into my plate of food. In the daytime we splashed around on the lake in a long-oared metal skiff, swam about, and fought off the horseflies. I was like a wounded World War I soldier, invalided out and now convalescent in dear old Blighty—taking the air for the first time, shuffling around the hospital grounds in slippers and striped dressing gown, summoning up, every now and then, a weak little traumatized smile.

And though I never gave her the details of my situation, Jo—butt of so many cruel jokes—was another godsend: it was she who supplied me with the name of the shrink who made calling me back from the abyss one of her pet projects for the year. I feel ashamed of my own bad satiric self when I reread a journal entry I made at one especially terrible point that spring:

> *Shocking depression. I went to see Jo in her office this noon—she gave me the names of some therapists. I told her something very bad had happened, didn't say what. She looked solicitous, but didn't probe. Put her arms round me at the end—I was on the verge of breaking down into sobs.*

The therapist I saw was a middle-aged Israeli child psychiatrist, by turns brusque and bracing—and a fair match for the Professor (or at least my mental image of her) in what I sometimes thought of as a Manichean battle over my survival. Malka had fought in the 1948 war, and in the role of psychological second did her best to inject me with her own brazen and bellicose spirit. I confess I was not too receptive at first, and when I objected, mewlingly, to taking an antidepressant—such reckless pill popping, I feared, would mess up my concentration and interfere with my schoolwork—she dubbed me Little Miss Sunshine and threatened to *stick me in the goddamned psych ward* until I complied. (Little did one know that thirty years later virtually every person on earth, not to mention one's pet gerbil, would be on psychotropic drugs of some kind.) While I continued to feel ashamed of my pharmaceutical "crutch," comply I did, and the drug's inspiriting effect on my hypothalamus was indisputable. After constant narcotic debauchery at the Professor's I had pretty much renounced dope-smoking—forever. But Tofranil, I have to say, has been a dear, dear pal of mine ever since: a sort of friendly and intelligent dolphin, on whose accommodating back I have ridden safely to shore after various major and minor shipwrecks. Though prone alas to getting stuck in fishing nets, dolphins—one somehow feels—seldom let themselves get entangled in unsuitable love affairs.

Various other pieces got picked up. I waited a year to tell Alice what had taken place—she had been puzzling, I guess, why she never seemed to hear from the Professor anymore. As it happened, Alice had not been entirely absent from my life during the Professor episode; I'd seen her once in fact just before its dolorous end. But given the Professor's grip on me then, the encounter had simply added a new element of nightmarishness:

At Alice's house, struggling to keep off misery. Invited to dinner. Alice has been asking me exhausting questions about Shelley and Spenser, the last things I feel like talking about. I can't talk to her about IT. [The Professor] last week: "I suggest you don't talk to Alice." While Alice and I were driving along today, A. said out of the blue, Do you have any erotic attachment to a man. I said No in a lame way. Alice again: aren't you attracted to men. I could have wept with frustration and pain. Told her I didn't really want to talk about it. Alice saying in any case—I looked like "I didn't take much joy in being a woman." I could have thrown up. She said I shouldn't "give up" on men "just because of your father."

I'd stayed mum thenceforth: not exactly the life of the party; nor, would it seem, was I making the most of my looks.

The following fall, however, Alice had finished her dissertation and was lecturing at a tiny Christian college in rural Wisconsin. Tom was still at the University; they lived apart for the year. One weekend I went to stay with her in one of the primitive on-campus trailers her college provided for visiting profs. The trailer didn't have a bath or shower so we were obliged to perform our late-night ablutions in a deserted classroom building, half-naked, at a pair of matching sinks in the women's restroom. Perhaps it was the intimacy engendered by these slightly self-conscious side-to-side sponge baths, but the first night I was there I found myself unspooling for Alice the story of my crack-up. She was predictably aghast—truly aghast—and having introduced me to the Professor, felt immediately to blame. I was hard pressed to convince her that the P. had not recruited me into unnatural love; that I had been already an eager, if somewhat un-fledged, practitioner at the time we met. The homosexual angle, one could see, clearly unnerved Alice, and later she told me she'd had to call Tom that same night around 2:00 or 3:00 a.m.—she had been too upset by my revelations to sleep. She came ultimately to accept the same-sex part of it, but remained deeply shocked by the Profes-sor's knavery and guile. Erotic deceit on such a scale was almost as disillusioning, I guess, as reading *Sartor Resartus*. And though Alice and I remained friends for many years I don't believe she ever com-municated with her former tennis partner again.

So what to say about the Dear Lady herself, now that more than three decades have elapsed? True: one feels a bit like Sir Walter Scott put-ting the question so sententiously. One imagines a title: *Dumped: Or, 'Tis Thirty Years Since*. Also true: that the matter evokes contra-dictory feelings in me. Having now described the fiasco with the Professor at length, I confess, I feel on the one hand a bit embar-rassed by its sheer triteness: my own sitting-duckness, my seducer's casebook callousness. As I expected, revisiting Ye Olde Journals has indeed been lowering—not least because they tell such a dreary old-hat tale. Who hasn't clawed at one's pillow in anguish at a lover's faithlessness? Had one jumped off a cliff that long-ago winter—Sappho of Lesbos–style—one would simply have ratified it: one's lack of originality; one's tedious by-the-bookness.

By not taking the chump's way out I suppose I threw in my lot, however feebly, with the ongoingness of life. I stepped back from my own little Sappho-plunge; avoided becoming a sentimental statistic. I veered away, somehow went on with things. And most of the time since I've been fairly glad I stuck it out. Had I not I would have missed out, of course, on any number of peak experiences: the entire Disco Era; my first withdrawal from an ATM machine; the fall of Communism; watching the O.J. freeway chase from start to finish in San Francisco in a bar full of drag queens; a cornucopia of royal sex scandals; the Red Sox winning the Series; Marianne Faithfull singing "Pirate Jenny" at the Fillmore (Jessica Mitford and her husband, who'd arrived in a Bentley, were in the front row); nude swimming with B. in the Ladies' Bathing Pond on Hampstead Heath; picking up Wally, then eight weeks old, from a morbidly obese lady dachshund breeder in a Modesto McDonald's parking lot; and indeed, my first exacting, artful, somewhat tremulous eBay bid. And how ever to forget thrusting a twenty-dollar bill in the general direction of Martina Navratilova, then gyrating and cavorting to boomy-bunny hip-hop at the lesbian rights fundraiser I attended at Fort Mason last winter? (I was that close to the stage—in the *lesbo-mosh-pit* so to speak: she leaned down, smiled, grabbed my sweaty twenty, and stuck it her sports bra, along with other tender offerings.). Even with regard to less-than-perfect moments—Wally and I subsequently flunking out of puppy school at the SPCA, the vomitacious and terrifying ride Blakey made me take with her on the New York, New York Roller Coaster in Las Vegas a couple of years ago—I am obliged to say with Nietzsche, *Yes, give it all to me again, exactly the same.* Even (*retch*) the double-loop-the-loop-upside-down part.

Yet on the other hand, it would be foolish to say the run-in with the Professor left me unchanged—or that its role in my life, however banal and muzzy from one angle, was insignificant. She was the Trojan Horse. She altered everything, the whole way one was *trending*. One doesn't want to discount other factors, but as I hinted at the outset of this shabby little shocker, the relationship and its aftermath no doubt helped to make me the figure of charity, selflessness, and erudite fun that I am today. Bestowed on me my sweet and sunny personality. Made certain bubbly characterological tendencies even more effervescent. And at this late stage it seems bootless to dream up counterfactuals or speculate on how things might have gone otherwise. What *if* the Austrian Archduke Franz Ferdinand and his wife had not been gunned down in Sarajevo in July 1914? What *if* Adolf Hitler had not allowed the otherwise doomed British Expeditionary Force to escape at Dunkirk in 1940? What *if* the Beatles had gotten back together? What *if* the Professor and I had not been introduced one ill-omened Christmas Eve? Don't even bother with this last one.

Granted, a certain amount of discomfort had to be endured. For five years I was entirely celibate—so scarified by the desolation that grown-up sexual desire had brought into my life that it seemed best, on the whole, just to *fuggedaboudit*. Bambi wore fawn-blinkers for quite some time—just couldn't cope. It was as if one had to start over again, work up to it—now with more ambivalence, more protective padding. One had tripped right out of the starting-gate.

If emotions were called for, they would now have to be dark ones. Mine was indeed a monkish, caustic, dyspeptic kind of chastity. In the matter of romance I became a sort of Swiftian misogynist: women, as lovers, were treacherous and bewildering. Impossible to trust Stella or Vanessa with one's adoration. Better to heap scorn and contumely—to wallow in one's abject, unsexed spleen.

Or at least that was the idea. For even as the rebuilding effort dragged on, and even though I continued to indulge, sometimes theatrically, in wholesale bouts of *contemptus mundi* (all too reminiscent of the perilous solipsism of adolescence), I also felt a subtle change in the atmosphere. Almost in spite of myself I was beginning to function, if not in the sexual sense, then at least rather more capably in social settings. Convening with other members of *homo sapiens*. Meeting the planetary locals in seminormal fashion. (Teaching, indeed, my first *students*, if only for a quarter or two, as an apprentice English instructor.) Joining the Human League, however belatedly—though not yet, perhaps, the Joy Division.

I continued to hang out every week or two with my feminist reading group; indeed one of the paradoxes of my misogyny, like Swift's, was that it coincided with a growing emotional connection with individual women, several of them in the group. (As I had done with Elsbet and Malka the Israeli shrink, I exempted these female paragons from my general excoriation of the sex.) This budding sense of relationship had nothing to do with the militant-sisterhood pipe dreams of my undergraduate years or indeed the hairy-legged velleities of lesbian separatism. Bye-bye, Pokey Donnerparty. These women—these new *friends*—were simply themselves: in need of no political reeducation by me, just open to life, and thoroughly nontoxic. Ordinary women (mostly straight, it turned out), with whom it was possible to talk and go on talking. Several of them were also, *ahem*, distinctly maternal. (*Awesome!*) I later told two of these friends about my imbroglio with the P.—I was still only slowly shaking off the Professor's demand for tomb-like discretion—and the sky didn't fall and that made me feel better, too.

My new Midwestern home likewise began to cushion and hold me somehow. I found I actually relished the meteorological extremes—especially the hot, glutinous, thundery days of summer. Riding my bike around the lakes or along the river past the old brewery was soothing—a balm to my prematurely ravaged soul. I moved to a new apartment, not far from my old one, and despite the ever-present company of a group of party-hearty cockroaches, several of them real no-goods, I was glad to escape the dismal reminders of the Professor still lingering at my previous domicile. *Farewell, O green shag carpet remnant. Farewell, O filthy old stovetop* (on which the corned beef had been boiled). *Farewell, O brainless spring-sprung bed.* Another wager on future happiness: I adopted a gray tabby kitten, subsequently named Iris (pretentiously enough) after Miss Murdoch. Iris—my Iris, that is, not the novelist—would meow in greeting when I came home from school; played happily for hours with the cockroach roommates (sometimes snaring and deftly consuming one); and would live with me for the next twenty years—almost, indeed, into the EBE (Early Blakey Era).

I attended, believe it or not, my first real party—one given by a droll fellow student, homosexual, with whom I became close in my last two years at the University. Being male, Derek was indeed a novelty in my world—a bawdy, quite unprecedented non-Terry. I found him endlessly amusing, a sort of human mood elevator. Physically speaking, he cut a wonderfully outlandish figure, being six feet six, pencil-thin, slim-waisted and swivel-hipped, with the longest legs I had ever seen. A dead ringer for Ichabod Crane. He smoked like a chimney, doted on hirsute redheads and rugby players, and would often entertain me by performing his own madcap version of the lewd chair-between-the-legs Bob Fosse choreography made famous by Liza Minnelli in the film *Cabaret*. I became for a while a sort of honorary (if chaste) gay man in his company. These were the early days of Clone Culture, after all—that glorious doomed era of Tom Selleck–style mustaches, disco balls, and bomber jackets. Even in the land of Norsemen and snowshoes, the fizziness in the atmosphere was contagious. Derek was the first man I had ever met who didn't wear underpants. His numerous erotic exploits—all pre-AIDS, of course, and typically acrobatic and arabesque—in turn helped to explode many of my sentimental notions about sexual love. One that he told me about somehow involved wrapping a number of greasy bicycle chains around his waist, hips, and crotch—to striking effect.

Elsbet stayed on, too, and our friendship deepened. I remember her coming over one hot afternoon: she was taking a photo class and had to do a series of black and white portraits. I was to be the model. I was a bit nervy and self-conscious; so we drank beer and put Lou Reed's *Berlin* album on the stereo to get in the appropriate *fuck-all* mood. Sweet sounds of glass breaking, drunken laughter, tinkly piano, a crowd counting to ten in German—then Lou, all bleary and would-be decadent. We hadn't talked about what I would do by way of posing, so I improvised: first, by dragging out some old photos of my parents from the fifties, just after they were married. These I held up to the camera, like biological specimens, while Elsbet took several close-ups of my hands holding them. (Caught forever in the lost light: I hold these family mementos with surprising delicacy.) Next I unearthed a somewhat garish five-by-seven color publicity shot of the Professor and displayed it in similar fashion. Garish because it showed her tanned (even a bit leathery) and draped in a sort of Mephistophelian seventies orange pants suit. She brandished her guitar mariachi fashion and had that same-old same-old wicked grin on her face I knew so well. A dark-eyed Queen of Spades look. Even now I can recall the moment she gave me this long-to-be-mourned-over souvenir. We were in the bedroom of my apartment one morning, getting dressed, I think, and when she took it out of her briefcase and handed it to me, I fumbled it clumsily. It wafted to the ground, landing face down on the dirty wooden floorboards—an ill omen, to be sure. While Elsbet snapped away, Lou's Weimar-sludge in the background, I mimicked tearing the picture apart with sharp little teeth, rabid-skunk style.

For the last part of the shoot, perhaps inspired by the dissipated soundtrack, I decided to cross-dress—something I had only ever done before in moments of ultrafreaky solitude. I suddenly really

wanted to. I wet my hair in the kitchen sink and slicked it back de-
cisively. I was already wearing jeans and a man's shirt, so the basic
sartorial items were already in place. To these I added a dark unisex-
looking jacket, aviator sunglasses (then the height of fashion), and a
gift from the long-lost Phoebe—a brightly woven Guatemalan belt
that I fashioned into something resembling a bizarre bulky tie. This
crude neckwear notwithstanding, I have to say I made a pretty con-
vincing man. Even a beautiful one, perhaps. Elsbet photographed me
for a good while in my get-up and I became ever more loose and free.
The resulting pictures—she later gave me a set of them—turned out
to be fairly stunning. She said afterwards that once I'd donned my
she-male duds my body language had completely changed. I'd relaxed somehow: unkinked, acquired a certain elegance. Ah, confident at last. Scrutinizing them nowadays I'm appalled by how young
and austere and baby-faced I look, but I can also see a little bit of what
she meant.

I put the Professor-sorrow to intellectual use. When the moment
came to choose an area for my Ph.D. work, I decided to specialize in
eighteenth-century British literature. It seemed a good way of getting far, far away from her. No more linguistics, no more ye olde
bloody folksongs. Yet that said, even with my Swift-identification,
it was also a somewhat peculiar choice. (The alternative was to have
been Gertrude Stein.) The scholarly subfield in question was then
pretty reactionary and male dominated; few female students were
ever drawn to it. Many of the age's canonical works remained spectacularly resistant to the new interpretive methods (Marxist, post-
Structuralist, and yes, *yawn*, feminist) then the coming rage among
American academics. But since I needed a break from women and
felt disinclined to jump on any more bandwagons, the pull the period
exerted on me was great.

The attraction no doubt also reflected the emotional contradic-
tions I still struggled with. At first—during my official mourning

period over the Professor—I identified mainly with the more dismal aspects of the period. I had taken a course on eighteenth-century fiction and had been stunned by the bleak, disaster-ridden novels of Daniel Defoe and Samuel Richardson. The stark psychological worlds described therein—harsh, harrowing, inhuman at times— seemed to evoke something of my own psychic life. The heroes and heroines in these books—Robinson Crusoe, Moll Flanders, Pamela, Clarissa—were as marooned and beset as I felt myself to be. They were cut off from love and companionship and locked in a ruthless Hobbesian battle just to survive.

The professor who taught the class, a man I hadn't encountered before, pursued these difficult themes quietly but profoundly. He was learned and intense and suffered, or so one sensed, from a sort of melancholia akin to one's own. Some long-term acquaintance with the baleful. In day-to-day life he was as shy, introverted, and conversationally awkward as the Professor had been smooth-tongued, outgoing, and flamboyant. Yet I found his reticence immensely calming. We were alike, I felt, in our unease—our inability to cheerlead. We were both stuttering through life. Yet halting though our conversations could sometimes be, they also hummed with a quirky and unpredictable intellectual excitement. Caught up in the moment, the stutterers forgot to stutter. (In this way I owe him everything.) He became my thesis adviser and I ended up writing my dissertation on Richardson's *Clarissa* (1749)—a massive, morally ambiguous, relentlessly tragic epistolary novel about an intelligent young woman who is tricked, seduced, and harried to death by a charming amoral rake. Gosh, I wonder what made me choose *that* for a subject.

It took longer for me to acknowledge the more amusing and playful aspects of my chosen period—though in the long run these were more significant, psychologically speaking, than anything else. However morbid my fixation on magnificent monster-works like *Clarissa*, a kind of basic Enlightenment optimism—not to mention some tiny motes of Johnsonian common sense—were also starting to take hold in me. For one thing, like a sort of baby-*philosophe*, I was on the way to making my own radical break with Credulity and Superstition: all the spells and symbols and matriarchal gobbledygook that I'd been in love with—well, since my barmy Phoebe days. (Not really that long before.) The little incense box filled with yarrow stalks—crucial for consulting the I Ching—somehow found its way into the trash pile one morning. The Great Mother, once so alluring, took early retirement and moved back to California. I stopped yammering on in seminars about Hermes Trismegistus and the Fairies Under the Hill. I liked the clear-cut sound—still do—of an Age of Reason. It was time to start thinking straight. And with the access of at least a *little* more mental clarity, a certain Voltairean gaiety kept threatening to break in, too. That Cock Lane Ghost? Just a very funny *hoax*.

Above all, reading the classic works of satire, lampoon, and burlesque was a tonic. Consoling indeed the realization that some illusions were *meant* to be shattered; that a clear comic light might be cast on the chaotic devil-murk of human emotions. Pathos could be turned to Bathos, and enlightenment unfold through wit, send-up, insouciance. Nothing was sacred, one found; even the grandest and most imposing monuments might be defaced. We were all rolling around in the muck like the Dunces anyway; one might as well get used to it. The way of the world demanded laughter as well as tears. One had to stoop to conquer. And in its highest form, I surmised, such rococo lightness and drollery could in fact be a pathway into something more profound. In the loveliest, most philosophical examples of eighteenth-century wit—Pope's *The Rape of the Lock*, Watteau's paintings, Samuel Johnson's burnished utterances, Mozart's operas, and indeed, at century's end, six modest and miraculous novels by Jane Austen—one felt it: a deep moral seriousness humming away at the core, along with the steady flow of beauty, intelligence, delight.

No: I didn't realize it at the time, but along with friendly counsel, such studies would eventually help me begin to exorcize that unholy mixture of conceit and insecurity—glum legacy of childhood convulsions—which had made me so susceptible to the Professor. Instead of merely confirming—like some of my intellectual fads of yore—a sense of isolation, my new interest in comedy suggested a way out of danger: an escape, of sorts, from the lonely and damaging egotism of adolescence. For master-satirists like Pope and Johnson and Austen, I realized, did not simply ridicule pretension and folly in others, even if that was what people hostile to such burlesque sometimes said. That if you lampooned something you must be setting yourself up as superior to it. That you were arrogant, epicene. Pretending to some higher authority. Yet the very greatest satire, I came to think—the kind that lives forever—ultimately grew out of a debunking attitude toward the self. To see the world mock-heroically was necessarily to engage in a sort of preliminary self-burlesque. You couldn't take yourself *that* seriously. You were part of it. All the Lilliputian preening and pomposity was, at bottom, one's own.

Obviously, even with such private revelations, a person like the Professor would hardly remain exempt from criticism—her behavior had been far from impeccable. But one definitely had to look a bit askance at oneself, too. At one's juvenile delusions of grandeur. At that painful, buffoonish susceptibility to hypnotic suggestion. The shocking neediness. (How indeed had this last gotten so bad? Little did I know I would spend the next thirty years in search of *that* particular Loch Ness Monster.) And once begun, the self-debunking process—otherwise known as self-examination—would have to go on . . . well . . . pretty much for the duration. Now, in my fifties, I'm at a point where I know (okay, . . . *sort of* know) that I'm far from perfect. I'm willing to accept that in the love-and-kindness department in particular, I may be—at best—only five or six inches high. Gulliver in the land of the Brobdingnagians. I'll cop to it: in order to play the harpsichord I have to run back and forth on the keys.

Madly. Panting with the effort. If a giant decided to micturate upon me I would be swept away at once, like a tsunami victim, or a daddy-long-legs that gets sucked down the drain when you start running the bathwater. I've been shrunk down so many times in the moral Rinsomatic I've gotten very tiny indeed. Homunculus-sized. Yet even so, I still feel impelled to wonder: Is there some very, very, very embarrassing self-knowledge stuff I'm *still* missing? Maybe other people can see it, glaringly: I'm really only *two* inches high. Or worse: only an *eighth* of an inch high. A measly *sixteenth*. Maybe I am even— eeek—*microscopic*.

Draconian judgments about other people can as a result be difficult to make. (Though not always, of course.) One gets waylaid by second thoughts, an unhappy consciousness of one's own follies and failings. In the early 1980s, just before I left Harvard for my new university job in California (I'd spent three years on a Harvard postdoc after finishing my Ph.D.) I visited my shrink of the time, the one who had taken up after Malka, for what I thought would be a poignant farewell. Said shrink was European, in her late seventies— Old World, reserved, and intellectually formidable. She had been a colleague of Anna Freud, and though now tiny, arthritic, and white-haired, remained a distinguished and imposing figure. All except, that is, for a bizarre, rainbow-colored set of plastic pop beads she always wore, somewhat incongruously, around her neck. I thought her an excellent psychiatrist despite her disinclination to smile or be nice to me. Once I asked her, fairly plaintively, if she thought I would ever escape from whatever Slough of Despond I was then currently wallowing in. She responded with a too-long stare; then stared a bit more; then said she *didn't know*. I got so mad at her for being honest I started to feel better at once.

And no doubt some of her mental associations were peculiar, notably regarding female homosexuality. I spent two years in therapy with her and yet something about the idiosyncrasies of my case repeatedly reminded her, it seemed, of a woman she had once analyzed whose preferred sex act involved being diapered and suckled by her female lover. I would object strenuously whenever my shrink mentioned this infantile lady: surely she didn't think I was like *that*. Yet again and again—each time forgetting that she'd ever mentioned her before, or indeed that I had ever complained—my psychiatrist would roll out Diaper Lady and playmate for our joint contemplation. Hard to forget the comical look of consternation that would appear on her face whenever she did so; or her oft-repeated expressions of wonderment—all the more memorable for being delivered in her weirdly-accented English: *Dey vore dia-peuhs! Dia-peuhs! Dey akchually vore dia-peuhs!*

Anyhoo, it's malignant. At our last session I was speculating on what my new life in California would be like—how I was leaving the nest, growing up, etc. etc. Partly by way of valedictory flattery, I suppose, I'd also said something about how far I thought I'd come in my conversations with her. *You have been so helpful; I will never forget.* Now, this psychiatrist had heard the story of the Professor numerous times—indeed, had once responded to some gory retelling of it, musingly, with one of her most pitiless pieces of moral commentary: *Vat a lot uff kvooked people dere are.* . . . Yet even so, I didn't see what was coming. I had made the mistake of asking her, rather too blithely, I'm afraid, what sort of person she thought I might become in my new role of college professor. As usual, she gazed at me for several seconds in silence, then replied, in a weary tone, *Vell, you know dat Pwuffessor who vas your luffer, den she abuse you? Vell, I tink you vill be a Pwuffessor and you vill meet a girl and do just da same.*

Now not everyone may find this comment amusing. But to me it's as droll as the business about the diapers, though I know the joke's on me. Was this prophecy correct? Well . . . [discreet throat-clearing]:

Yes and No. Yes and/or No. Yes but No. Erm. Not really.

Yes, one *was* the Professor; she *was* the Student. Which is to say such indeed *was* the off-kilter nature of one's first relationship in the new place. But other things were not the same. D. and I were almost the same age (just shading into our thirties); she had an advanced degree in another field when she entered the English program. We met during my very first teaching term. She was in my first graduate seminar that fall; we would get together about six months later. I played no role, ever again, in her academic work. We did not conceal our connection and colleagues and friends seemed to accept it, most very warmly. There were several parallel situations in the department at that time involving both gay and heterosexual couples. The social atmosphere was so much lighter. (It being a new day and the West Coast, the department had, among things, six "out" gay male professors.) Our relationship lasted for five years; D. and I lived together for four of them. I got tenure in the meantime; she finished her Ph.D. shortly after we broke up.

I leave it to the reader to judge whether by getting thus involved, I did *just da same as the Pwuffessor.* At the time I joined the faculty, my new university (like my old one) had no explicit policy regulating professor-student sexual relationships. True, certain attitudes prevailed. Pretty much everybody seemed to think that sexual relationships between instructors and undergraduates were a Terrible Idea. (Whether actual behavior reflected this virtuous sentiment, of course, was another matter.) While no doubt awkward and to be discouraged, romantic relationships with graduate students were felt to be intrinsically more ambiguous. Impossible—if at times just barely—to impugn outright. More likely to be "consensual." Age difference often not so extreme. Even *with* age difference (the gay guys particularly liked this one)—think of the Platonic conception of erotic pedagogy. Beautiful epigones, etc. Propriety still demanded, obviously, that certain hygienic protocols be maintained: whenever such a couple formed, it was considered the professor's

ethical obligation to inform the department chair and exempt himself
or herself from any supervisory role over the student in question.

Nowadays, of course, everything has been codified—more rigidly
at some places than others. On the issue of "consensual" relationships
between teachers and students, the sexual harassment policy currently
in effect at my own university has this to say:

> *At a university, the role of the teacher is multifaceted, including
> serving as intellectual guide, counselor, mentor and advisor: the
> teacher's influence and authority extend far beyond the classroom.
> Consequently and as a general proposition, the University believes
> that a sexual or romantic relationship between a teacher and a stu-
> dent, even where consensual and whether or not the student would
> otherwise be subject to supervision or evaluation by the teacher,
> is inconsistent with the proper role of the teacher, and should be
> avoided. The University therefore very strongly discourages such
> relationships.*

As "a general proposition" this strikes me as eloquent, sensible,
and true. But I'm also stuck with an autobiographical paradox: had I
punctiliously "avoided" my relationship with D. in the early eighties,
as per such a guideline, it is fair to say I would have missed out on
the first seriously *good* relationship I'd ever had, at precisely the time
I needed it most. For D. turned out to be a kinder and more generous person than I had previously encountered, a sort of female Bob
Cratchit to my twisty Mr. Scrooge. Emotionally speaking, she undid
a great deal of the Professor's devilish handiwork and fixed a number
of problems. (Her corny but unimpeachable motto: *never lose an opportunity to be thoughtful.*) I learned a great deal from her about trust.
I can't speak for my influence on her, of course, but it couldn't have
been *too* bloody awful. Though not close in any day-to-day sense, we
still stop and smile and hug when we see each other on campus: she's

a gifted administrator at my university, much loved and admired by many, including me.

All that can be said in the end, perhaps, is that a confusing sense of my own insufficiencies makes it hard for me to cast some final moral judgment on the Professor. I find it difficult to lay an eternal curse on her. There were parts of her then that I see all too well in myself. Not long ago, in fact, it even struck me—for the first time in thirty years—that the alacrity with which she cut me loose might be favorably construed. She knew, long before I did, that eternal bliss was not to be ours and that the sooner she left, the better. Yes, she administered the poison, but she also provided the antidote—distasteful as it was—with (arguably) a beneficial dispatch and aplomb.

And for better or for worse I had my chance for outrage—sometime in the late 1980s or early 1990s—and never took it up. It was the beginning of the Era of High Political Correctness and a lawyer from my old university called me. Some sort of sexual harassment charge had been lodged by a young female graduate student against the Professor. (I also got a pathetic e-mail, at some point, from the student herself.) As I recall, the complaint had somehow raised the possibility of a class-action suit—the legal office was, in any case, contacting former students, some from fifteen years or so earlier, believed to have had untoward romantic dealings with the Professor. Jo— still going strong, like a tugboat—had some part in the business, had taken the aggrieved student under her wing. *Did I wish to make a statement?*

I said no: it had all happened—I remember sighing—*such an unutterably long time ago*. But I also recall telling the lawyer that I wouldn't have felt entirely right doing so: I thought I had had my share in the imbroglio. Twenty-two years old might be young; but still, one had nonetheless been an adult. Yes, it had been a misfortune—but more like a car accident, I'd come to think, than being mugged. I may even have made some gay, Cole Porter–ish aside; that it was Just One of

Those Things. The lawyer thanked me but said that she, for one, was sorry I felt that way. I never learned the upshot of it all.

My decision not to squawk was no doubt due in some part to the fact that not long before the call from the lawyer, I had had a genuine comic catharsis—an altogether unexpected meeting with the Professor herself. I was attending a professional conference on the East Coast—a huge mind-numbing academic affair mounted every year after Christmas by a large scholarly organization to which I belonged. It was all the usual palaver: a bulbous cluster of convention hotels; doormen, taxis, and slush; plastic name tags, metastasizing panel discussions in so-called ballrooms, pompous "delegate" assemblies, alcohol-fueled crushes in various lobbies and elevators. Barf City: I was not enjoying myself. Trolling along one morning, however, through a drifting throng of rabbity academics—I was on the garish mezzanine level of one of the hotels—I was suddenly assailed, over all the hubbub, by the ear-shredding peal of a whistle. The whistle was one of those heavy-duty ones—the kind they give you if you are a Super Bowl referee—and someone was blowing on it forcefully, at regular screechy intervals. Alternating with every blast came a boomy cry, only slightly less loud: *WHEELCHAIR! WHEELCHAIR! WHEELCHAIR!*

The crowd ahead of me then parted like the Red Sea—if one can imagine a Red Sea, that is, made up of hundreds of mostly unprepossessing individuals wearing tweedy jackets, sensible shoes, and carrying book bags from Barnes and Noble. And suddenly the Professor loomed up before me—wheelchair-bound indeed, barreling forward in my direction, and yelling and blasting on the whistle as she did so. People on both sides had to jump out of her path; some were getting their feet run over. A red-haired, somewhat sallow-looking lady in her fifties trailed along behind her—a bit half-heartedly, it seemed, as if to push, or at least guide, the chair. But the Professor was moving ahead under her own steam; in fact sported some fairly grubby white fingerless leather gloves—the sort worn by paraplegic marathoners—and every now and then would give a firm and masterful spin with her hand to one of the wheels.

This juggernaut-like progress lurched to a halt, however, as soon as the Professor espied me. With a gasp and a clap and a deep shout of delight, she called out, *Terry! Wow! What are you doing here? What a surprise!* The woman with her, an unfriendly Slavic-looking lady who had once had a harelip, glowered at me suspiciously. She seemed to be some sort of lady's companion; she was carrying the Professor's briefcase and plastic bags full of what looked like Kentucky Fried Chicken leftovers. Perhaps they were boinking? The Professor, I noticed with a shock, no longer had her braid. (*Damn it! That missing piece has gone missing again*!) She now had a sort of bizarre, all-white, Barbara Bush-style flip. She looked happier, though, than I'd ever seen her before. What with the gloves and the whistle and all, life in the wheelchair obviously agreed with her.

It certainly did: she was there at the convention, it turned out, as a delegate from some national disability-rights-in-higher-education group. She was one of the head honchos in fact—was flying all around the country, would be taking part in meetings with this one and that one, *liaising* with the head of the Blah Blah Foundation. So what accounted for her being in the chair? She seemed nearly to rejoice as she explained: like some child-sufferers from polio, she had developed later-life post-polio syndrome—a sort of wasting condition involving the muscles originally affected. Her leg muscles had atrophied; her back had also gotten messed up. Final result: the P. would never walk again. I tried to look appropriately dismal when she said this last, but the response hardly seemed necessary. She appeared to exult in her paralysis, as if it had brought her some new and febrile kind of glory. Her deepest wish had finally come true. *And hey, Terry, you know, it's really fantastic: I'm in the best shape ever— working out with weights, playing Wheelchair Basketball every weekend;*

I'm training for the local disabled Olympics . . . —on and on she went. It was true—her biceps looked seriously ripped. As I walked alongside her and the companion toward the bank of elevators (they were on their way to some caucus session), the Professor began shouting again to people to move aside and blew on the whistle with renewed, even theatrical gusto. The whistle, I now saw, was on a sort of lanyard round her neck, like an athletic coach's. The scene was heroic, Gipper-like: WHEELCHAIR COMING THROUGH!

I had been shocked to see her, needless to say, but also found myself thinking, *This is fabulous, this is so insane I can barely take it in.* I felt mirthful, curious, and—I was glad to find—mostly unperturbed talking to her: if anything, she made me feel oddly elated. Intellectually speaking, I felt detached—Herr Isseyvoo in *Goodbye to Berlin.* I just wanted to hear her say more wild and surreal things. The uncanniness of the meeting was overwhelming: the face so familiar, but now haunted by inscrutable changes, a certain metaphysical blowsiness. No doubt she was thinking something similar about me. Yet she also seemed genuinely thrilled to encounter me—exhilarated in some unfeigned and child-like way. While the companion (who had been introduced but never said a word) continued to give me shade, the Professor bounced up and down with glee and burbled out an invitation: *Let's have dinner tonight—for old times' sake!* I assented instantly: I couldn't wait to get back to my hotel room, call various friends, tell them what had happened and what was still to come.

We met again in the lobby that evening and the Professor, now genteel, leather-gloveless, and *sans* companion, condescended to be pushed outside to a waiting cab. (We were going to a restaurant a few blocks away.) Here one had suddenly to credit the miracles one heard took place in the holy pools at Lourdes; for even as the cab-driver came over to help her, the Professor suddenly vaulted out of the wheelchair, folded it up, neatly and compactly, like a little campaign desk from the Napoleonic Wars, and before the driver could stretch out a hand, had shoved it into the open trunk, twirled around, and zipped back to me. Then she scooted herself into the back seat. She could obviously walk as well as I could—at least some of the time. In fact, when we got to the restaurant she didn't even bother unfolding the chair, just carried it in and then left it to be checked with our coats.

Our conversation was at first quite stunningly inconsequential. It was as if she had been declawed—had four soft paws now and was on my lap giving me little face-pats. Bizarrely enough, she seemed to regard me as if I were some former junior colleague—a student perhaps—who had gone on to do well and with whom she was just now belatedly catching up. She beamed at me proudly when I mentioned having published several books, as if she had seen my talent early on and pointed me in all the right directions. I was the protégée who had made good. What had been true all along, I now saw, was still true: that she was thoroughly dissociated. Lost in herself. Not available. Never had been. The smile was charming; the eye contact warm and intense; the alienation absolute.

There were moments of impinging hilarity, of course, during which I had to struggle not to give the game away. One had to meet the Professor's self-deception with one's own mask firmly in place: she had been one's tutor, after all, in slyness. The Professor was eager, for one thing, that I come to visit her ASAP and stay awhile. (*Really, Terry! I mean it!*) She wanted to get me out with her in a pair of chairs on the Wheelchair Basketball court. Then I would see *what's what*. The game was rough and nasty, I was informed; you had to have superstrong arms and could get pretty loused up in collisions. Not that you needed to be paralyzed or disabled to take it up. Able-bodied people did, too. All the time. *You've got to come this summer. You'll meet your match! I guarantee: your lower back muscles will feel like hell!* The Professor laughed and vamped and told me how fantastic it would be—not least of all, she crowed, *because it would be the one thing I could beat you at.*

And then there were the moments of feigned communion. I asked at one point what had become of Tina, and the Professor, suddenly less friendly-looking, went into some dark bad-memory zone and related the story of the unpaid loan, the detective, and Tina's subsequent bankruptcy. The Professor now looked paranoid: morose, hard, old, mentally addled. *She never paid me back. That was unacceptable. No way was I gonna let her do that.* But then, recollecting how effectively she had handled it, the P. regained her poise. She reverted to a more characteristic look—that of someone who had just received a best-in-show ribbon at the County Fair. Her begonias had obliterated everybody else's in the flower competition. Left them riddled. Ripped-up leaves and bits of pink and purple petal everywhere on the ground. Major vandalism. *Fuckin-fantastic!*

And then again, as if on cue—her expression softened and she turned a melancholy gaze on me. Garbo in *Queen Christina* saying goodbye to John Gilbert after their night of love in the inn. The chain of association had obviously triggered something: some ghoulish, poetical sensation of contrition. She had treated me terribly, she now confided; how could I even bear to think about it? She knew how much pain she had caused. *The things I did to you were unforgivable. I'm sorry, Terry—you know I mean that, don't you? I hope you can forgive me.* Then, out of the blue, More Good News: *You know, Terry, I would love to write a book with you. There would be so many things we could write about, don't you think? You can come stay with me in June. We can spend the summer together. I mean it: think about it. Can I call you when you are back home in California? I could make everything up to you.* The Professor's eyes glistened oddly; she sniffed a little, reached down for her napkin. Now, I admit it, I had never till then fully grasped the metaphoric spot-on-ness of the term *crocodile tears*. (Or, for that matter, the term *crocodile smiles*.) But here, all of a sudden, were the former: the conscious, copious tokens of grief—undeniably dampening the Professor's strong, still-handsome face.

One didn't say it in so many words, of course—one remained a paragon of good cheer throughout—but the sentiment *not on your bloody life, my dear, dear Professor,* was nonetheless delicately conveyed. The lady herself smiled winsomely in response—though not without a slight razor-glint—then gave me a cheeky, boyish wink. *Well, hey, keep it in mind, Terry: maybe one day you'll realize you have to stop looking in the rear view mirror all the time!* This final tweak was one of the very last things I remember her saying—we didn't stay in touch and I never saw her again. I think she ended up in some kind of hospice care organized by the nuns. Whatever Wheelchair Basketball skills I might have developed were sadly nipped in the bud.

Smiles and tears and a Parting Shot. Blakey and I celebrated our wedding in August, the one I mentioned in my proglomena a thousand years ago. (Lo, since I began this piece, many months of whingeing and moaning over it have come and gone.) The ceremony was surprisingly moving for us—deep, even. We both cried when the twinkie-gay-guy Justice of the Peace at City Hall read the vows and asked us to repeat them. Harvey Milk looked on (or at least his bust did); our friends and families stood by in a little circle around us. B.'s brother Adrian was one of the official witnesses when we went in to sign the registry; my baby sis was the other. My mother got weepy, but nonetheless managed to keep her knickers up in the Humor Department. She would never have dreamed, she announced loudly during a lull at the wedding brunch, that when the first of her two daughters got married, she (the mother of the bride) would be a wobbly eighty-two-year-old and the bride in question (an extremely weird English professor) pretty much past it too at fifty-four.

And yes, the November election has come and gone; and yes, the right-wing head-bangers did pass their stupid Prop 8 banning same-sex marriage in California. *Ugh*. The face-ache people at it again. B. and I think our nuptials are still binding, however: it appears that voiding existing marriages—as opposed to outlawing new ones—is close to impossible, or at least would require many court challenges, and possibly years, to bring off. So in the meantime—till death do us part in fact—we revel in our licit conjugalism.

It's been a big year all around, in fact, and not only on account of the Dearly Beloved stuff. We went round the world for the first time and that too was phenomenal—even if one's itinerary (owing to various far-flung conferences one was obliged to attend) was an oddball one to say the least: San Francisco to Aberdeen to Istanbul to Bangkok to Sydney to San Francisco. Bangkok, admittedly, was a bit of a low point—the fetid river canals and ubiquitous sex tourism got us down. But Sydney—lovely Sydney, our final stop before SF—was a different matter altogether. The Macquarie conference was fun; the city enchanting and easy and full, as always, of sweet, gleaming, carousing life.

No aggro at all—in fact—but, as we joked in our last e-mails back to the United States, lots of AGGRO! Aggro (her real name) was one of the more entertaining individuals we met on our trip, possibly even a new Best Friend Forever. Too bad she couldn't have come back with us for the wedding. Transport would have been a problem, though: Aggro is a seventeen-foot-long lady crocodile who lives under a sun lamp—stylishly enough—in a weedy faux-swamp at the Sydney Aquarium in Darling Harbor. We spent the morning with her our last day in Oz. And what an attractive nymph she is—svelte, greeny-yallery, with warm golden eyes, white scaly tum, and, yes, a big ingratiating smile for everyone. Alas, she suffers a little from Temperament: apparently in the past she has tried to eviscerate any other crocodile they put in the tank with her. Has a hard time getting close, in other words. Not especially nice to those whom she doesn't trust. (No real love life either, obviously.) Her favorite activity would seem to be dozing under her infrared lamp for hours on end, preferably while digesting some large and savory prey. When we first came upon her she was in fact relaxing in just this fashion. Someone said she was going to be fed again very soon, however, so with considerable excitement, we joined the little crowd assembled for the event.

From our first vantage-point, on one side of her glassed-in enclosure, we could see Aggro well indeed: sluggish yet majestic, stretched out at full length, both the parts of her above water and those below. She lay on a sort of shallow, silty underwater ledge, with only her eyes, brows, and big flaring nostrils showing above the water line. All very revealing, but after a few minutes we decided to move to the observation platform directly above her. (Sad to report, but Aggro had just delivered herself—rather indecorously, we felt, given her otherwise regal demeanor—of a large yellow torpedo of crocodile poo.) From above the view was less intimate, perhaps, but more pleasing overall. Nor did any safety glass block one's line of sight. While we waited for something to happen, B. and I took pictures of ourselves next to the *No Jumping or Diving!* sign gracing the platform: a truly horrifying pictograph, showing the Universal Stick Figure falling into the open maw of one of Aggro's brethren.

At last, from behind a padlocked door at the far back of the enclosure, Aggro's two keepers finally emerged—a pair of young and sporty-looking digger-girls with blonde ponytails, big rubber galoshes, and matching blue polo shirts. After a quick gander round to confirm exactly where Aggro was, they began moving silently and gingerly toward the edge of the pond—the one in front having attached and braced on her forearm, medieval knight–style, a sort of clear plastic riot shield, almost as broad and tall as she was. Behind her, the second keeper hung back slightly, stayed hidden as much as possible behind her colleague and the shield. She, the second girl, carried a bucket and was obviously concealing something large, wet, and scrumptious behind her back. As they proceeded—inch by inch, with utmost caution—the tension grew. Aggro had by now raised herself slightly out of the water, one saw, and was supporting her huge wedge-head and torso on her two tiny forelegs. Her finely marked features stood fully revealed now. She looked, by turns, pensive, feminine, intelligent, oddly expectant—the heroine in a Henry James novel waiting for the answer she both desires yet fears will never come. One's camera was at the ready; the suspense riveting.

Then—in a sequence almost too quick and fearsome to absorb: a Sudden Deranging Upward Lunge. The huge hoary form, vertical now and almost entirely out of the water, smashed up against the riot shield, powering its onslaught with a massive lashing tail. The keeper in front pushed back, reflexively and hard, struggled to keep her balance; her companion quickly braced her now from behind. The crowd of observers screeched at the blood-curdling shock of it all. And then again, just as fast as it had happened: a lull and a disengagement, a colossal slapping backwash. The monster had already slithered away in reverse, slipped easily down under the water. At peace too, presumably, having now been fed—though the residual water in the pond, so rapidly and violently displaced, still slopped from side to side, like that in an industrial washing machine.

There *had* been a fish, one gathered—Blakey says it was a big Aussie sport fish like a barramundi—but I never saw it at all. Not when the keeper thrust it up and over the shield; not the nanosecond flash of silver scales. My fault? Or a tribute to Aggro's balletic, crack-the-whip, zero-to-sixty? All I know is that the crusty little lady moved fast as soon as she saw what she wanted. Now, true enough: one had never entirely credited those gruesome stories one heard about alligators and crocodiles suddenly launching themselves out of lakes and rivers and snatching babies out of their prams. Or that someone's pet croc had suddenly appeared on a golf course at a resort somewhere in Florida, killed several golfers, then managed to abscond with a full set of golf clubs. Hard to accept, even from supposed eyewitnesses, that a pile of man-sized bones—now stripped clean—lay in shards and disarray at the fifth hole. Or indeed that a long greenish beast—huge, dwarf-legged, and dreadful, its booty hanging limp in its humungous jaws—had been seen hotfooting it back to its swampy home faster than an NFL wide receiver. But Aggro had had her lunch mauled and down her gullet before those of us in the peanut gallery had even registered its existence. This lady croc was one awesome predator. What a smile! What personality! What teeth! One couldn't help adoring her. It was lucky, Blakey and I agreed, as we packed up our suitcases that evening, that those two young Aussie girls at the Aquarium were buffer and butcher than they first appeared. They'd had the plastic riot shield thing down pat and were obviously familiar with Aggro's quick little feminine wiles. For all our tough talk and cynicism, the two of *us* would have been eaten alive.